The locals call it the Death House, but Carol and Marco designed the New Life House as a home for kids to *live*, safely removed from the stigmas and judgments of the outside world.

Seventeen-year-old Tyler arrives on the doorstep, hoping that he's finally found a safe place to die. His arrival causes the other kids to question the futures they've been promised, and Carol and Marco must convince them there is life after diagnosis.

Even through struggles with addictions and questions of sexuality, the residents could come to believe in the possibility of living.

LIFE
AT THE
DEATH HOUSE

Sean E.D. Kerr

A NineStar Press Publication

Published by NineStar Press
P.O. Box 91792,
Albuquerque, New Mexico, 87199 USA.
www.ninestarpress.com

Life at the Death House

Printed in the USA
First Edition
August, 2018

Print ISBN: 978-1-949340-55-6

Also available in eBook, ISBN: 978-1-949340-51-8

Warning: This book contains sexual content, which may only be suitable for mature readers, and the death of a character.

For Glen,

Thank you for believing in me, for believing in this project and for all that you did to make it possible.

Chapter One

October 1997

The air bit at his cheeks as he walked toward the house where he hoped he would die. After all this time, he'd made it. Tyler took a deep, satisfied breath as he slowly worked his way up the gravel driveway.

He found out about the New Life House on his birthday back in September, and had been trying to get there ever since. When he first saw the pamphlet, he nearly laughed. *Strange name for a death house,* he'd thought. The name just didn't make sense to him. There was no new life for people like him. There was only death and loneliness. And pain. That's all there was.

Despite his commitment to dying, his heart still raced at the thought. *A death house.* He'd already lost everything that ever mattered and then some. The only thing he had left to lose was his life, and he wasn't convinced that would be much of a loss. There was no one left to mourn him anyway. *I just don't want to die on the streets. I don't want to die like...* He couldn't even finish the thought.

Tyler held his breath to steel himself to the pit of guilt growing deep inside him. Why had he been the one who found the New Life House? Why couldn't they have found it together? He'd never expected how quickly things could change in a couple of years or even a few months. How many things and how many people he could lose in such a short time. He never knew just how real life could be until the day it happened. The day he didn't like to think about. The day he'd found he really was alone.

He stopped as he reached the edge of the paved section of the driveway, not far from the house but just far enough away so he could take it all in. It was huge. He cleared his throat and blinked as if to make sure it was really there.

The New Life House stood in the center of a two-hundred-acre piece of well-kept land. It was a large Victorian-style home with faded blue paneling, yellowing white trim, and a wraparound veranda with white paint, peeling and flaking away, revealing the graying wood beneath it. The last of the grass was fighting to be seen through spots of early snow and fallen leaves as winter edged its way in. The driveway was nearly half a kilometer of dirt and gravel, leading to the large circular patch of pavement around the front of the house, the same pavement he now hesitated to step onto.

Tyler looked over his shoulder to see how far he'd walked, but his view was blocked by a line of silver maple trees, sparsely decorated with what remained of their brightly colored leaves, that cut across the front of the property about halfway down the driveway. From where he stood, they resembled a really tall fence.

His attention drifted back toward the house. The sweet smell of rotting leaves mixed with the scent of a roast dinner filled the air, warming Tyler as he imagined what it would taste like. His mouth watered, and his stomach grumbled. He hadn't had a proper meal in days.

What am I doing? They're not gonna take me. This is stupid. He looked down at his worn runners, torn and caked with dirt, and wondered if his journey had all been for nothing. What if they could see right through his lies and could see what he truly was? What if they refused to let him stay? He couldn't take another rejection. He wouldn't let anyone have that power over him again.

Don't be ridiculous. You're going in. He did his best to give himself a pep talk. He was never very good at those either. The only thing he knew how to do was disappoint, but he would do anything to be allowed to stay...almost.

They agreed on the phone to let you come. Stop freaking out. They can't change their minds that fast. He took a deep breath, stepped onto the pavement, and began his walk to the front door.

He rang the bell and waited for what felt like hours for someone to answer. "Hi," Tyler said shyly, avoiding eye contact with the tall and athletic, bordering on beefy, man who greeted him.

"Hi there, you must be Tyler. I was expecting you about an hour ago," the man said, smiling and offering his hand to shake.

Tyler stared at it but shied away.

The man pulled his hand back but kept smiling, seemingly unbothered by Tyler's reaction. "Come on in. I'm Marco." His voice was loud, energetic, and slightly more high-pitched than Tyler expected.

"Thank you," Tyler said quietly. He looked around the foyer, in awe of its grandness. The room was large and dark with wood floors and features.

On a small table next to the office, a single lamp gave off a dim glow, lighting the first few feet of the darkened hallway that led toward the common areas of the house. Across from the entrance was a wide wooden staircase, lined with red carpet that led up to the second and third floors. The sounds of children giggling and chattering in the TV room drifted softly down the hall.

"I was beginning to think you weren't coming," Marco said. "Just put your shoes on the rack." He nodded toward a shoe rack already holding several other pairs of runners and boots.

Tyler did as he was told even though he was embarrassed that his socks were dirty, and both of his big toes stuck out of matching holes.

"Sorry I'm late." He chanced a quick glance at Marco. *He doesn't look like a doctor.*

Marco was wearing blue jeans and a Nirvana T-shirt. He looked like an old guy who hadn't accepted his age yet.

"Can I take that for you?"

Tyler flinched and jerked away defensively as Marco reached for his bag.

Startled by his reaction, Marco retracted his hand, immediately stepped back, and shrunk his stature. "It's okay. I didn't mean to scare you."

"You didn't scare me," Tyler said, straightening up. "I'm not a pussy."

Marco laughed. "I probably should have known that."

"How could you have known? You don't know me."

"Most young guys who have tattoos on their necks and piercings in their eyebrows tend to have a bit of a wild side," Marco said. "There's an element of tough guy that comes with that look."

"Hm." Tyler instinctively brought his hand up to touch the black tattoo in Chinese characters on the left side of his neck and forced the burgeoning tears to dry as he thought back to the day he'd gotten it. He smirked, pleased that he came off as tough. His blue jeans were baggy and tattered; he had a black hoody on, undone over his black T-shirt that read: *Do I Look Like a F*!#ing People Person?!* He had put great effort into crafting an appearance that would keep people at bay. He controlled what he could. Despite his great efforts to appear tough, he was cursed with blond hair and a baby face that, in his opinion, only served to make him seem vulnerable. That's why people always took advantage of him, but he wouldn't let anyone do that again.

"How old are you?"

Tyler stood a little taller. "Seventeen."

"I was pretty sure that's what you'd said on the phone, but you look a lot younger."

Tyler frowned and slouched again. "I know." He rolled his eyes. He'd heard these lines before. This conversation was going nowhere.

Marco ran his hand over his bald head almost instinctively, as though it would help him come up with something else to say.

Tyler despised small talk. It was only adding to his anxiety over whether they would let him stay or not. He took a deep breath and admitted what he hadn't on the phone a month before.

"I don't have any money." He said it quickly to get it over with. If it meant he had to leave, he wanted to know now.

"It's okay. We'll figure something out," Marco said, reaching his hand out for Tyler's bag again.

"I told you I don't have any money." Tyler pulled away and, for the first time, made full eye contact with Marco.

"And I told you we'll figure something out." Marco kept his hand outstretched.

Tyler cringed. He knew where this was going. It was just like all the others who said they wanted to help. It was never that simple. How could he have been so stupid?

"I'm not going to sleep with you so I can stay here," Tyler snapped.

Marco stepped back again. "That's not what I meant."

Tyler gave him a confused, distrusting look.

"Oh." He startled and clutched his bag tighter as a middle-aged woman with short, gray-blonde hair came in from the hallway. *Now, she looks more like a doctor.* She was wearing a beige sweater and tight, dark-green jeans. She had glasses on top of her head rather than over her eyes, something that had always amused Tyler. *What good do they do up there?*

"I thought I heard the doorbell ring," she said, smiling as she walked toward Tyler and extended her hand. "Welcome."

"Hi," he said, shrinking away from her.

The woman looked at Marco knowingly, smiled, and said, "You know the polite thing to do when someone tries to shake your hand is to reach out and shake."

She kept her hand extended, waiting for him to respond. "My name is Carol. What's yours?"

"You don't want to touch me," Tyler said. "What if you catch it?"

Carol's expression softened. "I'm not going to catch anything. That's a myth. Now shake my hand before my arm goes numb from holding it out here so long."

Tyler coughed into the crook of his elbow before shakily reaching his hand out to take Carol's, briefly meeting her gaze. "Tyler." He pulled his hand back and returned his gaze to the floor.

"That's a heck of a cough you've got there, Tyler. Sounded like it rattled inside your chest." Carol looked at him with concern in her eyes. "How long have you had it?"

"I don't know. A while, I guess." Tyler didn't look up.

"Well, I'm the resident nurse around here among other things. I do all the routine checkups and blood work, so we'll have to get it checked out. And then we'll find out what the doctor thinks, but I don't want to inundate you with logistics in your first five minutes here. Let's get you settled and fed before I bore you with all the details. I have a roast in the slow cooker. It should be ready in a couple hours." Carol and Marco exchanged glances. "But for now, how about you give your things to Marco? He'll put them up in your room while I take you in to meet the others."

"I don't want anyone going through my stuff," Tyler said, hugging his bag close to him and scowling nervously at Marco.

"Actually, Carol, I'll take him up to his room where he can put his things. I'll bring him down after we've gone through them," Marco said.

"Sure, sounds good. Welcome, Tyler." She nodded at him before turning and heading back down the darkened hallway.

"Let's head up to the second floor." Marco ushered Tyler toward the stairs. "I'm going to get you to open your bag and show me all of the contents. I won't touch anything. It's just for the safety of everyone here. We need to make sure there's no weapons or drugs in there."

"I don't have any of that," Tyler said.

"Yes, but I still have to check it out. I wouldn't be very responsible if I didn't. It's for the safety of you and the other kids, your roommate specifically."

"Roommate!? I don't want a roommate! He's going to go through my stuff. He's gonna steal—"

"He's four," Marco interrupted. "There's not much to worry about with him."

"Oh..." Tyler's voice trailed into a whisper. "Four?"

"Yeah, four," Marco said. "It's going to be his first day today too. Something for you to bond over."

"What do you mean, it's going to be?"

"He's being dropped off in about half an hour."

"That's fuckin' sad." They came to the second-floor landing and turned left down the hall. Tyler's room was the first door on the right.

"It is, but try not to swear, okay?" Marco pushed the door open and flipped the light switch.

Tyler followed him in, observing and scanning the room and the generic belongings. He judged the plainness of it all. The room was bright with pale-blue walls. There were two single beds, one on the left and one on the right. Both beds were done up in plaid, one with blue and the other with red. At the head of each bed was a desk with a lamp and fresh towels folded on top. At the foot was a dresser.

"How East Coast," he mumbled.

"Sorry?" Marco looked at Tyler to repeat himself.

Tyler shrugged, embarrassed that he'd been heard. "Nothing."

"Empty your bag out on the bed, please," Marco said, standing to the side and pointing to the blue bed.

The zipper to his bag screamed as Tyler pulled it open quickly and overturned it to pour the contents out. "I don't have a lot of stuff."

"That's okay." Marco eyed the contents on the bed. "Can I?" He motioned to touch the pile of belongings.

Tyler nodded. At least this way, he'd know if Marco tried to take anything.

Marco gently pushed things off one another to get a clear view. There were crumpled-up pieces of paper, candy bar wrappers, food crumbs, a couple pairs of socks and boxer shorts, some loose change, a book, a photograph, and a T-shirt.

"A Whistler fan, eh?" Marco said, pointing to the T-shirt.

Tyler nodded and looked away. He didn't want to think about that right now. He cleared his throat to chase the memories away.

"Can I hold it now that it's empty?" Marco asked, reaching his hand out.

Tyler hesitated but then handed the bag to Marco so he could finish the search.

Marco dug his hands through the pockets and shook it upside down before handing it back. "You're in the clear. I'll let you get cleaned up for dinner. The bathroom is down the hall to the left. I'll go find some clean clothes for you to wear. I think we have something that will fit you up in the attic."

"I don't wanna wear someone's hand-me-downs." The other kids would recognize their old things on him when he went down for dinner. *I'd be a total loser.* His stomach tied in knots as he realized that if he were to only wear his own clothing, he would be wearing the same outfit forever, which would also make him a total loser.

Marco laughed. "Don't worry. We just have extras. You'll see. The tags will still be on."

Relief. Tyler took a deep breath. "Oh, then that's okay." He stepped out of the way and lowered his gaze.

Marco stopped at the door. "I have to ask...what's with the choice of book?"

"What do you mean?"

"I remember having to read *Beautiful Losers* back in university. I'm just surprised that that's one of your only possessions," Marco said.

"It's one of the best books ever written. My sister gave it to me." Besides the photograph, it was the only thing he had to remember her by.

"Ah, okay. I'm impressed."

Tyler felt his face redden. Embarrassed, he turned away.

Marco pretended not to notice. "It's great to have you here. Oh, and one more thing. I didn't see any medications in your bag. Do you happen to know what treatments you're on? Doses or specific drugs?"

Tyler stared blankly at Marco, afraid to answer for fear of being kicked out for saying the wrong thing.

Marco again took the same nonthreatening stance he had in the foyer, this time leaning against the doorframe.

Tyler recognized the stance from the shelters in Vancouver. All the counselors and workers used to lean against walls and doors and anything they could just to keep their clients from feeling confrontational. It was so obvious, but it always seemed to work. *Funny.*

"It's going to help us figure out what treatments you need. The doctor will decide, but if you know what you're taking, I'm sure we can get you on some until you meet with him."

Tyler felt his face flush. He didn't want to admit that he'd never been treated, but he had to. "I wasn't on anything."

"Oh... How long have you known that you—"

"About a year." Tyler cut him off. He didn't want to hear the end of that sentence. He stared at his feet as he dug his toes into the carpet for distraction, squeezing and releasing.

Marco tried unsuccessfully to hide the concern on his face. "And how long do you think you'd been—"

"I think a year before that." Tyler hated it, but his eyes started to water. He refused to look up for Marco to see. He hadn't realized how ashamed he would feel when talking about it.

Marco took a deep breath and exhaled slowly and quietly. "It's okay. Let's not worry about that now. Carol will take some blood and do a general physical exam in the next few days, and then we'll get you in to see the doctor and all will be well." He clapped his hands together gently. "See you down there. I'll leave your change of clothes on your dresser while you get cleaned up."

Marco tried to hide his disappointment by forcing a smile, but Tyler knew. He knew it was too late.

Chapter Two

THE EXCITED CHATTER of kids came from the dining room. He stood in the shadows of the hallway, terrified. Carol shushed the kids and asked them to keep it down at the table, and Marco reminded them to listen to her. Tyler trembled as he flashed back to his last dealings with his own family. He shook the thoughts away, took a deep breath, and rounded the corner into the dining room. The other kids quieted and eyed him up and down as he stood in the doorway, looking for a place to sit. The room was bright; the table was full with food.

"Kids, this is Tyler. Make him feel welcome," Carol said, smiling up at him and pointing toward the only empty chair. "Take a seat between Bradley and Theo. Tyler's just joined us here today from Vancouver." Carol nodded toward the small four-year-old boy on his right. "Theo arrived while you were upstairs."

The kids collectively said, "Hi."

"Hi," Tyler said, nodding uncomfortably and taking his seat.

Bradley, who sat tall in his chair with broad shoulders and dark hair, looked like a jock, and Tyler immediately felt intimidated by him.

After half an hour, Tyler had filled and cleared his plate three times. The serving bowls with the various dinner foods sat in a semicircle around his plate, each one nearly empty. He barely said two words during the entire meal. He just kept eating as much as he could as everyone around the table watched in awe.

"You sure can eat," Carol said, chuckling as she poured the last of a bottle of red wine into her glass. The bottle sat by her plate, and hers was the only glass that had had any in it.

"Sorry…" Tyler said. He stopped eating and looked up to see everyone watching him.

"Don't be," Carol said. "I'm glad someone is finally enjoying my cooking."

"It's really delicious," Tyler said, returning to stuffing his face.

Across the table from Tyler sat Maggie, a red-haired pretty girl. He had spent the entire dinner avoiding eye contact with her and had barely looked up when she introduced herself. She reminded him of the type of girls who used to pick on him, but something about her seemed nicer.

The conversation moved to classes and other topics that Tyler didn't feel included him, so he tuned out. He waited until everyone was sufficiently distracted before he snatched up a couple buns and slid them into his pocket. Theo immediately snatched up a bun and stuffed it in his pocket, too, grinning from ear to ear. Tyler glanced around nervously to see if anyone had noticed Theo copy him.

When he felt the coast was clear, he smiled and whispered, "You're my roomie, aren't you?"

Theo looked up at Tyler but said nothing. He just blinked his big brown eyes at him.

"He doesn't speak yet," Maggie said from across the table.

"He's four. Shouldn't he have learned how at like two?"

"He knows *how* to talk. He just doesn't," Maggie said sharply.

"How do you know he can if he hasn't yet?"

Maggie blushed.

Tyler chuckled as Theo snatched up a couple brussels sprouts and stuffed them fervently into his pockets, giggling with delight.

Maggie giggled softly with them. "Theo...what are you—"

"Shhh. Let him," Tyler said, looking to Carol at the head of the table and then to Marco at the other end, afraid they would punish him. Carol was distracted by a conversation with Bradley, and Marco was engaged in one with Curtis who was sitting across from Theo.

Maggie watched quietly as Theo copied everything Tyler did. Tyler took his knife, cut a piece of butter, and stuffed it into a napkin, which he promptly folded and stuffed down his shirt. Theo snatched up a chunk of butter and stuffed it down his shirt.

Tyler laughed and tried to stifle a cough. "You're a cool kid, you know that?"

Theo lit up and giggled. He reached for his glass of milk, smiling as he pulled his shirt out and, with a splash, poured the entire glass inside.

"Theo!" Maggie cried out and rushed around the table to wipe him up.

"You've got a lot to learn, kid," Tyler said. His cheeks hurt from smiling. "Thanks for the laugh, li'l dude." His chest tickled as he exhaled. Phlegm bubbled in his lungs, and he coughed, barely covering his mouth in time. He looked to Carol and Marco shyly, afraid he might not have covered it properly.

"Okay, kids. Time to clean up. Up and into the kitchen with all of ya," Carol said with an air of amusement.

"Tyler, can you grab Theo's plate, please?" Marco asked. "I'm going to go get him into some dry jammies."

"Sure." Tyler stood up quickly, glad to get out of sight. The kitchen was through a double-action door behind where Maggie and Curtis sat, which swung noticeably between the two rooms with a swooshing sound.

Once they had all carried the dishes into the kitchen, Tyler quietly assessed the other kids. Maggie was at the sink, washing dishes. Bradley was standing with a damp tea towel, drying them and putting them away in the cupboards above the counters. Tyler tried not to stare, but he was instantly attracted to Bradley's dark hair and muscular build. *Wow, he's hot. He would be such a heartthrob if he didn't have...* Tyler stopped short of thinking up the three little letters that bonded them. He could feel himself staring too intently and looked away.

His attention then fell upon Curtis who stood with his back against the counter and a tea towel slung over his right shoulder. He was taller than Tyler by at least two inches with sandy-brown hair and a lean body. He reminded Tyler of home.

"You're on dry-duty," Maggie said, nodding at Tyler and pointing toward a large linen cabinet in the corner.

"Okay," Tyler said shyly as he walked to the cupboard and pulled out a faded tea towel.

Theo pushed his way through the swinging kitchen door, wearing Superman pajamas and carrying his empty cup. He looked around the room, wide-eyed. His face lit up as he spotted Tyler, quickly walked to him, and handed up his empty milk glass.

"Thanks." Tyler took the cup and handed it to Maggie.

Theo said nothing and immediately grabbed onto Tyler's pant leg as though it was filling the void the cup had left.

After a moment of sizing him up, Curtis asked, "So, Tyler...how'd you get it?"

Tyler stepped back defensively. His voice was tense and sharp. "How'd I get what?"

"Whoa, relax, buddy." Curtis put his hands up and fanned them slowly as a signal for Tyler to settle down. "We all have it. It's not a big deal."

"We like knowing each other's stories," Maggie chimed in from the sink, sounding almost nervous. "We aren't trying to be rude."

"Whatever," Tyler said as he grabbed a dish from the rack so temperamentally that he nearly dropped it. He dried it feverishly. His face grew redder as he tried to keep his cool by taking deep breaths and focusing on the dish. "What kind of question is that?"

"I came here when I was eight. It's been seven years for me now, almost eight," Maggie said, turning slightly to face him and offering a faint smile.

"How did you get it?" Tyler asked angrily.

"I got it from sex...or a dirty needle. I'm not sure which came first really." Curtis strained to force a smile at Tyler. "I was a little too wild, living so close to Toronto, and my dad had no control over me. A few bad decisions after turning fourteen, and here I am. Been here three years now."

"I came here by choice," Tyler said abruptly.

"Just on your own? Lame," Bradley said.

"What do you mean lame?" Tyler was becoming agitated again.

"I suppose you were just born with it too?" Bradley rolled his eyes as he took a plate from the dry pile and put it in the cupboard.

"This is retarded," Tyler said, pulling another dish from the rack and toweling it off.

"That's not a nice word," Maggie said.

"Well, this isn't a nice game," Tyler snapped back at her. "It's none of your business how I got it. Fact is, I have it, and that's that. Leave it alone."

"We all have it. You don't have to act like we're picking on you. We all have the same thing, and we all have to live with it, so why not embrace the things we've gone through?" Curtis said. He spoke deliberately and slowly. It reminded Tyler of how he used to speak to his younger sister, Rachel, when she was throwing a temper tantrum.

"You're older-brothering me," Tyler said, smiling. He didn't want this to escalate any further. He'd learned how to defuse tension through humor while living in downtown Vancouver. It was the most effective way he knew to get out of a beating.

"Lighten up, bud," Bradley said, snatching the bowl from Tyler's hand. He turned to Curtis and Maggie. "And if he doesn't want to say, he doesn't want to say. Drop it. Give the guy a nice first night."

Tyler looked Bradley over skeptically, unsure of why he would switch to sticking up for him so quickly after insulting him for being defensive. It felt out of place. The expressions of surprise on Curtis and Maggie's faces told him that it was.

"Looks like you've got a new friend." Marco's voice was loud and seemed to echo in the room, saving them all from the awkwardness of the conversation. He stood in the doorway to the kitchen, smiling down at Theo who was still clinging to Tyler's leg.

Tyler shrugged and followed Marco's gaze to Theo. "Yeah, I guess so."

"Can I talk to you a minute out here?" Marco asked, motioning for Tyler to follow him.

"Okay..." Tyler said uneasily. He pried Theo's hands from his pant leg and moved them onto Maggie. He tossed the towel onto the counter and made his way toward the dining room. Marco reached out to put a gentle hand on Tyler's shoulder, but as an automatic reflex, he jerked away, slamming himself into the doorframe.

"Whoa, easy there. I wasn't trying to scare ya," Marco said, pulling his hand back and freezing in motion, making room for Tyler to pass by. Tyler glared at him and continued moving into the dining room.

When they entered, Carol was still sitting at her spot. Her expression was blank, almost vacant. It was an expression Tyler was familiar with. It reminded him of his mother. He cringed at the thought.

"I'm sorry," Tyler said, bowing his head to Carol and then stepping back, keeping his eyes to the floor. He was sure they were kicking him out already. He hadn't even lasted one night.

"Sorry for what?" Carol asked. "For making a little kid laugh? Don't be silly." Her expression changed from absent to loving.

"Tyler," Marco started, "you're not in trouble. Relax." He leaned forward and crouched down to get a clearer look into Tyler's eyes but kept a respectful distance.

Tyler stood still, eyes quivering and glossing over.

"Don't worry, Tyler. We are not upset that you put the food into your pockets."

"Really?"

"Yeah, really."

"We just want you to know that this is your home now. You don't have to sneak food. You can help yourself to anything in the cupboards and fridge anytime you like."

Tyler was shocked. Not even his own parents had allowed him such freedom. If he had eaten anything that wasn't offered, his mom would send his dad in to teach him about manners. Even when he asked for something extra, she considered him ungrateful and would still send his dad in.

"We don't allow stealing," Marco added, taking a serious yet gentle tone. "This is your home, and we are a family, so let's all respect one another and keep this one incident of sneaking behind our backs as the only incident, okay?"

"Okay," Tyler said, glancing up at Marco and then at Carol before ducking his head back down. "It won't happen again. I swear." *They're not mad.* Tyler couldn't believe it.

"Good stuff. We're really glad to have you here with us," Carol said. "I think little Theo is gonna be all over you."

"Yeah, he's a nice kid," Tyler said, turning back to the kitchen.

AS SOON AS Tyler was gone, Marco turned to face Carol. "He's going to be a tough one."

Carol smiled. "No tougher than the next." She liked his edges and looked forward to smoothing them out.

Marco moved to where she sat and kissed her. "Your ability to love everyone and push forward no matter what inspires me," he whispered, sitting down beside her. "There's a lot to uncover with him. Have you read his file?"

"I skimmed it, but with everything that's happened, I've had a hard time getting to it. I just don't know where the time has gone."

"It's okay, beautiful. I was just asking. You'll get to it when you can," Marco said, rubbing her back. "Once you've read it, let's discuss financing his stay here."

This piqued Carol's interest. When Marco spoke with such little detail, it was because he didn't think she was going to like the decision he had made. It was typical for him to act and then steer her in the direction she needed to go to find out what he'd done. It was his way. She knew it, and she loved it.

"You make everything good," she whispered, closing her eyes and leaning her head on his shoulder. "If I ever had doubts about your commitment to this place, it's moments like these that put any of it to rest."

Marco looked at her and furrowed his brow. "Don't ever doubt my love for this house, these kids, or for you." He paused and cleared his throat. "I love these kids like they're my own. I know you don't like talking about it, but know that I'll miss Janie for the rest of time. And I'll welcome every new kid who comes here with open arms."

Carol flinched at the sound of Janie's name, but she leaned forward and kissed him. "I know."

Marco pulled her close. "Everyone deserves a family. Even us."

IT HAD BEEN a few hours since Tyler had arrived. He was tired from his travels and from the first full belly he'd had in what felt like years. He lay in his bed, nightlight on, staring up at the shadows it cast on the ceiling. He'd finally stopped coughing long enough to relax. It usually took him about an hour before the fluid in his lungs stopped tickling and causing him to cough. His eyes were focused so intently that they began to sting and get the familiar fuzzy feeling that comes before tears. He blinked the feeling away. All of his life, he had struggled to avoid crying. He remembered being emotional as a young kid, always crying about something. His dad and other kids used to call him a crybaby. He frowned as he thought about how hard he had become. His first response was anger now. Just as his mind started to race, he felt the presence of his young roommate.

Startled, he turned to see Theo standing beside him with his blanky clutched in one arm and a stuffed bear in the other. "Hey...you okay?"

Theo stared at him, moving in closer to the edge of the bed. He looked up at Tyler with his big, sad eyes; they appeared to quiver in the reflection of the nightlight. He turned toward his own bed and then back to Tyler again.

"Right. You don't talk," Tyler said, sitting up. "You should really say something. This whole not talking thing is a little creepy."

It was clear that Theo could understand everything Tyler was saying, but also that—as far as Tyler was concerned—he didn't give a flying curse word.

Theo coyly put his teddy and blanky on the bed next to Tyler, who laughed at the blatant suggestion.

"You want up?"

Theo nodded, so Tyler patted the spot next to him.

Theo made a little grunt as he climbed up, kicking his little feet as hard as he could and flipping himself onto his back to land as close as he could to Tyler.

Tyler smiled as he shifted over to make more room. Theo shuffled closer. "What's this guy's name?" Tyler asked, pulling gently on the hand of the teddy bear. "Is it something dashing like Tyler?"

Theo giggled and pulled the teddy closer, half-heartedly hiding it from sight.

"It has to be. If someone as cool as you named him, his name has to be good."

"I miss my mommy..." Theo said. His voice was tiny.

Tyler stared at him, unsure of what to say.

"I want my mommy..."

Surprising himself, Tyler said, "I'm sure your mommy misses and wants you too. I bet she's very sad that you're not with her right now." He didn't believe it. Normally, he would have said so, too, but this was different. He'd never had to lie to a four-year-old before, but he felt a strange need to be like a grown-up for him.

"Why doesn't she want me?"

"I...um..." Tyler struggled for the right words; his heart pounded in his chest as he searched. "She has some other things she needs to take care of right now." Theo was quiet. Tyler wished for him to say something to break the now awkward silence. He wondered if he had been convincing enough.

Theo tugged on Tyler's shirt. "Can I sleep here?"

"Oh, uh, yeah. For sure," Tyler said, clearing his throat. He reached over and switched off the nightlight before sliding onto his back. Theo snuggled close to his side. The silence was heavy. It felt like it was pushing him down into the bed, like a physical being was lying on top of him and trying to bury him. Now that it was dark, he didn't have to wipe the tears. He could hide in the dark.

"Clifford," Theo said.

"It's Tyler."

"No, silly," Theo said, giggling. "His name is Clifford."

"Oh, isn't it Clifford the Big Red Dog?"

"The big red dog is stupid. It's not real. Clifford the bear *is*. He's right here," Theo said, waving the bear in front of Tyler's face just as his eyes adjusted to the moonlight.

Tyler laughed. "Good to know. I'll try to remember that."

Chapter Three

THEY HAD BEEN at the New Life House for four days, and Theo had barely left Tyler's side long enough for him to use the washroom and shower each day. If Tyler wasn't behind the locked door of the washroom, he was fair game for Theo to be clutching his pant leg or hand as they moved from room to room. Tyler's favorite spot was the sunroom at the front of the house, next to the foyer. There was no back wall to separate it from the hallway, and the whole front wall was made of windows. Despite the lack of privacy, Tyler could often be found lounging on one of the window-facing couches or chairs, watching the birds and leaves dance in the wind.

It had become clear to Tyler that Theo's silence was deeply rooted in shyness, and that once he knew you were safe to talk to, he basically never shut up. They were sitting on the couch, enjoying the sun-filled view of the front of the property, Theo with his sippy-cup of milk and Tyler with a mug of coffee. Theo was nattering on and on at Tyler about something to do with nothing as he always did. Tyler had learned to smile, nod, and pretend like he understood regardless of whether he did or not. He already felt like a bad parent.

"Hey, guys. Are you ready?" Carol said, announcing herself from the hallway.

They turned around to face her. Theo closed his mouth tight and returned to his stoic self. Tyler stood and tapped him on the shoulder to encourage him to get up as well.

"It's nice that you two are getting along so well. Makes the transition easier, I'm sure," Carol said as they walked up the stairs to the examination room on the third floor.

The room was different than Tyler had expected. He hadn't expected it to be much different than any other room in the house. Instead, it had been made over to look exactly like an exam room in a doctor's office or a hospital. They had replaced the floor with white tiles and added the sterile counters, a small sink, and the typical examination table with the single layer of crinkly paper running up the middle of it. The walls were the stark contrast to a standard exam room. Carol had painted them canary yellow in an attempt to liven up the mood during routine checkups and needles.

"Have a seat up on the table," Carol said, pointing to it as she closed the door. "If you could—"

Tyler bent to lift Theo up and onto the table before sitting. "If I could what?" he asked as he sat beside him.

Carol pressed her lips together tightly, shrugged, and said, "—nothing, you already did."

Tyler looked at her curiously. "Okay...whatever you say," he said hesitantly.

"Just give me a few moments, and I'll get everything ready," Carol said, waving her hand to indicate that they should chat amongst themselves while she got organized.

"You gonna be a brave little man for the needle?" Tyler asked, leaning toward Theo and gently nudging him.

Carol turned toward them, supplies readied in hand.

"Take a deep breath. It's coming. Dun-dun-dunnnn..." Tyler teased, nudging Theo again.

"Ah-ah. I'm coming for you first, big guy," Carol said, winking at Theo.

Theo's giggle sounded like a whisper. He looked down after realizing he'd been heard.

Carol listened to Tyler's heart, took his blood pressure, and asked a series of questions to get an idea of his general health. "Are you experiencing night tremors or sweats? Bad dreams?"

Tyler shook his head. "No. None of that."

She moved the stethoscope to his back to listen to his lungs and asked him to take a deep breath. She frowned at the heavy sound of fluid buildup. "I'm concerned about your lungs. It sounds to me like an infection, but we will have to wait for the doctor to check you out. I can't diagnose, but I'm expecting that he will get you on an antibiotic. Have you noticed any spots on your chest or other areas of your body that weren't there before?"

"What? No. Like pimples?"

"No, not like pimples. These would be dark lesions. More like bruises," Carol said, glancing up from her clipboard for a moment to make eye contact with him. "They're a little scarier than pimples."

"No."

"Marco says you haven't been on antiretroviral treatments before. Just to double-check, is that true?"

Tyler hung his head and brought his shoulders in, curling away from what he expected would be a lecture. "I'm sorry. It's probably turned to AIDS by now."

Carol shook her head and placed a hand gently on his knee. "Don't be sorry. You didn't do anything wrong. I'll just make this note in your file so that when I scan it to Dr. Benson, he'll have an idea of what treatments you will need. I suspect he will want to have you on Combivir or some form of highly active antiretroviral therapy, which we call HAART. And don't try predicting the future. It never works. You're HIV positive. Let's stick to the facts until we know better."

She removed her hand and made a few notes before setting the clipboard down. "All right, let's get to the tough part then." She placed the vials for blood, a rubber band, a stress ball, and a small glass jar of medicine, with yet another needle next to it, beside Tyler. She readied her rubber gloves, blowing into them to make them easier to fit over her creased hands. "Let me see your arm, please."

Tyler held his arm out for Carol. She placed the stress ball in his hand and then tied the rubber band around his upper arm.

"Squeeze the ball to make your veins nice and big," Carol said, gently rubbing and patting the inside of his elbow to get the veins to stand out.

"You're going to be careful, right?" Tyler asked, staring at the needle in her hand.

"Are you afraid of needles?"

Tyler scoffed. "No, I'm not afraid of needles. I want to make sure you're careful so you don't get it." He stared at the needle with a sense of longing that he thought he'd long ago lost. "Not afraid at all," he said.

"You know how HIV is transmitted, don't you?"

Tyler looked down, ashamed that he still didn't know. He wanted to have at least some answer, so he said, "Sex and if my blood touches you."

Carol paused with her hands on his arm, just below the rubber band that was pushing his veins out for her. "You transmit the disease by allowing the blood, semen, vaginal fluids, or breast milk of someone with HIV into your own body. It would have to enter through your mouth, your butt, the tip of your penis, or cuts or breaks in your skin. It also enters through the vagina, but you don't have one of those, so no worries for you there." She winked, in an attempt to get him to laugh. "You don't transmit it by handshakes, kisses, hugs, or any of the things you may have been taught by hateful people. Blood or bodily fluids have to enter my body for me to contract HIV."

Tyler was surprised that she'd been so descript. He wasn't used to hearing a motherly figure say *penis* or *vagina*. It didn't feel right, so he squirmed in his seat.

Carol laughed, seeming to recognize his discomfort. "Oh, relax. They're just words."

Tyler chuckled.

"I do love these chances to properly inform you guys about the facts. Too often, you get here with a false idea of how you can pass the virus or even why you may have contracted it yourselves. It breaks my heart that so many of you are taught that the best way to keep from spreading it is to avoid physical contact altogether. Everyone needs affection to some degree. I would have told you more when we first met, but I felt like it was a bit much for a first handshake."

Tyler laughed loudly, surprising even himself. "Yeah, for sure."

She picked the needle back up from beside him. "And don't worry about me. I will be careful. The chances of getting infected through giving you a needle are pretty low, but I'll be careful regardless to eliminate the chances altogether. We have to take stock of what we're dealing with here, and the best way is by getting the blood work done here and couriering it over to Dr. Benson in town. They'll run it through the lab and then prepare the results and have you in for an appointment in a few weeks."

"Okay, the bad news comes then. Got it," Tyler said, bobbing his head and then breaking his fixation on the needle and staring at the wall straight ahead.

"Have you ever thought about the power of positive thinking?" Carol groaned and waved off Tyler's attempt at interjecting. "Yeah, yeah. I know. You're positive, so you always think positive. But forget about the puns for a minute. Have you ever wondered what would happen if you focused on a positive outcome, that maybe the energies in and around your body would help to steer your path in that direction?"

Tyler shrugged. "Sounds like desperation."

"It's not desperate. It's optimistic. Try it out sometime. You may surprise yourself."

Tyler groaned. He hoped she wasn't going to start forcing religion and all that crap down his throat. He hadn't pegged her for the type, but he'd been wrong before.

Changing the subject, Carol said, "I'm also going to give you both the flu shot. 'Tis the season after all. The other kids had theirs last week."

Tyler nodded but kept staring forward. Carol stuck the needle into his vein, and he gasped and nearly moaned at the familiar and comforting sting. He closed his eyes and took a deep breath as he tried to ignore the desire simmering inside him. His eyes burned wet beneath his closed lids.

"You okay?" Carol asked.

"Yeah, fine," Tyler said abruptly. "I'm fine."

She watched him curiously as she taped a cotton ball to the small puncture left by the needle. She kept her eyes on his face, waiting—he was sure—to see if he would reveal anything more, but he wasn't going to admit to anything. He blinked and moved his eyes away from her gaze.

Carol clapped her hands together as though she were wiping dust from them. "Okay, then. That's good. Theo, you're next." She slid her chair back to the counter to collect the vials and needles she would need for him. "Oh, one more thing, Tyler."

"What?"

"I'm going to need you to take out your piercings. We don't allow them here. I'm sorry."

Tyler frowned. He didn't want to take them out, but he didn't want them to tell him to leave either. He sighed as he removed the piercings. He couldn't help but feel like he was selling a part of himself for a roof over his head just as he had so many times before.

Carol slid her chair back over to sit in front of Theo this time. She reviewed his chart aloud. "So your doctor has you on HAART for now, Theo. Looks like you need to gain another thirty pounds or so before we can get you onto Combivir." She looked to Tyler. "You may not know this, but the other kids have all been transitioned over to Combivir. It's a new drug that has a lot of promise. I assume that's what Dr. Benson will put you on as well." She took a deep breath. "We're so excited about the new treatments. It's only been about a month since it was possible, but it's already bringing new hope."

Tyler forced a smile and nodded.

Carol turned her attention back to Theo. "I've got a couple questions for you, big guy. Do you notice if you're really warm or uncomfortable when you sleep?"

Theo fearfully looked up at Tyler, afraid to answer the question and pleading with him to step in.

"He doesn't," Tyler said.

"I do need him to answer the questions, but thank you for keeping a watchful eye on him." Carol scribbled a few notes on her clipboard.

"What are you writing there?" Tyler asked, leaning to try to peek at what she had jotted down.

"I am concerned that he is not speaking. It could indicate that there are other things at play. I need to get him to speak so I can eliminate any other concurrent disorders."

"Disorders? What disorders?" Tyler said defensively.

"Autism is my biggest concern. It doesn't mean he has it, but it is an indicator. I would need to run other tests and get the doctor to see him. The doctor would determine any results or diagnosis."

"Wow, just give him a little time. He just got here. He needs time."

Carol smiled. "Easy there. I realize he just got here. I do have to note it in my records; otherwise, I'd be pretty terrible at my job."

Tyler quieted. "There's nothing wrong with him."

"Of course there isn't. It doesn't mean he doesn't have any other obstacles to face. I'd like to make sure we're prepared for whatever life throws his way," Carol said as she clicked the button on the back of her pen to retract its tip. "I'll just take some blood, and we'll be done for the day." She arranged the needles and vials next to Theo. He whimpered as she slid the tiny needle into his arm.

"Ah, you got this, li'l dude. Breathe it out," Tyler said, putting his arm around Theo for support.

Theo's eyes lit up as Tyler reached out to protect him. He sat up straight and put on a brave face as Carol extracted blood and gave him his flu shot. Tears welled in his eyes and his lips quivered, but he didn't cry.

"All done. You were so brave." Carol taped the cotton ball on Theo's arm and then grabbed a sucker from the jar next to the sink. "Eh, voila!"

Theo grinned and grabbed the sucker eagerly.

"Great," Tyler said, hopping down from the table and turning quickly to catch Theo as he mimicked the jump. He caught Theo under the arms as his butt left the table. "Whoa, almost lost ya there." Tyler set him down on the floor. "Let's get going." He put his hand out for Theo to grab onto.

"See you for lunch," Carol said, waving to them.

Tyler looked back, still holding his hand out for Theo, who finally noticed it and excitedly grabbed on with both hands, squealing with delight. As soon as they were around the corner and out of earshot, Tyler said, "You need to say something to Carol, Theo."

"No, I don't."

"Yes. You do."

"*No!*"

Tyler felt his temper tightening in his chest. "This is ridiculous. *Yes, you do!* They're going to take you and give you to all sorts of doctors if you don't." They were on the second floor now and nearing their room. "Don't you get it?" he shouted, feeling embarrassed at how he was speaking to a four-year-old.

Theo shook his head defiantly, ran to his bed, and threw himself face down in dramatic refusal and let out a scream of toddler's rage.

"Oh, come on, don't do that," Tyler said, following Theo in and sitting down beside him. "I'm sorry. I didn't mean to shout. I'm not going to tell anyone. It's our secret, but I just want you to say something to someone soon so they don't make you see all sorts of doctors. You don't want anyone to think there's more wrong with you, do you?"

Theo sobbed as he hugged Clifford. He rolled away from Tyler, repeating, "No, no, no..."

And for the first time, Tyler worried they might take Theo away from him. Maybe something was wrong with how Tyler was interacting with him that made him less talkative. Maybe it was all his fault just like everything else always was.

Not giving up, Tyler messed Theo's hair. "You're going to have to talk to someone soon. I don't want them to take you away from me. I've grown to really like ya, so don't go disappearing on me."

Chapter Four

IT HAD BEEN nearly three weeks since Tyler and Theo had arrived at the New Life House, just long enough for Tyler to set himself apart from the other kids. He was sitting cross-legged in the papasan chair in the sunroom, drinking his third coffee of the morning and staring out the window, watching the world come alive. Small birds were balancing on the branches of the shrubs just ahead of the veranda while two hyper squirrels were chasing one another around the railing. He felt so much older than Bradley and Maggie, so much wiser, yet he was pretty much the same age. They seemed so immature, so innocent. He liked Curtis, but as far as Tyler was concerned, the other kids had lived a life of luxury and their immaturity radiated that fact. Theo was still pretty glued to him, which was a welcomed affection. Tyler couldn't remember a time when someone actually wanted to be near him. Ever since he found out he was sick, few people were willing to touch him except for the men who paid him. They were the most willing, but their touches and affection were not something Tyler wanted. He cringed as he pictured the things he'd done before coming to the New Life House.

"Hey." Curtis's voice broke through Tyler's thoughts. "What's up?" he asked, sitting down in the armchair next to the papasan. Curtis was wearing his signature faded, ripped blue jeans and a light-brown T-shirt with a wrinkled left breast pocket. He had this earthy, grunge style to him that Tyler had initially been intrigued by. His hair wasn't altogether long, but his bangs always seemed to hang casually across one of his eyes. He reminded Tyler of better days.

"Not much. Just chillin'," Tyler said, relaxing back in his chair. He felt uncomfortable now, not because Curtis made him feel that way, but because he didn't know how to behave when talking with people face-to-face. He didn't know where to put his hands, what to do with them, or where to look. He'd dart his eyes from Curtis's face, to his shoulders, to the window, and back so quickly that the twitch in his eye made him feel cross-eyed, which only served to increase his feeling of insecurity. Habitually, he coughed long and deep with each burst rattling his windpipe and burning his chest and throat. By now, everyone had grown used to his constant coughing.

Curtis was the oldest kid at the house. He turned seventeen a few months before Tyler. The two had been bonding over shared stories of their misguided youth and a love of Nirvana and Green Day since a few days after Tyler arrived.

"I'm not used to this yet," Tyler said, fidgeting in his chair. "I can't figure out if I'm bored or what."

"Bored," Curtis said, laughing and putting his feet up on the coffee table. "It takes time to get used to the slow pace."

"It's funny because it's cool, but it's long. You know?"

"Yeah," Curtis agreed. Both boys quieted and stared out the front window at the long driveway. The world at the end of it seemed an impossible journey away.

"I wish I knew how to put it into words," Tyler said, sighing. He stared intently at the few orange and yellow leaves that remained on the line of maple trees that cut across the property, offering a sort of protective shield from the outside world.

"No worries. I know what you mean. I was new once too," Curtis said, offering a friendly smile. They sat in silence for a few more moments before Curtis stood. "We have our math lessons today, so you'll probably wanna take a leak before we go. Carol doesn't like when we leave during class."

Tyler sat up in his chair. "Why do they do that?"

Curtis appeared perplexed. "Do what?"

"Why do they homeschool us? Why don't we get to go to school in town like everybody else?"

Curtis chuckled. "Because we're not like everybody else. Or at least, that's what everybody else thinks. Carol thinks we're safer here. She doesn't want us dealing with the locals. Apparently, they won't like us because we're HIV positive."

Tyler scoffed. "Who cares?"

Curtis shrugged. "Carol's a little overprotective. You'll get used to it."

Tyler slouched back in his seat, disinterested.

"I think with what happened last year..."

Tyler's ears perked up. This sounded intriguing.

Curtis shook his head before Tyler could ask him to tell him more. "It doesn't matter." He continued, clearly bothered by whatever he had almost brought up. "I think it just proves there's a cost to total isolation too."

CAROL AND MARCO designed the New Life House so the kids could avoid the public school system by obtaining their homeschooling certifications, convinced that allowing them to go to the school in town would subject them to awful teasing and prejudice. Carol held several degrees, as did Marco, so they saw the extra certification as a form of "icing on the cake."

Carol's father had been a major contributor to Dalhousie University in Halifax, leading her to achieve all of her accreditations from that university. She spent many years trying to live up to his dream of what she could have been while never feeling quite like she'd succeeded. She was now a registered nurse, held a bachelor degree in social work and a PhD in psychology. She went to school right up until she was nearly forty years old, and spent the next few years planning and getting ready to open the New Life House.

Marco was also a registered nurse. It was at Dalhousie that, while studying for their degrees in nursing, they had first met. They started the New Life House while he was finishing his BA in psychology and Master of Social Work. They felt that if they both held several degrees in fields related to running the house, they would be more impressive to the agencies and companies they were seeking funding from.

The kids were all working on various levels of curriculum; however, they had their classes at the same time, in the same room, similar to how one-room school houses functioned in the past. Specifically, they had their classes in the library of the house, which had been converted into a classroom. The only entrance from inside the house was through the door next to the stairs in the foyer. They were forced to add an exit door from the library to the side yard of the house in order to meet the fire safety codes.

Depending on the subject, Carol or Marco would lead the lessons of the day, working one-on-one with any of them who needed extra help. Marco taught history, French, wellness, and geography while Carol taught English, social studies, math, and science and supervised online electives in art or gender studies.

TYLER FELT EMBARRASSED every time he needed to raise his hand. He hadn't been in school for so long that he was two grades behind his age group. The lesson was in algebra, and Tyler was frustrated. "This is stupid," he said, slamming his pencil down on his desk. "We're dying; why the hell do we need to know this shit?" His eyes lit up with emotion as he stood from his seat. A wave of heat fuzzed through his body and flushed his face.

"Tyler, that's enough," Carol said sharply. "We don't speak like that here. Sit down and tell me what you're having trouble with, and we'll figure it out."

"I can't do this," Tyler said, sitting down and shoving his desk forward.

"Whoa, buddy," Bradley said, mumbling. "Take 'er easy."

"Oh, screw you," Tyler shouted, jumping up and stomping toward the door. Bradley reminded him of everything he hated back in high school. It was the jocks that made fun of him for his supposed homosexuality and anything else they could come up with. He had taken his fair share of schoolyard beatings from Bradley's type.

As he stormed from the library, Tyler could hear Carol scolding Bradley.

"Enough," Carol said, looking at Bradley to quiet down. She pulled the door to the library shut and walked back to the front of the room to continue helping Maggie.

"Hey, I didn't do anything," Bradley said, smirking.

"I heard you, Bradley," Carol said. "Just lay off him. Try to remember what it was like when you first got here and have some empathy."

LATER THAT EVENING, after a sullen and quiet dinner and after the kids had done their evening chores, Carol found Tyler sitting out on the back veranda. "Hey," she said quietly, stepping out of the screen door, letting it creak and then slam behind her. Its hinges were failing, making it impossible to go in or out quietly. "Do you want to tell me what that was all about earlier?"

He was sitting on the rickety, squeaky old porch swing, facing the back fields with a blanket wrapped around his legs and the hood of his sweatshirt pulled up over his head. The moonlight shone in his eyes, making it obvious that he was crying. He said nothing, but shifted in his seat to make room for her.

"You're going to have to talk about it if you want it to get better," she said, sitting down beside him. The sky was dark; the moon was bright. The songs of crickets and a distant owl bounced chaotically around the veranda.

"I don't want to have to do this stuff. What good is all this schooling going to do for me?" Tyler said, staring straight ahead. "I may not even live long enough to use any of it. Then what was it for?" He was angry and his voice was sharp. The light from the moon bounced more and more rapidly in his eyes as he spoke. A thin line of spit stretched between his lips each time he opened his mouth.

"You don't know that," Carol said. "It's not a death sentence anymore. Forget about what you see in the movies or in the news. They're just propagating hate and fear. Ignore it."

"HIV isn't..." Tyler said in a hushed tone, protesting her reassurance.

"You don't know that it's advanced past that, Tyler," Carol said, leaning back into her spot on the swing to stare out at the sky with him. "You're worrying yourself over this when you don't even know what the outcome will be."

"I didn't do any treatments for two years. I ran around the streets using drugs and having unprotected sex for a little over a year after I was infected, and before you get all worried, they knew I was positive," Tyler said. The line of spit broke. "I've read about the symptoms. It's pretty obvious to me. I didn't do anything to stop the virus." He had been worrying himself with the details of HIV versus AIDS and what it all meant for weeks. As if on cue, he fell briefly into a fit of phlegmy coughs.

Once he had gotten himself back under control, Carol said, "Let's not worry about that. Let's live in the moment."

"What do we do when we find out that it's AIDS?" Tyler asked, turning to watch her expression. He wanted to be able to see if she was lying when she answered.

"Then we accept it and move on. The medicines and advancements in the field are full of promise, and we look toward those. I refuse to accept that you don't need to learn or expand your horizons just because you have HIV...or even AIDS. You'll suck it up and keep going forward." Her convictions passed his test; he believed her.

"It's not that easy."

"Sure it is," Carol said. "You only get one shot at life, so make the most of it. What if you do find out you'll die in a year? What then?"

"I don't know," Tyler said, stunned that she had put it out there to him.

"You like straight talking. I'll give it to you straight. You can either live out the rest of your life ignoring your feelings and closing yourself off from all the things that make life wonderful, or you can buck up and grab the bull by the horns and enjoy the ride. You're a teenager. These years are supposed to be filled with learning and laughing and celebrating life. Because you still have one. It's not over."

Tyler crossed his arms and sulked back into the swing. He wanted to live. He wanted to be the fun guy. He wanted so badly to be anything but what he was. He just wanted to be normal, but how could he ever say that to her? How could he admit that all of this anger was really fear? And did he even need to? He sighed and stared at the ground as he rocked the swing with his feet again, refusing to reply.

Chapter Five

THE DRIVE INTO town to meet with Dr. Benson was mostly quiet with Tyler staring blankly at the passing fields and farm houses, convinced the results of the tests were going to confirm that his disease had advanced beyond HIV and into AIDS. He had somewhat fantasized about it over the last two years. It embarrassed him that despite the fear and the pain this caused for so many people, he actually fantasized about being sicker. He longed for it. Many times, he had daydreamed about arriving on the front stoop of his family's home in Vancouver to chastise his father and confront him and to blame him for his illness. *It's all their fault.*

"Tyler…Tyler," Marco said, interrupting his thoughts.

"What?"

"Where'd you go just now?"

"I'm sitting right here," Tyler said, looking at him impatiently. Tyler wished it was Carol who was taking them to their appointment, but it was Marco.

"You know what I mean," Marco said, briefly meeting Tyler's gaze before looking back at the road.

Tyler glared at him. "Obviously, I don't."

Marco laughed under his breath. "You were a million miles away. What were you thinking about just then? Want to talk about it?"

"No," Tyler said, crossing his arms over his chest. He wasn't sure he would know how to say it even if he did want to. He stared out the window again, hoping it would excuse him from further discussion.

Marco drove with one hand on the steering wheel, the other resting casually on the door beside him. He had a half smile on his face. He cleared his throat and said, "What do you think you're going to hear today?"

"That it's advanced."

"You know you can't predict the future, and if you try to, you'll just put yourself through all this agony for nothing. Let the doctor do his job," Marco said.

"I'm not predicting the future. I'd rather be prepared for what's coming than not. I'd rather not set myself up for a fall by expecting things to be fine. I figure I'll be less affected by bad news if I go in expecting it. Anything else will be an improvement."

"Hm. I get that. I do," Marco said, "but have you ever heard of the concept of positive thinking helping to improve your health?"

"No. That's stupid."

Marco just laughed, scoffing at Tyler's blunt response. "Well, ha, looks like I've been told. It's not stupid though. You should try it out." He laughed again.

Tyler scowled out the window, refusing to engage any further.

"How 'bout you, Theo?" Marco asked, glancing in the rearview mirror to make eye contact with him.

Theo simply stared back, blinking.

"Tough crowd." Marco looked ahead again. They drove the rest of the way in silence with the exception of the Top 40 radio station that Marco turned on to fill the emptiness.

When they neared the doctor's office, Marco switched the radio off. "When they ask for your health card, just don't panic. I understand you don't have one yet, so we'll take care of that later. We can send an application in once we have your identification sorted through your home province and parents."

Tyler stiffened. "What do they have to do with anything?"

"They're your parents. They have everything to do with you," Marco said. He slowed the vehicle down and turned into the small parking lot of the medical center, which had barely enough room for four cars. The soft gravel and dirt crunched and popped beneath the tires.

"They have everything to do with suffering for sure." Tyler fixed his attention on the structure of the medical center. He considered it so stereotypically East Coast and so painfully "small town." The siding was a light-brown plastic. The building was more like a residential bungalow than a medical center. "That's lucky. We don't have a line up to wait through," Tyler said, nodding to the empty parking lot.

"Yeah, they like to give us their full attention when we come and to leave their other patients for other times." Marco switched off the ignition.

They climbed out of the car and walked to the front door of the medical center. "Let's just hurry in and hurry out," Marco said. "I don't enjoy being in doctor's offices any more than you do, so let's make this quick and painless."

"The needles were done already, so it shouldn't be too bad." Tyler clicked his tongue twice and winked for snappy effect.

Inside the center, Tyler was amused to see that the exterior of the building was a perfect match for the interior. When they first walked in, there was a boot tray with a small box of hospital-issue, blue booties beside it. On the wall, no higher than a foot or two off the ground, a sign read: *Please remove outdoor shoes and boots. Please use booties.*

Marco removed his shoes and donned a pair of booties before removing Theo's shoes. He had decided to carry him since the booties were all too large for his tiny feet.

"Aren't they going to need to burn or throw out the ones I wear? That's a total waste," Tyler asked, hesitating as he considered whether or not to remove his shoes and wear a pair of booties. Even though he was pretty sure defiance was the only way to play it safe, he looked to Marco for a cue.

Marco chuckled. "No. It's not a waste. They'll just wash them after you're done. Same as with everyone else."

"Really?"

"Really. You should read up on the disease. You have a lot of misconceptions about it."

"Yeah, yeah," Tyler said, kicking off his shoes and pulling on a pair of booties.

Once inside the waiting room, they were greeted by a short, stout woman in white nurse's scrubs and white sneakers. The sides of her shirt were stretched tight over her rounded waist. She had straw-blonde hair, pulled into a bun at the back of her head.

"Good morning, Marco. It's nice to see you again," the nurse said as she approached them. She shook Marco's hand. "And you must be Tyler," she said, turning her kindness toward him and offering her hand for a shake. He shook her hand and retracted it quickly, looking down at the floor to avoid eye contact. "And you, you must be Theo. Carol was telling the truth when she said you were a cutie-pie. My name is Crystal Conrad. Most people just call me CC. Unless you prefer formalities, I'd prefer that. I work with Dr. Benson."

Tyler watched as CC, whose voice reminded him of Glinda the Good Witch from *The Wizard of Oz*, spoke to Theo, bringing out smiles and nearly a laugh. She pulled a sucker from her pocket and handed it to Theo. "Usually, I wait until after the appointment for these, but you're a special one, so you can have one now."

Theo's face lit up as he grabbed the sucker; though, his smile faded as Dr. Benson walked into the room. He was intimidating just by the sheer size of him. He stood about six feet and four inches tall with a solid build, not fat but not fit either. His dark-brown mustache was beginning to see an invasion of gray. He wore big square glasses that appeared to be squeezing his nose so tightly that they were the cause of its redness.

Tyler kneeled so he could whisper in Theo's ear. "I think this is Rudolph's human cousin, so we should be extra good."

Theo's eyes widened, and his tiny hand squeezed the sucker a little tighter. He stared up at Dr. Benson and then at Tyler. His fearful expression dissipated.

"It's true. I'm sure of it," Tyler said. He grinned. It was easy for him to try to protect Theo. He wanted to make sure everything went well for him. The fact that Theo would only talk in front of him made him feel like he had something special to offer, and it was something he took seriously.

"Let's get you two into the exam room. I'll do a few physical checks, but I see that Carol did a pretty extensive round of them with you when you arrived at the house, so I won't spend too much time on that or keep you anxiously waiting for the results too long." Dr. Benson ushered them from the waiting room to one of the small rooms in the back. Tyler lifted Theo up onto the examination table, the crinkly white paper echoing loudly, and then sat beside him.

Dr. Benson excused himself from the room to collect his stethoscope.

"Rudolph, eh?" Marco said, snickering.

Tyler blushed.

Dr. Benson returned to the room with CC in tow. She stayed only for a moment to record their blood pressure and temperature. "See you shortly," she said as she exited and closed the door.

"Why close the door if nobody else is here?" Tyler asked.

"It's just customary. Standard procedure really," Marco said.

"If it's safe for us to be around normal people, why do you make it so no one else is here during our appointments?"

"Tyler—"

Dr. Benson raised his hand to silence Marco. "It's not that we are keeping people safe from you. We're keeping you safe from the people."

"What's that mean?"

"The people in this town are somewhat narrow-minded, not well educated. They fear what they don't understand. Often in an irrational way, so we're just sparing you the displeasure of their acquaintance," Dr. Benson said, frowning. He scooped up his otoscope, which appeared far too small for his hands, flicked the light on, and peered into Theo's ears and then Tyler's. "How are you doing, little tyke?"

"He doesn't talk," Tyler said quickly, trying to keep Theo from feeling pressured to say anything.

"Ah, a quiet one, are we?"

Tyler glanced from Theo's face to the doctors. "Yeah, he doesn't talk."

Dr. Benson nodded as he scribbled into Theo's chart. "Marco, keep an eye on that. Make sure to let me know if there's any change."

"For sure, we will," Marco said, straightening up from his lean against the wall as though he were stepping forward to a call for action.

"Why? What does it matter? Maybe he just doesn't like talking." Tyler's eyes began to sting as he spoke. "Isn't there enough wrong with him already? Why do you have to go looking for more trouble?"

"Relax, Tyler. He's not looking for trouble. He's a doctor, and he needs to make sure Theo is healthy."

"Ha. That's funny. Make sure the kid with HIV is healthy. Good one," Tyler said, glaring at Marco.

"I have to rule out other possibilities such as autism or a speech impediment before simply declaring that he's not a talkative boy. I would be an irresponsible doctor if I didn't do my due diligence." Dr. Benson spoke softly to combat Tyler's abrasiveness. "I haven't said anything is wrong with him in the first place. Having HIV doesn't mean there is anything wrong with you. It simply means that you—and he—will get to have a different life experience than most other kids. I think it means that you'll have the joy of discovering gratitude and zest in life earlier and deeper, and there's nothing wrong with that."

Tyler stopped arguing for a moment, considering what the doctor had said. It felt like it was a standard sales pitch, but it seemed genuine. It could also be that it spoke to Tyler's ego, reminding him that he's going to have something better than the "normal" kids. He found himself at a loss for words despite his desire to refute this far too simple statement. "Hm," was all he could muster.

"That's a nice tattoo you've got there," Dr. Benson said, nodding toward the tattoo on Tyler's left forearm. It was done in all black, Old English font and read: *Karma*. "What's the significance?"

"It reminds me to be a good person. No matter what."

"Good reminder. I like that."

"Thanks."

"So let's get to the results. The part of this that you're probably all most concerned about," Dr. Benson said, rolling his chair back toward the door so he could swivel to face all three of them. "These are never the fun parts of a checkup, but let's just rip the Band-Aid right off."

Tyler's chest tightened, his breathing quickened, and his back and underarms started to sweat. The sound of the clock ticking in the corner felt like it was slapping his temples with each second that passed. Ever since his initial diagnosis, he had avoided medical attention and continued using drugs through injection, smoking, snorting, swallowing, and any other way he could. He tried to pretend it wasn't real for so long that it became a nagging fear that he fought to ignore. It wasn't until he quit the hard drugs and started hitchhiking across Canada that the fog cleared enough for him to brave another diagnosis. He saw a flyer for the New Life House and dreamed that they would take care of him while he died, so he wouldn't end up like... He forced himself to avoid the memory he was drifting toward. He just wanted someone to take care of him as it all ended.

Dr. Benson reviewed Theo's chart first. "Theodore Lukas Brookes. A fine name," he said. He winked at Theo. When he spoke, he directed his gaze and words to Marco. "His viral load is quite low. I'm pleased to see the HAART treatments his previous doctor had him on are working quite well. I think we'll continue with those treatments and monitor him and his weight to determine when we can safely switch him over to the newer treatment. For all intents and purposes, he's quite healthy."

"That's great, little man. Did you hear that?" Marco said, leaning forward to give Theo a high five. Theo clapped his tiny hand against Marco's, barely covering half of his palm.

Tyler waited for Theo to turn his attention to him before whispering, "Way to go, Theo. You rock." He braced himself for his results, wringing his hands and taking short breaths.

Dr. Benson set Theo's chart down and opened Tyler's. "Tyler James Nickels. I'm afraid my news for you is not quite as cheerful."

Marco's smile faded as he, too, absorbed what Dr. Benson was saying. His breathing quickened; he stood a little straighter and looked from the doctor's face to Tyler's.

Tyler stared blankly at Dr. Benson, blinking in an attempt to keep the tears at bay.

"Your viral loads are quite high. I'm concerned that you might be dealing with an advanced case, commonly referred to as AIDS. It is typically quite rare to advance so quickly being that you were only diagnosed a little over two years ago, but your CD4 counts are very low. They're hovering around 100. I want to reexamine you in a few weeks' time. What we'll do in the meantime is get you on antiretroviral therapy. That's what you'll hear your friends at the New Life House refer to as A-R-T." He spelled out the acronym for Tyler. "The specific medication I'm going to prescribe is the Combivir tablets. They're easier to take. It's a pill that you take twice a day by mouth, breakfast and dinner."

Tyler stared blankly at the doctor, still trying to think of something to say.

"Have you been noticing any swelling or discomfort in your lymph nodes? Sweats or chills?" The doctor wore a solemn expression now, one of care and concern.

Tyler shrugged and nodded. "Just the sweats. I have to change my sheets in the morning sometimes." He glanced at Marco but then back down to the floor, embarrassed. "I thought Theo pissed in my bed the first time."

The doctor frowned. "I see." He scribbled on Tyler's chart.

"Is it because I was on the streets?"

"I'm not sure. That could play a factor. You weren't taking any medications or living in a lifestyle conducive to nurturing or improving your health. It is not common for such a quick progression; however, it is not the first. It does happen that some people's immune systems have a harder time combatting the virus especially when left untreated. I do, however, believe that the lifestyle you were living plays a role, considering the lack of good nutrition, drug use, and stress. Were you aware that you also have hepatitis C?"

Tyler's face lowered toward the floor. "No," he said quietly. He felt a wave of shame come over him as though he were being diagnosed for the first time again.

Marco bowed his head as he listened.

Tyler was blankly accepting everything the doctor was saying, nodding and blinking, giving the odd *uh-huh* and visibly trembling as he harnessed his emotions and held his composure. Despite all the preaching he had been doing about expecting the worst-case scenario, nothing could have prepared him for the actual moment. "Am I going to die?"

Dr. Benson offered a comforting smile. "We're going to get you on some tough meds and a healthy meal plan. I think we can avoid such dire results, in an immediate sense, if we ensure you are active and committed to a healthy lifestyle."

"I thought it was a death sentence...AIDS..." Tyler said. His voice faded as he said the last word as though saying it any louder would unleash the gravity it held.

"Don't get ahead of yourself just yet. We haven't crossed that bridge. There are higher risks once it advances and there are times when you will be more uncomfortable, but with proper care and your new lifestyle and medications, anything is possible," Dr. Benson said, closing the file. "Never underestimate the power of science. You never know when someone will find a cure to this thing."

Tyler coughed. Phlegm wet the edge of the fist he used to cover his mouth. He wiped it on his chest.

Dr. Benson's face lit up as though he'd just remembered something. "Yes, that cough. Carol had mentioned she was concerned about it. Let's take a look."

Tyler lifted his shirt so the doctor could listen. He let out a faint gasp as the cold metal of the stethoscope touched his skin. He could feel the phlegm gurgling in his lungs as he did the requested breathing—inhale, exhale and inhale, exhale. He closed his eyes so he wouldn't have to see Marco's face. He didn't want to see that sickening look of pity anymore.

When Dr. Benson was done listening, he removed the earpieces of his stethoscope from his ears and hung them around his neck. He looked at Tyler with apparent compassion. Tyler couldn't tell if it was real or if he was trained to do this as a doctor. "You've got an awful lot of fluid built up in your lungs. Carol was right to be concerned." He turned to Marco. "I'll draw up a prescription for an antibiotic for that as well. Keep an eye on it, and let me know if it gets worse."

Marco nodded his understanding. "Maybe you and Theo can go wait in the lobby for a few moments while I speak with the doctor."

Tyler knew this was more of an instruction than a request. He stood and lifted Theo onto his hip, balancing him with one arm. "Come on, Theo. Let's go." Theo stared intently at Tyler and kept still in his arms, breaking from his usual squirming and giggling. He reached his hand up and placed it against Tyler's cheek as if to comfort him.

"I'm sorry the news wasn't what you were expecting, Tyler," Dr. Benson said, standing to shake his hand.

Marco exhaled a big, shaky breath and cleared his throat to keep himself from crying. "I'll be out soon." His voice wavered as he called after them.

IN THE WAITING room, after CC had given them their suckers, Tyler and Theo sat side by side, with their backs to the window, facing CC's desk. She was quietly sorting through files and entering data into her computer.

"What did they mean? AIDS?" Theo asked, clutching and staring at the two suckers CC had given him. He was sitting on the edge of his chair, swinging his feet back and forth rapidly.

CC looked up from her computer, surprised to hear Theo talk. Tyler raised his finger to his mouth in a friendly "shhh" motion. She smiled and went back to her computer, sneaking a peek at the two of them every few seconds.

Tyler took a deep breath. He could feel tears dancing around in his eyes, itching to burst out. "It means that everything's gonna be okay," he said. Theo was looking up at him now. Tyler tousled his hair playfully and changed the subject. "Look at you with two big suckers. That's the best loot ever."

"Suckers, suckers," Theo said gleefully, staring back down at his prize.

Tyler looked up just in time to catch CC watching them again; she quickly looked back to her computer screen. He could see that she, too, was fighting tears.

WHEN MARCO WAS finished speaking with Dr. Benson, they both came to the waiting room so the doctor could shake their hands once more and to, again, offer his apologies for the bad news. Tyler couldn't wait to get out of there and back to the house where he could hide.

They drove mostly in silence. Marco didn't push Tyler for conversation as he had on the way into town.

Tyler mused at how Marco's whole diatribe about having a positive outlook on life was used up and now he had nothing to fall back on. *That's the problem with blinding yourself to reality.* He rolled his eyes and fixed his gaze on the farm fields that blew by as they sped out of town.

Marco shifted and fidgeted in his seat as he grappled with what to say to break the silence. After a few false starts, he said, "Now remember what the doctor said. It's not certain to have advanced yet. Anything can still happen." He forced a half-hearted smile. "I'm going to need you to tell me how to contact your parents."

"Why can't you just leave it alone?" Tyler yelled out of frustration. He thought he'd made himself clear on the drive into town.

Marco startled at Tyler's reaction, but held his ground. "It is illegal for us not to inform your parents that you're living with us and that your health has changed. You're still a minor."

"They're not going to give you any money. They're not going to do anything," Tyler shouted, slamming his fist against his door.

"Quit slamming things. I understand that you're dealing with some pretty wretched news, but you still have to respect that Carol and I are acting as your guardians. That means you have to at least feign respect for us from time to time. And it's not about money."

"Just leave me alone," Tyler said, mumbling and crossing his arms across his chest. "Just stop." He folded his arms tighter and turned to look out the window, watching as the New Life House and its property line came into view. Their little fortress sheltered from the horrors of the outside world. Horrors like the one he'd had to face today.

"All right, I'll leave it alone for now. But you have to realize that we can't legally keep you here without informing your parents. I'd rather talk to them than lose you," Marco said as he slowed the car to turn into the laneway.

Tyler said nothing and made no gesture to show that he had heard.

"I guess I'll take your silence as confirmation that you heard me."

When they got back to the house, Tyler went straight upstairs to bed without stopping to speak to anyone. Carol brought him a sandwich and a glass of milk for lunch, and when he didn't come down for dinner, she brought him up a full plate with roast chicken, mashed potatoes, steamed carrots, broccoli, and a dinner roll. He wouldn't roll over to greet her or answer her when she asked if he wanted to talk, but the empty plates when she returned to gather dishes satisfied her enough to let him be.

As Marco and Carol prepared for bed, Tyler slipped a small piece of paper under their bedroom door.

Nancy and Bruce Nickels
1-604-481-3444

Chapter Six

IT WAS A Sunday evening when Marco chose to call Tyler's parents. He remembered Tyler talking about how religious they are, which led him to want to call on a Sunday. Hopefully, they had learned about forgiveness and unconditional love at the morning's sermon. He could hear the faint echoes of the laugh track from an evening sitcom the kids were watching in the TV room. He was in the office, spinning in circles in the desk chair as he considered what he was going to say to the Nickels'.

The room was cluttered. There were files, notebooks, boxes of old medical records, frames with degrees waiting to be hung on the walls, empty Tim Horton's coffee cups, and all kinds of random office paraphernalia. The chaos mirrored how Marco felt inside: overwhelmed.

"You want me here for this?" Carol asked from the doorway. She held the newest novel she was reading in her hands, standing with a small knitted blanket over her shoulder.

Marco looked up at her. "You're primed and ready to read while they watch. Go ahead. I'll be fine."

"Okay. Good luck," she said before turning toward the TV room and disappearing from sight.

"Okay, you can do this. Just suck it up and make the call," Marco said, attempting to give himself a pep talk. The desk drawer shrieked and grunted as he slid it open. Inside the drawer was a jumble of pens and random, previously used, stick-it notes. He never understood why he and Carol never made the extra motion to throw them in the garbage once they were done. It's not like the garbage was far away. It lived right beside the desk. They simply tucked it away to be dealt with later, a time that never seemed to come. Amidst the chaos was the small piece of paper with Tyler's parents' contact information. He snatched it up and slammed the drawer closed harder than he'd meant to, sending huge drops of his of tea splattering about the top of the desk. "Shit." He grabbed several tissues from the box beside the monitor and dabbed hastily at the spill. Before dialing, he rummaged through the papers sind files on top of the desk in search of his glasses case. "What a mess," he said as he finally found it.

After a few deep breaths, he dialed the number. And after a few rings, a man answered.

"Hello?"

Marco sat forward in his chair as if to come off more formal. He thought himself silly considering Tyler's father clearly couldn't see him through the phone. "Hi there, is this Mr. Bruce Nickels?"

"Yes, this is he. Who's this?"

"My name is Marco Costa—"

"Hm. You don't sound very Spanish," Bruce interrupted.

Indignant, Marco responded, "I'm Italian. You won't be hearing any Spanish today, sir."

The line went silent save for the sound of a woman, who Marco assumed must be Mrs. Nickels, asking Bruce who was calling. "Ah, so no Spanish for me today. Too bad. What can I do for you?"

"I'm calling from the New Life House out in Nova Scotia."

"Nova Scotia? What does someone from way out there want with me?" Bruce began sounding impatient. "I don't have time for these telemarketing scams. Nobody does."

"I understand. I don't either. This is not a telemarketing scam. Trust me," Marco said.

"Sure. I'll repeat my question. What does someone in Nova Scotia want with me? I'm a little more than a stone's throw away here," Bruce said. His tone softened.

"I'm calling about your son," Marco said, bracing himself for the aftermath. Bruce said nothing. The sound of heavy breathing encouraged Marco to keep going, so he continued, "He's come to live with us here. His disease has advanced quite rapidly and aggressively—"

"Look. I don't know what he's telling you, but I don't have a so—"

Marco interrupted Bruce this time. "Sir, with all due respect, you *do* have a son, and he is very sick and—"

"No, you listen here, Mister. With *all due respect*, I told that dirty little faggot to get out of our lives and to stay out. He's got what he deserves, and God is doing *His* justice. It's no fault of mine that he chose to sin and receive Holy punishment. That's on him," Bruce shouted.

Marco had to pull the phone away from his ear. He brought the phone back slowly so he could speak when the shouting stopped, but Bruce started in again.

"You queer lovers out there keep him, and don't bother me with this again. And don't bother my family either. I don't want to hear from you again." The line went dead, filling Marco's ear with the hateful hum of the dial tone.

"Wow," Marco said, confounded by the hatred Bruce had spewed at him. He hadn't imagined there would be such an adverse response. Suddenly, all of Tyler's refusals to speak to his family became clear.

THAT NIGHT, AFTER all the kids had gone to bed, Marco went outside to join Carol. "Oh, good. I'm glad you're still smoking one," he said, sighing as he stepped outside and onto the veranda. The screen door did its usual clatter-and-slam routine.

Carol grabbed her chest and whipped around to look at him. "Jesus, you scared me half to death."

He giggled. "A little stoned are we?" He walked over and sat beside her heavily. The springs of the swing creaked as they adjusted to his added weight.

Carol shot him a mischievous glare. "I don't know what you're talking about."

"Gimme that," Marco said, playfully tackling her to take the joint away. "I think I'll be confiscating this contraband." He squinted at her in jest as he took a long toke.

Carol relaxed back in her seat, watching Marco with curiosity as he smoked. His brow was furrowed and his eyes dark. He rarely showed his anger. She reached out to run her fingers along his shoulder and arm.

He kept his eyes on the night sky and smoked the joint in silence until it was gone.

"It went that bad, eh?"

Marco looked at her, startled from his thoughts. "Yeah, it was pretty dismal."

She sat up and tucked her feet onto the swing to face him, inviting him to tell her more.

"That's not my God," he said, almost in a whisper. "My God teaches forgiveness and love. I know you don't think so or believe in any of it, but I believe. I believe God is loving, not hateful."

Carol nodded. "I know."

Marco was glad she didn't take this time to go off on one of her rants about religion or God. In fact, he was glad it was something they rarely discussed because they sat on such opposite sides of the spectrum. She was an atheist, and he was raised Catholic and still held many of his beliefs even though he didn't go to church and rejected the hate-based teachings. He appreciated that she sometimes tried to respect the fact that he had taken what he needed from the religion and had left the rest.

"Like, how can someone so devout in his religion be filled with so much hate? And it's not just hatred for some random person; it's for his own son. He hates his own son," Marco said. The stars reflecting in his eyes appeared to tremble as he spoke. "That asshole kicked his son out and forced him onto the streets where he got worse. Tyler's health could be so different if his stupid father had learned anything in church."

"I'm sorry, Marco. I know you were hoping there would be some sort of excitement or gratitude for news about Tyler." Carol soothingly stroked his neck with her fingers.

"I just thought that love for his son would be more important than his hatred for gays or whatever." He pointed angrily at the emptiness beyond the veranda. "I thought family would be more important."

"Some people are assholes. Let him hide behind his misconception of the bible. He'll be the one who regrets it in the end."

"You know they're never going to send a cent for Tyler to be here, right?"

Carol nodded. "I gathered that much."

"I want to pay for him to stay. I don't want to send him out to be part of some ill-prepared foster home. His place is here." He was crying now.

Carol said nothing.

"I need to do this. I don't care if I have to pull it from my own savings. I just need this. I can't explain it." He sounded frantic, desperate.

"Never mind that," Carol said, waving her hand dismissively. "We're going to do this together. Everything's going to be okay."

Marco smiled and sniffled, wiping at the tears and snot that had run onto his face. He leaned into her arms, rested his head on her chest, and whispered, "There's always tomorrow."

Chapter Seven

CAROL AND MARCO had given strict instructions to everyone that they were to have a group therapy session before dinner. It wasn't Wednesday, so this was an extra session. Apparently, it was being held so they—the kids—could address any feelings they might be having about the news Tyler received earlier in the day head-on. In Maggie's opinion, it was cruel and unfair to force Tyler to listen to everyone talk about it before he even had time to process it on his own.

Earlier in the day, Dr. Benson confirmed that Tyler had advanced to AIDS. At the appointment, the doctor informed Carol and Marco that because of the length of time Tyler had gone untreated and the lifestyle he had kept before seeking out the New Life House, his body had had little strength to fight the virus. Now, with three AIDS-defining illnesses—hepatitis C, a lung infection, and night sweats—and an extremely low CD4 count, Dr. Benson was certain Tyler's case had advanced.

Marco, Carol and Tyler had broken it to the others soon after they got home from the appointment, a few hours before this therapy session was called.

"Okay, everyone, let's get started," Marco said, motioning with his hands for everyone to settle down.

The chairs in the library were arranged in a circle, making for a more intimate and supportive setting. They sat in a similar order every week. Marco and Carol were sitting side by side at the head of the circle, and from Carol's left around to Marco's right were Maggie, Theo, Bradley, Curtis, and Tyler.

"Tyler, why don't you start tonight? You've been to a few of these now. You should have the hang of it," Carol said.

He crossed his arms and slumped down in his chair, clenching his lips together in refusal.

"I can start," Maggie said, trying to get Tyler off the hook.

"Sure. Kick us off and we'll go around in a circle clockwise." Carol leaned back in her chair, preparing to listen. She had a pad of paper in her lap, which she used to jot down notes on specific things everyone mentioned. She did this so she could reference any concerns that arose during their one-on-one sessions later in the week.

"I'm just struggling with hope right now. I know it's insensitive considering…" Maggie glanced at Tyler shyly. "I just find it hard to have hope that we're all going to be okay when we see that it won't be for someone in the same situation as us." She hated having to choose her words so carefully. She really wanted to talk about Janie and how she'd lost her hope along the way and felt like she had no one to talk to about it. And after what happened with her, now Maggie was feeling the same way, and it scared her. She didn't want to end up like that. But she knew she couldn't talk about it around Carol. She hated how superficial her problems sounded and knew that if she were just able to talk about what she was feeling, she would be better off.

"There's still hope for Tyler," Marco said. "He is on Combivir like the rest of you, and you never know what the world of science will discover today or tomorrow or the day after that. There's always hope."

Maggie smiled her fake smile, knowing she would never get anywhere with what she was saying and said that she agreed and that she'd finished sharing for the day.

"Theo, are you gonna say anything today?" Marco asked, shrinking his stature down to meet Theo's terrified gaze and frantic head shaking indicating an emphatic "No."

"You know, I'm sorry to bug on your news, Tyler, but I need to talk about it," Bradley said, his voice jumped out of him as though he'd been anxiously waiting to speak for hours.

Tyler shrugged and kept his eyes focused on the floor.

"I don't wanna steal your feelings from you, but it really has me freaked out."

Tyler shifted in his seat. "Ha, nice," he said sarcastically.

"No, not in that way. It's not an insult, man. I've been having a hard time with it because it's like I've been living here all this time and ignoring the fact that I'm sick."

Carol and Marco both sat up in their chairs to listen closer.

"I've been walking around like this is some kind of boarding school or glorified foster home or something, but it's so much more than that. I could *die*. You could die. We could *all* die. It's like I forgot this disease could advance because I've been living in this protective bubble out here."

"You're not living in a protective bubble out here, Bradley," Carol said. "Forgive my interjection, but I feel it is important for you to understand that you've been living a quasi-normal life out here because this disease is not a death sentence. A few years ago, it was a different story. There are treatments now—as you know and are on—that practically guarantee you a full life. You can live a normal life. Just imagine where we will have advanced to in another few years."

"How do you explain Tyler then? I'm sorry, man," Bradley said, pointing at Tyler. "I know you have to be feeling that this whole 'it's not a death sentence' thing is a bit tired too."

"Bradley, it's not tired. Every case is different. You can't assume that because one person's viral load is high, another person's will be as well. You know that. No one is the same. That's what makes us unique," Carol said. "I understand that you're afraid and that Tyler's recent news brings up fears you thought you had dealt with, but everything will be okay. There's always tomorrow."

A shadow of a smile crossed Bradley's face as Carol finished. "There's always tomorrow," he whispered, leaning back in his chair and crossing his arms over his chest. "It's so frustrating."

"You know, Bradley's right," Curtis said.

"He is?" Marco asked, sounding surprised.

"Yeah, he is. I think he's just having a hard time expressing it properly."

"Okay, give it a go." Marco grinned slightly, a proud glint in the corner of his eye.

Curtis straightened in his chair. "We all have this disease for whatever reason. Be it that we made some poor life choices or that someone else's poor life choices had an adverse effect on us or some tragic accident, who knows? We all have it is what matters."

Bradley nodded along as Curtis spoke. Maggie nervously looked from Curtis to Tyler to Carol, unsure whom she should be siding with. She wanted to agree with all of them and to stop them from forcing Tyler to listen to their fears about him.

"We live in this house with people who are like us and are being raised by you two." He pointed at Carol and Marco. "And we don't get to experience a social world outside of this. We hear about HIV and the statistics all the time, and we comfort ourselves with them. We forget that this disease is still very real and that it can take a turn for the worse without any notice. That's the bubble. And Tyler being diagnosed with AIDS, I think, just woke us all up to that."

TYLER SCOFFED UNDER his breath as he watched Marco and Carol nod proudly. For the first time, he found himself irritated by Curtis, mostly because he was probably right.

"You don't get diagnosed with AIDS. HIV advances to AIDS, but it is not a diagnosis," Carol said, frowning as she did.

"Well spoken, bud," Bradley said, pushing on Curtis's knee.

"You know, I never told you how I got it," Tyler said, sitting up straight and gripping his seat tightly. The room quieted, and all eyes focused on him. The tension in the air was palpable as he spoke.

Carol was sure Tyler was going to snap and storm out like he had in class. "Tyler, you don't have to say this."

"My family is very religious. We went to church twice a week and said family prayers every day. I figured out that I was bisexual when I was around twelve. Started rebelling and doing drugs and doing everything I could to rebel against God. I was angry with Him for making me rotten." Tyler ignored Bradley's noticeable cringe as he admitted to being bisexual. "I was experimenting in life and got infected with HIV by sleeping with a guy. My father beat the hell out of me when I told him I'd gotten it and that it was from gay sex. He screamed about HIV being a gay disease and how I deserved it. I was tossed out in the front yard with a backpack and a few pieces of clothing at barely sixteen years old." He struggled to fight off tears, taking a deep breath to try to calm himself down.

Carol tried to interject, but he continued. "I told my mom first. I thought she would be the one to protect me because my dad had always been so abusive. She freaked out and told me I was disgusting and that I was against God and that this was punishment for lying with another man." Tyler made air quotes with his hands as he said this. "She refused to hug me or do anything to help. She said I was dirty and that I would give it to her if I even touched her. I never even got to say goodbye to my sister." He stiffened in his chair as he thought of Rachel.

"I spent a little over a year living on the streets of Vancouver, using drugs and booze. I had a real problem with smashing coc' and heroin, but I got off about two months before coming here. Went to detox. I was prostituting myself for money for food and a place to sleep at night."

Maggie began to cry, dabbing at her eyes with a tissue.

"I heard about this place by accident. At a shelter one night, I heard about this house in Nova Scotia where kids with AIDS could come to die."

Carol inhaled aggressively. "You come here to live," she said abruptly.

Tyler paused to consider this, but continued without correcting himself. "I hitchhiked here from Vancouver. When I got here, I had barely eaten in two days. I weighed, what, barely over a hundred pounds. Hadn't showered in a week. I made the call on my birthday and got here a month later. That was my birthday present to myself. Pathetic."

"Tyler, are you sure you want to be saying these things like this?" Marco asked. "You might want to find some healing for some of this before revealing it to everyone at group. Maybe during your one-on-one sessions would be better?"

Tyler shot Marco a fierce look. "I have nothing to lose now. I'm dying, so I may as well forget about later and get it all out in the open now. What does tomorrow matter for anymore?"

Carol attempted to interrupt again. "Tyler—"

"You know, I gave up when I was out there. On the streets. I remember a john forced himself on me and tried to get away without paying. I kneeled on the fucker's throat until he couldn't hurt me anymore. I wish it was my father instead of that man—"

"Tyler! That's enough," Marco said angrily, cutting Tyler off midsentence. "Theo is too young to hear this, and this is not the type of thing you should be sharing in group. Let's save this for one-on-one."

Feeling like he'd gotten the upper hand, Tyler smirked and sat back in his chair, satisfied. He wasn't going to be shushed. And he loved the look of discomfort on Bradley's face as he told the story. *Good*, he thought. *Good.* He glared first at Bradley and then at Marco as he waited for group to be dismissed.

THE HOUSE WAS quiet and dark with the exception of the glow from the joint Carol was smoking on the back veranda. Marco had gone to bed and had ensured that all of the kids had as well. It was part of her regular routine to finish the night off with about half a bottle of Chianti and a joint. Today she was drinking a full bottle and partaking in a planned two joints, but had brought her stash and rolling papers down just in case the need for more were to arise. She had been struggling with accepting Tyler's test results ever since they'd heard them, and now that this group session had brought it all up in the kids, and with the intense outburst from Tyler, she was emotionally tapped out. The only way she felt she could get through this without yelling at someone or breaking down was to retreat to her familiar spot on the veranda to watch the stars dance on the horizon and for a double dose.

"Hey, you got room for one more?" Tyler said, stepping out onto the veranda. He held the door and closed it gently to keep it from squeaking and slamming.

Carol could feel herself start to panic with the joint in her hand. She contemplated throwing it over the veranda, but didn't think fast enough as Tyler was already sitting beside her.

"Relax," Tyler said, chuckling. "I've seen a joint before. You don't have to trip out."

"Well, Jesus. I've never been caught by one of the kids."

"I'm not a kid," Tyler said, snatching the joint from her hand and taking a toke before she could grab it away from him. "I'm not like the other kids here."

"I know you're not," Carol said, reaching farther to try to get the joint from him. She watched him carefully as she half-heartedly tried to stop him from smoking it. Maybe she was higher than she'd been in a while, but she wasn't sure she wanted to stop him. She hadn't had company to get high with in so long. Marco rarely partook.

With indignation Tyler said, "Relax."

"You shouldn't smoke this." She could barely take herself seriously as she said it, and it was clear he didn't either. She reached for the joint again.

He pulled it out of reach quickly and took a long toke. "Hey, I'm the one who's dying. It's you who shouldn't be smoking this shit," he said through a smoke-filled cough. He smirked and handed it back to her. "Besides, I need something to make all this touchy-feely group shit bearable."

She took the joint, sizing him up as she took a long haul. She was speechless. She felt like she was having an out-of-body experience as she handed the joint back to him. *What the hell am I doing? Is this happening?*

"I won't tell anyone, so don't worry. I just got off the streets. I have a code," he said proudly, handing her the joint after taking another few puffs.

Carol stared at him, bewildered with the situation. "I never thought I'd be smoking a joint with one of the kids that live here. I feel like this is a horrible dream, like I'm not really making this stupid mistake." Years ago, before Janie died, she would have sent Tyler back inside and reprimanded him sternly for the intrusion. She shook her head as the reality of the moment sunk in.

"It's not a mistake. Whether you'll admit it or not, I've got less time left than the other kids do. And I'm from the streets. I've smoked a lot of dope. It's not like I'm going to go inside and trip out like the rest of these kids would."

"Try not to put yourself too highly above them. They all have stories too," Carol cautioned. "Just look at Theo. He's here because his mother is an addict who can't care for him. He comes from a pretty messed up background. Nobody's life was perfect before coming here."

Tyler seemed to disregard her words of wisdom. He smirked. "Yeah, I guess Curtis would be fun to toke with."

"Stop it," Carol said. She could feel the effects of the weed and wine kicking in. She was light-headed and beginning to grin like it was her first time again. She knew she should be ashamed that she was getting high with one of the kids she had sworn to protect, but she felt good. She watched—almost as though she were standing beside herself, looking on—as she handed him the joint and he took it in slow motion. If she were being honest with herself, she would admit that she enjoyed the company. She felt comforted—and even more satisfied by the drug—in Tyler's company. It was kind of like the rush of adrenaline that came from breaking the rules was making the experience even better.

"You know, it's strange. I came to understand and accept my sexuality when I was pretty young. It's my parents who were ashamed. They really hated me for being bisexual. In a way, I think it was their refusal to talk to me about it that got me into trouble in the first place. Most kids get the sex talk, but because my parents were so afraid I'd have sex with a dude, they didn't tell me anything. I didn't learn about the real dangers from the people who were supposed to protect me. It was their job, and they failed at it, and I'm paying the price."

"They never even talked to you about sex? What about in school?" Carol asked, lighting the second joint.

"We went to a very strict Catholic school. There was no such thing as sex ed. Our parents were very concerned that we look good at church and in the eyes of God. There was no such thing as sex before marriage as far as they were concerned."

She passed the joint to Tyler. "How did they know to fear that you might sleep with a guy?"

Tyler laughed, choked, and coughed as he inhaled smoke from the joint. "I never knew how to delete the stupid internet history. Turns out they knew how to look."

"Ha!" Carol took the joint back again. "That's funny. Good ol' internet. You guys had it early."

"What do you mean?"

"Well, it seems like the internet craze is only really just starting out here." Carol still didn't quite understand the whole phenomenon.

Tyler shrugged. "I guess so. I never really thought about it." After a brief pause, Tyler added, "I didn't kill that john like I said I did."

Carol smiled, amused. "I was pretty sure it was a lie. Why'd you say it?"

"Bradley was so freaked out that I was bi that I figured I'd freak him out even more."

"You'll have to come clean with everyone. That's a serious claim to make, so you'll want to set it right."

"Ugh, that sucks, but I will. Also, I think you should know that Theo's been talking. He's been talking to me nonstop since the first day. I promised I wouldn't tell."

"Really? That's great. I'm glad you did. I was getting really worried."

"I know. That's the only reason why I'm telling you. I hate telling secrets."

"It's safe with me." She reflected on the brotherly bond Tyler and Theo had been forming since they moved in, apparent in every action, word, and look they gave one another. She wondered if Tyler would have started letting his guard down this early had Theo not been his roommate. *A sad thought*, she decided, *that a four-year-old having HIV was meant to be.* She hoped Marco's God had more beautiful things planned for "His children" than this. Running the New Life House had pretty well secured her atheism years ago.

Tyler smiled; his eyes were red. "I never imagined this would be my life."

"It's been a rough day. Try not to give up."

"I'm living at a hospice. I think that ship has sailed."

"Don't call it a hospice," Carol said, frowning.

"Why?"

"Because you don't come here to die. You come here to live."

"Hm," Tyler replied, handing the joint back to her.

His indifference unsettled her. She felt like he knew something she didn't. She watched him as he stared off into the stars. No wonder in his gaze, just the soft glistening of his wounds. She smoked the joint in silence as she watched him observing the night sky. After a few tokes, she choked and sputtered and passed the joint back.

"To tell you the truth, I never thought this would be my life either," Carol said. They sat, side by side, staring out at the sparkling emptiness.

"You didn't?"

"No. I imagined I'd have kids and a husband and my own office as a psychiatrist making the big bucks."

"What changed?"

"Everything."

Chapter Eight

"WHY IS IT called a sunroom?" Theo asked. He was sitting next to Tyler with a firm grip on Clifford the Bear, twisting him about and changing his perspective of the room over and over as he, too, tilted his own head to see the room from all of its possible angles.

"Because the huge window faces where the sun sits and allows all sorts of heat and light in. It's basically the place to enjoy the sun. It's like a church for the sun in your house," Tyler said, pointing at the window.

"What's a church?"

"A place where scary people go."

"But we're not scary. Why are we here?"

Tyler laughed. "No, we're not scary. Sunrooms are the church for the good people, not the scary ones."

"Oh," Theo said. He paused, stopping Clifford in midspin as he considered his next question.

Tyler took another gulp of his coffee. He liked the silhouette that the sun cast over the row of maple trees that divided them from the realities beyond. The only connection to the outside world was the thin stretch of gravel driveway that snuck between them. Snow now covered most of the property. The snow removal company had come through and cleared the concrete section of the driveway so the ice and freshly fallen snow glistened on the dark cement. "Look how exciting this all is, Theo. See the snow gathering on the trees way out there?" Tyler said, tapping Theo's shoulder and encouraging him to look where he was pointing.

"Where?"

"On the trees way out there. It's just like the trees from the start of the Rudolph movie." He pointed to a collection of pine trees huddled near where the driveway slipped through the maples.

"I can't see. Where? Is it too far?"

Tyler sighed. He sometimes forgot he was talking to a four-year-old. "It's magical anyway."

"Can we watch Rudolph?"

"Maybe later."

The floorboards creaked in the hallway behind them.

"I can watch it with him if you want to stay here and relax," Maggie said from the doorway.

Tyler spun around quickly in his seat to face her. "Are you spying on me!?"

"Wh-what? N-no," Maggie said, stammering and taking a few steps backward.

"Well, how do you know what we're talking about then? I'm not a fuckin' pedophile," he seethed.

"What are you talking about?" she said curtly. "I never said—"

"Just because you all find out I'm bi doesn't mean you have to start spying on me. We share a room for fuck's sake."

"Stop talking to me like that." She cleared her throat and balled her hands into fists. "I don't think any of us care that you're bi. Well, maybe Bradley, but no one else does."

"Why are you spying on me then?"

"I wasn't spying." She stepped back into the room. "I was passing by and saw you two in here talking. I hadn't ever heard Theo speak. It kinda drew me in."

"So you did listen to us."

"But it wasn't spying. I had no motive." She walked around the couch, lifting her chest and perking her breasts out as she did. "I thought it was sweet."

"Sweet, eh?" Tyler said, smiling and leaning back into the couch. "Sorry I freaked out."

Maggie blushed. "It's okay."

"No, it's not. I shouldn't have yelled at you." He took a big sip of his coffee.

"Thank you. I guess it makes sense. You've had a rough week."

"You're right about that. It's been brutal," he said.

"Why did you tell us all that stuff yesterday?"

Tyler didn't respond. He sat quietly with his eyes focused on the line of distant trees. Calmly, he took a deep breath and looked back at Maggie. "Because I found out I have nothing left to lose anymore, so why not be honest about who I am and stop hiding?"

Maggie kept his gaze. "But were you telling the truth about that...you called it a john?"

Tyler smirked. "What do you think?"

She smiled awkwardly. "I have a hard time thinking it could be true, but you do have an angry streak. And if you say you were telling the truth..."

"You'd believe me?" he said without intending to sound indignant. "I mean...you would for real? Just because I say it's true?"

"I believe in trusting someone until they've proven that I shouldn't." She sat up proudly, seemingly committed to her convictions.

"Hm. I like that," Tyler said. "You wouldn't survive one week on the streets."

They both laughed.

"That's for sure. It would be a big change from where I come from." She watched him take another sip of his coffee. "You know that's decaf, right?" She pointed at his cup.

Tyler followed her motion, bending his head down to stare at the mug he was cradling in his hand. "Are you kidding me!? No wonder I'm still exhausted."

Maggie giggled and leaned back into the cushion of the armchair, shifting to get comfortable. She pulled the knitted blanket that was folded on the back of the chair down and draped it over her legs, making sure to carefully wrap her feet. "Try adding an extra scoop of sugar. At least you'll get the sugar high to mimic the caffeine."

Tyler chuckled. "Yeah, and I'll add diabetes to my list of problems." They paused in awkward silence. "Do you think less of me now from what I said yesterday?"

"No.".

"It's okay. I judge myself most days."

Maggie took a breath and a moment to think of what she wanted to say before speaking. "I think that when you notice you're judging yourself, you should actively think of something to love about yourself. There's nothing wrong with being bi."

"Seriously? You don't think?"

"No. Not at all. I think everyone's curious. I think you can be bi when you're single, but when you're in a relationship you're either gay or straight depending on who you're with. I think I've got a pretty open mind."

"Interesting. Hey, Theo, can you go find Carol for a bit? I think she wants you to go see her," Tyler said. He felt guilty for lying to him and sending him away in such a juvenile way, but he wanted to spend some time talking to Maggie alone. To his surprise, Theo put up no argument, grabbed his sippy cup of milk and Clifford, and playfully stomped out of the sunroom in search of Carol.

"So—" Tyler paused and flashed a mischievous grin. "—how'd you get it?" He tried to sound as fake-sexy as possible, adding an exaggerated wink for effect.

Maggie giggled, covering her mouth shyly as she did. "Answer my question first."

"What question?"

"Did you really kill someone?"

Tyler shook his head. "Nah, I was just trying to freak Bradley out. I did kneel on the guy's throat though."

"Oh?"

"I wanted to kill him, but I couldn't. I was imagining my dad as I was attacking him, and it's like I woke up or something. You know, like from some sort of awful dream. And I saw what I was doing and got all freaked out and took off."

Maggie's eyes were wide as she listened. She hardly succeeded at appearing compassionate.

"Johns weren't supposed to be violent. The guy tried to rip me off, and then he punched me. It just brought somethin' outta me that I don't think either of us expected," Tyler said. He surprised himself with how matter-of-fact he could talk about the experience. He hadn't thought any of the therapy sessions had been effective. He was always so irritated by Maggie and the other kids when they talked about their issues in such a grown-up, controlled way. *Easy habit to form*, he mused.

"It's crazy, but I get it. I think it's probably a normal reaction."

"Ha. I doubt any normal person would find themselves in that mess in the first place."

"Given the circumstances, I'd say it was pretty normal," Maggie said, blushing. "Sorry. I'm not trying to make excuses for you."

Tyler shrugged. "No worries."

"I was born in Toronto. That's where I got it," Maggie started. "I was sent here when I was six."

"Wow. That's really young," Tyler said.

"Yeah, it was." Maggie sat up straighter in her seat. "My family was very wealthy."

"They're not anymore?"

"Not what?"

"Rich."

"They're not my family anymore. My family was rich when it was them, but now this is my family."

"Are you kidding? Carol and Marco are loaded. Aren't they?"

Maggie smiled. "It's different though. In Toronto, it was like a socialite family. We had more money than anyone I knew. My dad is the CEO of a big company and my mom came from money, and I got HIV from a needle at a park when I was six."

"What were you playing with a needle at six for?"

"My nanny had taken me to the park to play. I had my doll, Alice, with me. She was sick," Maggie said, laughing and rolling her eyes. "I was administering a cure for her to feel better. I had her in my lap and stuck the needle into her, and it went straight through and into my leg."

"Wow," Tyler said, gasping. "Talk about an unfortunate way to get it."

"What do you mean? Aren't all the ways unfortunate?"

"Well, yeah. But you didn't lose your innocence to get it. You got it *because* of your innocence. You know?"

Maggie pondered that for a moment. "I guess...yeah...it is sad. I've done a lot of work to accept it, though."

"Of course. You'd have to," Tyler said, pulling his legs up so he could sit on his feet. "Keep going though. Sorry I keep interrupting."

"Gosh, no worries." She waved his apology away. "My nanny still works for my parents. They were so afraid that people would find out I had gotten it that they kept her on staff to keep her from telling anyone, and they sent me here."

"Shitty."

"Yeah, it was pretty shitty," Maggie said. "They've told everyone that I'm away at some fancy boarding school and that someday I'll be the CEO of the family business. Like they think I'll come back someday after ten or twenty years of being hidden away to save their reputation."

"Would you?"

Maggie scoffed. "No. They haven't spoken to me in years. I receive a Christmas letter every year, and Carol and Marco receive a bunch of money for me. That's all they do. I would be too tempted to ruin them if I went back."

Tyler chuckled. "Feisty. I like it. Revenge is something I can relate to."

"I was the first kid here. It was just me for a couple years before anyone else showed up. Then my friend Janie came. She was a few years older than me. Simply put, she was amazing. She made me feel alive, you know? She challenged my reserved nature and desire to be proper and taught me to be bad. It was always exciting with her around. I got to reinvent myself;

though, since she's been gone, I'm back to being the same old me again. I wish she were still here to keep me from becoming so boring."

"You don't need to reinvent yourself if you're happy with who you are, and I think there's a lot you should be happy about."

Maggie blushed. "Really?"

"Yeah."

"Thanks. I appreciate that, but there was this carefree and bold attitude she brought out in me that I miss. I miss the way she made me feel."

"Hm."

"Hm, what?"

"Is that why you accept me for being bi?"

"No, no. There was nothing like that between us."

Tyler looked her over suspiciously. "But you loved her."

"Of course, she was my best friend."

"It sounds like more than that to me."

"It wasn't," Maggie said. "We were both boy crazy. She was so wild and free. That's why we were all so surprised when she did it."

"Did what?" Tyler asked. "Wasn't it..." He lost the confidence to say it out loud. He had heard only a little bit about Janie but nothing about how she died. He'd just assumed she'd been lost to AIDS, kind of how like how he thought they'd all go.

Maggie frowned. "She killed herself last spring, six months ago. Carol found her."

"Holy shit, I'm really sorry," Tyler said. "I can't imagine..."

"You don't want to. Carol won't talk about her at all. It's too much for her," Maggie said. "Sometimes, I really want her to. I know she has a hard time because of how she found her."

Tyler was curious but hesitated to ask.

"She hung herself in the basement, and Carol found her. That's why we don't talk about it. Carol had a big emotional meltdown, and it's just not something anyone wants to ask her to talk about."

"Jesus. I guess she'll talk when she's ready." Tyler tried to imagine how Carol felt, and his mind wandered into his own experience with death. He closed his eyes and cleared his throat to turn it off.

Maggie pointed to the tattoos on Tyler's arm. "New subject: what do they mean?"

He had three tattoos on his arms. He first pointed to the one that ran up the inside of his right forearm—four vertical lines with a diagonal one slashing through them, representing the number five—and said, "This one is kinda morbid. It's supposed to symbolize the days as I wait to die. I got it to remind me to embrace the moment and, I think, to justify my drug use at the time."

Maggie nodded as she listened intently. "That one's sad."

Tyler smirked. "Yeah, I guess." He then pointed to the tattoo of the word *Karma* written in Old English on the outside of his left forearm. "This one is my reminder to be a good person. Sometimes I feel like I'm being punished for all the shitty things I've done, so I got this tattoo to remind me to start doing things to end the cycle."

"Nice," Maggie said.

Tyler blushed. "I like my tattoos to have significance. I don't want to just ink myself up without any purpose." The tattoo on his left bicep was partially visible. He lifted the sleeve of his T-shirt to reveal the remainder of a black-and-gray snake that wrapped around his arm, facing down toward his hand, with a big red apple in its mouth. The apple had yellow liquid oozing from the holes where the snake had bitten it. When his sleeve was down, all that could be seen was the apple. "This one for sure represents my dabbling in all things anti-God."

"Wow, it's very nice."

"Thanks. I like this one. I like that I got to take some religious symbols that are so important to my parents and ink myself with them. You know? It's the snake biting the poison apple. And I bit a lot of apples," Tyler said, taking a moment to admire it.

"What about the one on your neck?" She pointed to the Chinese lettering on the left side of his neck.

He instinctively brought his hand up and ran his fingers over it. His eyes lowered as he thought back to the day he got it.

After a minute, Maggie said, "You don't have to tell me if you don't want."

His eyes lit up with tears, but he coughed to knock them back. "It means: forever in love." He forced a smile.

"That's beautiful."

"Thanks. I wish I could get more, but I don't think that'll be happening anytime soon."

"Probably not," Maggie said. Maggie's eyes grew wide as she looked over Tyler's head toward the hallway. She started to fidget in her seat and motion to someone behind him.

"Curtis, are you okay? Do you need a room?" Carol asked as she came into the hallway.

Tyler turned around to see what Carol was talking about, and wondered why Curtis was hugging himself.

Curtis dropped his arms to his sides and stood up straight. "No thank you, Carol. I'm okay. I was just—"

"Being a brat," Carol said, finishing his sentence. She stopped beside him to peer into the sunroom.

Tyler waved awkwardly. "Hey..."

Curtis blushed and returned the greeting quietly. He beamed a boyish smile that reminded Tyler of lost love before turning and moving quickly toward the foyer. Carol shook her head and followed after him, smiling. "Kissy faces? Really?" She laughed as she moved out of earshot.

"What was that about?" Tyler asked, turning back around to Maggie whose face was redder than the apple on his arm.

"No idea. I hear he was dropped on his head as a child," Maggie said, shaking her head and refusing to make eye contact with him. "I have to go," she said, standing and rushing from the room.

Tyler smirked. "Okay, see you later, I guess." He turned to give a little wave, but she had already run to the stairs and disappeared.

Chapter Nine

"TY-TY?" THEO asked in his tiny voice, tugging at Tyler's shirt sleeve. It was morning, and he was standing beside Tyler's bed with Clifford clutched under his arm, wearing an expression of sheer panic.

Tyler blinked, trying to focus his eyes. "Hi...Theo?" he asked. "What are you doing up?"

"I had a bad dream."

"Come on up, li'l dude." He moved over and lifted the covers so Theo could climb up, as he often did, to sleep next to Tyler with Clifford between them. He told Tyler once that Clifford needed to be in the middle and tucked under the covers so he didn't get cold. He got colder than humans apparently. Once they were settled and both lying on their backs staring up at the ceiling, Tyler asked, "So what's wrong? What'd you dream?"

"Is Santa gonna find us?" Theo asked, clutching the blankets and pulling them close to his chin. "What if Santa doesn't know we're here?"

Tyler smiled. Amidst all the changes, he had entirely forgotten about Christmas. "Santa knows where we are. He'll find us."

"But how do you know?"

"Santa knows everything. That's what makes him Santa."

"We never even sent him any letters. How will he find us if we didn't tell him we moved?" Theo was beginning to speak quicker and louder than his usual whisper.

"Let's do that later today. We can write letters and get everyone else to write one too," Tyler said, turning toward Theo as he spoke, and as he did, a tear slipped from his eye and soaked into the pillow. "You're a great kid, Theo. There's no way Santa would forget about you."

Theo grinned and closed his eyes to drift off to sleep, trusting in Tyler's plan.

"A really great kid," Tyler whispered, turning to look at the ceiling again. This small boy putting so much faith in him and believing in every word he said was still so overwhelming. He was used to people crossing the sidewalk with their small children when they saw him. People would walk by and take a few steps away as they passed for fear that he would hurt them. Now, here he was sharing a bed with a four-year-old who thought the world of him and basically only spoke to him because there was something he trusted in him, something special. "Maybe I'm not such a bad person after all," Tyler said aloud, startling himself as he had intended to simply think it. He'd been thinking it for weeks. Maybe Theo was the only one who could actually see him. Maybe he wasn't someone to fear. Maybe there wasn't anything wrong with him at all. Maybe, contrary to what his father and mother had always told him, he was capable of loving someone other than himself.

LATER THAT MORNING, as promised, Tyler enlisted Maggie's help in gathering colorful pencils and crayons, as well as construction paper and other crafting materials, so they could have a house 'Letters to Santa' activity in the fancy living room.

The kids called it the "fancy" living room because it had no television and was basically 'boring.' It was filled with large less-comfortable couches and armchairs with wooden frames, dark cherrywood coffee tables, big book shelves, and a matching pedestal desk. None of the furniture lined the walls. The only feature on the wall, besides paintings, was a large fireplace in the center of the back wall. The room was rarely used except for special occasions or if someone wanted quiet time for studying or reading.

Tyler was surprised at just how eager everyone was to participate. Even Bradley, whom Tyler thought would be the one to ruin it, got down and put a lot of effort into his letter and spoke as though Santa was real.

"IT'S FUNNY. IN a million years, I never thought I'd see Bradley crawling around on the floor searching for glitter for a letter to Santa," Carol said as she sipped her wine. She had made eggnog for everyone, and after finishing her own "special" glass of that, she moved on to her signature red wine. She frowned as she filled her glass with Chianti. As the deep reddish-purple liquid neared the brim of her glass, she pushed the memory of her earlier declaration from her mind and justified her decision to drink. "It's fine. It's a special occasion. Tomorrow, I won't drink anything but water," she told herself.

"It certainly feels like Christmas in this moment," Marco said, moving to stand behind the love seat where she sat. "Did you see mine?" he asked, holding his letter in front of her so she could see.

She laughed but not from the heart. She was too conflicted with guilt over the glass of wine in her hand. "It's beautiful."

"Liar," Marco said, kissing her neck. His card was a piece of beige construction paper that had been folded in half with big block letters that read "DEar SaNtA" on the front and, inside, he had drawn a crude attempt at a red lingerie set.

"Oh, jeez," Carol squealed and hurried to close the card before one of the kids could see it. "You're such a shit," she said as she tucked the card under her bum and kissed him on the cheek.

Marco grinned. "Eh, make sure that gets to Santa, though. I've been a good boy, so I'm sure he'll get me what I want."

"Hey, Carol, Marco, look over here," Maggie said, calling their attention to where she sat, cross-legged. She held up her letter that she had constructed out of white glitter and silver gems on red paper.

"Very nice, Maggie," Marco said. "Always an impressive feat when you get into the arts and crafts."

Maggie smiled shyly, glancing over at Tyler to see if he had noticed the compliment or her letter. He was focusing his attention on Theo, giggling and whispering things to him as they colored on their cards. For a moment, she appeared disappointed that he hadn't noticed and lowered her card. Her smile was quick to return when Tyler looked up from Theo's card and nodded his approval at hers.

Tyler and Theo's cards were more rudimentary in style with block letters done in marker and crayon. They hadn't included any glitter, ribbons, or stickers. They simply colored a few pictures of reindeer and elves. Curtis had cut and folded his into the shape of a tent that opened two front flaps to the contents of his letter. Bradley had taken Curtis's lead and had made his circular on white construction paper and had cut out octagon-ish shapes from a black piece to make his into a soccer ball.

"Seriously, kids. You've all done great jobs. I love that you both shaped yours," Carol said, pointing toward Bradley's and Curtis's letters. "That's great. Very creative."

"Thanks. Curtis copied my idea," Bradley said.

"Whatever, *bud!*" Curtis said, shoving him and laughing. "You couldn't come up with that genius if you tried."

"Yeah, yeah," Bradley said. "You're just jealous." He jumped up to avoid a second shove.

"Let me have those before you wreck them," Carol said, chuckling and taking Bradley's letter and then Curtis's. "I will make sure to drop these in the mail so Santa gets them right away."

Theo jumped up with his and waved it around so Carol could take it. She smiled down at him and patted his head as she took the letter. "I bet he's going to be thrilled to receive yours, Theo," she said as she ran her fingers through his hair. He was leaning against her, standing on his tippy-toes and stretching his tiny hands up and pulling at her shirt.

"Someone gave him sugar," Tyler said, blinking at her and giving her a feigned innocent expression. "I have no idea who, though." He handed her his letter.

"Sure you don't," Carol said, rolling her eyes playfully. "Good thing he sleeps in your bed when he has nightmares."

Tyler paused. "Awe, crap. Sometimes I wish I thought things through the whole way. Do you think salt would counteract the sugar?" He winked.

Carol laughed. "No!" She lightly nudged Tyler to get his attention, leaned in, and whispered, "Your love for Theo is a beautiful thing."

Tyler seemed to stumble on the word *love*. "I like him. He's a good kid. I just want him to be happy."

"Okay then, like. Your *like* for him is heartwarming."

He blushed and shied away awkwardly.

Chapter Ten

SNOW AND ICE clung to the edges of the windows in the sunroom, creating a frosted vignette of the world outside. The veranda and all of the windows were lined with multicolored Christmas lights; a giant, plastic Frosty the Snowman sat on the front lawn beside the walkway; Christmas wreaths hung from every external door, and several lined the railing of the veranda; the banister inside the house was wrapped with lights and fake snow; the hallways and all common rooms were filled with mistletoe and various colors of sparkly garland; the backs of every chair in the dining room were lined with green, leafy garland; and the door that connected the dining room to the kitchen was lined with lights. Christmas Eve had arrived and exploded all over the New Life House.

"W-o-w..." Theo said. His eyes were wide with amazement as Tyler led him down the stairs in the foyer. Carol had been planning this for weeks. She had given everyone specific instructions on how to decorate. The goal was to bring the magic of Christmas to Theo. They put him up in his room for his nap for an extra hour to give them all time to decorate and splash Christmas around every corner and surface of the house.

"Santa's gonna love this place when he sees it," Tyler said, lifting Theo up and carrying him down the last few stairs. "Wait till you see the outside." He pulled the front door open and let it swing into the door stopper with a loud *thud* and reverberating *clang*.

Theo gasped joyfully and clapped his hands together when he saw the giant snowman surrounded by a jack-in-the-box, a white elephant with red polka dots, and several other toys from the island of misfits from the *Rudolph the Red Nosed Reindeer* movie that he had now succeeded in getting the house to watch up to thirty times.

"Just wait. It gets better," Tyler said, walking down the walkway to get far enough from the house for a good look. When he turned around to show Theo, he was pretty sure his ear drum popped from the pressure of the high-pitched shriek Theo let out when he saw the house. The railings and posts of the veranda each had a giant candy cane on them, and every window and edge of the house was glowing from string lights. Some of the lights were flashing, creating an effect that they were dancing to welcome Santa.

"Santa's coming!" Theo squealed.

Tyler laughed, not looking at the house but focusing solely on the joy on Theo's face. "He sure is. Let's get back in there. There's more magic waiting for you."

Elvis Presley was singing "Jingle Bell Rock" from the radio on the table outside Carol and Marco's office. The song brought Tyler back to his childhood when he and his sister and their parents would decorate the Christmas tree while listening to these same familiar songs and hymns. His mother had insisted they treat the holiday as a time to be thankful for their blessed lives as well as for the celebration of Jesus's birthday. In their home, Santa was an afterthought, but not because their parents didn't want them to experience the magic. They wanted them to appreciate the religious meaning first and foremost and then to enjoy the magical side of it as an added bonus.

Tyler brought Theo to the kitchen to report for duty. Maggie had prepared a Christmas cookie baking event of sorts. She had premixed all of the batter and put dishes out with the various toppings, red and green sprinkles, gum drops, and sprinkles in the shape of Christmas characters. She also set out cookie cutters shaped like reindeer, Santa, stockings, Christmas trees, gingerbread people, and the North Star.

Carol had asked everyone to bake cookies and prepare other hors d'œuvres while she and Marco readied the living room, which was hidden behind a set of double doors down the hall from the TV room.

By the time the sun started to set, they were all anxious for the big reveal. They lined up outside the closed doors, chattering and giggling with festive spirit. When Carol opened the door, the kids all stared in awe and made approving sounds, oo-ing and aw-ing, as they entered.

Earlier in the day, Carol and Marco wandered into the forest at the back of the property to cut down a tree and, somehow, managed to get it into the living room without anybody noticing. The mantel over the fireplace was decorated with a single string of white Christmas lights. There were three large plastic bins on the floor in front of the Christmas tree, which contained all of the decorations for the tree. A large jug of eggnog sat on the small desk off to the side of the room beside a tray of fancy glasses. Carol and Marco stood side by side, smiling from ear to ear, as they watched all of the kids enjoy the Christmas scenery they had prepared. The warm glow of the freshly stoked fire created a yellowish-orange hue to everything in the room.

"We wanted to do things a little differently this year," Carol said, motioning toward the Christmas tree and the bins laid before it. "We thought we could, as a family, decorate the tree while feasting on snacks this year rather than having Marco and I hog all the fun by decorating it ourselves."

"Really?" Maggie said excitedly, eyeing the bins.

"Yep," Marco said. "The more the merrier, really."

"Oh, yeah! Turn that up!" Bradley said emphatically as "The Little Drummer Boy" came on the radio. "This is the best Christmas song."

Maggie turned and twisted the volume dial. The kids, along with Carol and Marco, danced and started pulling decorations out of the bins.

"It's funny; when Rachel and I were growing up, we used to sing blah-blah-blah in place of all the words to the hymns at midnight mass. My mom used to get so upset. She took that mass of all masses to be so serious," Tyler said.

Maggie pulled an ornament with a miniature nativity scene from one of the bins and handed it to Tyler. "It seems like this would be the best one for you to hang up then."

Tyler placed the ornament on a branch. It hung lopsided. "Ta-da!"

Maggie hung a purple Christmas ball made of glass beside the nativity ornament. "So does it feel good to have a Christmas again? It must have been hard not having one last year."

"It does. I did have a good Christmas last year when I was out there, though."

"Really? How did... I thought you were homeless," she said. She quickly tried to soften it. "I'm sorry. That was way more abrupt than I'd meant to...to..." She stumbled over her words, trying to fix the question and to seem less shocked. "A shelter?"

"My good friend saved up a bunch of money to get us a hotel room. It was a surprise for me. There was a beautiful Christmas tree in the lobby. We stayed up almost all night in front of it. It's one of my best memories." He paused to stare at this tree while thinking of the one tucked away in the past. A rush of sadness waved over him.

Maggie looked deep in thought as she wrestled with what to say next. Finally, she cleared her throat quietly and asked, "Was it a prostitute friend?"

Tyler's eyes began to sting and fill with tears.

"I'm sorry. Can I take that back?"

Tyler cleared his throat and forced a smile. "It's okay. And no. I didn't do that until I was alone. Last Christmas is one of my last happy memories before coming here."

"Well, I'm glad you didn't have to spend a Christmas by yourself." Maggie awkwardly shrugged, trying to act as nonchalant as possible. "Merry Christmas."

"Merry Christmas."

"THIS IS ONE of the things I missed, you know," Tyler said, stepping out the back door and onto the veranda to join Carol. She was wrapped in a blanket. The night air gave life to her breath as she exhaled a cloud of smoke.

"You just had some the other day," Carol said, laughing but handing him the joint she had already smoked half of.

Tyler took a couple tokes of the joint and, without exhaling, said in a quick release of words as he tried to hold the smoke in, "I didn't mean the joint. I meant *this*. Christmas. The whole day was just out of this world." He coughed and filled the air with another cloud of smoke and frozen breath. It felt good to cough without any phlegm coming up. His throat burned as he took another couple tokes before passing it back.

"I'm glad, Tyler. That's what this place is all about. It's about creating a family for those of us who don't have one and celebrating life because that's something we do have," Carol said, taking a toke of the joint. "You should get to bed, though. Marco and I can't go to bed until everyone's fallen asleep."

"Seriously?"

Carol winked at him. "It's part of the magic. Here, finish this. Merry Christmas." She handed him the joint and went inside, the screen door creaking and slamming behind her.

Tyler stayed on the veranda and found himself staring at the stars, drifting to his familiar thoughts. *What if this is the last Christmas I get? What if I never see Rachel again?* And, now, some new worries came to him. *What will happen to Theo when I'm gone? What if I die before he's old enough to miss me?* These new ones surprised him. He wondered if his father had these same worries but about him. Maybe his father was watching the stars above his home in Vancouver, wondering if he would ever get to see Tyler again before he died.

WHILE THE HOUSE slept, Carol and Marco donned their festive costumes. Marco dressed in a Santa suit, complete with stuffing for his belly, and Carol dressed as Mrs. Claus in a red dress with the traditional white apron. They both wore wigs and spectacles to hide their identity in case Theo was to wake up and try to sneak a peek while they stocked the tree and stockings. They giggled hysterically as they bumped into tables and rattled the Christmas tree when they got caught on branches and miscalculated distances for their unnaturally resized bodies.

Carol laughed as Marco pried his beard loose from the branch it had snagged, nearly toppling the tree over. "I love this part," she said, beaming with childlike joy as she began hanging the Christmas stockings, which she had stuffed full with candies and chocolates and small gifts, above the fireplace. They had fastened a hook to the front of the mantel for each stocking years ago, recently adding one more as this was the first time they had five kids for Christmas.

"I can't wait to hear Theo say, 'Santa came! Santa came!'" Marco said excitedly as he hopped over beside Carol. "It's just gonna be great."

She leaned into his shoulder as they stood to appreciate the tree surrounded by wrapped presents. Little red embers hissed in the fireplace below.

"This," Marco said, wrapping his arm around her. "This is what I love the most."

Chapter Eleven

WITH CHRISTMAS OVER and a new year begun, the charms of El Nino arrived to help welcome new beginnings. The temperatures were hovering around ten degrees Celsius. The kids had all received new winter coats, snow pants, snowshoes, toques, and mittens for Christmas and, thanks to this warm spell, had yet to use any of them. Today, they were outside in jeans, sweaters, and hoodies.

"At least we thought ahead enough to get them all a few games," Carol said, sipping her coffee. She and Marco were sitting side by side on the wicker love seat adorned with a cushion at the front of the veranda. They were wearing the sweaters Maggie had knitted for them for Christmas, hers a beigey brown and his a blueish green.

"Brilliant call on the football," Marco said, smiling as they watched Bradley, Curtis, and Tyler tossing it around in the driveway. Maggie was sitting off to the side with Theo tossing a much smaller Nerf football just in front of the veranda, barely visible from where Marco and Carol sat.

"Thanks. It's worked out better than I ever could have imagined." Carol loved the Christmas season, and she loved the months that came afterward. She found joy in watching the children make use of their new items—clothes, toys, skis, or whatever winter sport item they got that year. In the early days of every new year, she and Marco found themselves reinvigorated with a zest for their efforts at the house and a stronger love for the children in their lives. "Sometimes, I think this is better than having kids of our own," Carol said, leaning over and resting her head on his shoulder.

"Yeah it is," he said, hugging her close. "And neither of us had to suffer through you going through labor." He winked.

"Seriously." She laughed, almost cackled.

MAGGIE WAS HALF-HEARTEDLY playing catch with Theo while she watched the older boys. Bradley had lit up when he saw how excited Theo got over his Nerf football, so he'd insisted they all go out to play catch. She smiled as she thought of the innocence behind Bradley's excitement. As she watched him—he was wearing his favorite charcoal-gray hoodie, unzipped over his staple, tight-fitting white T-shirt—she wondered why she never got physical with him when they were dating. She wouldn't even let him put his tongue in her mouth. Janie used to call Maggie crazy for not jumping his bones. He was hot after all, and for Janie that would have been enough. Maggie wanted something more, something with meaning.

"Come sit in my lap and watch the guys play." Maggie left the Nerf ball in the snow beside her and motioned for Theo to come closer. "Let's see what we've got out there." She knew he wouldn't understand or care about this, but she wanted to enjoy the sights with someone. "I still think that waiting for the right guy is important. The right moment," Maggie said, gushing in Tyler's direction. "Just because they're pretty doesn't mean they're bed-able."

Theo watched her with big doe eyes, clearly not following what she was saying.

She hugged him close. "You can never tell Tyler I said that." She looked back out at Bradley again. "I've known Bradley for three years. And that body." She felt a twinge of guilt for talking to a four-year-old like this but shrugged it off. "I barely know Tyler, and I'm thinking about how he might be the right guy for me. He's not even that nice to be honest."

"Ty-Ty's fun," Theo said in his tiny voice.

Maggie smiled. "He is fun. You're right. He's pretty abrasive and defiant a lot of the time." She knew she should use words Theo wouldn't be able to say. Plus she figured it was a good way for her to practice her vocabulary.

She looked back to Bradley again as he tossed the football to Curtis. His flexed muscles appeared to stretch his shirt in an unfairly exaggerated way. It was as though his overdeveloped torso would burst out of the seams of his T-shirt any minute. She blushed when she thought of what Janie would say: *Those muscles just make me want to jump on and ride.* "Gross," she said aloud, shivering at the thought.

"TYLER, GO LONG," Curtis said, motioning for him to back farther away in the circle. "Longer!" He waved for him to keep going.

"I can't catch that, jeez," Tyler said, looking behind to see that he'd reached the edge of the cement and was now pressed against the four-foot-high snowbank. "This is crazy."

"You can do it, Tyler!" Maggie called out to him.

"You got this." Curtis wound his arm back and then grunted as he threw the ball.

Tyler, nervous but excited by Maggie and Curtis's confidence in him, raised his hands and jumped as the ball neared him. His fingers grazed the edge of the ball as it flew by, and the force of it toppled him backward into the snow.

Curtis and Bradley hooted and hollered from the other side of the driveway, Maggie giggled, and Marco let out a cheer for the effort. "Great toss, epic miss!"

Before climbing out of the snowbank, Tyler rolled over to where the football had landed and scooped it up. "Damn thing," he muttered, scowling down at the ball. He climbed out of the snowbank and took a few steps before tossing the ball to Bradley. "I'm done."

"Oh, come on. It's not that bad," Bradley said. "Don't wimp out on us now."

Tyler stopped near Maggie and Theo. "No thanks. I'm tired. You guys have fun."

"That was an awesome almost-catch," Maggie said, smiling up at Tyler. The green in her eyes seemed to flicker in the sun. Framed by her red hair and the crisp white snow that edged up against the house, she was prettier to him now than she had been in all the time he'd known her.

"Thanks. You know, I almost had it," he said, brushing some of the snow off his sweater and jeans. "Pretty sticky stuff."

"Let me help you." Maggie swept the snow off his back while he brushed his front and arms. "You're right; it is really sticky."

Tyler chuckled. "That's what she said."

Maggie giggled and blushed, shoving him gently. "Don't be gross."

"Hey, fag!" Bradley shouted from across the driveway, whipping the football at Tyler.

Maggie let out a scream as she and Tyler ducked out of the way. The ball hit the edge of the veranda with a bang and bounced, spiraling back into the driveway.

"HEY! BRADLEY! WATCH your language. You don't speak to people like that here, and you don't throw things either!" Marco yelled, jumping up from his seat. He moved quickly, hoping he could catch up to the boys before they came to blows.

Ignoring Marco's intervention, Tyler started toward Bradley, shouting, "Fuck you, asshole! Come say that to my face!"

"Tyler, don't," Maggie protested, pulling at his arm. "Just don't."

Tyler shook his arm free and stomped over to come face-to-face with Bradley. "You got a fuckin' problem, bud?"

Bradley laughed, pressing his chest against Tyler until their noses were inches apart. "You think you can do anything about it? You're dreamin', brah."

"Bradley, don't be such an asshole!" Maggie shouted from the sidelines.

"Hey! Enough!" Marco shouted as he reached the two of them. He slid his arms between them and pushed them apart. "Stop it, right now!"

"Tyler, let's go. Come on, let's walk it off," Curtis said, patting Tyler on the back while gently pulling him toward the house.

"Fine. Keep your mouth shut, bud, or I'll shut it for you," Tyler said, pointing at Bradley.

"Oh yeah, *bud*," Bradley said, mocking Tyler and mimicking fear. "Think you're tough. Talkin' like a big man. I'm shakin'."

"Cool it," Marco said with his hand on Bradley's shoulder.

Bradley quieted and met Marco's gaze briefly before lowering his eyes to the ground. "I'm sorry."

"They're going for a walk. Let's me and you go for a walk too," Marco said, using his hand on Bradley's shoulder to direct him to walk around the other side of the house. "What's up with all that?"

Bradley shrugged and pursed his lips as they walked. They stopped to face each other once they got to the side of the house near the car and fire exit to the library.

"You can look me in the eyes when we're talking. Remember that that's how we promote respect in our conversations."

Bradley looked up. "She's known him like five minutes," he said, angrily waving his hand in the direction Tyler had been. "He's sicker than me!"

"Ah," Marco said. The episodes between Bradley and Tyler over the last few months clicked together in Marco's mind. "Jealousy is a wicked beast."

"I'm not jealous. I'm angry." He looked back to the ground.

Marco leaned down to again meet Bradley's gaze. Placing both his hands on his shoulders, he said, "I know it's hard for you that things didn't work out with Maggie, but just think about it. It's not Tyler's fault. He's new here, so you need to make more of an effort to be nice to him."

Bradley lifted his head, tears in his eyes, glaring at Marco. "Are you even listening!?"

"Yes, I'm listening." Marco removed his hands from Bradley's shoulders. "I have heard you tell me that you're not jealous, but you're angry at Tyler because Maggie likes him. I think you need to work on that. You'll be leaving for college at the end of the summer anyhow, so you only have to deal with him for another eight months and then you'll only have to see him on holidays, so relax. You'll find another girlfriend someday, and you can then flaunt her in Maggie's face to show Maggie what she's missing."

Bradley rolled his eyes. "Yeah, because girls are just dying to date a guy with HIV. Wake up, Marco."

"No, you wake up. The world isn't as dark and hateful as you think it is. Sometimes I wish we would let you kids go to the public school so you could see it."

"I'll try," Bradley said.

"Try what?"

"To be nicer."

"Good. Let's give it our best, yeah?" Marco said, giving Bradley a friendly slap on the shoulder. "You'll feel better for it too. Honest." He was sure Bradley was just telling him what he wanted to hear, so he pushed a little further. "Do you remember how much it bothered you when Janie pushed you away when you first got here? She hated you just because you were what she called a 'dumb jock,' remember?"

Bradley's eyes watered. He looked up at Marco again. "That was different."

Marco chuckled. "Was it?"

Bradley shrugged.

"I don't think it was so different. She didn't like you because you reminded her of something she didn't like about her own past. Maybe there's something in your past that Tyler reminds you of." Marco squeezed Bradley's shoulder gently, feeling like he'd pushed far enough.

"He doesn't remind me of anything," Bradley said sharply.

He decided to let it go for now, so Bradley could think about it on his own. "Maybe not right away, but think about it. And let me know if you think of some way you might be projecting onto him."

"Sure." Bradley rolled his eyes and forced a smile. "I'm cold. Can we go inside?"

Marco sighed, sure that he'd gotten nowhere with him, and conceded, "Yeah, let's go."

TYLER AND CURTIS sat on the porch swing on the back veranda. Tyler, still fuming from the altercation, was rocking the swing with quick, jolting movements with his feet planted firmly on the wooden floor.

"You're gonna bust this thing off its hinges," Curtis said, using his own feet to try to stop the motion. The rubber of his shoes squeaked on the wood as he failed to steady the swing.

Tyler slammed his feet down, bringing the swing to an abrupt stop and nearly flinging Curtis over the edge of the veranda. "What the fuck is his problem?" He turned to face Curtis who was hunched forward, bracing himself on the swing with his hands.

"A little warning please." Curtis sat back up. "Bradley can be hotheaded. You get used to it after a while."

"Fuck that. Next time he pulls that shit, I won't warn him. I'll drop him."

Curtis laughed, leaning back in the swing and looking out over the back field. "I know you're speaking with that whole testosterone-induced anger right now, but really. You have seen how ripped he is, right?"

"The bigger they are, the harder they fall."

Curtis shook his head. "You're nuts, man. If you think you can get the better of him, you're dreamin'."

Irritated by Curtis, Tyler started to rock the swing again. "I'm not scared of him."

"I'm not saying you are or should be. I'm just saying that he'd pound you. He's a big guy. And besides, aren't you always saying that you're better with your words than you are with your fists? Where's this change of philosophy coming from?"

"I don't like being picked on. Calls me a fag. I'll show him what a fag can do," Tyler said, slamming his feet down again and bringing the swing to another abrupt stop. Curtis, still not prepared, nearly toppled out again.

"You gotta stop that. Serious." Curtis put his hand out, signaling for Tyler to stop rocking.

"Sorry," Tyler said, relaxing in the swing. "I'm just pissed."

"I know. Bradley's pissed too. You know he and Maggie used to date, right?"

Tyler took a second to process it and then slowly smiled. "Ohhh. No, I didn't know. Interesting."

"Yeah, he really liked her too. You know, he even used the 'love' word a few times," Curtis said, leaning back to face Tyler. "She never reciprocated the sentiment, though. I think it really bugs him."

"Of course it would. He's the hot jock who expects people to love him." Tyler smirked and rubbed his forehead as though he were kneading his thoughts. "It all makes sense now. He's been threatened by me since day one because she's been so nice."

"She likes you but not him. That drives him crazy."

"He's used to getting the attention and doesn't like that it's going to someone else." Tyler smiled wider now.

"Yeah, I guess," Curtis said. "But let's just... I don't feel right talking about their personal stuff too much more without them here. Hopefully, it will all come up in group."

"No worries. Truthfully, I think he's more upset about losing out on the attention than missing out on Maggie unless there's some kind of exciting personality she keeps really well hidden," Tyler said, laughing and slapping Curtis on the thigh. "I won't tell him you told me their history if you don't tell either of them that I think she's kind of boring..."

"Deal," Curtis said, standing. "So you won't pursue anything with her?"

"Nah, I'm not saying that. Knowing that she rejected him but likes me just made her a little more interesting." Tyler flashed him a devilish grin. "I guess for now I'll be interested in girls."

"God, bisexual guys are double the pig." Curtis laughed and helped Tyler to his feet. "That hardly seems fair, but whatever. Do what you gotta do."

MAGGIE AND TYLER spent the afternoon watching television with Theo, who won most arguments, much to the disdain of everyone else, forcing them to watch *Rudolph the Red Nosed Reindeer* for the fifth time that week. Even Christmas coming and going couldn't save them.

Curtis and Bradley chose to spend the afternoon in the den or, as Carol and Maggie often referred to it, the "man cave" up on the third floor. The den had a mini fridge, a microwave, and an Xbox. The kids would sometimes go upstairs to have *Mortal Combat* marathon competitions. Each of them would draw character names out of a hat until all the fighters were assigned. Marco often won. Carol described his ability to reign victorious over a video game marathon at forty years old as more of a testament to her than to him, for without her patience, he would never have the time to master all of the special moves and fatalities.

All throughout dinner, it felt to Maggie as though everyone was whirring by as she lingered in slow motion. Her only focus: Tyler. He seemed to be moving at the same pace as her. She could hear every word he said, but nothing from anyone else.

"Maggie, could you please join us?" Carol said from her seat at the head of the table.

"What? Oh." Maggie bowed her head, embarrassed, and slowly made eye contact with Carol. "I didn't mean to be rude."

"You weren't being rude. You were just off in some other world. I thought it would be nice if you joined us for dinner in spirit as well as body," Carol said. "What projects are you planning for this week?"

"Oh, I don't know. I think I'm going to start reading a new book. I just got one of the new *Fear Street* books last week. Maybe I'll start knitting a new blanket. I haven't given it much thought actually."

"That's not like you. You always have your weeks planned," Marco said, stuffing a forkful of mashed potatoes into his mouth.

"That's not true. I can be spontaneous."

Curtis snickered. "Sure you can, and I can take us on a camping trip without planning anything ahead of time." He chuckled some more as he drank some of his milk. "That's rich."

"I'd like to see that," Carol said, laughing,

Indignant, Maggie glanced over at Tyler. "I *can* be spontaneous. They don't know what they're talking about."

Tyler smiled, amused.

After dinner and cleanup, Maggie found herself irritated by the usual 'family time' they all spent watching the evening news followed by a movie. Some of the kids would play a card game of some sort—UNO, cribbage, canasta, or the like—and some would watch the film. She usually loved this time of the day. Today, however, she wanted nothing more than for everyone to go to bed so she could talk to Carol about Tyler. She needed perspective.

Finally, after what felt like days, Carol excused herself to the sitting room, which acted as a sort of buffer between the hallway and the bedroom she shared with Marco as it was the only way to enter. It was where they held one-on-one counselling with the kids. They made it as comfortable and welcoming as possible, adorning it with a couch and a couple armchairs for lounging and pillows for hugging during conversation.

Maggie knocked lightly before popping her head in the door. "Can I come in?"

Carol waved her over. "Come on. Have a seat. Marco's gone to bed." She was sitting on the couch with a cup of tea. A second tea cup, a pot of tea with steam gently sliding from the spout, and a matching sugar bowl sat on a silver tray on the coffee table. "I made peppermint. Your favorite night cap."

"You knew I was coming?" Maggie asked, closing the door to the hallway behind her and then taking a seat beside her.

"Maggie, I've known you a long time. I've learned to know when you need and want some advice."

Maggie liked that Carol had grown to know her so well. It made her feel noticed. She poured herself a cup of tea, added two sugar cubes and stirred.

"You don't hide when you're anxious very well," Carol said. "Your expression grows so serious, and you purse your lips and blank out to the room. Your patience gets thin. These are all things that tell me you need to talk." Carol smiled as she spoke. She leaned back into the couch and pulled her feet up, pressed her knees to her chest, and held her cup of tea and its saucer close. This position and level of comfort had been nurtured and fed for years.

Maggie had been coming to Carol for advice and heart-to-heart chats since she moved to the house. Being the first child to come live at the New Life House, she had a few years as the *only* child who lived there. This time taught her to open up to Carol as though she were her own mother, a role Maggie had generally welcomed Carol into with open arms.

Facing Carol, Maggie took the same position, kicking her slippers off so she could dig her socked feet in between the cushions. She blew gently on her tea. "I know I shouldn't like him, but I do." She blew on her tea again and then took a delicate sip, slurping as she did. "You know what I did the other day? God, it was awful."

Before Carol could respond, Maggie started into her story. "When we were talking in the sunroom, I actually puffed my chest up and stuck it out for him as I walked by. I can't believe I was so cheesy. I kind of wanted to die as I did it."

Carol couldn't hold it in any longer. She roared with a boisterous laugh that threatened to wake the entire house. "Oh, jeez. Maggie. Ha. I'm sorry, but that's too funny."

"Oh, I know. Embarrassing, right?" Maggie slapped her forehead with the palm of her hand and groaned.

Carol patted her knee. Her laughs faded into chuckles and then petered out. "I think we all have these kinds of stories in our tickle trunks. I'm glad I got to hear this one of yours. Thank you." She wiped at the tears that had gathered in the corners of her eyes. "Thank you."

Maggie continued to laugh at herself for a moment, her face a deep red. "I just get so nervous around him that I want to be cool. And I want to be attractive because he's…" Her confidence to finish the sentence left her.

"Tyler is a good-looking guy," Carol said.

"He's infuriating," Maggie said. "I often just wanna clobber him for the things he says. He can be such a jerk, but he's sweet more than he is not."

Carol laughed. "He's a man. That's normal."

"I just wish Bradley wasn't so mean. I don't know how to make him stop."

"I think you need to sympathize and even empathize with Bradley. He's also lost a lot of people in his life. Rejection is a big deal for all of us, specifically those of you who live in this house."

Maggie sipped her tea, listening to Carol and trying to consider her views. She wanted perspective more than anything, and Carol was the only person in her life that had ever been able to give it to her in a direct, respectful way.

"And you know that Bradley feels rejected by his family, his friends, his sports teams, his idea of the future, and, most recently, by you." Carol kept her tone flat and direct, devoid of emotion.

The consideration hurt Maggie to realize, but she knew it to be true. She had done more harm than good by dating Bradley. They had dated for almost eight months before she told him she didn't want to date. It suddenly made sense to her why Bradley was being so dramatic about her interest in Tyler. "I feel guilty that I told Bradley I didn't want to date anyone in the house, and now I'm falling for a guy who just moved here."

Carol's tone was warm, soft. "You can't control your heart sometimes, but it is a delicate situation. We all have to live here as a family, so I want you to be really sure that you feel for Tyler before going down this road. It would be difficult for you if the same outcome came of this as it did with Bradley."

"Okay. I know." Maggie nodded automatically, trying her best to mute the arguments flying around in her head so she could hear what Carol was saying or at least make it seem like she was. She had no intention of following the advice, but she didn't want to be rude. She was going to etch her own sketch, and she was going to prove them all wrong. If anyone could make it work, she figured it was her.

"You are more mature than any girl your age I've ever known. You'll make the right choice for you and everyone involved. I think you just need to allow yourself the time to think about it all from a rational perspective. The heart is not rational, so if you let your brain intervene for a while, you'll make the decision that's best."

"Do you think I should talk to Bradley?"

"I'm not sure that's going to help right now. Maybe eventually, but for now, I think you should work on talking to you."

"You're probably right."

"If you do decide to date Tyler, you will keep me in the loop of any intimacy, won't you? I don't want to be that woman who tells you not to be intimate and expects that you'll listen. I was a teenager once too. I just want you to know the risks involved where your health is concerned."

"My health is already compromised," Maggie said defensively.

"It can always get worse. You're a smart girl. You have to make smart choices."

"I am a virgin and intend on being one for a long time, so you don't have to worry."

"Good. That's a smart choice," Carol said, smiling and placing her saucer and cup down on the tray. "We should both get to bed. Class is going to come early tomorrow morning if we're not careful."

Maggie drained the last sip of tea from her cup and set it down beside Carol's. "You're right. Science tomorrow or English?"

Carol's eyes widened in surprise. "Wow, you really do like him. You're usually the one keeping *me* on track." She stood up and wrapped Maggie a hug.

"I'll check my agenda," Maggie said, pulling away from the embrace. "Isn't it something that there's a guy who actually makes it so I can't think?"

"It's terrifying." Carol laughed nervously and waved as Maggie turned to skip down the hall to her room.

Chapter Twelve

ABOUT A WEEK had passed since the fight in the driveway, and neither Bradley nor Tyler had taken the time to talk about it. They shrugged off Curtis's nagging advice to speak to one another and took up opposite corners of the house whenever they had a choice. Tyler spent most of his time hiding in the sunroom with Theo and Maggie or in his room while Bradley spent most of his time in the TV room or the man cave playing video games.

Fed up with what he deemed to be an immature and childish avoidance game, Curtis decided to stage a meet up and forced reconciliation. They had all received a pair of snowshoes for Christmas, and Curtis had been dying to get out and use his. He figured that if he could get both Tyler and Bradley to agree to indulge him on a hike separately, neither would be bold enough to pull out at the last minute. He asked that they meet him down in the foyer with their snowshoes at 11:00 a.m. on Saturday morning.

"What are we waiting for?" Bradley asked. "I'm burning up here." He unzipped his coat and sighed, making known his agitation. He leaned against the front door in frustration.

"Just give it a minute, all right?" Curtis waved his hand at Bradley dismissively.

"Whatever," Bradley said. Pouting, he let his snowshoes clatter to the floor.

Curtis rolled his eyes and took a deep, exaggerated breath. "Seriously, dude?"

Tyler appeared at the top of the stairs with his snowshoes under his arms. His hair was a mess and pointed in all directions. He stopped when he saw Bradley. "Whatever, man. I'm not coming. Not happening."

Bradley stood up straight and puffed his chest. "What?"

"Come on, Tyler. Don't worry about it. It'll be fun. Just the boys out for an afternoon snowshoe," Curtis said, stepping toward the stairs. "Just come on."

Tyler glared at Bradley and then turned it toward Curtis. "I'm not some kid you can trick into doing what you want. Maybe you can pull that shit with him, but not me."

Curtis rolled his eyes and tossed his hands up in frustration. "God, this is so ridiculous."

"Whatever. I'm out," Tyler said, turning and walking back to his room.

"Fuckin' stupid," Curtis groaned. "I hate this drama shit." He turned toward the door to face an irritated Bradley. "Don't you start too."

Bradley pursed his lips and raised the palms of his hands in a gesture to show that he wasn't going to say anything. "Let's go," he said as he picked up his snowshoes and pulled the front door open.

Curtis forced a half-hearted smile. "Sure. Let's." He grabbed his snowshoes and followed him outside. The slam of the door echoed through the empty foyer and up the stairs.

A FRESH SHEET of snow had come to cover the forest the night before, blanketing their path. For Curtis, this was always a beautiful sight. He had been participating in outdoor activities since he was a toddler and felt closest to home when he was in nature. He took a deep breath, sucking in the sweet scent of the snow-covered pine trees. They smelled differently to him when they were smothered by snow, as they also smelled differently when they had been freshly rained on or been heated up on a dry summer's day. He had gotten ahead of Bradley and was enjoying the peace and quiet of the forest with the odd—and welcomed—interruption by birds and squirrels chirping in the branches above.

When Curtis was still living at home with his dad, he had been involved in his school's outdoor adventure club and any other local clubs he could find. His mother left him and his dad when he was three. His only memories of her came from photos his dad had kept. His dad and he were closer to best friends than they were to father and son. He could remember their weekends in the summer being spent out camping or white-water rafting. They even went winter camping a few times every year. The snow crunched and squeaked beneath his feet as he plodded along through the forest. The air had a calming clarity to it that invited him into the familiar state of reflection that the woods often brought him to. "I love it here," he said to himself, stopping to glance around at the shaded forest. On a day without a fresh snow, the sun would creep in through the branches to light up the paths, but today, everything was sheltered by a snowy hood.

He hadn't called his dad in a while. Being in the forest reminded him of that. He kept his relationship with his father quiet from everyone except for Bradley, Carol, and Marco. He didn't want the other kids to feel resentful because most of them had sadder stories. Curtis had been lucky.

Bradley's parents had visited him a few times during his first year at the house, but had all but disappeared since.

The aggressive stomping of snow as Bradley caught up to Curtis pushed his thoughts away and brought him crashing back to reality. As he stomped, Bradley grabbed twigs and branches in his path and snapped them off, grunting eagerly for each one. "I can't believe that little pussy just backs out like that. What a prick," he said as he grabbed at a healthy branch and attempted, unsuccessfully, to rip it from the tree it belonged to.

Curtis sighed and turned toward him, preparing to counsel him as he often had to.

Bradley raised his hand to keep Curtis from interjecting. "Seriously, though? Does he think he's so much better than me that he can't lower himself down to snowshoeing with me? What the fuck is that all about?"

Curtis started to interject.

Bradley raised his hand to silence him again. "Does he think we're gonna beat him up or something? What the hell is his problem?"

"Br—"

"I will knock him if he doesn't start acting like a fuckin' dude," Bradley shouted. He took a long deep breath.

Seeing his opportunity, Curtis quickly asked, "Can I?" He held his hand up as though he were in school waiting for the ornery and chatty teacher to acknowledge him.

"Well, yeah," Bradley said indignantly.

"You nearly knocked him out the other day. And you called him a fag. You know his story. You know how his parents treated him about it. Of course, he's gonna think you're a jerk and want to avoid you."

"Wow, don't hold anything back. Let it all out. I can take it." Bradley's voice dripped with sarcasm.

Curtis took a deep breath. He knew that dealing with Bradley was sometimes taxing. It was one of the reasons why he chose to have the talk in the woods. He knew he'd need the strength of the forest. "You know, my father used to say that part of being a man is to sometimes swallow your pride and extend your hand in kindness toward the person you dislike the most," Curtis said, scanning the trees for animals and birds. "It's about humility and embracing it even when you don't want to. That's what separates boys from men."

"So being nice to Tyler for the greater good of the house despite the fact I want to slap him around most of the time?" Bradley said, sighing.

"Yes, that's what I'm saying. It won't kill you to be nice. You don't even have to live with him for a full year anyway."

Bradley paused and gave Curtis a curious look. "What do you mean by that? He's not that sick."

Curtis shook his head. "No, no. Not that. College," he said. "Tyler's here another couple years, but you and I get to go off and make a life for ourselves."

Bradley's laugh sounded angry. "Yeah, right. I'll be a soccer or rugby star, and you can be a rock-climbing guide."

"Something like that, yeah," Curtis said. "I have big plans for the future."

"My plans are pretty well ruined. No one will want to play sports with a guy who's positive. They'll be afraid that if I get hit or cut, they'll get it. My future doesn't look as bright as it used to."

Curtis took a deep breath and turned away. He had little patience for the pity parties Bradley always threw when they talked about the future. Curtis felt the depression and doomsday period should only last for the first year or so after diagnosis. After that first year, he expected people to jump on board with a positive outlook. If plan A wasn't going to work, the obvious choice would be to find a plan B. The defeatist attitude the other kids at the house subscribed to, Bradley especially, was draining for Curtis.

"I miss being back home lately," Curtis said. "I can't wait to finish my high school credits here so I can move back near my dad."

"How is he doing?" Bradley asked, following along behind. The sleeves of his coat swished as he moved.

"I'm not sure. The last time we spoke, he was fine. He's actually dating someone."

"That's cool. Good for him."

"Yeah, I guess. It kind of reminds me that life is still going on out there. Beyond the trees," Curtis said. He stopped as he reached a large maple. It was the largest tree in the forest on the property, and it was his favorite. He called it the "Knowing Tree" because it always helped him clear his mind and make the right decision. He made a point of finding it every time he came out on a hike. Once, in the middle of summer, he hiked out to this tree and fell asleep for almost an entire afternoon. Carol and Marco were livid when he got back. They thought he had run away. He found something comforting about this tree. This tree that, he guessed, based upon its size, had survived for hundreds and hundreds of years and had nurtured all kinds of life as it now nurtured him. He breathed in deep and exhaled slowly. Being near it made him feel alive and like he could do anything.

Bradley stopped talking as they stood before the tree. He knew how Curtis felt about it, and he knew that this part of the hike always involved a mandatory moment or two of silence, a pause for reflection.

They were the same age and had come to the New Life House within months of each other. Curtis had come first. And they had shared a room for the entire three years they'd been there. Curtis was an only child at home, so he welcomed the chance to have a brother and really took the role to heart, and Bradley was used to being a younger brother, so he took to that role with ease. There was little they didn't know about each other.

Without turning away from the tree, Curtis started into his planned heart-to-heart. "What is it about Tyler you hate so much?"

"I don't hate him," Bradley said. He turned his attention to Curtis, forgetting about the tree. "We fought. Big deal."

Curtis still didn't look at Bradley. "The things you said to him, though..."

Bradley frowned and looked back at the tree, ashamed.

"You know he's bi, but you still called him a fag. That's pretty hateful."

"I know," Bradley said, taking a deep breath. "I regretted it as soon as it was out of my mouth, but by then it was too late."

"It's never too late to apologize to someone," Curtis said, finally turning to face him.

"I know."

"So do something about it." Curtis returned his gaze to the tree. There were still a few leaves stuck in the branches above, a phenomenon he was often struck by in winter. *Why do these ones get to hold on but the others don't?* he often wondered.

"But he pisses me off," Bradley protested. "Everything about the guy. He's a punk. I try to be nice to him and he gets that whiney tone and bitchy look on his face like he's a girl or something—"

Curtis started to interrupt, but Bradley waved him off, saying, "I know, I know. I just can't stand when he whines. And those tattoos, and it just sucks that Maggie likes *him*," he said, seeming as surprised as Curtis felt by that last bit of honesty.

"So it's jealousy?"

Bradley blew off the idea. "I'm not jealous," he snapped. "There's no way I'm jealous of that loser." He stared at the tree in defiance. "And stop looking at me like that."

"Like what?"

"Like you think you know everything."

Curtis laughed. "You just listed a whole bunch of superficial reasons to dislike him, and every single one of them relates to your feelings for Maggie and the fact that she doesn't feel the same way."

"Whatever," Bradley said, reaching out and pushing on the tree with his closed fist. The tree didn't budge.

"I thought you two sorted all that out."

Bradley stepped back from the tree and turned to face Curtis. "Apparently, everything she said was a lie."

"What do you mean? She told you she didn't want to date you. That's still pretty true."

"She said she didn't want to get involved with anyone at the house. That she wanted to keep things as a friendship so there'd be no tension."

"Oh," Curtis said. He hadn't realized Maggie had lied. Even if her reasons were to spare Bradley the pain of knowing that she just wasn't interested in him, she had still lied.

"She's all over the guy now. You know? How am I supposed to feel?"

"Like shit," Curtis said. "I expect you feel like shit."

"I do. It sucks. I really liked her."

"She's not the only girl you'll ever meet," Curtis said. "She's actually pretty dull. I picture you with someone a little more wild than her."

"Yeah, like any normal girl is going to want me."

Curtis knew that Bradley meant *negative* girl rather than *normal*. "She's not the only positive girl in the world. And besides, you don't have to limit yourself to positive people."

Bradley rolled his eyes. "Oh, fuck. What kind of world do you sleep in at night, bud?"

"There are mixed relationships and marriages all over the place. In some ways, this house being so far into the middle of nowhere is more harmful than good. In the city, it's not as big a deal. You obviously can't lie about it, but the number of more open-minded people is huge."

"I don't wanna talk about this," Bradley said.

"Okay, fine," Curtis said. "If you can at least consider that Maggie not liking you has nothing to do with Tyler, give the guy a chance. He's not that bad."

Bradley took a deep breath but said nothing.

"You only have like eight months left. Suck it up." Curtis chose to go with the tough love approach because it often worked with Bradley. He didn't like resorting to the tactic, but he liked knowing that it was always on standby for when he was being especially pig-headed. "You know Janie would kick your butt for being a dink to him."

"Yeah, she would. She'd kick Maggie's butt for liking him."

Both boys laughed.

"I know you don't like hearing it, but I think we all need to be nice to one another. Janie died feeling like she was all alone. I don't think it's fair for us to make someone else feel that way," Curtis said, lowering his head as he did. He hadn't intended on bringing her into this. He had barely said her name since she died.

"Okay, fine. I'll work on it," Bradley said. He nudged Curtis gently, making brief eye contact so Curtis would know he meant it. "For Janie."

Curtis frowned. "I'm sorry. I'm not trying to use her death like that."

Bradley slapped Curtis's shoulder. "Hey, it's gotta be good for something."

Curtis forced a smile. "I guess it does."

They continued admiring the Knowing Tree in silence, contemplating their conversation and what their next statement might be. Curtis was content with his arguments, and was confident that Bradley was more affected by them than he wanted to be.

After a few moments, Curtis clapped his hands together. The nylon of his gloves made a loud pop as he did, jolting Bradley from his thoughts. "Let's head back. I'm starving."

They walked back to the house in almost complete silence. The only sound was the swishing of their coats, the crunching of the snow beneath them, and the dry splatter of snow flung from the backs of their snowshoes against their snow pants as they moved.

"Are you sure I have to be nice to him? Like seriously?" Bradley asked, flashing Curtis a bright-eyed grin as they approached the front door. "Like seriously, seriously?"

"Get in there," Curtis said, snickering and pushing him against the door. "Jackass."

Bradley's laugh was boisterous and deep as they flung the door open, spraying snow from their boots onto the floor of the foyer. The house was quiet. They could hear the soft hum of the television coming from down the hall but no laughter or conversation.

"Wonder where everyone is?" Curtis said, unzipping his coat.

"Who cares? I'm goin' for a nap," Bradley said as he kicked off his boots. "I'll do all the touchy-feely apology garbage later."

"Charming," Curtis said, following him up the stairs.

Chapter Thirteen

THE HUM OF the television drifted down the hall and into the foyer. Bradley had roused from his nap early to see if he could find Tyler and get "the talk" over with before anyone else could show up to witness it. He found him in the TV room sprawled out on the red, leather chaise longue with his arm relaxed and stretched over his head, watching old tapes of *Party of Five* that had been recorded on blank VHS tapes.

"Whatcha watchin'?" Bradley asked from the doorway.

Tyler looked up, embarrassed, and said uninvitingly, *"Party of Five."*

Bradley stifled a laugh. He stepped into the room and headed toward the couch. "Oh, that's cool," he said without making eye contact. He focused his attention fully on the TV. The entire Salinger family was fighting with Bailey, trying to convince him to get sober. "I remember this episode."

Tyler looked over at him curiously. "You watched this show?"

"Well, yeah. Janie was obsessed with it. It was always 'Bailey this, and Bailey that.'" He laughed. "Maggie too. I would watch it with them every now and then..." Bradley said, smirking and slapping Tyler in the leg as he tossed himself back onto the couch.

Tyler flinched as Bradley slapped his leg.

"Relax, buddy. I'm not gonna hurt ya," Bradley said in a tone unfamiliar to Tyler. He sounded as though he were offended.

"I'm fine. Whatever," Tyler said, resuming his relaxed pose and looking back to the television. "I have a feeling you watched this show a little more than a few times if you remember this specific episode."

Bradley grinned. His eyes flashed as he chuckled. He sat up on the couch and snagged a few potato chips from the bowl on the coffee table.

"Are you flirting with me?" Tyler asked as Bradley smiled and flashed his boyish grin again.

"Seriously? Let's not make it weird or anything," Bradley said, grabbing another handful of chips. "You swing both ways. I swing one. Let's just leave it at that. Sound good?"

"Sure," Tyler said suspiciously. "You're just acting really strange... so...what's up?"

Bradley smiled again. "I think we need to iron some things out."

Tyler sat up. His defenses were on. He was ready for a fight, knowing Bradley would likely throw accusations at him rather than apologize. He was certain he knew where this talk would go, but he found himself reflecting on what Carol and Marco had been trying to teach him in therapy, that he needed to practice responding rather than reacting. It had something to do with listening to what was being said and considering it before calmly replying rather than hearing what he wanted to hear and yelling and flying off the handle. He couldn't remember the whole technique, but he figured he'd give it a try. *Weird. Guess this whole therapy thing is working*, he thought as he took a deep breath and tried to open his mind to whatever ridiculous thing Bradley was about to say.

His attempt to clear his mind was thwarted when Bradley nudged his leg again and flashed another of his best grins.

"I'm sorry for being a dick before."

Tyler laughed. "No worries." He was uncomfortable with hearing apologies from men. He wanted this to be over before it got started. As he listened to Bradley and watched him gesture and nudge his leg, he tuned out the words. He simply stared as Bradley appeared to flirt with him, but was he? *He can't be seriously flirting with me?* Tyler thought. *God, he's hot. Okay, Tyler, focus. Focus.* He blinked and turned his attention back to what Bradley was saying and less to what he was doing just in time to hear him finish.

"So I wasn't trying to hurt you with the ball necessarily."

"Okay," Tyler said. He could only assume that Bradley had just justified the entire episode in the driveway. He felt his mind drifting off to a sex fantasy.

"Hey," Curtis said, announcing himself. "You two are talking. Fancy that." He walked across the room and sat at the foot of the chaise longue.

"Sure are," Tyler said, shifting his legs to give Curtis more room. "We've established that we both overreacted and that if I lighten up, he'll nice-en up or something like that."

"Oh, good. I'm glad. I really want the two of you to get along better so we can all chill," Curtis said. He got up and sat beside Bradley on the couch, grabbed a handful of chips, leaned back, and put his feet up on the coffee table.

Bradley laughed and slapped Tyler on the leg again. "Just don't be such a pussy all the time."

Exasperated, Curtis let out a defeated, whiny sigh and covered his face with his hands.

Tyler paused, watching Curtis's reaction and trying to decide how to respond. He couldn't help but see the hilarity in Bradley's earnest attempt to be nice and Curtis's frustration with the failure. He laughed. "You suck at this." He laughed again and shook his head.

"Fuck, I know that," Bradley said, roaring boisterously. "I'm bringing out all my best charm, so just go with it."

Curtis peered between his fingers. Once he determined it was safe, he joined in the laughter. "What are we watching?"

"*Party of Five*," Tyler answered. "I can change it and put something else in."

"No, don't do that. I remember this episode," Bradley said, winking at Tyler and offering up yet another award-winning smile.

Tyler settled in his seat. "Fine with me," he said. He felt himself blushing as he looked from Bradley, who was now watching the show intently, to the TV in fevered repetition. *I'm sure he's flirting with me.*

"You guys enjoy. I'm gonna go up and play Xbox." Curtis waved as he left the room and headed to the foyer.

"HEY. HOW WAS the hike?" Marco asked as he stepped out of the office, casually putting his hand out to signal Curtis to stop and chat.

"It was great, thanks."

Marco took a step back to observe Curtis in full. "You're awfully happy," he said. "What's up?"

"Oh, well. You know," Curtis said, pretending to downplay his success.

"Nope. I don't. But you do. And you're going to tell me." Marco laughed. "You heading up to the cave?"

"Sure am. Care to join me?"

"Yeah, I'll bite."

"I think I might have to consider being a counselor or something," Curtis said as they started up the stairs.

"Oh yeah? Why's that?"

"Would you believe me if I told you that Bradley and Tyler just made up and are watching old episodes of *Party of Five* right now?" His pride was palpable.

"Really?" Marco said in disbelief. "You're serious?"

"Yeah." Curtis pointed toward the TV room. "Totally serious."

"Wow. I'm impressed."

"Turns out I'm pretty awesome at this therapy stuff. Think I found my calling."

Marco cautioned, "Let's not get too far ahead of ourselves, big guy. There's plenty of time for them to start fighting again."

Curtis shook his head. "Nah, I think they'll be fine."

Marco smiled. For all of Curtis's maturity, he still lacked the realistic approach to life that would center him as an adult. Curtis took everything at face value because that's how he offered it. What you saw was what you got, and that's how he expected everyone around him to function. This was something that often concerned Marco, and he was pretty sure that it was this blind trust in everyone around him that landed Curtis at the New Life House in the first place.

Chapter Fourteen

ON THE SURFACE, Bradley and Tyler's truce had been going for a little more than a week now. Due to his pride about how well his maneuvering had worked, Curtis was blind to the glares and the snide remarks Bradley was making under his breath every time he saw Tyler and Maggie together.

Admittedly, Bradley knew he could have been more honest with Tyler about why he was upset in the first place, and then maybe he would tone down his doting over Maggie, especially now that they were "friends."

On Maggie and Tyler's part, they had been spending most of their waking hours together. They held hands everywhere they went and giggled about nothing and everything.

In Bradley's opinion, they were moving way too fast and had gone from kind of liking each other to full-fledged love in a matter of days. "They parade around here with Theo like they're some kind of happy little family," he grumbled to the empty room. He was in the dining room eating breakfast, alone. He rolled his eyes as Tyler and Maggie walked by, each holding one of Theo's hands. He gritted his teeth to keep from saying something he would later regret. He didn't want Curtis to know that he was still angry, so he swallowed his words and his pride and tried to let it go. He was mostly angry that he'd tried to appeal to Tyler on an emotional level, and now it seemed like the relationship was being thrown in his face anyway.

Bradley grumbled. He was used to getting what he wanted from people, especially when he flirted with them. He wasted some of his best moves with Tyler—a *guy*—and it had achieved nothing. Flirtation was always his go-to solution whenever he needed to have a difficult conversation. He had developed earlier than most boys his age and was considered very attractive everywhere he went, and he knew it and how to use it. He used to brag to his friends that he wasn't above flirting to get what he wanted. And he still wasn't. Yet despite all this, Tyler wasn't backing off. "Asshole." He took a gulp of his orange juice and slammed the glass back down into place with a satisfying thwack. He stared at his burnt toast with peanut butter spread thickly atop it and frowned.

"Hey, buhhhh-dee! Goo-oood mornin!" Curtis announced himself loudly and slammed his binder onto the table across from Bradley.

The bang pierced the air, jolting him back to reality as though it had slapped him. "What the fuck?" he shouted, irritated. "I hate that shit."

"Jeez, someone woke up on the wrong side of the bed," Curtis said. "Did you not have your midnight snack last night or something?"

"Ha, ha. Very funny, asshole," Bradley said, turning gloomily back to his toast and taking a big bite. Peanut butter oozed off the toast and onto his upper lip.

Curtis grimaced. "God, that's nasty." He had long hated peanut butter, the smell, the taste, the sight, everything about it, and Bradley loved to taunt him with it.

"One day, when you're a real man, you'll like it," Bradley said, moaning as he licked the peanut butter from his fingers.

"It looks like you're eating shit."

Bradley laughed and stuck his covered tongue out. "You'd know."

Curtis closed his eyes in disgust. "Yuck."

Bradley took another big swig of orange juice. "Didn't you eat like an hour ago?"

"Sure did, but I didn't have near enough coffee yet." Curtis took a mug from the stack in the center of the table and filled it from the carafe.

"Is there ever enough if there's no caffeine?"

Curtis poured cream and two scoops of sugar into his cup. As he stirred, he added, "It's all in the mind, and my mind hasn't been convinced yet." He opened his binder and began reviewing some notes.

"Do we have a test? Why are you studying? Holy shit," Bradley said, starting to panic. "When did we find that out?"

Curtis laughed. "We don't have a test. I'm reading about some camping activities we can do this summer."

"Summer? Already? Seriously?"

"Yeah, of course. I'm not allowed to take us winter camping because of the risks, so I get to start researching ideas of what we can do and learn now. It helps make sure the trip is as awesome as they always are."

"You're kidding, right?"

Curtis looked at him, confused.

"Camping is not fun," Bradley said, staring blankly at him.

"Whatever, man. Just because you cried like a baby last year doesn't make it not fun. That actually made it quite fun for the rest of us."

Bradley mimicked Curtis, saying, "Meh, meh, meh...meh, meh."

Curtis looked back to the sheets in his binder. "It was hilarious."

"Seriously. I will destroy any bug that touches me this year. I want netting."

Curtis laughed.

"Seriously. Include that in your wish list for the trip."

"I'll think about it," Curtis said. "Right now, I'm researching ways that we can learn to make fire without any tools except sticks and how to build our own shelters rather than use tents. I think that would be great."

"You think Carol will allow us to build our own shelters?"

"I don't know. She might if I can come up with a way to make them warm and relatively dry."

"She's going to get all freaked out about pneumonia, and that'll be that. Sorry to be the shadow of doubt, but you know what she's like."

"You never know. Life is full of surprises. I'm not fond of having regrets, so at least I'll know I tried," Curtis said. "Have you done much planning for the summer kick-off games?"

Bradley shook his head. "No." The summer games were the annual event that Bradley had been in charge of for the last three years. This would be his fourth and final year to plan them before leaving for college. The games usually involved one to two days of various sports and track and field events. It was a way of reminding Bradley that he could still participate in and love sports while giving him something positive to focus on each year. Carol and Marco hoped he'd start to believe in a future as a professional athlete again, but he was sure the dream was dead.

"Are you going to wait until the last minute again like last year?"

"Sure am," Bradley said, smiling and taking another huge bite of his toast.

"Maybe planning would help keep your mind off other things," Curtis hinted.

Bradley scoffed. "What other things?" He tried to play innocent.

Curtis leaned forward. "I think it's great that you're giving this truce with Tyler a go. Really, I do. I'll never believe that you got over it just like that. Your face betrays you every time."

Bradley felt his face change to an expression of irritation before he could force it not to. His facial expressions had been his downfall in many arguments over the years. Sometimes he would think he was smiling despite his frustration when, apparently, he was scowling. "Oh, whatever." He stood with his now empty mug and plate. "At least *I'm* trying."

"It's your chance to be the bigger man."

Bradley snickered. "Pfft, like that's even a competition." He rolled his eyes as he turned toward the kitchen. "I was born the bigger man."

Chapter Fifteen

"WHAT ARE YOU guys doing out here? It's freezing," Marco said, walking over to Tyler who was in the circle with Theo.

Tyler wore a genuine smile as Marco approached. "Theo insisted on coming out to ride around on his tricycle, and I would pay money to see someone win an argument with him. So here I am, freezing to death."

"Ty-Ty, keep looking!" Theo called from his tricycle. "I'm over here."

Tyler looked back to Theo. "I'm looking. See?"

Marco chuckled. "How was class?"

"It was good. I think I like writing. And I don't think I'm as bad at school as I thought."

"Good. I'm glad to hear that. It's amazing the things we discover we're good at when we have the support of the people around us—" He hesitated to finish the sentence, fearing that Tyler would recoil from the sentiment. "—of our family."

Tyler nodded. "Yeah. It's crazy."

"You didn't have a lot of support growing up, did you?" Marco put his hands in his pockets and chipped away at some ice with the toe of his boot.

Tyler looked at him and took a deep breath. "Is this gonna be therapy?"

Marco laughed. "No. It's bonding. They're similar, but more of a two-way street of information sharing."

Tyler smiled. "All right then. Yeah, my parents never really told me that I was smart. And once they thought I was an immoral sinner, they stopped saying anything nice really."

"Hard to feel like you're capable of anything when you have parents like that."

"Yeah, it was rough," Tyler said. "But I got by."

"I'm sure you did."

"What's your story then? You know, I sit with you and tell you all my stuff, but you've never told me anything about you."

"Fair," Marco said. "I don't find that therapy or group sessions are really the time for me to be taking the stage. I like to let my stuff come out through conversation and genuine life moments."

"Okay, so...help me relate to you then?" Tyler said, winking as he mocked some of the terminology that Marco and Carol regularly used in both group and one-on-one therapy sessions.

"Well, I grew up in Italy until I was ten. We moved to Toronto after that. My parents were very religious."

"Catholic?"

"Yep."

Tyler mocked a shudder. "The worst kind."

Marco laughed. "I still believe in God and the Bible."

Tyler cringed.

Sensing Tyler's discomfort, Marco added, "But don't worry. I don't subscribe to the hate-based teachings."

"Phew," Tyler said, "I've had enough crazy religious wing-nuts in my life. Been there, done that."

"I imagine. Your dad sounds like a piece of work."

"My mother too. She was no picnic."

"Ha! You know how in Italian families, there's this machismo attitude where the men have to be God-fearing yet strong and fierce and tougher than everyone else?"

"No, I didn't know that."

"Okay, well, that's how it is. And I never really fit into that. I wanted to be a social worker, and I wanted to work with kids. I like feeling things and sharing that with others. My father never got it. He felt like I was only half a man. We've never really recovered."

"Really?"

"He still lives in Toronto. My mother passed away a few years ago. I don't really talk to my brothers either. I do get to see my sister every few years, though."

Tyler frowned. "I'm not sure I'll ever get to see mine again."

"You don't think? Is she still living with your parents?"

"Yeah, she's still there. You know, she and I were great. We used to do everything together. I always wished I could have kept in touch."

"That's great that she didn't take the same stance as your parents."

A boyish smile slid onto Tyler's face. "Yeah, we actually hated the religious crap they threw at us. We used to goof off in church all the time. We'd get in such shit." He chuckled. "We used to mock all the chanting and the silliness. I remember this one time when my dad whipped us both. Rachel never really got the belt, but she did that day."

"What did you do?"

"A bunch of people went up to the front and started speaking in tongues and dropping themselves on the floor. And then other people started just dropping all over the place. It was like a hilarious movie. We lost it. And...so did my dad. But he wasn't laughing." Tyler's eyes lit up with happy years.

Marco watched as Tyler drifted into memories, appearing genuinely happy. He liked this look for him. It was an expression he hadn't seen him wear yet. It was a rare occasion where he didn't want to chastise him for swearing, and so he let it slide. "Sounds like you had a good relationship with her. Hopefully, once she's out of there, you two can link up again."

"If I live long enough."

"Oh, stop that. They're coming out with new medications and clinical trials all the time. I have faith that we'll get you on one of those and you'll skate on into adulthood virtually unscathed."

Tyler laughed. "What a salesman."

"I believe in science. It's not over till it's over."

"Hm." Tyler shrugged.

"How are you feeling lately? Have you noticed any changes we should talk to Dr. Benson about?"

Tyler shook his head. "I still get night sweats sometimes, but it's not so bad."

Marco rested his hand on Tyler's shoulder. "You'll let us know if anything changes or if you notice the sweats happening more frequently?"

"Yeah, yeah."

"How are things with you and Maggie? It looks a lot like love."

Tyler squirmed and chewed on his bottom lip, appearing to fidget in his own skin. "'Love' is a big word..."

"I'd say it looks a lot like you guys are playing house. It's hard not to notice."

"Yeah, I guess so. It's nice to have someone that likes me."

"I do want to make sure you two are careful that you don't ostracize everyone else."

"We're not," Tyler said quickly.

"Okay, sounds good. I'm not saying you are. I'm just hinting that if you two spend all of your time together, you won't allow for any quality time with the others. And if you break up, you'll have no relationships or friendships to fall back on to soften the blow."

Tyler scowled. "What's with all the negativity? We aren't going to break up, and we're not pushing anyone away."

"Fair enough. Let's not get angry with each other. I'll drop it," Marco said. "I don't want to ruin the conversation we've been having." He was amused by the defiance Tyler showed toward the idea of breaking up. It struck him as odd that despite the horrors these kids faced in life, they still had all of the optimistic, blind pitfalls of adolescence.

Tyler turned his attention back to Theo, who was still cycling in circles. "I'm out here with you and Theo, and Maggie is inside. This is time that anyone could come and hang out like you did. There's lots of times when we're not together."

"You're right. Let's just forget it then." He had learned a lot about Tyler in the short time he'd been at the house. Specifically, that if Tyler felt confronted or cornered, he'd lash out and push back, but after he calmed down and had time to think about it, he usually came around with a more open mind.

Chapter Sixteen

CAROL WAS SITTING on the swing on the back veranda, smoking a joint. She had come prepared with an extra one just in case Tyler decided to join her, and she hoped he would. She had been coming prepared for his company ever since the first night they smoked together. Marco hadn't seemed to notice that she was taking longer or taking more down with her than usual, so she felt pardoned by his ignorance. Tyler didn't join her every night, and she couldn't help but notice that she felt like something was missing on the days when she remained alone.

"Knock, knock," Tyler said as he stepped outside.

Carol looked up. "Oh, hey. Come have a seat." She shifted over to make room for him beside her.

"I am so glad you're out here tonight. I really need a toke," Tyler said, letting out a deep sigh as he tossed himself down beside her. He grabbed up some of the blanket she wore on her lap and covered his legs with it.

She handed him the lit joint. "Here."

"Yesssss," Tyler said, taking a long haul. "What a day." He leaned forward to pass the joint back. "Marco came out and was talking to me and it got a little heated because I thought he was saying I spend too much time with Maggie."

"Mmhmm," Carol said, nodding.

Tyler paused. "You think so too?"

Carol, sensing that he wouldn't like what she had to say, passed the joint back to him before answering. "I think you both should try to bond with the other kids and keep those friendships going as well as spend time together."

"In case we break up?" he said in a childish voice. "Why is it that everyone wants us to plan for the worst?"

Carol smiled. "We're just trying to show you that we care. I think you and Maggie make a cute couple. You balance each other nicely." She was sure that a compliment would keep this from ruining their visit. She didn't normally tiptoe around a conversation, but she truly liked these visits with

Tyler and didn't want them to change. They sat in silence for a moment, pondering the conversation and smoking what was left of the first joint.

"I was looking forward to this."

"Me too," Carol said. "I can't believe I actually look forward to smoking with you. My father would be rolling over in his grave if it were possible." As she laughed, a cloud of smoke erupted around her, obscuring her features.

Tyler laughed with her. "Don't worry, I'm not going to say anything. I have a code."

Carol raised her eyebrows at him. "Ah, yes. A code."

Tyler smiled proudly with an air of arrogance. "Yeah. A code. And I love these talks. I feel more like me during these talks than I do any other time of the day."

Carol rolled her eyes. "So I guess you think I should dope up all my patients before therapy? Help them find their true selves?"

"Ha," Tyler said. "That would be hilarious. I can just imagine everything Maggie would be pouring out to you."

"Oh, dear," Carol said, cringing. "I'm not sure I could handle all that. All I need is a liberated Maggie spraying all sorts of sexual desires at me."

"Oh, gross. Spraying?" Tyler laughed. "I just inhaled." He choked and sputtered. "Awful timing."

"*Spewing*! I meant spewing!"

They roared hysterically for a few moments, both gripping their chests with awkward squawks emerging from their throats as they tried to gain control.

"I can't even look at you. I'm gonna pee," Carol said, squealing. "Oh, shit. Ffffff." She gained control for a moment but again lost it when she saw that Tyler was still giggling. "Stop. Stop. Stop. Get a hold of yourself already. Oh, my chest hurts." She took a deep breath. "I haven't laughed that hard in years." She turned away. "I'm leaking," she said, wiping tears from her cheeks.

"Me either. I damn near shit myself," Tyler said, which was met with another burst of hysteric giggling.

"Okay, seriously. I'm going to piss myself if we don't stop. Stop," Carol said, holding her hand out to silence him as she sat up straight in her seat and took several deep, measured breaths. "Tell me something I don't know that won't make me laugh."

"Theo started talking to Maggie."

Carol cleared her throat. "Oh? That's great." She lit the second joint.

Tyler shrugged. "It's okay, I guess."

"It's not?"

"Well," Tyler said. "I kinda liked when I was the special one."

Carol snorted. "A relationship is all about sharing. Guess you'll just have to share Theo."

"I'm not much for sharing."

"Well, forget about that. This whole game of house you three are playing requires a lot of it." She playfully flicked the ashes of the joint at him.

"*That* was not in the brochure," Tyler said. His expression was troubled.

"What were you just thinking?"

"Hm," he mumbled, passing the joint back to her. He shook his head and pressed his lips together tightly. "I don't want to have to share everything with her, with anybody."

Carol kept her eyes on him as she smoked the joint. "Do you like her?"

"Yeah, she's nice. I feel good when I'm around her. Like, she makes me feel like a good person."

"Shouldn't that be what you focus on then?"

He shrugged. "I guess."

"Maggie's been here a long time, you know. She was my first. She's very special." She paused for effect to catch his attention, waiting for him to make eye contact before continuing. "She's been broken before, and I want you to be careful with her."

Tyler's smile faded. "Okay," he said, intending complete sincerity. "I like her. I do."

"I know. I just want you to understand that she's not like the girls—or boys—who you were with on the streets. She's innocent and still believes in the type of love she sees on TV, so you need to be careful that you don't lead her on." The change in Tyler's facial expression told Carol that she had been more forward than she'd meant to be. She had planned this conversation in her head earlier, and it had sounded so much more polished then.

"Lead her on?" He sounded hurt.

Carol smiled warmly now. "If you tell her a sweet nothing, it will be a sweet *something*. So just make sure you mean what you say because she will take you literally." She had a knack for softening her voice and warming her expression in just the right way to smooth over any offenses she made.

She had learned over the years that a simple change in tone and expression could easily help someone forget she'd overstepped a boundary. It was a lesson that had served her well many times over with all of the hormonal teenagers she spent her days with.

"I always mean what I say. That's why I have a hard time making friends."

"Well, yes. There's a difference between being truthful and being brutal," Carol said, laughing. "It's a fine line really."

Tyler nodded in agreement. "It really is. It really, really is." He passed the last of the joint to Carol. "Finish this. I think I'm good."

She laughed. "Let's not get ahead of ourselves here. You're stoned. If we were defining this by Maggie's standards, you'd be pretty bad."

"Really? She doesn't like drugs?"

Carol shook her head. "Noooo, no. She does not. Don't ever tell her that I smoke or that you do. She's very wholesome."

"I like that she thinks I'm a good person, you know? If I'm being honest, I'm not sure which I like more. The fact that she sees something good in me or her as person. I'm still figuring that out. All I really know is that she makes me feel like my parents were wrong about me."

"Good, that's half the battle," Carol said. She butted the joint and stuffed it in the Clorets tin that she carried back and forth from her room every night. "I'm going to get to bed. See if I can focus enough to read something."

"God, good luck," Tyler said, leaning back in the swing. "I'm too stoned for that. I think I'll sit here for a bit. I don't think I can handle having Theo wake up and force me to talk to him and Clifford before they can sleep. Shit trips me out every time."

"No doubt," Carol said, stepping inside the house.

TYLER LAUGHED AS he heard her muffled scream as the door creaked and slammed behind her. *I like it here,* he thought. *Why couldn't life have been like this back home? Would I even have to be here if it was?* He gazed into the stars, spotted the little dipper emptying into the big one, and smiled.

Chapter Seventeen

TYLER

Two and a Half Years Ago
June 1995

"Ty, you're gonna get in such shit," Rachel said, giggling as she followed him out the front door.

"Shh, shh," Tyler said, holding his finger up to his mouth. It was just after midnight, and they were sneaking out of the house again to meet their friends in Stanley Park. He flashed a devious grin at her as he slowly pulled the door closed behind them until it clicked.

Their parents had decided to keep their bedroom in the basement because it was fully finished with its own bathroom and living room. They hadn't taken into consideration that they had two teenagers who, every Friday and Saturday night, would wait until they had fallen asleep before sneaking out to party with their friends.

"Why's it just me who's gonna get in shit? You're here too," he said, laughing.

Rachel smirked. "Because I'm sweet Rachel. Look at this face." She fanned her hands in a circular motion under her chin. "How could this face do any wrong?" She fluttered her eye-lids in mock innocence. "The preacher loves me and always says how good a girl I am in Sunday school." She giggled as they scurried off down the street and into the darkness.

Chapter Eighteen

TYLER

Two and a Half Years Ago
July 1995

"Shh," Chad, a tall sixteen-year-old boy, said as he ushered Tyler into the shadows in one of the hollowed-out, old-growth trees in Stanley Park forest. A big group of kids had met in the park again to get high and play hide-and-seek.

Tyler looked around him, checking to see if anyone was nearby before following Chad into the tree. "What are we doing here?" He shifted awkwardly and put his hands in his pockets to keep himself from fidgeting. Chad was the "hot guy" that Tyler often fantasized about in the shower. He was tall and athletic with sandy-brown hair and dark eyes and usually had a dark tan. For Tyler, a personality trait that attracted him was masculinity coupled with dominance and charisma. He was a small guy himself, so he wanted to feel like he could be protected when needed and lifted and carried when desired.

Chad smiled and rubbed his chin. "Well, we're playing hide-and-seek," he said. Seemingly shy and unsure, he giggled. "I thought it'd be fun to hide here...together."

Tyler blushed and found himself thanking God for the darkness in the hollow of the tree for it helped conceal the erection he had sprung. He shifted, in an attempt to be subtle, and glanced down at himself to make sure he was indeed hidden by the shadow. When he looked up again, Chad had moved so he was standing right in front of him. So close that he could feel his breath on his forehead. "Cool," was the only thing he could think to say.

"Yeah?" Chad said, smiling and tipping Tyler's face up to his. "You sure?"

Briefly, he forgot how to talk. He'd had a crush on Chad for so long that he was sure he might be dreaming or being tricked. So he nodded.

"Cool," Chad said, smiling bigger now. He leaned down and kissed him. The kiss started off slow and soft, but as they pressed against each other and became more excited, it grew more intense.

Tyler took his hands from his pockets and put them on Chad's hips, partly to steady his balance as Chad leaned into him harder and partly so Chad would know he wanted to keep going. He let out a gentle moan as Chad reached his hands around and grabbed his butt, squeezing gently. Chad pushed his tongue into Tyler's mouth, which was something he'd only ever dreamed of doing before.

The kiss broke for a few seconds so they could catch their breath. Chad smiled again, looking in Tyler's eyes and breathing heavily. "I'm glad you're into this," he said as he started kissing him again. He spun Tyler slightly so he could lean him against the wall of the tree, grinding their erections together. "Really glad."

Tyler still didn't know what to say, so he continued kissing him and moaning quietly. Chad pressed harder against him and also moaned, giving Tyler the courage to move his hands down from Chad's hips to his erection.

He moaned and stopped kissing as Tyler rubbed him. "Let's just kiss for now," he said, kissing him deep again.

"Okay," Tyler said between kisses, embarrassed that he'd started to take it further. "I'm sorry."

"Don't be sorry," Chad said. "That was hot. Seriously hot." He kissed him again, and moved his hand to Tyler's erection to return the gentle squeezes. "I just didn't want you to think I was going to try to have sex with you at the same time we first kiss."

"Cool." They kissed again. The sound of crunching twigs and leaves startling him. He tensed and tried to move away from Chad but wasn't quick enough. There stood Rachel, smiling as she saw him with his hands pushing against Chad's stomach.

"Ooooh," she said before singing in her girlish voice, "What do I see? Chad and Tyler standing in a tree...k-i-s-s-i-n-g."

Chad laughed, and Tyler stopped pushing him away, dropping his hands to his side.

"This is not what you're supposed to be doing during hide-and-seek," Rachel said, crossing her arms over her chest and raising an eyebrow at them.

"Rachel, I..." Tyler stammered for words to say, looking from Rachel to Chad for some hint of what he could say to pretend they hadn't been kissing.

Chad just laughed and leaned over and kissed him on the cheek.

Startled, Tyler jerked his head away.

"Hey. She doesn't care," Chad said, stepping closer to Tyler and sliding his hand onto his back.

"She's my sister," Tyler said quietly, not meeting either of their gazes.

"So?" Rachel said. "What's that got to do with anything?"

Still jittery from the panic of being caught, Tyler's eyes darted from their faces to the ground in fevered repetition. "Well...um...well."

"Well, um, nothing," Rachel said. "I've been watching you two check each other out all summer. It's about time if you ask me." She rolled her eyes and walked away with her nose in the air. "I don't care if you're gay. The seeker is headed this way. You're about to lose the game," she called back as she disappeared into the forest in search of a better hiding spot.

"But I'm not—" He started to protest but stopped as Chad took his hand and kissed his cheek again. Giving up, he said in a whisper, "I don't know what I am."

"You're hot," Chad said. "That's what I know."

Tyler smiled and blushed, turning his face so he could kiss Chad again just in case it was his last chance.

Chapter Nineteen

TYLER

Two and a Half Years Ago
August 1995

The music had gotten so loud that Tyler could barely hear Rachel when she was talking. It was a little past midnight on Saturday. A heatwave had blasted Vancouver for most of the week, so some of Chad's friends had decided to throw a party they aptly named "The Heatwave." Rachel's birthday had just passed, so she and Tyler had decided to stay out and party all night regardless of the consequences. As far as they could see it, she'd only turn fourteen once.

They were standing on the stairwell, leaning against the railing and looking down for familiar faces in the living room that had been converted into a dance floor. Their view of the faces was distorted by a disco ball, green laser lights, a smoke machine, and a strobe light.

"Ty," Rachel said, finally being able to raise her voice above the music. "Where's Chad?"

Tyler shrugged and leaned down and spoke into her ear as loud as he could. "I don't know. I lost him a while ago. It's crazy how many people are here."

Rachel, liking this technique, stretched up and said, "I am going to go find Britney. You go find Chad."

"You're okay separating? This party is way crazier than we thought."

"Quit doing the protective older brother thing," Rachel said, punching him in the arm. "I can probably take more of these people than you could."

He laughed. She probably could. "Okay, I'll go find Chad. Don't leave without me, though. I'll wait for you either way."

"We're here till the sun comes up, remember? If all else fails, meet me at the pool when you see the sun," she said, "I need to smoke a joint and Britney offered earlier, so I'm going to go find her. That strobe light is tripping me out." She waved and trotted down the stairs. After a few flashes of the strobe, he lost sight of her.

He decided to check for Chad upstairs, away from the strobe light. The house they were in had three floors. The main floor, which had the dance floor, games room, kitchen, and backyard with a pool; the second floor, which had another kitchen, a living room which had been converted into a pot smoking section, and, in some corners, a make-out lounge; and the third floor, which had several bedrooms. He found Chad in the second-floor living room, smoking a joint with a group of kids his own age and a couple girls Tyler had met during their hide-and-seek game earlier in the summer.

"Oh, hey! Ty," Chad said when he noticed Tyler stepping into the living room. He waved him over and made room for Tyler to sit beside him. "Where's Rach?" He put his arm around him and leaned back into the cushion of the couch, pulling Tyler with him.

"She went to find Britney. Apparently, she was promised a joint and wanted to cash in."

Chad kissed him. "Fun. So she's okay for a little while?"

"Yeah. We agreed that if we don't meet up throughout the night, we will meet at the pool when the sun comes up."

Chad's eyes flashed with excitement. "Do you want some of this?" He reached past Tyler and took the joint from the girl, Hannah, who was beside him. "It has PCP in it, so it might cause some hallucinations."

"Sure," Tyler said, trying to sound confident. "That sounds like fun."

"You sure?" Chad asked, watching Tyler's face for any sign that he wasn't comfortable.

"Yeah, totally. I haven't done it before, but no time like the present." He took the joint and took a long toke.

"That's hot," Chad said, kissing him as he exhaled the smoke and sucking it into his own lungs.

"Oh, get a room," Hannah said, laughing and slapping Chad on the shoulder.

"Okay," Tyler said. He hadn't meant to sound quite so eager, but he liked the look of surprise on Chad's face.

Chad pulled back to look at him fully. "Really?"

Tyler nodded, biting his bottom lip flirtatiously and ignoring Hannah's giggles.

"Yeah, let's go." Chad jumped up from the couch, taking Tyler by the hand and pulling him up. "Oh," he said, turning and grabbing two red plastic cups from the table. "I got you a drink. It's probably super warm by now. I got a little side-tracked when I was looking for you." He blushed and grinned innocently.

"No shit, that was like an hour ago," Tyler said, referring to the time when Chad had said he'd be back with a drink in a minute. He smiled and took the cup.

"I got you a gin and Pepsi. It's great. Tastes like lemon-flavored Pepsi kinda." He kissed Tyler again and nudged him to move toward the stairs to the third floor. As they walked, he pressed himself against Tyler's back and pulled him hard against his erection. "I wanna make sure you're sure. You're sure, right?" He breathed heavily, erotically, in Tyler's ear in anticipation of what was coming.

Tyler's breathing matched Chad's as he leaned back into him. He took Chad's hand and slid it down to his crotch. "Totally sure."

Chad moaned. "Hot. Mmm." They made it halfway up the stairs to the third floor before they stopped to make out.

Tyler felt dizzy as Chad pressed him against the wall. He hardly noticed the railing digging into his back. The effects of the PCP started flowing through him, making him feel like his skin was vibrating.

Chad stopped kissing him and leaned his head back to look at Tyler's face. "You sure you're sure?" He was smiling and breathing hard.

Tyler kissed him again and pulled him close. "Yes," he said between kisses, "I want this." They continued upstairs and ducked into one of the bedrooms.

Chad locked the door behind them and turned on the light. "I want to see all of you," he said, moving quickly to Tyler and kissing him passionately, grunting as he pressed against him.

Tyler moaned as Chad squeezed his butt, knowing that this time there would be more than just squeezing. He grabbed at the bottom of Chad's T-shirt and tugged it up over his head. It was the dark green one with "Whistler" written across the front in navy-blue block letters outlined in white. He was pretty sure Chad wore it because he knew it was Tyler's favorite.

As Tyler tossed the shirt to the floor, Chad reached his hands up and held his face, kissing him and pushing his tongue into his mouth. "You know," Chad said. He kissed him again. "We." He kissed him again. "Should stop." And again.

Tyler pulled at Chad's belt, unbuckled it, and moaned as he kissed his neck. "Stop what?"

"I don't know." Chad shook his head. "I'm high. Forget that." He laughed and continued kissing Tyler's neck. They pulled each other's clothes off with frantic excitement and had sex for the first time. Chad was gentle, and then passionate and aggressive, just how Tyler had imagined it. He kept slowing down to make sure Tyler was okay because it was his first time.

Chad had brought only one condom with him for the party, hoping they would have sex. He hadn't expected Tyler to want it more than once. Before they had sex the second time, Chad said, "We need to go steady after this. You okay with that?"

Tyler nodded. "Yeah. I want that."

Chad kissed him lovingly and, as he referred to sex without a condom, made love to him for the first time.

Chapter Twenty

TYLER

A Year and a Half Ago
September 1996

"Ty, are you okay?" Rachel asked, sitting beside him on the bench where he'd asked her to meet him in Stanley Park. When he'd called her, he had been crying. "You've never sounded like that before. You scared me," she said. She leaned over to give him a hug, but he jumped away, raising his hands in self-defense.

"No, don't," he shouted. "You can't touch me."

Startled, she pulled away. "What's wrong?" she asked again, this time more deliberate and assertive. "You scared me on the phone."

Tyler frowned and sat on his hands. He stared at the ground as he dug the toes of his shoes into the dirt, pushing the sand and pebbles around aimlessly. He shrugged. "I don't even know how to say it."

Rachel kicked a bit of dirt at his feet. "What do you mean? Don't be such a bitch."

He startled as the dirt hit his feet and looked up at her. His eyes were red and puffy. When he saw the concern in her face, he looked away again. "I can't believe this happened to me. I don't even know what to do."

"What are you talking about?"

"They're going to call and tell Mom and Dad."

"Tell them what? Tyler. You're scaring me."

"*I'm* scared," he said. Tears, mixed with dust from the dry September wind, now stained his cheeks. He looked at her again. She still looked so innocent and perfect. His parents had done a good job at correcting the mistakes they'd made with him. She'd always teased him that she was their saving grace after they'd realized the mistake they'd made by having him. He'd always believed it to be a joke until now.

"Scared of what, Ty?" she asked. "You're freaking me out."

"Dad's going to kick my ass so bad. I don't think I can go home."

Rachel began to cry. "You have to come home. Don't talk like that." She grabbed his arm and resisted his attempts to struggle free from her. "You can't leave me. *Tell me.*"

He relaxed in her grip and then told her. "I have HIV or AIDS or whatever." He sobbed as he said it. "I... What am I going to do?"

Rachel instinctually let go of his arm. "What? Are you sure? How do you know?"

"Chad is so upset. He was talking all crazy like he deserves to die or something."

"What? What do you mean?"

Tyler choked down saliva and mucous, so he could speak more clearly. "He didn't know he had it. He got it sometime before we started going steady. It's not his fault. He just didn't know."

"You're defending him?" she said angrily. "He did this to you. How are you not angry?"

"He didn't know," Tyler said, shouting and startling a group of pigeons into flight from the path behind them. "I love him." He looked away and took a deep breath. He continued in a matter of fact tone. "He went to the doctor because he's been feeling so sick lately. He had no idea. As soon as he knew, he told me. And now I went to the doctor and they checked, and I have it too." He buried his face in his hands in frustration. "I'm so stupid."

"You're not stupid," Rachel said. "Dad will understand. They have to."

"You know that's not true," Tyler said. "They hate me for being gay. They've been trying to pray it out of me ever since they found those stupid porn sites." His tears dried as he grew angry, making him feel stronger. "He hates me already. He's gonna kill me." He paused. "What if they go after Chad?"

Rachel looked to the ground. She sat still as she tried to think of something to say that would make it better, but she couldn't come up with anything. Her face twisted in a knot as she struggled for something, anything to say that would help.

"It's okay. I don't think I can go home. You understand, right?"

"No, I don't," she said defiantly. "I think your family is supposed to support you. If you leave, how will you ever know what they'll do? I think they'll try to understand."

"Because they love you, they would try to understand."

"They love you, too, Tyler." She rolled her eyes as she always did when he threw his pity parties. "I get in trouble, too, you know. Remember who sneaks out with you every weekend."

"When was the last time he smacked you?" Tyler said, seething with anger now.

"You're a boy," she said. "That's why he does it to you."

"That doesn't make it okay."

"No," she said, shaking her head. "No, it doesn't. But we know he's an asshole. You know? Maybe this will make him lighten up."

Tyler stomped his feet. "Fuck!"

"I don't want to lose you," Rachel said. The conviction in her voice was fading. "Please come home."

"What do you think their God is going to say about it? Won't there be some reason to cast me out in their stupid bible?"

"Fuck their God," Rachel said angrily. "He's done nothing for us. He's only given them a reason to punish us, so fuck him. He doesn't make my decisions. You're my brother, and I want you to come home." Her voice grew tiny and babyish. "You won't be able to get better if you don't come home." A wave of dimples trembled across her chin as she fought to keep herself from crying too. Her eyes filled with tears that trembled along with her chin as she begged him to stay. "What happens if you don't get better?"

Tyler forced a smile. "I'm gonna be okay. I'll come home. I'll get better. I think I'll wait here a while, though." He looked around the park at the myriad of people passing through, at all the couples, singles, men, women, and children continuing on with their lives as he faced the end of his. His focus stopped on an elderly homeless man sitting beside a shopping cart filled with garbage. "I'll meet you there. Just let me build up to it."

"Will you come tonight?"

"Yes." He nodded. "I will come in a bit. I just want to be alone right now."

"Okay," she said. "If you don't, I'll kick your butt." She stood and hesitated to hug him. He looked her in the eyes, afraid for her to touch him, so she settled for an awkward wave. "Bye."

Chapter Twenty-One

TYLER SHOOK HIS hands in an attempt to get them to stop trembling as he passed through the door at the bottom of the stairs and into the hallway that led to the library. Remembering the techniques Carol had been teaching him to use when he felt overwhelmed, he stopped for a moment to slow his breathing and concentrate as he inhaled and exhaled deliberately and deeply.

He could barely remember anything Maggie had been saying to him when he was in the den with her. She had been nattering on and on to him about feeling inadequate for close to two hours before he just got up and walked out. He didn't even tell her where he was going. And they didn't fight. He just up and left her sitting in the den with Theo. Maybe it was his decision to wear Chad's Whistler T-shirt that gave him the gall to do it. Maybe it was all the dreams he'd been having. He'd been dreaming more and more about Rachel and Chad and his parents. For the first time in a long time, he wanted to go home to Vancouver.

"I bet she'll feel ignored now," he muttered as he stomped into the library. The chairs were still arranged in a circle in the center of the room from their group therapy session the day before. He was beginning to hate those. The memories they were stirring up in him were nearly unbearable. When he thought enough about it, he was sure the therapy sessions were the cause of all his emotional struggles right now. And at any rate, he needed something to blame.

He sat in the leather chair at the desk in the corner of the room and closed his eyes to collect his thoughts. After a few moments of slow breathing, he opened his eyes and picked up the phone. His palms were clammy as he dialed the number. He'd rehearsed what he would say to his father if he answered and to his mother if she answered, but he hadn't thought of what he'd say to Rachel. He expected her to be angry that he never went to visit her after being kicked out. He didn't want her to get it, so he disappeared. How would she ever understand? More than anything, he wanted to make things right with her, but the longer he'd stayed away, the more afraid he was that she'd never forgive him. As he dialed the last digit, he started to doubt his resolve. He took a deep breath when the phone clattered on the other end as someone picked up the receiver. His father's angry voice pierced his ear.

"Look Mister Marco, whatever-your-name—is, I told you not to call here and that he's *not our son*. Leave us alone, or I'll press charges for harassment!"

The phone clicked and the sound of his father's insolence was replaced with the irritating hum of the dial tone. He sat still, listening to the hum for several minutes before hanging up. When he finally stood to leave, his legs were shaky and his head pounded as blood pulsed through his temples. He took a deep breath and slowly walked from the library.

"Hey, Tyler. You okay?" Curtis asked as he passed him in the hall.

Tyler nodded. "I'm fine." He felt stunned. He hadn't expected his father to still be so angry. All his hopes of talking to his sister were dashed in just one call. There'd be no way he could call from a Nova Scotia area code and get the phone passed to her.

Curtis looked Tyler over, assessing the blank expression on his face and the breathless sound of his voice. "Are you sure?"

"Mmhmm." He continued walking, leaving Curtis to continue on his way toward the library.

"I'm gonna make a call, so if anyone needs me, can you just tell them I'll be back up in a bit?" Curtis said, waving at Tyler who disappeared around the corner without acknowledging him.

Instinctually, Tyler went back to the den. "Where's Theo?" he asked. He was out of breath and anxious. It felt like every part of his body was pulsing as the adrenaline from the confrontation with his father still rushed through him. He wished he'd shouted back.

"Where were you?" Maggie asked as he walked into the room. He looked at her but didn't answer, prompting her next question. "Don't you think it was rude to just walk out? I was talking, and you just walked away. It wasn't very nice." She looked down as she finished her sentence, seemingly made uncomfortable by the unusually confrontational manner in which she went at him.

"I had something to do downstairs, so I left. I'm back, so let it go," he said, sitting down beside her. His voice was sharp and quick as he spoke. He took a handful of ketchup chips from the bowl on the coffee table, picked up the PlayStation remote, and started up the Mario Kart game. As he raced with his Yoshi Kart around the rainbow level, he kept falling off the edge of the track. His constant failings raised his anxieties as he refused to look at Maggie. He could feel her eyes on him as though they were burning into the side of his head. His eyes began to sting as they filled with tears, and his vision blurred as he stared harder at the television.

"I've never met anyone so moody before," she grumbled, folding her arms across her chest and turning her attention to the video game.

Tyler felt his chest tighten as he fought off the urge to scream at her. His breathing was short, shallow, and rapid as his face grew redder. He didn't even know how to verbalize what had just happened, and he wasn't going to be pressured into repeating the things his father had just said to him or into trying to name whatever these feelings were that he was drowning in. He needed time to process it all, but he didn't want to be alone. He wished she would just sit quietly with him and allow him the time to breathe.

Frustrated, Maggie turned back toward him. "Don't you think we should be able to tell each other what we do when we wander off?"

"For fuck's sake," Tyler said, louder than he'd intended.

"What?" she said, leaning back in surprise at his reaction. "You always do this. Freak out every time I try to talk about something important."

"God dammit, Maggie! I feel like I'm losing myself here. I want to have my secrets. I want to have my thoughts and my feelings and my life. I don't owe any of it to you. It's mine. I don't like that you're making me report to you what I'm going through. That's my fucking business," he shouted. He felt an odd sense of pleasure at the pain that spread across her horrified face as he yelled. "You want me to be someone I'm not. This isn't a TV show. It's real life. It's not all about you and making your perfect little world more perfect." He glared at her, fidgeting where he sat as though he were getting ready to jump up and stomp out of the room.

"Tyler—" she tried to interject.

"You're way ahead of me. I need space to breathe. You're smothering me."

"I am not," Maggie said, balling her fists by her side to emphasize her protestation. "I am trying to help."

Tyler sighed impatiently. "Maybe we shouldn't be spending so much time together anyways. You know? We're too young to be so serious. You're gonna go off and get married someday, and that's not me."

"So you're planning for this to fail?" Her voice was shrill and emotional now. "Am I the only one who actually wants this to work?"

"Fuck," he said angrily. "Have you not listened to me at all?"

Maggie leaned away as he shouted, and as he raised his hand to point angrily at nothing, she held her breath to keep from crying.

"*You* are the only one who has a fucking future," he screamed. "What's the point in getting excited about a future with someone who might, *might* have three years left?"

She started to protest his analysis, but he put his hand up to dismiss her. "I have read the statistics. I am being realistic. I don't want to be the stupid fool who goes around thinking that life's going to work out perfectly. Nothing is perfect. Ever."

"So you're just going to give up?"

"Just go," he said, turning away and searching for something to distract himself with. "I don't want to talk anymore. Just leave me alone." He stood and started walking away, having found nothing he could use as a distraction. The sound of Maggie weeping overwhelmed him as he rounded the corner and jogged down the stairs. Once in the safety of his room, he slammed the door and dove onto his bed in tears. "You're such an asshole," he screamed at himself, covering his head with his pillow and slapping it until the rage settled down and his ears started ringing.

MAGGIE BURST INTO her bedroom, sobbing from the confrontation with Tyler, and slammed the door behind her. She wished she could have said more to get her point across. She wished Tyler weren't such a jerk. For an instant, she wished she'd never met him. "How could he be so hateful?" she said, tossing herself onto her bed in a huff and burying her face in her pillows. Her mind flashed back to the argument again. "So pathetic," she mumbled. She hated that she was turning into one of those girls she cringed about on TV. She hated when they would lose themselves so totally in a guy that they'd fall apart when he pushed them away. She hated that he could be so dismissive of their love like it never mattered to him in the first place.

"He wouldn't even care if he broke my heart." She was glad for having her own room. No one could hear her griping and moaning and talking to herself.

Next time, I'm going to be the mean one. I'll dismiss him, and we'll see how much he likes it, she thought, comforting herself with bitter rehearsals of future arguments. She would win. She would forget her nagging desire to make him happy and she would win.

As she rehearsed the ways she would dismiss and outwit Tyler in their next dual, her tears dried and her cheeks flushed as a deep, indignant rage brewed inside her. She lay on her back, eyes fixed on the ceiling with the imaginary arguments swirling and repeating in her head until the adrenaline faded and she fell asleep.

Chapter Twenty-Two

BRADLEY APPROACHED TYLER, who was sitting with Curtis on the wicker bench on the front veranda, aggressively with his hands balled into fists by his side. "So ya feelin' big or what?"

"What?" Tyler said, looking up at him. "No bigger than usual." He laughed and looked at Curtis for a hint.

"Don't ask me," Curtis said, shrugging.

"You like making girls cry, huh?" Bradley's chest was puffed up now, and he was standing in front of Tyler, towering over him.

Realizing that Bradley was here to fight, Tyler stood fast and bumped Bradley with his chest, pushing him backward. "You think I'm fuckin' scared of you?"

Bradley swung his fist as he stumbled back, catching Tyler in the jaw.

"Woah! Woah!" Curtis shouted, jumping up and running to get in between them as Tyler lunged forward.

"Stay out of it," Tyler said, knocking Curtis away and charging at Bradley. He slammed into him with both fists punching into his chest. "Fuck you!" He hit hard and sent Bradley stumbling down the stairs at the edge of the veranda to the driveway.

"Stop!" Curtis yelled, running up behind Tyler.

By now, Bradley had regained his footing and had advanced on Tyler, punching him in the stomach. "You got Maggie in there in tears because you treated her like shit. I told you what I'd do."

The punches knocked the wind out of Tyler. "Oh, what the fuck do you know?" Tyler said between his gasps for breath. He was hunched over, trying to hold Bradley off with one hand. When Bradley paused, Tyler punched him as hard as he could in the stomach.

"HEY! HEY! ENOUGH!" Marco's voice interrupted them almost as fast as his strong hands did when they grabbed Bradley and moved him away.

"Don't you hit him again." Marco was angry as he stared Bradley, who was now also wheezing for breath, in the eyes and moved him into the driveway.

Curtis kept Tyler by the stairs to the veranda.

"You know better than this, Bradley," Marco said.

Bradley frowned. "I know. I'm sorry."

"Sorry. You're *sorry*." Marco sighed and took a deep breath. "I thought you and Tyler were getting along. What's this all about?"

"Maggie's in there bawling her eyes out, and this guy's out here telling jokes with Curtis like nothing happened." Bradley pointed angrily at Tyler as he shouted. "What kind of guy treats a girl like that? That's messed up."

"That's their business," Marco said. "I will go in and talk to Maggie to see how she's doing, but you don't solve problems with violence. You know that. That is not how we do things here."

Bradley looked away.

Marco kept at him. "Don't shut down on me. This is not news. We have never allowed violence to solve problems. Ever. You don't know what is going on for Tyler and Maggie. I think you need to stay out of other people's business."

"But—"

Marco interrupted him before he could finish. "But, but, but. But nothing. You come to me or Carol if you have serious concerns, and we will deal with it. I don't want to see or hear of this kind of fight again. It is unacceptable."

"Okay. I'm sorry. I said I'm sorry."

They stood in silence for a minute as Marco stared at Bradley, who refused to make eye contact, and tried to consider a punishment. At last, he sighed and said, "Let's just cool it for now. We can talk about this and how we can best learn from it later. Go on inside and clean up for dinner."

Bradley sighed and nodded in agreement reluctantly as he moved begrudgingly toward the house, glaring at Tyler on the way by. He stomped his foot down hard on the step beside Tyler to give him one last scare as he passed.

"Curtis, go on inside please. Go help Bradley." Marco nodded, directing Curtis to follow. "Thanks for your help."

"Sure," Curtis said, standing up and jogging up the stairs.

Marco sat close to Tyler and nudged him with his shoulder. "What's up? This isn't like you. You're not a fighter."

"Nothing." Tyler stared straight forward with tears in his eyes.

"Okay," Marco said, "Let me guess then. It has to be something big considering you actually got into a fist fight with Bradley of all people. The guy's not exactly in your weight category, but you know, small guys sometimes win. Why'd you engage? You're not normally physical."

Tyler shrugged again, taking a deep breath and holding it.

"You can't tell me it's nothing. Talk it out. Be blunt. Just let it out. I don't care how it comes out as long as you just let it out without fighting."

Tyler looked at his hands, focusing on them as he squeezed the tip of his pointer finger to distract himself from crying, watching the color of his nail go from white to pink with each squeeze and release. His back rose and fell as he steadied his breathing. "My family doesn't want me," he said. His voice was quiet and weak, defeated.

Marco frowned and put his hand on Tyler's back and rubbed. "I'm sorry, Tyler."

Tyler looked up at him now. "I called. I just wanted to talk to Rachel." His voice cracked as he began to cry. "He said I'm not his son. He can't choose that. What is it going to hurt for me to talk to her? She's not going to get it by talking to me on the phone."

"I know, Tyler. Your dad has a lot of learning to do. We've actually signed their address up to receive information packages about HIV and AIDS. I'm not sure if they're reading them, but they receive a lot of information in the mail."

"That probably has them freaking. Now the mailman knows." He smirked through his frown as he said it, enjoying the thought of his parents panicking.

"Probably not totally ethical, but they can cancel it. We just thought they should get some information."

"They're probably too scared to touch it," Tyler said. He paused and then continued, "And *Maggie. God.* She's driving me crazy. I don't have to tell her everything. I told her to leave me alone because she kept prying. That asshole in there comes at me like it's a bad thing to set boundaries."

"Was it a healthy boundary?"

"Yeah, it's healthy. I just want her to give me space, so I can have my own secrets and my own life that she's not always needing to pick away at."

"I get it. I do. But that's not what I meant. I meant to ask if you were respectful in setting it."

Tyler thought for a moment. "I could have been nicer about it, but I've tried being nice. She keeps pestering me. And I'd just called and got freaked out at. I was a little emotional and just wanted quiet company."

"Maybe you're realizing that you aren't fully ready to be in a relationship," Marco said, feeling a momentary flash of guilt for using the situation to steer them apart.

"I don't know anything right now. I miss Rachel. I miss Ch—" He stopped himself from saying it. "I just miss my life. Everything is so different now. I miss how things were."

"I know," Marco said. He put his arm around Tyler and squeezed him in a gentle, one-armed hug. "It's okay to miss it. You're allowed to mourn the life you left behind. Just don't forget to embrace the one you have now."

Chapter Twenty-Three

"ALL RIGHT, EVERYBODY. Let's get settled and plan a time to meet back here," Carol said, snapping her fingers to get their attention. They were in the food court of the mall, sitting at the circular booth table in front of A&W. Carol was wearing her glasses on the end of her nose, appearing authoritative and bossy while trying her best to smile and come off as motherly. This was the first time they had all come to the mall at one time. Usually, they would bring one or two of the kids and would stick by them the whole time. She liked being in control of how the world interacted with them. Today, she was nervous. Once she had everyone's attention, she continued, "Let's say three o'clock."

Marco leaned forward to chime in. "Finish off your burgers and then pair off in groups. Bradley, Curtis, and Tyler in a group; Maggie, if you want to take Theo up to Toys "R" Us, Carol and I will go see what trouble we can get ourselves into." He watched Bradley for any sign of irritation for being paired off with Tyler. When Bradley said nothing, he said, "Let's all make sure we get along. This is our first outing where we separate like this in town. Let's be on our best behavior please."

"Sure, sure, Marco. You're the biggest troublemaker here. No napping at Sears this time," Bradley said, tossing a french fry at Marco; everyone laughed.

"What's that about?" Tyler asked.

"They like to tell these lies that I abandoned them with Carol to have a nap in the beds at Sears." Curtis and Bradley heckled him as he talked, but he spoke over them. "I was just trying to see which beds were going to be best for the house when we upgraded them."

"You almost got kicked out," Carol said, taking a sip of her A&W root beer.

Marco smiled and turned toward her. "Thanks, dear. I appreciate your taking my side."

Carol shrugged as the kids laughed. "I can't help your reputation." She fluttered her eyelids to feign innocence.

"Yeah, yeah. Let's get this thing started," Marco said, waving everyone out of the booth so he could stand. "See you all back at three." He tapped his watch for effect. "You all have sixty bucks. Spend it wisely."

Maggie waited until the boys were out of earshot before asking Marco and Carol if they would consider taking Theo instead. "I was hoping to shop at some girls' clothing stores and Claire's. I didn't want to make a big fuss about it, but I wanted to get my own things."

"Sure, we can take the big guy," Marco said.

Carol stepped over and linked arms with Maggie, puffing her chest up proudly. "I'll join you. I could really use some girl time."

Maggie leaned into Carol's embrace. "Great."

"All right then. Looks like it's just me and you, big guy," Marco said, putting his hand out for Theo to give him an exuberant high five. "We'll go buy all sorts of guy stuff." He hugged Carol tight and kissed her. "See you soon, love."

Carol pulled away from the hug, waving as she and Maggie again linked arms and set off toward the clothing stores.

"So where do you want to go first?" Carol asked, smiling big and proud. "I'm actually really glad we get some time together."

"Me too," Maggie said. "We used to get so much more girl time, but it's just been so tough lately."

Carol squeezed Maggie's arm lovingly.

"How about we go to Guess?"

"Sure, you lead the way. Oh wait..." Carol stopped and pointed toward Delia's. "What about there? You and Janie used to love that place. Remember that pair of camouflage bellbottoms she bought? She had that slinky top to match, the one with only one strap." Carol drew the line of the strap on her own body.

"I do. I got a pair of dark-blue ones. No camo. They were cute." Maggie followed Carol to the store, grinning. It was the first time Carol had brought up a fun memory about Janie since she'd died.

As they walked into the store, Carol asked, "How are things with Tyler?"

"They're okay, I guess."

"There's a story there..." Carol looked at Maggie expectantly, waiting for her to say more. She already knew about the fight, but wanted to hear it from Maggie's point of view.

"He just gets so mad. He screamed at me the other day because he said I was too clingy, but I was just trying to find out what was wrong. I thought I was being supportive."

"Well, he shouldn't be screaming at you. I hope you screamed back." Carol didn't really want any of them screaming at each other, but she did want them to stand up for themselves no matter what. And she'd be damned if she raised a girl to take abuse from a man, so it was even more important to her that Maggie stand up for herself.

"I think he did most of the screaming, but I'm embarrassed by how I acted. I just wouldn't let it go. I kept badgering him to tell me what was wrong because he came back to the den all emotional."

Carol's expression said that she knew more about the argument than she was letting on. "Sometimes the best way to be supportive is to offer quiet comfort." Carol squeezed Maggie's arm gently. "You know, offer a gentle pat on the back and sit quietly with him. He's still new to all this. He hasn't had all the years of experience in opening up and sharing his feelings like you have. You have to be patient with him and try to understand that we all deal with things differently."

"I know. It's just that I feel like I'm pushing him away, and it's like I have no control. All of a sudden I'm saying and doing things that are embarrassingly clingy, but I can't stop once I start. We're both so tense." She picked the first yellow dress she found that was her size and looked like it might fit from the rack. It was a shade or two under neon yellow and kind of hurt her eyes to look at, but she turned around to show it off to Carol. "How's this?"

Carol shielded her eyes from it, pretending to go blind. "It's pretty bright and also pretty short."

Maggie nodded. "Perfect. I was hoping to find something different and edgy, something that will catch Tyler's eye. Maybe give him a reason to be speechless for once." She ignored the look of surprise on Carol's face and made her way toward the fitting rooms.

"I'll wait here," Carol said, pointing to the dresses she was looking at but had no intention of trying on. "Just make sure it covers your butt the whole way."

Maggie laughed. "What fun would that be?" She disappeared behind the curtain to try the dress on. When she came back out, Carol gasped at the dress.

"Wow, Maggie, you look amazing."

"Oh my gosh, it fits better than I ever thought it would," she beamed as she stepped farther into view. The dress framed her nicely, showing off her hips and curvy figure. The straps covered her shoulders, the stitching in the chest perked her boobs up, and the bottom landed a comfortable four inches above the knee.

"That is going to make the boys go wild," Carol said. "Poor Bradley."

Maggie blushed. "Thank you. I'm hoping Tyler likes it too." She brushed her hair behind her ear as she looked down at herself. She cupped her breasts and giggled. "And what are these all about? I don't even recognize them. Like, what the heck?" She bounced them playfully.

"I think everyone will like it, and I don't think you need to grab at those to get their attention." Carol pulled Maggie's hands from her breasts and put them by her sides. "Let's find you a sweater and some track pants. Don't you think that would be nice? It's often very cold out." She winked.

Maggie curtsied. "I think this is the one."

TYLER MOANED AND rubbed his stomach. "I love coffee-flavored frozen yogurt, but maybe that was a bad idea." He groaned as he sat up straight. "Let's get going. I need to walk this off."

"Did you really need dessert after two burgers?" Curtis said, eyeing the now-empty, large Yogen Früz cup that sat in front of Tyler.

"I wanna go check HMV for new movies," Bradley said as they moved from the table. "We gotta go through the other way for that." He pointed back through the food court to the other side where the giant pink "HMV" letters glowed brightly.

"Cool. Sounds good," Curtis said. "Green Day's *Nimrod* CD just came out before Christmas. I need it." They got up and followed after Bradley.

As they moved through the food court, they came across a group of teenagers sitting near a dividing wall that cut the food court in half in order to make it appear larger. They were wearing blue team jackets with yellow lettering and numbering from Pembden High School.

Bradley smiled at a pretty girl with long dark hair who was sitting at a table with two other girls and four boys.

The girl looked to her friends wide-eyed as though she were afraid, mocking him.

One of the boys caught her expression and glanced over his shoulder at Bradley and quickly turned to his table of friends and said, "Watch out.

If you make eye contact with them, it'll be you sent up to the death house next."

The pretty girl was more uncomfortable now as the others laughed. "That doesn't make any sense."

"Sure it does," the boy said. "They're from that big house outside of town. You know. The Death House. I'd recognize a bunch of faggots like that anywhere."

"Hey, fuck you," Bradley said. "Who you callin' a faggot?" He stepped toward their table, chest puffed up and hands balled into fists by his side.

"Bradley, just leave it," Curtis said, stepping in behind him and putting his hand on his chest to pull him back. "It's not worth it. Let it go."

"Yeah, let it go, pansy," the boy said, snickering. He stood to meet Bradley's gaze, staring him down. "Go back up to your little hideaway."

Tyler looked on at the impending fight from behind Curtis and Bradley. He hadn't moved inward toward the confrontation. He looked over at the kids sitting around the table. They hadn't stood to defend their friend, and each had varying expressions of fear on their face. The pretty girl whom Bradley had smiled at was leaning away from the argument.

"Do I look like a faggot?" Bradley shouted. He bumped his chest against the boy.

The boy bumped back. "Yeah, you do. Problem?"

"Kyle, how do you know he looks like a faggot?" one of the other boys asked. "He looks like a dude to me."

The boy Bradley was confronting—Kyle—kept his eyes forward but spoke over his shoulder to his friend. "It's not hard to figure out they're not from here. They're totally from the Death House. They have the gay disease."

One of the other girls, the blonde one, looked away. "It's not a gay disease. Stop being an asshole."

"What did you call me?" Kyle said, turning to the girl. "I'm just trying to keep you girls safe." He turned back around and shoved Bradley.

"Bradley, don't!" Curtis shouted, getting in between him and Kyle before Bradley could swing his fist. "Seriously, man. You know Carol will take away our privileges, and I don't want to be punished for this douchebag." Curtis kept his hands on Bradley's chest, pushing against him to move him backward and knowing fully that if Bradley wanted to, he could knock him out of the way without much effort.

Bradley noticed the look of fear in Curtis's face and let his chest deflate and his shoulders drop. "Fine."

"Oh, fuck that," Tyler said, pushing past them.

Kyle was laughing and putting on a show of bravado for his friends, feeling like he had won. His expression turned from jovial and smug to one of fear.

Tyler winked as he approached, causing Kyle to take a step back, but he was blocked by the chair and table behind him. "You think you're so cool, huh?" Tyler said, anger pulsing through his veins. He reached his hand out and grabbed onto Kyle's face and squeezed.

"Hey, don't touch me!" Kyle said. His voice was shrill now. All of his machismo bravado faded as Tyler used his hand to push the boy down into his seat. His friends were now gasping and standing up, trying to move away and whispering as they witnessed Kyle's tears start.

"Tyler, what are you doing?" Curtis said as he and Bradley turned to see what the commotion was about.

Tyler smirked and leaned in real close so he could whisper in Kyle's ear. "You know...I hate that word. Faggot. And I hate when morons go around thinking that anyone with AIDS or HIV is gay."

Kyle was crying now, feeling trapped in his chair and afraid to touch Tyler in return. He kept his lips pressed tightly together to keep from ingesting anything off Tyler.

"You should know that *anyone* can catch it. *Anyone.*"

Kyle's friends were moving away from the scene. "Please let him go. Just let go of him," the pretty girl said, still standing near the table. "Don't hurt him." She watched helplessly.

Tyler glared at her. "Don't worry." He looked back to Kyle's eyes. "You can't get it from touching us, lover." He kissed the air in front of Kyle's now tear-stained face and said, "Get the fuck outta here." His voice was sharp and angry as he said it. He pushed Kyle's face away and stepped back to let him stand, pointing toward the pretty girl.

"You're fuckin' crazy," Kyle said, standing and moving quickly to the girl. "Let's go. Let's go," he said urgently as they speed-walked through the food court in the direction their friends had gone.

"Better get tested," Bradley said, sneering at him. "Maybe we'll let you come live with us if you got it. Maybe we won't. Maybe we'll let you just die alone."

Curtis stared in total amazement at Tyler. "I can't believe you just did that."

Tyler acted nonchalant and as though it meant nothing, shrugging for effect. "I lived on the streets. I'm not afraid of some punk-ass bitch like that."

Bradley turned to face him. "He's three times your size. He could have kicked your ass."

Tyler shook his head. "Not with you here. I had my back up." They laughed. "And besides, he was afraid to look at us for fuck's sake. I'm pretty sure he'd be terrified to really hit any of us. Wouldn't want to draw blood."

"Good point," Curtis said. "That was awesome. Wow."

Bradley put his hand up to get a high five from Tyler. "That was more than awesome. It was epic!"

Tyler clapped his hand to Bradley's. "My sister woulda loved that." He puffed his chest up as he walked, feeling taller and bigger than he had in months. "She was a total badass. Everyone thought she was this sweet and innocent little angel, but she was a total wild child."

"What happened to her?" Bradley asked.

Tyler looked at him with a confused expression. "What do you mean?"

"Well...you said *was*, so I thought maybe..."

"Nothing happened to her. I just haven't seen her in a long time. She's part of the past now, which makes her a *was*."

"Hm," Bradley said with an air of doubt. "I don't think she's as in the past as you say."

"Tell that to my dad."

"What does he have to do with anything?"

"I tried calling the other day. He answered, screamed at me, and hung up. He's watching the phone. I don't know if I'll ever get through to her."

Bradley frowned. "Some people suck."

"Tell me about it," Tyler said, shrugging. "That's why I hit you when you went at me about Maggie. She was trying to force me to talk about it, and I just wasn't ready. I just wanted to be left alone, and she kept hounding me, so I kinda lost it."

This was the first time Tyler had opened up to him. Bradley looked Tyler over curiously, seeming to see something he hadn't before.

Feeling Bradley's eyes on him for too long, Tyler shied away. "Whatchu lookin' at?" He turned around to see if there was something behind him. When he turned back, Bradley was awkwardly half smiling at him.

"Nothing. I guess I just never paid attention to how rough you had it before," Bradley said. "You always act so rough around the edges and moody that I never really stopped to think about why you are that way."

Tyler puffed his chest up, trying to act as butch as he could. "Ah, whatever, man. Don't make a big deal out of it. I'd rather you think I'm a jerk than a victim. Deal?"

"That's a pretty easy deal." They laughed as they walked into the HMV to catch up with Curtis who was hurriedly searching for something to spend his money on.

CAROL LOOKED FOR all of the kids as she and Maggie approached the food court. They met Marco and Theo on the way. Marco was carrying a large Lego set they had purchased. Carol's mind wandered to imaginations of Tyler screaming and hollering as his feet found stray pieces left on the bedroom floor. The thought made her snicker softly. The boys were walking back through the food court with HMV bags in their hands, carrying on like they'd been up to no good. "You all made it. Good job," she said as they converged together in an exuberant cluster of chatter.

"I can do without a trip to the mall for a little while," Tyler said, laughing slightly. "These normal people are nuts." He mocked a shudder and moved closer to the center of the group.

Carol chuckled. "It's nice to see everyone getting along." She took Marco's hand as they started to walk toward the exit to the parking garage.

"So how was it?" Marco asked, nudging Curtis. "How'd they do?" He smiled as he said this, making sure both Bradley and Tyler heard him asking. "You all seem pretty pumped."

"They did good. I think they may even be friends after today," Curtis said, winking at them. "Male bonding at its finest."

Marco looked him over suspiciously. "Do I want to know?"

Tyler interjected. "No. You don't."

Marco looked from Tyler to Curtis. Both boys wore almost guilt-ridden expressions. He turned his attention to Bradley to see if he could get a better read on him, but he looked away. "Now I think I want to know. What did you get up to?"

"Secret's in the mall," Tyler teased. "Maybe next time you can break off with us guys." He stopped abruptly as a tall, muscular police officer stepped into his path. "Excuse me." He stepped to move around him, but the officer moved to block his way. Another officer stood a few feet behind him, assessing the group.

"Officer, what's the problem here?" Carol said, letting go of Marco's hand and moving to Tyler's side. She looked at each of their faces, trying to recognize them with no luck.

"Excuse me, ma'am," the officer said. "Could you please step back." He held his hand out to get her to step away.

"No, I can't. What is the problem here?" Her voice was more assertive now. "These boys are with me. I won't step away."

"Ma'am, there's been a complaint about an assault. We're going to have to ask these three to come down to the station with us." He pointed his finger at Tyler, Curtis, and Bradley.

"What?" Carol said. "I don't think so. What assault?"

"Ma'am, if you don't allow us to take them, we will have to arrest you for interfering with police business. You can meet them down at the station to find out what happened." The officer tapped Tyler on the shoulder and nodded for him to follow his partner.

"Carol, we didn't assault anyone," Tyler said, looking to her for protection. "We didn't do anything."

"Let's go," the officer said, interrupting. "All three of you." He tapped Bradley and then Curtis on the shoulder as well, indicating for them to follow Tyler. "The rest of you can meet us at the station."

Chapter Twenty-Four

THE POLICE STATION was quiet with only two desk clerks on duty and a vacant holding cell in the back corner. Adding to the subdued atmosphere were the gray walls and dark, faux-wood furniture. When Carol and Marco arrived with Theo and Maggie, they entered through the front door into the small waiting room that was separated from the rest of the station by a standing reception desk. Carol went straight to it and tapped the bell so hard that it barely made a sound, so she angrily hit it over and over until the female officer got up and slowly walked over, rolling her eyes to her colleague as she did. She appeared to be in her forties with short reddish-brown hair that had clearly been dyed. She walked with a masculine strut, leaning her shoulders back and bouncing slightly at the hip as she moved.

Before the woman could speak, Carol raised her hand to silence her. "I want those boys out here now! You do not have any right to take them into custody without first explaining to me, their legal guardian, exactly what you are accusing them of. This entire ordeal is ridiculous and unethical." She slapped the top of the desk as she finished.

The woman, Officer Clarke, put her hands up to signal Carol to calm down. "Just relax, ma'am," she said. She was chewing gum, smacking her lips as she did. With every chew, the sound of spit squishing from the gum into her mouth made Carol's eye twitch.

"I'm not calm. I will not be calm. I want to get in there with my boys." She pointed to the interrogation room at the back of the station. She could see the two arresting officers yelling and pointing at the boys who were sitting side by side at a table through the open blinds. The anguish on Bradley's face was sending her into a rage. He looked like he was going to start crying any second.

Officer Clarke turned toward the interrogation room, and then turned back and smirked. "They're being questioned at the moment, ma'am. How about you take a seat over there, and we'll let you know when you can go in there." She pointed to the seats that lined the wall of the waiting room. They were black, plastic chairs with rust stains on the metal frames that held them together.

Carol smiled bitterly and twirled her finger on the desk. "You don't seem to understand, Officer Clarke, that I am simply being courteous by making these vocal demands. I haven't even begun to lose my cool, and if you deny me one more time, you will see me lose my cool."

Officer Clarke straightened her posture and said, "Are you threatening me ma'am?" Her voice was firm and deep. "I won't tell you again. Go sit down over there, and we will tell you when you can go back there."

"You know, my father—Edmund Taylor—he was good friends with Mayor Beckett. And I still know the mayor quite well and his wife. And if you deny me one more time, I will make a call to him and then to my lawyer; you might know him too... Albert Blackburn." Carol smiled as she saw the smug look fade from the officer's face. Her lawyer, Albert Blackburn, was the best lawyer in their county. He tried most of the cases for the police station and rarely lost.

Officer Clarke swallowed deep. "Yes, I know them." Her voice had changed again. She was softer now.

"And you know I run the New Life House out on the fifth concession. You know the place, I'm sure. And I think you also know that it is incredibly illegal to take a minor into custody and refuse them their right to speak to their guardian or their lawyer."

"Yes, ma'am," Officer Clarke said. She sighed. "I'll go tell them that you're going to go on in."

Carol waved her hand to dismiss her. "No, no. You won't. I'm just going to go on back there." She started past the desk. She stopped as she passed by and said, "I used to be really well connected here, and I'm sure I could make a hefty donation to some cause the mayor deems important in return for a favor to have you turned into a meter maid." She smirked arrogantly. She hadn't pulled her father's name or used her former social status for anything in a long time. She had forgotten how good it felt.

"I'm sorry for the confusion," Officer Clarke said, lowering her gaze and taking a deep breath.

"Good," Carol said curtly. She walked past the older, slovenly officer who had not moved from his chair but who had watched the confrontation intently. As she passed him, she kept her eyes on the door to the interrogation room. She turned around and called back to Marco, "Call Albert, please."

Marco nodded and pulled out his cell phone. He flashed a smile at Officer Clarke, who now stood with an obvious air of nervousness at the desk, as he searched through the contact list on his phone.

"Maggie, can you go on and sit down with Theo over there? We'll be a little while." He nodded and pointed toward the seats.

Officer Clarke watched them as they sat and eyed the Lysol container and roll of paper towels sitting on the table in the corner.

Marco followed her gaze and shook his head in disgust. "Hi, Albert. Yes, it's Marco..." He plugged his free ear and moved outside to where he could talk in private.

"You kids try not to touch too many things," Officer Clarke said, eyeing them wickedly.

"We're not touching anything," Maggie said. "We're just sitting here."

"All the same. Try to keep it that way." Officer Clarke remained at the reception desk, refusing to take her eyes off of them.

"Stop talking to them right now," Carol said as she barged into the interrogation room, sending the papers they had on the desk scattering in the breeze caused by the door.

"Hey, you can't just come in here," the same officer who had been so rude to her during the arrest said. His nametag read: Officer Carlson.

"You can't question these boys. They are invoking their right to have a lawyer present. I will be pressing charges and personally requesting that the mayor conduct an investigation into the process that you refused to follow during this arrest." Carol was forceful, tactful, and aggressive in her approach.

"Excuse me?" Officer Thoms—the other arresting officer—said, standing up.

Carol raised her finger to him. "Don't try to pull the same intimidation tactic with me. I'm not a teenager. It won't work." She glared at him.

The boys sat completely still. Each of them stared at her in awe, somewhat afraid that this same anger would be coming to them later.

Officer Carlson raised his hand to the boys to signal them to remain seated. "These kids are not going anywhere. They committed a serious offense."

Carol's head snapped in his direction so quickly that he startled slightly. "Oh, did they? What was that offense? Maybe we can start obeying the law as a group now. Starting with *you*."

"We didn't assault anyone," Tyler said. "Those kids were picking on us and pushing Bradley around. They pushed us first. We didn't do anything—"

"Enough." Officer Carlson slammed his hand on the table. "You don't get to speak until I tell you to." He leaned forward to intimidate them again.

"Who do you think you're talking to?" Carol said, leaning so she could see the officer's face. "You do not speak to them like that. They're minors. You speak to *me*." Her voice was loud and sharp now.

"Why are those other kids not here under arrest? Tell me that. Enlighten me as to your process and duty to protect." She crossed her arms over her chest.

"Those kids wouldn't have attacked them."

"Why not? You take their word but not theirs?" She pointed to Bradley, Curtis and Tyler. "It's he said, she said. This is a joke. It will never hold up. You're wasting everyone's time and *my* tax dollars."

"Because...he's got AIDS," Officer Carlson said. "The people in this town might be hicks, but they're not dumb. They're not going to go endangering themselves."

Carol's face flushed a deep red. She took a deep breath.

"Oh, shit," Curtis said. He clearly meant to say it under his breath as he shrunk in his seat, wide-eyed, when everyone turned to him for a brief second before Carol started in at the officers.

"This is complete discrimination. We're leaving. You will be hearing from my lawyer. Expect a call from the media as well. I'm going to create a firestorm out of this one. You will regret the day you went after these kids and pissed off a Taylor. If you think you can arrest kids because they're HIV positive, you have another thing coming. I've never been so angry. I feel sick just looking at you."

"He grabbed his face," Officer Carlson defended, pointing at Tyler. "That kid grabbed another boy's face and tried to give it to him."

Carol laughed in an almost maniacal way. "I didn't realize that hands had penises. Maybe that's this new-wave hick thing you're talking about. Can you all get your wives pregnant by sticking your fingers in their mouths too?"

The officers grew silent, looking to one another uncomfortably.

"This is a total case of us versus them. You can't prove that they weren't pushed first. And you certainly can't prove that he tried to give him AIDS by touching his face. You'll get laughed out of court and off this force for saying dumb shit like that." She laughed cruelly again. "Your mother should be so proud. I used to know a Carlson. I wonder if he's your father. That would explain a lot." She knew she was moving off base, but she wanted to lash out and hurt him the way he'd hurt the boys, *her boys*.

"Ma'am. Hurling insults is not going to get to the results you want," Officer Thoms chimed in from behind Carlson.

"There is no discrimination here. He grabbed his face and attempted to infect him with a deadly disease," Officer Carlson said.

"Oh, wake up. Can you even hear yourself?" She rolled her eyes and waved for the boys to stand. "Stand up and go on out there to Marco, guys. We're leaving."

"Excuse me, you can't—"

Carol raised her hand to silence Carlson from speaking. "Just stop," she said sharply. "You need to read a book, browse the interweb, or do *something* to educate that tiny little brain of yours about the realities of HIV and AIDS. What you're claiming is impossible. When my lawyer is done with you, he'll have you transferred to the Northwest Territories. You can't get HIV or AIDS from being touched. Touching someone does not exchange bodily fluids. Just wake up." She tapped Tyler, Bradley, and Curtis on the shoulder, assisting them out of the interrogation room.

The officers didn't try to stop her. "Ma'am. We will be in touch for questioning them."

"Oh, save it," she said. She waved her hand again as she followed the boys out to the waiting room.

CAROL AND MARCO ushered the kids out to the car, and as they were leaving the front door, Officer Carlson called after them, "We don't take kindly to violent behavior in this town. Maybe let this be a lesson to you on how to conduct yourselves."

Marco kept his hand on Carol's shoulder to keep her from going back in to respond. "Oh, shoot. I'll be right back. I still have her pen," he said as he noticed it in his hand. He turned and jogged back into the station. When he stepped in, Officer Clarke was on her knees, wearing rubber gloves and spraying the chairs where the kids had sat with Lysol and scrubbing them down. She paused briefly and looked at the pen in his hand.

"I'll just keep it," he said, frowning. His eyes filled with tears. For a second, he thought he saw remorse in her eyes, but she seemed to sigh with relief when he said he'd keep it and went right back to scrubbing the chairs. He pressed his lips together to keep from saying anything that might dignify her, and turned around and left.

Chapter Twenty-Five

"CAROL," BRADLEY SAID, knocking on the back door of the veranda. "Can I talk to you please?" He stepped outside before she could answer.

She did her best to swallow the smoke in her lungs, standing up and moving over so she could blow some of it away before he made it to her. She tossed the roach over the edge of the veranda and sat on her supply tin. "Sure. Come have a seat." She tried for the calmest tone of voice she could muster, coughed and took a big sip of her wine to mask her breath.

"Are you okay?" he asked as he sat.

"Yeah, of course. Why? What's up?" She could feel how wide her eyes were despite her best efforts to act normal.

"You look like a deer caught in headlights." He eyed her suspiciously.

She shook her head and blinked to relax her eyes. "No, dear. I'm just processing everything that happened in town today. How are you holding up? You seemed really freaked out earlier."

He lowered his gaze and frowned. "I just... Is it fair?"

"Is what fair?"

"For me to ask you not to report the police?" He frowned as he said it and squeezed his left thumb in his right hand, massaging it.

"After everything they did, why don't you—" She stopped short of finishing the question. "Ah," she said. She patted his hand. "You're afraid that it will result in unwanted attention for the house."

"I know you need to have people know about the house, so media coverage is good, but I don't want to have my picture taken or have anyone know that I...that I have it. You know?"

"Don't worry, honey. They won't take your picture or anyone's. They'll simply give the police force a hard time." She gently touched his brow, which was crinkled up like a worried old man's, and then slowly ran her hand through his hair before squeezing his shoulder. "Don't stress yourself out about it."

He looked up at her, anger and tears in his eyes. "Please let it go. *Please.*"

His seriousness caught her off guard. "Okay. I'll talk to Marco if you feel that strongly about it."

"I do," he said, keeping his eyes fixed on hers. "I really do."

"Okay." She nodded. She appreciated the maturity he was showing in coming to her to get it stopped rather than resorting to his usual emotional outbursts.

"Thank you." He smiled now, but something about his expression told her that he was still shaken. It was in his eyes. He sniffed the air and wrinkled his nose. "Gosh, that smells awful. Do you smell that?" He sniffed the air again. "It smells like—"

"Skunk." She finished his sentence in a hurry. "There was one wandering around out here earlier. It must have sprayed something." She hated the obnoxious grin she was wearing now. Feeling like he was going to call her bluff any second, she started to giggle.

"It stinks." He looked around in search of the skunk. "Try not to get sprayed out here."

"I'll be careful," she said. Her eyes were watering as she stifled a full belly laugh. "You go on in to bed."

"Yeah, I don't want to get sprayed. Yuck." He shivered and returned to the house. "Thanks, Carol."

She waved before he disappeared into the house. "Thank God you're pretty, honey," she said aloud, snickering to herself. She checked over her shoulder to make sure he wasn't in the kitchen waiting to come back out. When she felt the coast was clear, she tossed the blanket to the side and ran down the stairs to the bush where she'd tossed the joint. *What if there really is a skunk out here?* she wondered, turning her head sharply to look around at the shadows being cast by the house and nearby shrubs. She giggled again as she imagined how ridiculous she must look. "There you are," she said, bending down to pick up the joint that was, miraculously, still lit. "Come to mama." She took several deep hauls off it to get it smoking again and returned to her spot on the swing to finish it off.

No sooner had she finished the joint did the guilt and fear of being caught set in. She found herself standing near the toilet, preparing to flush the remainder of her stash. As she stood, breathing heavily and trying to work up the courage to dump it, she caught a glimpse of herself in the mirror. Her face was tired yet wild. Her hair was a mess about her head, and her wrinkles seemed more pronounced than usual. "You're just tired, Carol. You're acting crazy. There's no reason to flush it." She hugged her bag of marijuana to her chest and stepped away from the toilet. "Stop jumping to such extremes. You just need a few days off. You don't have to get rid of it all." She scolded herself for being so rash while staring in awe at her haggard features. "You just need to get some sleep. Bradley didn't notice. You aren't in trouble. You're tripping out."

She came out of the bathroom, still clutching her bag of weed, and stopped to stare at Marco who was sleeping peacefully. She stuffed the bag back up onto the top shelf of their closet and slipped into bed next to him, wrapping her arms and legs around him and nuzzling into his neck. He stirred and leaned back into her as she hugged him, offering her the unintended, silent consolation she needed.

"Everything is fine," she whispered as she drifted off to sleep.

Chapter Twenty-Six

"HEY, THERE YOU are," Tyler said, taking a seat beside Maggie in the sunroom. She was sitting on the couch, watching the squirrels prance about on the railing of the front veranda.

"Hey," she said. She sat up a little straighter and folded her feet under her legs. "How'd you sleep?"

He yawned. "Not too bad. I'm wiped, though. What crazy day."

Maggie smiled. "Yeah, it was pretty crazy."

"I haven't been in trouble with cops in a long time. I kinda felt like I was back in Vancouver again."

"Did you get in trouble a lot before?" Maggie watched him closely to see if she could guess whether he was telling the truth or telling a tale. She wasn't confident that his whole 'bad boy' routine was anything more than a routine. Something in her gut told her that he was sweeter than he let anyone believe.

Tyler shrugged. "Nah, not really, but when I was tricking, they would give me a hard time. They never caught me for it, but they knew what I was hanging out there for. And they nabbed me a couple times for shoplifting but let me go."

She liked when he told her the truth about his life. It made her feel closer to him when he wasn't exaggerating for effect. She folded her hands in her lap and turned to face him, looking him in the eyes. "I'm sorry about the other day," she said, offering a gentle smile. "I shouldn't have pried so hard. You have a right to your privacy."

"Thanks, I appreciate it." He scratched the side of his head nervously. "You know, I've been meaning to talk to you about a lot of stuff anyways."

She held her breath, feeling her stomach turn in anticipation of bad news.

"I just think we might be going too fast."

Her heart sank. She looked down at her hands and started wringing them.

"I just need to be honest about what I'm thinking. I don't want to hurt you." He lifted her face so he could see her eyes.

"Are you…" She stopped short of finishing her sentence for fear of the answer.

"I'm just…I'm confused. I don't know what I want and you do. I still don't know if I want to be with a boy or a girl."

She started to cry when he said this, not wanting to hear anymore, regretting that she'd brought the other day up at all.

"You know that I'm bi. I've never lied about that."

She nodded, sniffled, and wiped the tears from her face.

"I don't know who I am. I don't know what I want. And I feel all this pressure to be this perfect person for you when I don't even know how to be a person for me. I don't even know how to make that make sense." He sighed. "I just don't know," he said a little softer now.

"I'm sorry for pressuring you," Maggie said. Her voice wavered as she spoke. She wanted to scream at him. She knew he was bisexual, but she didn't know he was struggling with knowing whether he wanted a boyfriend or a girlfriend. This was news to her, and she wanted to slap him for it, but she held back for fear of pushing him away altogether.

TYLER HOPED HE would find the right words to make her smile. "I don't want to hurt you. I'm not saying that I don't want us to happen. I'm just saying that I don't know if it's the forever kind of love, and I need you to slow down. I'm not sure about anything in life." He paused to see if she would respond.

She remained silent.

"I like you, Maggie. I like figuring out who I am with you, but I don't want to be making promises that I don't know I can keep. Is that fair?" He felt guilty for lying, but decided that it was better than breaking her heart so blatantly. He wanted to like her, but the more he thought about Chad, the more he wanted to be gay. And he knew he could never tell her any of that. She would never understand.

She nodded. "Yes. That's fair."

He touched her chin, turning her face up so he could see it. "Let's be in the moment. There's a lot of good things that can happen in the moment." He leaned in slowly and kissed her, keeping his eyes open to watch hers and knowing that she believed him when she closed them.

Chapter Twenty-Seven

IT HAD BEEN two weeks since the incident at the mall, yet it seemed like the wounds were still as fresh as if they'd happened the day before. At the time of the event, only Bradley seemed visibly shaken; however, all of the kids—along with Carol and Marco—had been struggling to come to terms with it ever since. Bradley seemed to be having the most difficulty. Carol had taken notice that ever since the night when he begged her not to make the whole ordeal public, he had practically been hiding in the shadows of the house. He rarely joined the others for movies or television nights; he came to breakfast late so he could avoid sitting with the other kids and went straight to bed after evening chores. She didn't like seeing him so lost. He had always been somewhat cantankerous, and *that* she could handle, but he had gone from that extreme to completely subdued.

"Where are you?" Marco asked from his side of the bed. He leaned in and stroked her cheek with his forefinger. "You're a million miles away."

She took a deep breath and set the book she was pretending to read in her lap. "Had the events remained between the kids and never involved the police, I bet this would have blown over much differently," she said. "It's almost like, by the police getting involved and furthering the prejudice, we all took it as the voice of society. But how could we not?" She looked to Marco for a response that would help her compartmentalize it all. She hadn't been this angry with the police or the "outside world," as the kids would call it, in years.

Marco smiled in the same way he always did when she jumped right into the middle of a conversation that she'd been having in her head, expecting him to catch up on the spot. "You know I wasn't a part of the first half of that, right?"

She blushed slightly. "Well try to keep up, would ya?" she said, jokingly as she rolled her eyes playfully. "Sheesh." They both laughed for a brief moment before she caught him up on the conversation, concluding with, "I'm worried about Bradley. He's taking it really hard."

Marco sighed. "I see. I think it would be tough for anyone to handle—"

"Hasn't it been hard for you?" she asked, interrupting him.

He frowned. "Of course it has. I don't like seeing the kids or you struggle with anything, and this was a huge thing. I hate seeing this kind of small-mindedness."

Carol crossed her arms over her chest. "This town is too religious for a house like this."

"It's not about religion. It's about small-mindedness. We should think about trying to get information sessions set up in town to inform people about us and what we do. Maybe that would help spread the word around."

"The kids couldn't handle that. That would be too risky," she said, shaking her head.

"I don't mean that the kids should do it, but we should, as medical professionals. It is our responsibility to hold workshops to educate the locals about what we do and the real implications of encountering someone who is HIV positive. You know...dispel some of the myths that seem to be swirling around about this house. Maybe that was part of our mistake in starting this place. We should have started educating people from the start. Instead we hid ourselves and the kids away, and let all the rumors take control rather than addressing them head-on. We took overprotective to a whole new level."

"We can't blame ourselves for the ignorance of those people," Carol said. She felt her body temperature rising as she grew defensive. Little beads of sweat began to form under her arms and above her lip. "This was not our fault."

Marco took her hands in his. "I'm not saying it's our fault," he said calmly, slowing his voice and mellowing his tone. The technique was deliberate and obvious, and one that he often used with her and she knew it. It was his way of trying to keep her from overreacting. "I am just saying"—he spoke with emphasis on each syllable—"that we have a role to play. We cannot simply expect the world to understand what we're doing if we don't do anything to help them."

She remained silent, processing what he'd said and considering whether she should try to refute it or let it stand. She found herself struggling with her desire to prove him wrong and the small feeling of doubt she had in her own resolve. *Maybe it is our fault*, she thought.

"I think we can fix this, though," he said. "I think we should make a point of hosting, somewhere in town, some community engagement sessions where we inform the adults and community members about the house and what we do. We need to educate people about HIV and AIDS and let them know that they have nothing to fear in us or these kids."

Carol nodded reluctantly. She didn't want to host anything for the townspeople. The thought of wasting any time or money on them infuriated her, but the thought of neglecting her duty as a professional and a caretaker for these kids felt worse. "You're right," she said at last, stunning Marco. She laughed when she saw him pause in mock surprise at the sound of those two words and shoved him. "Oh, get off it. You're often right as much as it pains me to admit."

Marco smiled. "Love you." He kissed her on the cheek quickly before she pushed him away again. "I'll talk to Dr. Benson and the mayor and see about setting up some sessions somewhere. It won't be right away. We'll need to do a lot of planning—"

"Which is right up your alley," she interrupted.

"Exactly," he said, kissing her again and then tucking himself under the covers and rolling over to face the wall. "Have a good sleep. Good night."

"Good night." She sat for a few moments, still pretending to read before giving up with a sigh. "I'm going to go down to the veranda. I'll be back up in a bit." She leaned over Marco and kissed him on the cheek.

"Sounds good," he mumbled. "Try not to stay out there too long. You'll catch a cold."

"I'll bundle up."

TO CAROL'S SURPRISE, Tyler was already waiting for her on the swing when she got outside. "Hi there... What are you doing out here?" she asked as she stepped out the kitchen door and moved to sit beside him. She felt at odds with him being there already, expectantly.

He shrugged. "I'm actually just watching the stars. You know? I don't know how to explain it, but I feel different today." He turned his head to face her for a moment. After he was done assessing her, he smiled and looked back to the stars.

"Different how? Are you feeling sick?" She stopped in motion, clutching her Clorets tin. She hadn't checked in with him lately to find out if he was feeling any symptoms that should be treated or could indicate some kind of infection. She felt a sudden rush of anxiety wash over her as she thought of all of the possible answers he could give that would confirm her negligence.

He shrugged again, still smiling, and said, "It's nothing like that. I feel different in this house. It's like I actually belong here since I stood up for us." He smirked as he thought of it again: the mall, the supposed assault, the cops, and the cop station. "It was a really simple thing for me. I don't mind telling an asshole when he's been an asshole. You know? I'm proud of myself. And I think Bradley actually likes me now. And I finally feel like I belong here. Like I'm one of the 'gang,'" he said, making air quotes with his hands.

Carol was instantly relieved. *Oh, good. It's just teenage bravado*, she thought. She pulled a joint out of the tin and lit it. "I was worried you'd been feeling sick or noticing symptoms."

He shook his head. "Nope. None of that. I'm actually feeling great." He took the joint from her. "Is it weird that I'm actually kind of pumped up since that whole thing?"

"No," she said, laughing. "It's not weird at all." She liked his tenacity. He reminded her of herself when she was his age. *Only a little more lost.* "I think I'd be feeling the same way," she said. She watched as he accepted the answer. He seemed pleased by it.

"So you gotta tell me something," he said.

"What?"

"Why in the heck is there no caffeine here? It's like you get off on some kind of twisted torture." He flashed a bratty smile at her.

She laughed. "Believe me. It's not fun for us either."

"Then why don't we have it?"

"It's a depressant. And we don't want to take any risks. Kids dealing with the troubles that you are all dealing with are prone to depression—"

"Wouldn't anyone be?"

"—we don't want something as silly as coffee making things worse," Carol continued, "And yes. I think anyone would be at a higher risk of depression in your situation."

He nodded. "So you told me once that you started this place because *everything* changed. What did you mean by that? What's everything?" He passed the joint back to her.

She leaned into the swing and tucked her feet up onto the bench. "I knew you'd ask me that eventually," she said. "I was kind of hoping you wouldn't."

"Why's that?"

"Because I wasn't planning on actually opening up to you about any of that stuff."

Intrigued, Tyler pulled his feet up as well so he could face her. "Well, now you *have* to tell me."

She didn't want to, but at the same time, she did. She took a deep breath before beginning her long and uncomfortable story. "I've told you about my father and how I grew up, right?"

"Yep," he said, nodding.

"Okay, good. So you know that my dad was the doctor in town. We also come from old money, so there was always a link to the upper class in town. I always felt a lot of pressure to be just like him. I wanted to become a psychiatrist. I would have been the first in town and the first woman in town as a doctor. It would have been an impressive feat for the family."

"You are a doctor, though. Aren't you?"

"I have my PhD so, yeah, I am a doctor in that sense. But I don't have an office or a patient list. I'm not invited to the social events in town. I've basically let our family name fall out of the circuit. And that was something that was always important to my parents. Mostly my father, but I think it mattered to my mother too." She paused to reflect before continuing. "The things that changed were mostly life circumstances."

"Like what?"

"Like, I found out that I wouldn't be able to have a child of my own." She paused after saying it. It was a reality that had never lost its sting for her. She and Marco had rarely spoken of it after they'd found out. It was what prompted them to open the New Life House, so they could still have children in their lives. "It really hurt because Marco and I both really wanted to have a family. We love kids, so it really shook us both."

Tyler did his best to appear apologetic and said, "I'm sorry. That sounds really shitty."

She looked at him through her tear-blurred vision. "It's okay." She took a deep breath. The tears melted back into her eyes without falling. "I just haven't talked about any of that in a long time is all. I'm so used to doing all the listening."

"Doesn't listening get boring?" he asked, taking the joint from her and sucking a long haul into his lungs. "I think I'd hate having to listen to all of us whiny kids all the time."

She laughed. "It gets tough sometimes, but like I said, Marco and I always wanted kids. We wanted a family of our own. After my father died, we did a lot of soul-searching and came to the decision that we'd like to arrange our lives so we could give homes to kids who didn't have a family.

It's like we felt like we were reverse-orphans who couldn't have kids, and actual orphans who didn't have parents would be the best fit for us."

"How did you decide to pick dying kids?"

Unfazed by his bluntness, she answered, "We were in medical school. We were studying cases of HIV and how the infections are passed and learned that children become infected and are sometimes submitted to hospitals or children's aid rather than kept in the care of their parents. That's a really rare thing, you know, for kids to be willingly sent away by their parents."

"Great, so we're the lucky ones," Tyler said, waving his hand in the air fancily as though to include himself and the other kids in fake celebration.

"Yes. You are. I'd say you're lucky to end up here." She winked to get him to laugh. "It isn't common, but there are some shitty parents out there who abandon their kids for it and there are good parents who simply aren't capable of caring for the child once infected. Parents like Theo's." She frowned. "Sometimes the parents are just as lost as the kids. And that's why we decided to start this place."

"Aren't you scared that you've found a way to pick kids who are all going to die?"

She shook her head and sighed. "No, sweetie. I'm not worried, and neither is Marco. As I've told you a hundred times, this is not a death sentence. Almost all of you will outlive us by many decades." She felt guilty as she said it. In her gut, she didn't believe he would. And she didn't think he believed it either, but to his credit, he didn't react. He simply forced a tight-lipped smile and turned his gaze back out to the stars.

After a few moments of listening to nothing more than the sounds of one another smoking the joint followed by deep exhalations and the odd cough, Tyler asked, "Why did you call it that? The New Life House?"

"Because that's what you get when you come here." She took the joint and turned her attention to the stars as well. She wondered if the name was offensive to someone like Tyler whose life may not last long enough to leave the house.

"Hm," he said. "I feel like both names have their place."

Carol turned toward him. "Both what names?" She handed the joint back to him.

"The New Life House *and* the Death House." He didn't look her in the eyes as he said it.

The words stung as she heard them. She'd heard whispers about the nickname the locals had come up with for the house, but she'd never actually heard it said. "The Death House?" she said. She blinked repeatedly to try to keep the tears from escaping. "That's an awful name." She found herself recalling Marco's push to hold community engagement sessions. *How is he always so right?*

Tyler pressed his lips together in an attempt to smile but frowned instead. "I'm sorry, but I see it as both."

"How is it a death house? Don't you feel alive now that you're here?"

"I feel more alive now than I have in years, possibly ever," he said. "Don't get me wrong. I love it here, and I think it does offer a chance to have a new life. But you can't escape the fact that some of us will die here. Some of us will come here, experience a new life, and die."

He spoke in such a matter of fact tone that it calmed her down at the same time that it riled her up. There was something ironically comforting in the rationale he used to defend the disgusting nickname. "Why do I feel so safe with you?" she asked rhetorically. "I don't open up about anything with anyone. But with you, it's like all the walls I've put up just shatter."

"Good. I feel the same way about you. It's really easy talking with you. You know? It's almost like I crave these conversations. They're so brutal and honest, and I think they're the one thing that's keeping me connected to who I think I am. I like that I don't have to sugarcoat things when we're here. It's freeing."

"These talks are great, aren't they? Not exactly legal or ethical, but God, they're good for the soul."

"Sure as shit are," Tyler said, nodding in agreement and leaning into the swing, pulling the blanket up to his chin. "This is the most content I've felt in a long time, probably since I had to say goodbye."

"To who? Rachel?"

Tyler shook his head. "Someone else. Someone I loved." He spoke softly, almost mournfully.

Carol looked him over curiously, wanting to know more. "Really? Do tell."

Tyler looked at her with tears in his eyes, but still with a warm smile. "Not tonight."

Chapter Twenty-Eight

TYLER

A Little More Than One Year Ago
December 1996

Tyler leaned into Chad as they walked, pressing against him and squeezing his hand. He didn't want to let go, ever. It was the fifth straight day of misting rain. The dampness and the cool temperature stuck to Tyler's skin like sweat, making him shiver. He scrunched his eyes against the mist as they moved through the crowd of junkies in front of Knowlton Drugs on East Hastings Street in downtown Vancouver.

Tyler's eyes fluttered as he felt the effects of the MDMA wearing off. He hated this part, the part where his body seemed to be shutting down. Despite his best efforts, his eyes couldn't focus. The only thing that kept them from rolling around in his head was keeping them closed, but that always made him fall asleep. One day, a few weeks back, he and Chad took a break to sit on a bench in Dr. Sun Yat-Sen Park. When they first sat down, the sun had been up and when they next opened their eyes, it was dark and nearly four hours later.

"Heyyy." Jackie's familiar, flirty voice came rasping at them from amidst the crowd in front of the store. She was in her early twenties, but looked older. Up close, her green eyes looked dead. Tyler always felt like there was something missing from them, like the color was fading. Jackie had taken both Tyler and Chad under her wing when they'd come down to East Hastings.

Tyler forced himself to smile but closed his eyes as the sudden movement of her and the people in behind her made his eyes twitch.

"Hey, sexy lady," Chad said. He leaned over and hugged her tight. "That was a lot of fun last night. Thanks for inviting us along."

Jackie giggled and poked at Tyler's stomach to get him to look at her. He blinked, opting to keep only one eye open. That seemed to make the twitching less severe.

"You got the twitch again?"

Tyler nodded. He covered his right eye with his hand to keep the lid from twitching again. He hated the feeling, and felt like screaming every time someone pointed it out because it made it feel that much stronger.

Jackie laughed again. "You boys looking to fix?" Her whole body spasmed. Her head bobbed jerkily to the right. She corrected herself and squirmed where she stood as though she were fighting the urge to twitch again. Her eyes wandered past them to the cars driving by.

"Nah, we're sketched. Think we're just gonna go get some sleep." Chad put his arm around Tyler and squeezed him gently.

Tyler grinned. His stomach filled with the feeling of butterflies flapping against the edges. He suddenly felt warm despite the cold. He tucked in closer to Chad. "Ye-yeah." His voice stuttered and his jaw chattered. "I need t-to get some gum-m."

Jackie swung her small, green purse around in front of her, dug into it, and pulled a package out. "Here you go, sweetie."

Tyler took a piece and popped it into his mouth, instantly relieved by the sweetness and the ease of tension on his jaw. He had been chattering his teeth since they'd started partying the night before. "I have been dying for some of this." He held the pack back to her.

"Honey, don't you worry. I have you covered. Take that. I'll get another pack later. I'm working tonight." She perked her breasts out, rested her hands on her hips, and turned sideways. She was wearing tight jeans, stained and slightly torn; a sparkly, silver tank top; and a shiny, red leather coat. "Think I'll catch a few like this?" She smiled big, revealing the few teeth she still had to be a yellowish-brown.

Chad and Tyler both nodded emphatically. "Absolutely," Chad said. "You look amazing."

Jackie pushed him playfully, running her hand down his chest. "You're too sweet, Chad. I can't get my hair to stay the fuck down." She groaned and started fussing with the mess of frizzy hair on top of her head. "You'd think the fucking rain would weigh it down, but *no*." She continued trying to flatten it.

"You look pretty," Tyler said.

"Thanks. But who cares really, right? They don't care what my hair looks like as long as my mouth and pussy work fine." She laughed her obnoxious laugh at the look of disgust on both Chad and Tyler's faces. "You two. You two. I'll see you later." She kissed the tips of her pointer and middle finger on both hands and then pressed them against each of their cheeks before strutting down the sidewalk toward Main Street, wagging her hips and stumbling every few feet.

"Let's go." Chad leaned into Tyler to nudge him toward Carrall Street where they shared a couch with Jackie in a corner room at an old, derelict factory that had been cleared out of most of its interior walls and furniture, basically gutted. The people there called it "The Spot." Not a very original name, but—apparently—the people who coined the name thought it would be hard for the cops to figure out where it was if it had an innocuous name. It seemed like a ridiculous rationale to Tyler because the cops came wandering through nearly every day. They never gave anyone much trouble, but they made themselves known.

They turned down Carrall Street and made their way to the alleyway beside the Gospel Mission and Carrall Street Church. It was the only way to get into The Spot. They walked down the now-familiar alley toward their home. The path itself was colorful with the crumbling and chipped backs of red brick buildings, green dumpsters and graffiti.

The windows were bricked over and had bars on them. They were shaped like how Tyler imagined the openings at the top of a horse stall, wide and arched. He could picture Black Beauty and Ginger sticking their heads out of them...if they weren't closed up. He liked being near there because it made him feel closer to Rachel. She loved that movie. They'd seen it in theaters as a family when it came out a couple years before.

"You know it's not going to be like this forever, right?" Chad asked, bumping Tyler gently with his shoulder as they walked.

Tyler half shrugged. "I guess."

Chad frowned. "I mean it." He stopped and pulled on Tyler's hand so he would turn to face him. "I'm gonna give you a good life. I promise. This is just a stepping stone. Temporary."

Tyler smiled and fidgeted on his feet. He liked hearing Chad talk about taking care of him and making sure he had a good life. He felt kept. "What will we do?"

Chad smiled now and kissed Tyler, pressing against him. He pulled his head back to look him in the eyes. "And where will we go?"

Tyler kissed Chad again and then shivered. "Somewhere warm. *Please,* somewhere warm." He motioned to keep walking, and pulled Chad along by the hand.

They came to the big, brown, and rusty door marked with a giant, spray-painted *T* and *S* about halfway down the alley. This marked The Spot.

Chad grunted, and the heavy door squeaked as he pulled it open and then ushered Tyler inside. They made their way across the large, open room quickly. The couch and small room they shared with Jackie was on the other side of the building, near the front. As they moved through, they passed by several metal burn bins with small fires going and a couple people standing with their hands over the flames. There were boards up on most of the windows, allowing bars of light through. The light was mostly dim these days as it had been misting rain and lightly snowing for nearly a week. Tyler liked how dark it was in there because it helped his eyes relax. The pressure was instantly lifted.

"Hey, boys," Little M—a large, elderly man—called out from next to one of the fires. His voice was scratchy and sounded like an exaggerated stage whisper. "No one's givin' you any trouble, are they?"

Chad waved and beamed proudly. "No, sir. Not a chance. Not with you around." Everyone at The Spot had taken to watching out for them since they'd come down to live there. At times, it felt like they had adopted twenty new parents and siblings. Jackie always said that the young ones were the people everyone wanted to protect because there was something more tragic about them being there.

When Little M had first learned about why they were down there, he threatened to beat down Tyler's parents' door to force them to take him back, but Chad managed to convince him that it wouldn't solve the lack of love. At least with Chad, Tyler had love. And at The Spot, they at least had a family. Little M accepted this begrudgingly, but he had taken his role as family seriously. Tyler actually feared what would happen if someone outwardly hurt either him or Chad while Little M was watching out for them. Just because his name was Little didn't mean he was in fact *little*.

Tyler could hear the faint murmurs coming from a few people who were sleeping in the shadows near the walls, and the groans of a few people who had likely just injected themselves with cocaine. A lot of people at The Spot and in the Downtown East Side were doing it these days. After they shot up, they would roll around on the floor screaming and groaning like they were in pain. It terrified Tyler. He couldn't understand the appeal.

Garbage littered the floor throughout the building, but it was home. Jackie's couch was in a semi-private corner. It had been an office of some kind once upon a time. There was no door to their room anymore, and one of the walls had crumbled away at the top, leaving a four-by-six-foot hole in the left corner. Jackie said she liked it that way because it felt like they had a real window, like it was a real apartment.

"I have been looking forward to this," Tyler said, plopping himself down on their tattered yellow couch. The fabric was browning from dirt and filth, and it had white stuffing poking through dozens of rips and tears. It looked like someone had taken a knife and used the cushions to practice stabbing someone to death.

Chad kicked the bottles and wrappers out of his way as he stepped around Tyler's leg to sit on the side closest to the wall, lifting his feet onto the overturned plastic milk crate they used as a coffee table. He slid his hand onto Tyler's leg and kissed his cheek. "I love you." He smiled and leaned back against the arm of the couch, pulling Tyler close to him.

"I love you too," Tyler said. He eagerly leaned back against Chad and swung his feet up onto the couch. He held his hand up with his fingers spread, so Chad could gently tickle the back of his hand and his fingers. He closed his eyes and relaxed, feeling like his insides were falling back into Chad in waves.

"Where would you want to go?" Chad said, speaking softly into Tyler's ear.

"California. I've always wanted to go there. It's so warm. And we could be in movies. It would be awesome." Tyler kept his eyes closed and tried to imagine what it would be like on Hollywood Boulevard.

Chad grinned and nibbled Tyler's ear. "Totally. And if we couldn't get into real movies, we could always do porn." He chuckled.

Tyler stiffened. He didn't want to imagine Chad being with anyone but him.

As though he noticed Tyler's discomfort with the idea, Chad added, "But only with each other. No one would be in it but us."

"Better not be." Tyler playfully elbowed Chad in the stomach. "Porn with you would be great. But you're so hot you'll be a real movie star. They'll love you." Tyler sat up so he could turn and kiss Chad.

The sound of a man snorting deeply, swallowing, and then clearing his throat right outside their doorway interrupted them. Tyler sat up and moved his legs off the couch.

"Hey," Chad said cheerfully. He waved at the man who stood watching them. "You need something?"

The man smiled but something about it made Tyler uncomfortable. "Hey, I'm Rick," he said, stepping into their room and out of the shadows. He was tall, at least a foot taller than Chad and much taller than Tyler. He was wearing a dark-blue jean jacket over a white button-up shirt that was tucked into his pants. The buttons at the top of the shirt were open, revealing most of his chest, which was covered in short black hair. His smile was big and shiny, his teeth white and perfect. His black hair was slicked back, and his beard was closely cropped.

Tyler couldn't help but to feel like Rick didn't belong in The Spot. He'd never seen him around before.

"I'm Chad and this is Tyler." Chad put his arm around Tyler almost as though he were laying claim to what was his. Tyler blushed.

Rick pointed to the spot on the couch next to Tyler. "Can I sit with you guys? I'm just looking for a place to poke." He smiled again, giving them a look that seemed an attempt at being flirty.

"Yeah, sure," Chad said.

Tyler breathed in an overpowering, but nice, scent of spicy cologne as Rick sat beside him. He smelled good. No one in The Spot ever smelled good. Tyler could feel the warmth of Rick's body as he leaned back into the couch with his shoulder very close to him. "What's that accent you have?" Tyler asked.

Rick turned his head to look at Tyler with his gray, almost silver eyes. "No accent, really. I'm Italian, but I've lived in Vancouver my whole life."

Tyler nodded as though this made perfect sense.

"What are you doing down here?" Chad asked. "You look a little well-dressed for this place."

Rick chuckled. "Yeah, yeah I guess I am." He reached into the inside pocket of his jacket and pulled out his kit—a small toiletry bag. "You guys mind?"

Both Tyler and Chad shrugged. "No."

Rick flashed his mischievous grin again. "You guys ever smashed before?" He pulled open the kit and removed a blackened spoon, a piece of a sponge, a lighter, a small plastic baggie filled with powder, and a rubber band. He placed each item neatly in his lap.

Chad sat up and leaned around Tyler to see what Rick was doing. "No, we haven't. Is that..." He pointed at the small plastic bag of powder.

"Heroin," Rick said quickly. "It's not coc. I wouldn't want to be out there moanin' and groanin' like all them fools out there." He nodded toward the other room where they could still hear several people panicking over a bad trip. "That shit's scary."

Tyler nodded. "Yeah, I'm afraid of shooting up coc."

Rick smiled and leaned back against the couch again. This time, he leaned closer so his arm rested on Tyler's. "Call it smash. You'll sound a lot cooler." He chuckled and looked Tyler in the eyes again.

Tyler swallowed. "Okay."

"You two wanna try? It's the greatest. I love being there for people's first time. I miss the first time. It's never the same, but it's always perfect. It's like the warmest day, and the most exhilarating ride. Like you're sliding down a warm water slide filled with cushions. And then you land in them, and they hold you tight and squeeze you comfortingly. Every touch is like a massage, like your skin is on fire, but fire the feels good. It's like you're never alone, and you never want to be. You'll love it."

"Yeah, I'll try some of that. I've always wanted to," Chad said.

Tyler looked at him, surprised to hear him say it. "Really?" He didn't like that Chad hadn't told him this before. He thought the fear of needles and injection drug use was something they shared.

Chad nodded. "Yeah. I've always thought it seemed like a lot of fun. The way people describe it. It just sounds so nice." He took his arm from around Tyler. "It'll be fun." His eyes flashed. "Didn't that sound great?"

Tyler agreed that he would try it too.

Rick sat up straight, excited. "Awesome. I'll get it ready, and we can all go together. I'll give you both a poke before I do me." He emptied some heroin into the spoon and proceeded to cook it. "Fancy rubber band, huh?" He picked it up and placed it on Tyler's leg.

Chad reached over and picked it up. "It looks pretty official."

"It should. I snagged it from a doctor's office. Nothing but the best for me and the people I smash with." He smirked. "I take care of my friends."

"I like that. We're new down here, so we need lots of friends." Chad watched intently as Rick placed the sponge into the spoon to soak up the cooked heroin and then proceeded to pull the plunger up, filling the body of the syringe.

Rick looked them over, eyeing them up and down. "You boys think you'd wanna do some work for some cash sometime? I can take you boys somewhere to get cleaned up, showered and shit, you know? And then I can get you in with the right clientele. Cute boys like you will make a good buck."

Chad chuckled under his breath. "Thanks, Rick. But we're good. We're lovers, so we don't want to do anything with anyone else."

Rick pursed his lips and then smirked again. "Suit yourselves, boys. How about I leave the offer on the table? You guys ever get tired of being down here in The Spot without any money, food, or a warm place to sleep. And you come see me. Till then, we can be friends, yeah? I like smashing with cute guys." He pressed his leg against Tyler's. Then he looked at Chad. "You want to go first? I can make my way down the couch that way."

Chad nodded and leaned back to get into position. Tyler watched, intrigued by the process and a little off put by Chad's nervous excitement. He felt like he was watching a B movie of someone else's life.

Rick got up off the couch and swung the milk crate in front of Chad and used it as a chair. "Just relax, and let it take you." He tied the rubber band around Chad's arm and rubbed the inside of his elbow to get the veins to stand out. "Perfect," he said.

Chad turned his head to face Tyler. He beamed excitedly. "Another first." He squeezed Tyler's hand.

"Keep your arm relaxed," Rick said, eyeing them.

Chad released Tyler's hand. He closed his eyes and moaned; his legs curled upward, and he breathed in deeply as Rick slid the needle into his vein and slowly pushed the plunger.

Rick laughed. "He's a natural. Look at that." He smiled as he watched Chad, and then he turned to Tyler. "He looks happy, doesn't he?" He carefully untied the rubber band from Chad's arm, causing another gentle burst of moans.

"He does." Tyler watched Chad's face, trying to discern if he should be concerned, but Chad kept smiling.

"Sounds happy too." Rick chewed his bottom lip and patted Chad's knee. After a brief moment of pause, he shifted the milk crate so he was in front of Tyler, with his legs on either side of Tyler's knees. He leaned with his arms on Tyler's legs as he prepped the heroin, lighting the flame beneath the bowl of the spoon.

Tyler tried not to stare too hard at Rick, but he was strangely drawn to him. He darted his eyes back to Chad.

Rick smirked. "You're nervous around me."

Tyler shook his head. "No. I'm not nervous."

"Sure you are." Rick smiled arrogantly. "You've got nothing to fear in me, my friend." He filled the syringe. He set the needle on the couch and moved closer so Tyler's knees were against his crotch.

Tyler shifted in his seat a little, looking to Chad and then back at Rick who was staring intensely at him, his gray eyes seemed to flicker.

"If you guys ever need anything. I mean anything. You just let me know." Rick slid his hands onto Tyler's thighs and pushed closer to his knees.

Tyler could feel that Rick was aroused. "I don't—"

"Don't answer now. Just remember that you can come to me anytime, for anything."

"Chad's my boyfriend. I don't want to," Tyler said, stopping short of finishing his sentence. He felt like he might cry. He was embarrassed that he had an erection. He didn't want anyone to do that to him but Chad.

Rick lifted his hands from Tyler's legs. "You don't have to do anything you don't want to," he said in a serious yet calming tone. "Nothing at all. You can't blame me for trying, though." He winked.

Tyler breathed, relieved that Rick had stopped touching him. To change the subject, he said, "Is it gonna hurt?"

Rick shook his head. "Not with me." He smiled and picked up the needle, tapped it twice, and then rubbed Tyler's arm. He gently slid the needle in and pushed the plunger, slowly removing the rubber band as he went.

Tyler gasped and moaned. His eyes shot open and then closed. He felt himself falling comfortably backward into the cushions of the couch. Then he felt Rick's hands on his crotch, squeezing. He moved his hand up to Rick's to try to get him to stop, but all he could do was hold on. The rush was pulsing through him so strong that even though he didn't want Rick touching him, the physical contact was waking all of his senses in a way that he had never experienced before.

Rick took Tyler's hands and pulled him forward so they were face-to-face. Tyler opened his eyes again and stared into Rick's mouth as he was whispering something to him. He couldn't make out what it was. He smiled as it started to become clear. "You're a beautiful young man, Tyler." Rick kissed him. "I can't wait to have you." He then stood up and swung around to sit beside Tyler on the couch. He took Tyler's hand and placed it in his lap. Tyler didn't fight it. He closed his eyes as Rick kissed his cheek and then his neck.

WHEN TYLER WOKE, he was still sitting between Chad and Rick. He had a hand in both of their laps, and they both had a hand in his. He quickly pulled his hand away from Rick and leaned closer to Chad.

Chad groaned slightly. "Mmm." He stretched and opened his eyes. He kissed Tyler above the eye. "That was so amazing."

Tyler nodded. It had been the best feeling he'd ever known, despite Rick's advances.

"I love you, Ty."

Tyler grinned, forgetting any discomfort with Rick. "I love you."

Chad squeezed Tyler's leg. "Before he goes, we gotta make sure Rick tells us how to find him. We have to do that again. It was so good."

Chapter Twenty-Nine

CAROL HAD ASKED Tyler, before they'd finished on the veranda, to reach out and try to help Bradley back out of depression. She had decided that sending Tyler, rather than Curtis this time, might catch Bradley off guard enough to actually work. And just as asked, Tyler waited to have his breakfast. By the time Bradley skulked his way down the hall, Tyler's stomach was in knots. "Jesus. I'm starving!" he said, frantically jumping off the bed, tossing his magazine and blankets around in a jumble of action as he made his way out into the hall.

The attention startled him, so Bradley backed away and put his hand up to signal that he didn't want Tyler to get any closer. "What do I have to do with you being hungry?"

"Everything," Tyler said, laughing lightly. Bradley looked at him curiously as they started down toward the kitchen and dining room.

Bradley walked with his head down, his hands in his pockets and his shoulders hunched, as he had since the arrest.

"You know you're more attractive with your head up and your shoulders back," Tyler said, raising his eyebrows in an over-exaggerated gesture aimed at getting a laugh and nudging him gently with his elbow. He made a clicking sound with his tongue for extra effect.

Bradley laughed, and said playfully, "Fuck off." He pushed him away. "Like I need you telling me how to be hot."

"Hey, I've got the best of both worlds. I know what chicks dig and what guys dig, so you'd do well to learn a thing or two from me."

Bradley rolled his eyes. "Oh, brother. I don't wanna know," he said. "You know, it's taken a while, but I'm finally used to that."

"To what?"

Bradley waved his hand at Tyler, indicating all things Tyler. "*That*. There was a time where I would have freaked out about you saying shit like that. I used to reassure myself, childishly, that I was too strong for you to rape." He snickered. "What a loser, hey?"

Tyler just laughed.

"It's like I finally realized that being gay or bi, or whatever you are, doesn't make you a monster." He slapped Tyler on the shoulder.

Tyler winced at the slap but smiled. "Thanks, Bradley. That's actually really nice. Are you feeling okay?"

"Fuck off." Bradley laughed again as they turned into the dining room. They went into the kitchen to prepare their cereal and toast, talking about trivial topics—things like what they wanted to do after breakfast—and ignoring any serious conversation. Bradley remained subdued, only offering the cursory grunt or *mmhmm* as Tyler would finish a sentence.

After Tyler had finished scarfing his bowl of cereal and two pieces of Cheez Whiz–drenched toast, he began to fret the conversation he was supposed to have. *How do I even bring it up?* He sat for a moment in silence, considering how to start. Nervous, he gulped down half of his coffee with the hope that he could finish it all and have an excuse to go to the kitchen to regroup. He strained to remember anything he'd said in the last ten minutes.

Bradley, finally fed up with the false pretenses, said, "Listen, I don't get why you're doing this." When Tyler looked at him with a confused expression, he added, "We don't do this." He pointed at Tyler and then back at himself. "We've never had breakfast and hung out. Who told you to do this? Curtis? That dick. I told him to let it go."

Tyler raised his hand to stop Bradley from talking. "Curtis didn't say anything to me." This admission seemed to calm Bradley down slightly. Tyler took another sip of coffee. "You're depressed. That's obvious."

"It's not obvious," Bradley said, scoffing and leaning away from the table. "I just want to be alone for a bit. Is that so bad? I have to spend all my time with you people. Sometimes I just want to be by myself."

Tyler rolled his eyes. "Uh-huh. That's why you avoid every group activity or meal that's not mandatory?"

Bradley shrugged and looked away.

"Why are you so upset? I thought you'd be happy that I stood up to those assholes."

"I'm not upset about that," Bradley said. "I'm upset because now the whole fucking world is going to know about me. *I don't want to wear this shit like a fucking badge everywhere I go!*" he shouted, leaning forward and slamming his fist on the table.

"Who said anything about that?"

"Carol wanted to go to the paper and make a big deal about it. What if the paper writes a story about it anyway? Our names will be linked to this forever. There'll be no escaping it," he said. Again, he was shouting.

"It's illegal to link our names to anything," Tyler said.

Bradley calmed down. "What do you mean?"

"We're minors. They can't print our names because we're under eighteen."

Bradley's eyes widened as he made sense of it. "Seriously?"

"Yeah. How could you not know that? I thought it was common knowledge."

"I was fourteen when I came here. I missed out on a lot of stuff," Bradley said, frowning and crossing his arms. "It's not like I was researching this type of thing. I guess that's why my name never appeared in the paper when..." He shifted in his seat uncomfortably.

"When what?" Tyler asked. "Surely you don't think they'd write an article about you being infected with HIV. That's not exactly newsworthy or ethical."

"Yeah, I guess not," Bradley said, shrugging. "Either way, I'm glad they didn't."

"No kidding," Tyler said, laughing.

They sat in silence for a few more minutes before Bradley broke it. "You ever feel like there's no future? Like every time I think I know where I'm going, something gets in the way and then I'm going nowhere again."

Tyler looked Bradley over, contemplating the question and how he could answer. "Hm. When I was on the streets, I felt like that, but now I'm here. I think this is my future. You know? Like. My future is going to end here probably."

"You can't say that. You have no way of knowing what medicines will come out or anything."

"Sure I can," Tyler said. "My viral load is crazy. I don't know that I'll die tomorrow, but it's not like I have fifty years or more left at this rate." He looked into the hall from where he sat. A framed picture hung on the wall of all of them on Christmas day, gathered in front of the tree, holding their respective stockings. "This is the only future that I have now, and I'm okay with it. I wish I could go off to college after this, but I don't see the point. I read that I would have three years to live with AIDS, sometimes less if my luck sucks, and I can't say I've had the best of that. It's all really confusing. I'm taking the treatments now, but if they can't get my viral load under control, what happens then? It's scary feeling like I could die tomorrow."

"It is scary, but you could get hit by a bus tomorrow. You never know when your time is up. Why not live like you've got everything to look forward to?" Bradley paused for a minute to think on this. "And you ended up here. That's lucky enough."

"Wait…" Tyler scratched his head in jest and pointed at himself and then Bradley as he leaned forward and scanned the room as though he were searching for someone hiding behind a chair. "Who's pep-talking who?"

Bradley laughed. "I blame Curtis."

"Me too." Tyler gently slapped the table. "Look at us finding common ground in uncommon futures."

Chapter Thirty

TYLER TOOK A deep breath and closed his eyes as a small smile crept across his lips. He'd taken a solo walk after breakfast to reflect on Bradley, on Carol, on the kids in the mall, on his sister...on Chad. His mind was a flurry of excitement and disagreements and heartfelt commentaries. After breakfast, the conversations he was reliving were so vivid that he decided to take a walk, to try something different.

He stopped by the line of maples midway down the driveway to watch two blue jays tussle over something high up in the branches of one of the trees before settling and sharing the coveted prize. He exhaled and felt the steam from his breath warm his face as he walked through it.

It was the first time he felt like he was part of a family in years. Even at home with his parents, he felt out of place and disconnected. The only other time he felt this way was with Chad, but he was gone now.

"It's been a year today." He took a deep breath and considered what it meant. "You always said it could be like this, that there were people like this." He laughed at himself as he talked to the great nothingness around him, but in his heart, he knew he'd been heard.

When he awoke in the morning, he had expected to be miserable. He'd almost planned it. He even wore Chad's Whistler T-shirt—again—so he could hold on to the memory that he'd once known love, real love. But instead of feeling lost and broken, he felt peaceful, content. He turned his gaze skyward again, welcoming the calm that washed through him. He finally felt permitted to live.

The sound of the snow and ice crunching beneath his boots reminded him of his significance in the world. He stopped to reflect on this feeling, the feeling that he did, indeed, matter. And for a brief moment, everything seemed different. The trees smelled different. The air felt different. The birds sounded different. Everything was different. He continued back to the house with an unfamiliar skip in his step, relishing in the sounds of purpose.

Chapter Thirty-One

BRADLEY

Two and a Half Years Ago
September 1995

Bradley's parents were visiting for the fourth time since he'd arrived at the New Life House a year before. His mother kept telling him over the phone that their schedules were simply too chaotic for them to get over more often than they did, but he knew the real reason for their absence. She was just too nice to say it.

His dad, tall and built like a football player, was leading the conversation as usual. "The summer training camps were packed this year. It was quite the thing to watch the seniors take their turns training all the freshmen. You would have loved it." It wasn't hard to see where Bradley got his looks. His father had been one of the blessed to have his looks from infancy straight into adulthood, and Bradley resembled him nearly as much as a clone would have.

Bradley sighed. "Yeah, it would have been great. I wish I could have been."

His dad frowned. "You know, I was watching all the other fathers and sons out there."

"David—" Bradley's mother tried to shush his father.

David groaned and shrugged her off. "Ah, come on. He made big boy choices, he can have big boy conversations."

Bradley closed his eyes to keep from crying. "It's okay, Mom."

Diana—his mother—reached her hand out and gently squeezed his. "Sweetheart, don't—"

"Let me finish my sentences before you swoop in to tell him that I'm the bad guy. I'm not the bad guy here." David was red-faced and irritated now. He was pacing, having left the edge of the desk where he'd been leaning for the start of the conversation. Diana glared at him, but kept Bradley's hand in hers.

"You finished?" David quipped condescendingly. When she said nothing, he said curtly, "Good." He walked back to the desk at the back of the room. "I *feel* left out. I feel sad as I watch all the other fathers and sons tossing the ball around and showing up to camp together. That was my dream. That was my life before…before you lost your head. What were you thinking? What is wrong with your head?"

Bradley clenched his teeth as tears began to slip from his closed eyes. "I know."

"You know what?" David stomped toward Bradley and stopped in front of him, staring down at him. "Open your eyes, and look at me like a man. Stop this crying bullshit. I want an answer."

Bradley opened his eyes. They were bloodshot and wet with tracks from fallen tears beneath each. "I don't know. I trusted him. I thought he was helping me."

"And you needed the help? You needed to cheat?" David grabbed onto Bradley's face so he couldn't look away again. "Why did you take our dreams away? You were going to be somebody, and now you're nothing. It hurts after all the sacrifices I made for you."

Bradley pulled his face away from his father's grip and slid his chair back so he could stand up. "I'm sorry it's been so hard for you. I fucked up, okay. I fucked up." His voice was high and shrill.

David rolled his eyes and tossed his arms up in defeat. "I can't do this. Do you know how hard it was for me to watch all those games this year, knowing that if you were there, you'd be the star? You'd be the MVP. Instead they gave it to Cody Wallace. That halfwit. It should have been you. It should have been *me* running out on the field to congratulate you, not his good-for-nothing father."

"I said I was sorry. What the fuck does it even matter to you? I have it. You don't. You have your life still. I know the consequences. I have to live them. You don't." Bradley felt like throwing up after screaming at his father. He'd never stood up to him before. In truth, before he'd gotten HIV, they'd never even argued. They practiced soccer, football, baseball, and nearly every sport they could together. Bradley had always regarded his father as his best friend and his dad, citing it as a win-win.

"You ungrateful little prick," David shouted, stepping forward with his fist raised. His arm twitched as he contemplated striking him.

"David! Don't you dare," Diana said, jumping to her feet and standing between them. "Step back. Step back." She pointed toward the desk angrily.

Defeated, he obliged and moved back. "You gave it all up for *him*. We put so much into your future. We just wanted you to go off and have a successful career in sports. What university is going to give a scholarship to you now? What team is going to take you? It's all over now. And you did it. You chose this." He stared at Bradley, challenging him to say something. "Now you can hide up here, away from all the sports and glory like some little wimp. You're lucky I let your mother talk me into this place." He pointed around the room. "If I'd had it my way, you'd still be home and forced to deal with it instead of being coddled up here."

"David, we agreed he would be best to have anonymity. You know how small towns are. He would never have escaped it. At least now he has a chance to be somebody after all the gossip fades away."

"That's the funny thing about being anonymous, dear. You never become anyone. You're nothing. You're nobody." His tone was cold and spiteful. He glared at Bradley.

Bradley frowned and looked at the floor. He didn't know how to dispute what his father was saying. He knew it was his fault and that he'd lost everything. It's all he'd thought about since it happened. "I didn't know it was bad. I trusted him. He said it wasn't bad." Bradley spoke quietly, sheepishly.

"You should have said *no*."

"I'm sorry, sweetie," Diana said as David stormed from the room. "He's just hurting. We all are." She rubbed his shoulder. "I'll try to talk to him."

Bradley began to cry as she wrapped her arms around him and squeezed him tight. "I love you, Bradley. And your father does too. He just wants to be mad at someone. Give him time. Your brother and sister, they miss you too. It's been tough on all of us but know that we love you very much." She kissed him on the cheek and left him standing there, crying, as she went to join her husband in the car.

Bradley's chest rose and fell rapidly as he tried to calm himself down. His eyes searched the room for something to lash out at, but couldn't find anything but the glass his father had been drinking from. He lunged forward impulsively and flung it as hard as he could at the door his mother had just exited through. Water and glass exploded with a loud *bang*. "Ahhhh!" he screamed and stomped his feet. Throwing the glass didn't give him the relief he'd wanted. He continued screaming as he grabbed papers and books from the desk and threw them to the floor. He spun around wildly, tipping chairs and throwing anything he could get his hands on. As he got to the bookshelf and began ripping books from it and tossing them to the floor, Marco's strong arms grabbed him from behind.

"BRADLEY! BRADLEY!" MARCO shouted in hopes of startling him out of his fit. He wrapped his arms around him tightly, barring him from throwing anything else.

"Ahhh-ahhh!" Bradley screamed again. His voice trailed into a whimper. He let himself sink into Marco's arms, and they fell slowly to the floor, leaning against the bookshelf. He could barely get his hands high enough to cover his face for how Marco was holding him. He began to wail. "Fuck!"

"It's okay. It's okay. We're gonna get through this." Marco kept his arms flexed as he held him, not wanting to have to chase him down if he were to get loose. He looked around the room at the overturned chairs, the broken class, and the papers and books littered across the floor.

Bradley continued to cry, heaving and coughing.

"I know. I know. Just let it out." Marco felt Bradley relax in his arms.

Carol came quickly into the room, but stopped short when she saw the mess and then as her eyes came to them huddled in the corner. She held her breath as though it would keep Bradley from noticing her and exchanged an understanding look with Marco, knowing what he wanted her to do. She closed the door and left them to sort it out, ignoring her own deep-rooted desire to fix it.

Chapter Thirty-Two

"OKAY, LET'S GET this started. We never should have missed group last week. I apologize for that. It's clear we all have a lot to discuss." Carol pushed her glasses up closer to her eyes and did her best to smile invitingly. She was expecting—and dreading—an overly emotional session. "Bradley, get us started."

Bradley teared up as soon as he started talking. "All I've ever wanted is to be a professional soccer player. Or play for the Jays." He took a deep yet shaky breath and sat up straight as he thought of what he wanted to say. He rubbed his forehead and sighed as he struggled for the words. "I worked my whole life toward that. You know? I was on every team possible. I didn't do drugs. I obeyed the rules. I was good. I was *good*." He wiped at a single tear that escaped and began to slide down his cheek. "I was going to be somebody. I never really talked about how I got it with all of you. Carol knows. Marco knows." He nodded toward them. He looked at Curtis. "And Curtis knows. But the rest of you think I got it by shooting up with some of the other players on my team. I *never* did drugs. My coach did it. He was doping some of us up because he wanted to have the best team. The best high school team. How sad is that? Turns out he had some kind of sick sexual pleasure in it too. He was shooting himself up with the same needle he was using on me. He didn't do it to anyone else. Share the needle I mean. He went out and got sick and then gave it to me."

Tyler took a breath and tried to look at Bradley without being noticed.

"Why me? Why did he choose to do that to me?" Bradley said, tears blurring his vision. "I thought I was being a good athlete by letting him give me enhancements. He said they were natural. I can't believe I believed him." He shook his head and pinched the bridge of his nose and pressed his fingers against his eyelids.

"Bradley," Marco said softly, leaning forward. "Your coach was a sick man. Trying to understand why he chose you and not the others will simply torment you."

"I know." Bradley looked up, having gained control of himself again. "At the trial, he just kept saying that it was our connection and that now we're bonded for life. It's disgusting." Tears welled in his eyes. "He doesn't even care what he did. He's in prison now, and I'm here."

"Which is a lot better than prison," Marco said in an attempt to cheer him up. "They don't look kindly at people like him in there. I'm sure he hates his life."

"Why does it matter if he cares?" Tyler asked hotly.

Bradley turned sharply toward him and said, "He was my *coach*." Spit bounced from his lips. "Don't you get it? Your coach is supposed to take care of you. Your coach is supposed to be your best friend, your mentor, your surrogate parent. He's supposed to be everything." He stopped when he realized he was shouting. "I'm sorry. I'm not trying to scream at you."

"No worries," Tyler said, forcing an attempt at a comforting smile. "I didn't realize your story was so tough. I just thought you were a perfect jock with a perfect life who partied too hard and got sick. I'm just..."

As though he hadn't registered what Tyler said, Bradley continued, "And you know the worst part? The worst part of the whole thing?" He paused and looked around the room at everyone. They were watching with baited breath seeming as though they were about to join him in tears. "I would have been one of those kids in the mall."

Carol began to shake her head to keep him from going down the road of blame and hatred, but he waved her off.

"No. It's true. I would have picked on all of you because I was one of them. I was that stupid jock who would have called you names for having the misfortune of being sick with...with—" He stumbled over the word. He'd always hated saying it out loud. "—with HIV," he said angrily. "And now I'm a nobody. I'm just a guy who could have been something, but I'm nothing. I'll never get to be on the Jays or any of the teams I dreamed about playing for."

"Bradley," Marco said softly. "We've talked about this. You know there are no policies in place in any sports league that would stop you from following those dreams. You just need to believe in it again. The ball is in your court, and we're here to help."

"Whatever." Bradley slouched back in his chair and crossed his arms over his chest.

The room fell silent for what felt like an eternity. No one wanted to chime in and take away from this reveal that had taken Bradley three years to make. After another few moments of awkward silence, Carol stuttered her way through a transition to the next person to share. "Thank—thank you, Bradley." She paused and stared at him, willing him to look up and into her eyes, but he kept his head down. She forced a half-hearted smile and continued, "I know that was hard to share. We're all here for you." She waited another few seconds before asking Curtis to take his turn.

Curtis seemed to struggle for the words to say before beginning. "I feel like everything I've been telling myself—telling everyone—isn't true. I've been so eager to rejoin the outside world that I felt like it was as ready for me as I was for it. The more I think about it, the more wrong I think I was."

"You weren't wrong," Marco said. "You *aren't* wrong. Yeah, some people are frightened by this disease and by the people who have it, but not everyone is. One of the pitfalls of us being out here in the country is that you don't get to see that city people are different and a lot more accepting. It takes time for the country folks to get it."

"Don't get me wrong. I'm still excited to go to college and to get out there. I'm just a little shaky about it now. I thought everything was going to be so easy." Curtis took a deep breath and again tried to think of the right thing to say. When he came up with nothing, he concluded with "I don't want people to be afraid of me."

Carol smiled warmly at him. "When you're in the city, it will be up to your discretion who you tell. No one will know unless you tell them."

Curtis nodded. "I know. I think I just need some time to process it all. I'll be fine. It's like I know what I'm feeling, but I can't figure it out in words. I think I just need to take a hike to the Knowing Tree."

Carol loved how this tree out in the woods was sometimes better for him than therapy. It had always impressed her how much healing he could do out beneath that tree, sometimes it even left her feeling slightly inadequate.

"Are you done?" Maggie asked, raising her hand meekly. When he nodded, she started. "I don't think I'm having a negative reaction to what happened at the mall. I'm spending a lot of time reflecting on it and, to be honest, I'm just imagining how much Janie would have loved it." She giggled lightly and quickly apologized to Bradley for giggling so soon after he had been crying. "I'm trying to find the humor in all of this. That's what Janie would have done. That's how she would have coped. And I've been imagining her helping Tyler beat up those kids—"

Uncomfortable with staying on the topic of Janie, Carol coughed and cleared her throat, distracting Maggie briefly from her point. Carol waved off the distraction so Maggie would continue. She had done her best to compartmentalize Janie, the suicide, and her failings therein; however, she still felt like she would fall apart at the sound of her name. She would never forget what she looked like, dangling there in the storage room in the basement, her eyes bloodshot and her neck purple and swelling over the noose. She took a deep breath and forced the image out.

Maggie looked at Carol hesitantly before continuing. "I'm worried because I know that Janie used to feel trapped into being positive and joyful all the time. She didn't share her feelings because she was afraid she'd make the rest of us sad. I just need to remember her sometimes, you know? I can't just pretend like she never existed." She cleared her throat and sat up straight in her chair, wiping imaginary dust from her pants. "I'm sorry. I don't know where this is coming from. This is not what I'd planned to say."

"It's okay. Keep going," Marco said.

"I'm not sad about what those cops and those kids said and did because I'm enjoying memories and imaginations of Janie. I like wondering what she would have done or said. It gives me strength." Maggie was visibly struggling to keep her composure; her chin was trembling as she fought off tears.

Carol closed her eyes as Maggie was speaking, breathing quick, shallow breaths and trying as hard as she could to imagine anything but the last look on Janie's face, the look of death.

"I just feel like because we're ignoring how she died, we're also ignoring how she *lived*. I told myself I wouldn't cry, but she was my best friend, and I miss her. And I want to be able to say it. I want to be able to laugh about the silly things she did, and I want to be able to grieve and mourn and scream her name at the top of my lungs."

"Thank you," Marco said, nodding at her. "I think we can all agree that we would like to keep her in our hearts and in our thoughts. I'm sorry you've felt conflicted about cherishing her memory." He looked to Carol, who was still sitting with her eyes closed, and said delicately, while keeping his eyes fixed on her, "It's going to take time until all of our wounds are healed, but I think you raise a good point that we need to work on as a family."

Maggie agreed and passed her turn to Tyler.

Tyler shrugged and grinned. "I'm actually happy for once." He looked around the room at the others, who were all in various states of sadness or emotional conflict, and smiled. "It's interesting being the only one who actually feels good about life for once. I'm happy I told those assholes where they could go, and I'm happy they freaked out and tried to blow it up into something it wasn't. I'm just happy. Maybe that's the last time they'll fuck with us."

"Tyler," Marco said sharply. "Watch your language. You can't curse like that here."

Tyler rolled his eyes. "Fine. I have no regrets. I'm not sorry, and I'll never be sorry. So it drew some attention to us. Who cares? Maybe the attention will help the morons in this town wake up."

Marco took a deep breath and leaned back in his chair. "I just want to remind everyone that we are here to heal. The intent of a sharing circle is to encourage us all to find solutions to the things that may or may not be bothering us. Curse words are not healing words. They are problem words that we use when we're avoiding the true feeling behind what we're saying. Take the time to find the words and the emotions that you want to express rather than taking the easy way out and resorting to cheap language." Marco had never been a fan of cursing, and he had even less appreciation for it during counseling.

"Sure thing," Tyler said, crossing his arms. "Still won't break my mood."

Carol straightened in her chair, slowing her breathing as she considered how to address the kids. The tension and turmoil each of them was dealing with was palpable. She knew they were proud of standing up for themselves. She was proud of them too. She didn't want to discourage them from doing so again, but she wanted to find a way to take their focus away from that particular moment in time. There were better things to concern themselves with, and, as far as she was concerned, they were renting way too much space to those little bastards in the mall. She looked from face to face, still at a loss for what to say. Then it came to her, the simple yet effective phrase that she and Marco had employed with the kids, and in life, since day one. "Everything's going to be okay. There's always tomorrow."

Marco met Carol's gaze before adding, "We're always here for you. That's never going to change. We just wanted to avoid any further fights or hurt feelings by having all of us open up about how we're feeling since the day out at the mall."

"How are you two feeling?" Tyler asked with a touch of attitude. "You don't often share about how you're doing. Why is that?"

"Because we're the counselors here," Marco said. "We don't want to muddy the waters. We do share sometimes, though."

"I'm feeling overwhelmed," Carol said, surprising even herself as she spoke. She had intended just to think it, but now that she'd committed, she continued, "Sometimes I allow myself to get lost in the chaos of helping to keep this place organized, and mixing up my emotions with the emotions of all of you. Another reason why calling this circle was important was so that all of us, including me, could figure out what we own and what we don't." She blinked and focused past Maggie's gaze, knowing that she was expected to respond to her. She wasn't ready. She didn't want to address Janie yet. She, instead, looked into Theo's unbiased eyes.

Marco listened attentively as Carol spoke. He hadn't known they were going to share in the circle. When it was his turn, he said, "I guess I've been feeling detached from myself and from Carol. We have so many things pulling us in different directions that I feel like there's little time for us to sit down and relax together. That's been tough but manageable. Now that it's out in the open, my solution will be to initiate more downtime."

"And thankfully, for us as well, there's always tomorrow. These are just growing pains," Carol said. "All of these things that we're experiencing now are breathing strength into us. Pretty soon, there'll be nothing we can't all handle."

CAROL'S HAND SHOOK as she brought the joint up to her lips and sucked a long toke into her lungs. She almost wished she hadn't called the sharing circle. *God, Carol. What are you doing to these poor kids?* The voice inside her head mimicked her father's.

She had organized her life at one point to please him. She always felt that she needed to jump through hoops and be a specific way in order to earn his acceptance. He wanted her to be a psychiatrist, so she started to follow that path. She never fully lived up to his dreams for her. She wondered if he would have supported her decision to turn their estate into the New Life House. He was a well-respected doctor that had the support of the entire community and was invited to nearly every event the town held. She had been a lousy daughter. She spent her teenage years rebelling and partying. When she went to university, it wasn't to follow any dream of her own but to earn her father's love and approval. It wasn't until he died that she decided she wanted to chase after other degrees. And it wasn't until she learned that she couldn't have children of her own that she decided she wanted to offer a home to kids who weren't wanted in their own. Her dream had grown from a series of tragedies.

"How much good are you actually doing?" she asked herself aloud. "These kids are killing themselves. Would they really be so fucking sad if you were any good at what you're doing?" She took another deep haul off the joint. The cold winter air grabbed her exhalations and froze them in motion around her in dramatic fashion as she sat staring out at the black abyss beyond the light cast by the veranda. "If you were any good at all, you would have seen the markers in Janie. You would have seen through the mask." She paused to take a toke, inhaling shakily as she fought off a surge of sobs. Her cheeks burned as the tears slipped out, freezing against her skin. "You couldn't even dignify Maggie by saying something, anything," she snarled. "Holy shit, Carol. Get a grip." She sat up straight and tried to take a toke of the joint. By now she was crying so hard that she could barely get anything off of it. She was so caught up in her self-hatred and doubt that she didn't hear the sound of the floor boards creaking in the kitchen, or the sound of the screen door opening and closing as Tyler snuck down to join her for their now routine evening visits.

"Hey," he said, whispering as though he were afraid to be caught. He knocked lightly against the outside of the door to announce his presence.

She didn't even look over to him before sending him off, saying, "Not tonight, Tyler. I need to be alone." She felt ashamed that he knew to find her there for drugs, ashamed that she had been smoking with him in the first place, and now she felt trapped, afraid that he would turn her in if she were to deny him.

Surprised by the answer she gave, he stood for another moment before saying, "Okay. I'm sorry that you're upset." He went back inside before she could reply.

Carol looked toward where he had stood but only after he had left. She stared blankly, thinking of nothing as the joint burned away between her fingers. She leaned back in the swing and pulled the blankets up around her. *I should go in before I fall asleep out here and freeze to death. Then again, maybe that wouldn't be such a bad thing.*

She shook the thought almost as instantly as it crossed through her mind. "Wouldn't that be a mess? Bet you'd be proud of me then, hey, Pop?" She stood and groaned as she did. Guilt waved over her as she made her way into the house, feeling like a hypocrite. *What kind of caretaker for kids with degrees in psychology fantasizes, for even a second, about suicide?*

"A damn shitty one," she answered aloud. "You should know better."

Chapter Thirty-Three

THE CENTER OF the library was cleared of its usual semicircle of chairs, and in their place was a round cushion, with several feet between them, for each of the kids and one in the center for Carol. Carol believed there needed to be ample space for the positive energy and thoughts to properly flow around, allowing for maximum healing. She was already sitting on her cushion with her legs crossed and her hands resting on her knees, palms facing up. Jasmine-scented incense was burning from its stand on the desk at the front of the room.

Carol watched as Tyler, Maggie, Bradley, and Curtis filed into the room with their water bottles in hand. Almost instinctually, they all took a deep breath as the sweet and inviting scent of the incense surrounded them.

Tyler looked around the room and then at Carol. "Is this why we were told to wear sweatpants?"

Maggie nodded excitedly. "Yes! Finally. I've missed music therapy." She skipped over to a bright-pink cushion.

"Music what?" Tyler followed her across the room and sat on the orange cushion next to hers.

Maggie beamed at him. "It's where we sit and listen to music and meditate. While the music is playing, Carol will call out positive messages to each of us. The idea is to allow those messages, and the meditation and music and the vibe of the room fill your body and mind with healing powers."

Tyler's expression said that he thought she was nuts but he said nothing. He just scoffed.

Maggie rolled her eyes. "What? Are you afraid to try something new? Scared that you might actually feel better for once?" She smiled again and squinted her eyes at him.

Tyler puffed up his chest and sat up straight. "I fear nothing," he said in a Russian accent.

Maggie giggled. "See. You're already uplifted."

"Where's Marco?" Bradley asked as he dropped his water bottle beside a yellow cushion and lowered himself onto it.

Carol was pleased to see that Bradley appeared to be in an affable mood. She swore she could see the happy spark in his eyes that had been missing for a while. "He and Theo are having some bonding time. I figured this would be a little too much sitting still for that one just yet." Carol was trying to say it as diplomatically as possible. She was certain Theo would be counterproductive to music, quiet, meditation, and basically anything that required any focus.

Curtis stretched and yawned. He leaned so he could see Tyler. "This is what I was telling you about the other day."

Tyler looked at him with a confused expression on his face. "Huh?"

Curtis chuckled. "Side effects. I always found that the side effects of the meds feel less extreme after music therapy. So you'll feel better."

"You're feeling side effects?" Carol said. This was the first she had heard about it.

Tyler shrugged. "Yeah, I guess. My stomach a bit. Kinda nauseous sometimes. Usually in the morning."

Carol nodded knowingly. "We'll get started then."

Curtis clapped his hands together and rubbed his temples.

Noticing his behavior, Carol asked, "Curtis have you been experiencing any side effects?"

He kept his eyes closed. "Yeah. I've been having a headache the last few days and have been really tired."

"Is the music too loud?"

"No, no. It's good. I'm all set for feeling better." He relaxed his body and placed his hands on his knees.

"You will notice that there are five candles burning. One for each of us. The candles are intended to represent our spirit during this exercise, undaunted and burning brightly." Carol's eyes moved to Tyler and she nearly lost her focus when she saw the look he was giving her, as though he thought she'd gone mad. For an instant, she felt self-conscious as though she was making a fool of herself. She closed her eyes, shook her torso and head to clear away the negative feeling, and found herself smiling again. "It's been a while since we all did this," she said, keeping her eyes closed and her head turned toward the ceiling. "If you could all get into position. Tyler, that means to just assume the same position you see me in." She opened one eye and looked at him to make sure he was participating. To her surprise, he was getting into form.

"The first thing I want you to do is to focus on the music. Let the soothing sounds of the violin and the harp carry you into a place of calm. The sounds should lift you. Clear your mind. Now take deep, intentional breaths. They should be slow and steady. Focus on your breathing."

Their breathing became rhythmic as they naturally began to breathe in sync with one another.

"Feel your body relaxing. First, your feet and then up your legs and to your waist. Now concentrate on your tummy. Sit up straight to stretch it out, and relax the muscles." Carol opened her eyes again to ensure that everyone was following along. Each of them was. She closed her eyes. "Feel the relaxing and positive energy flow into your chest and shoulders. Let it slide its way down your arms, by your elbows, and into your fingers. Take deep breaths. Let yourself relax."

The music came to a violin solo, filling the room with an intensely melodic riff filled with emotion. Carol breathed deep. The music felt as though it were vibrating through her chest and out her heart.

"Let any of the side effects or discomforts you are feeling wash from your mind and your body. Let the music and the positive energy of the room boost your spirits."

When the violin stopped and the subtle sound of the harp took over, Carol continued giving instructions in a soft voice. "I want you to allow yourself to drift toward sleep. Embrace the calming feeling of the harp and let the music make you afloat."

Carol opened her eyes to watch each of the kids as she spoke words of inspiration and confidence-building to them. "Tyler, you are bold, courageous, and tenacious. You bring a sense of excitement into the lives of the people around you. You make us feel alive.

"Curtis, you are kind, gentle, and wise beyond your years. You are there for anyone who needs you, and you never put yourself first. You make us feel loved.

"Bradley, you are strong-willed, caring, and funny. You can always be counted on for a smile or a laugh, and you defend the honor of others. You make us feel safe.

"Maggie, you are brave, intelligent, and fair. We can all count on you for objective insight and moral guidance. You help us treat others with kindness."

Carol enjoyed as each of the kids sat a little taller as she called out their individual compliments. It was all the evidence she needed to see that music therapy was an exercise that she must once again incorporate into their schedules on a regular basis. She closed her eyes and relaxed as the harp finished its solo. "All right, take your time opening your eyes. Hold on to the energy that you've just taken hold of."

The kids began to stir and stretch.

"Thanks for this, Carol," Bradley said. He took a deep breath. "I feel better. Truly. This was just what I needed, I think. So thanks."

Carol's eyes welled up with tears. She loved knowing that her alternative methods were helpful. She wished she'd continued them after Janie died, but she had lost faith in their effectiveness after what happened. She worried that she might be relying too heavily on healing energies and not enough on science. "Positive thinking leads to a positive life. It's important that we keep our minds focused on the good. That's how we heal. That's how we get the upper hand."

Bradley nodded in agreement.

"How's your headache, Curtis?" Carol asked.

"It's okay. I think it's still there a bit, but it's on its way out, which is awesome."

Tyler snickered, lightly snorting as he tried to hold it back.

Carol gave him a look that dared him to say something, but was glad when he smiled and remained silent. She continued, "Now let us carry these positive thoughts into the week ahead."

Chapter Thirty-Four

"GET UP!" CURTIS said, snapping the blinds above Bradley's bed up to allow the bright midmorning sun to accost and abruptly wake him.

"God, what is wrong with you?" Bradley groaned, pulling the blankets over his face and rolling away from the window.

"Get your lazy ass out of bed. It's time to get our college applications written and submitted. Get up! We're two weeks late!"

Bradley groaned again. He wanted to tell him to go to hell, but he clenched his teeth. He angrily flung the blankets off his face and scowled at Curtis for being so perky and optimistic about everything. "Why bother?"

"Because you're never going to *be* somebody if you don't *act* like somebody."

"What time is it?"

"It's time to fill in our applications. Meet me downstairs in the dining room in ten. And bring these with you," Curtis said, tossing a heavy pile of college brochures onto Bradley's stomach, knocking the wind out of him. Bradley coughed, but before he could protest, Curtis darted out of the room and down the hall.

"I hate you." Bradley pulled the blankets back up over his head, sending the pile of brochures into a whooshing mess all over the floor. "God, seriously?" He threw the blankets off and sat up in frustration. "What the fuck?" he said angrily, stomping his feet on the ground. He was furious that Curtis was forcing him to wake up, and now he had to clean up this mess. He was pretty sure he would have punched him if he were still in the room. His eyes moved from the mess of brochures still caught up in his blankets, to the smearing of paper all over the hardwood floor, and, finally, to Curtis's half of the room, which was painfully organized and neatly put together, including a crisply made bed with the corners tucked in military style. "I seriously hate you."

THE NATIONWIDE DEADLINE of February 1 for equal consideration to college programs had come and gone, and Curtis was now in full-on panic mode as he feared that his chances of getting into the programs or colleges of his choice were ruined. He had been planning to apply before the deadline but had been thwarted by all of the recent drama. And, according to Curtis's accounts, Bradley hadn't sent in any applications yet either. Since the mall incident, Bradley had lost all hope that the future was even possible. He'd spent most of his time moping around feeling sorry for himself. Curtis, on the other hand, was not one for sitting idly on the sidelines while life passed him by.

By the time Bradley got downstairs with the jumbled-up pile of brochures spilling out of his arms, Curtis had begun filling out his first application. Bradley stopped at the foot of the dining room table to stare in disbelief at the neat piles of brochures and pamphlets Curtis had piled all around him. He sat on the left side near the head of the table. A spot with brochures, pamphlets, and applications had been set up neatly across from him.

"Oh, hey," Curtis said, flashing him a mischievous grin. "There's coffee on; you look like you need a cup."

"You're such an asshole." Bradley dropped the pile of brochures in a heap on the foot of the table. "I can't believe you made me pick all this shit up."

"It seemed like the only way to make you wake up would be to piss you off. You're too easy."

"I don't know why I like you."

"Because I'm the only one who doesn't put up with your shit." Curtis laughed as he picked up a brochure for Nova Scotia Community College. "There's so many awesome options for tourism and adventure-related programs. I don't know which one to apply to."

Bradley rolled his eyes and shuffled into the kitchen to pour himself a coffee, but before exiting, he glanced down at Curtis's half-empty mug. "Do you need a top-up?"

"Sure, please," Curtis said, guzzling what remained in his mug and then handing it off to Bradley. "Thanks."

"Yeah."

When Bradley returned with a coffee for each of them, Curtis had taken to sifting through several different brochures at a time. The programs he was focusing on were in the tourism and outdoor adventure categories. He had been applying to a variety of different cities, always making sure that his choice would lead to a large city where nobody would have to know that he was sick. His dream was to move on with his life and to blend in with society and only let people that he was close to know about him.

Curtis had always held the belief that he could live a normal life once he moved from the New Life House and got away from the small town where everyone knew that he was from the "Death House." This college application process was his golden ticket to go somewhere big and crowded.

Bradley, on the other hand, was always so doom and gloom. He wanted the fame and fortune that would come with being a professional soccer player or a first-baseman player for the Toronto Blue Jays. He had the skills to be successful, so when he had been diagnosed with HIV, it came as a tremendous blow to his world. Despite what everyone told him, that he would be able to do those things still, he gave up. He was so afraid that people would find out he was positive or that he might bleed on them that he decided his dream was over. He eventually overcame the depression, but had never grabbed onto a new dream.

"Aren't you going to look at any of the brochures?" Curtis nodded toward the untouched stack of brochures.

Bradley continued to lean back in his chair, unengaged. He sipped his coffee and then set it down with a dull thud. "I don't see the point in any of this."

"The point is that it is normal," Curtis said. He folded his hands on top of the application he was working on, taking a break for the first time since Bradley came downstairs so he could pay full attention to the conversation he knew was coming.

"Do you not get that we're not normal? We don't fit the bill, bud."

"Sure we do. We have as much right as anyone else to go to college, get a job, and have a family. There's nothing separating us from that."

"Three letters for ya... H—I—V," Bradley said condescendingly. "It's depressing to be looking at this shit when we can't do anything anyways."

Curtis just smiled. He kept his calm, positive composure that Bradley always looked up to. "I refuse to give up on the life that I wanted before I met those three letters. HIV isn't stopping you from living life, Bradley. The only thing stopping you is you. I will not chain myself down because of an illness that can be kept in check with proper medication and a healthy lifestyle. Come on, Mister Fitness, I can have a life and so can you, so get over yourself and check out some of these brochures." He grabbed the brochure for Fanshawe College and tossed it in front of Bradley. "Check out this one. They have a ton of really great broadcasting courses and even some golf and golf club management courses. If you don't want to play, I think you'd be great at sports broadcasting. And it's near Toronto, in London, not too far from my dad."

Bradley took the brochure and flipped through it. "Hm."

"What?"

Bradley shrugged.

"And if we choose the same school or at least schools in the same city, we could share an apartment. Just think about it. We could be roommates still. That's pretty cool, hey?"

"Yeah, that is cool. I'd be down for that." Bradley smiled reluctantly as the thought of moving away with Curtis sunk in.

Curtis chuckled as he watched Bradley try to hide his excitement. He knew Bradley wouldn't want to let on that he'd given in too easily and was enjoying watching him try to keep up the charade.

"That school you're looking at now, Fanshawe, that's one of my top picks. It has a great adventure tourism program."

"Hm," Bradley said, considering the options, putting his hand out and thumbing through the pile of schools. "When's the deadline again?"

"February first."

"Shit, that's like two weeks ago!"

"Exactly. Now you know why I was freaking out. We have a lot of work to do, so get busy!"

Bradley leaned forward and began reading through the brochures with more intent now. "Jesus. I wish I'd listened to you earlier than this."

Curtis smirked and thought, *I think we'd both be lost without each other, Bradley.*

Chapter Thirty-Five

CAROL PULLED THE door open before Madeline—Theo's worker from the Children's Aid Society—had a chance to knock on it. "Good morning. It's nice to see you." She ushered her into the foyer.

Madeline was wearing the same gray blazer and matching skirt with a light-purple blouse that she seemed to wear every time she came to the New Life House. Carol wondered for a moment if this were the only outfit she owned or if she had read somewhere that purple and gray were the best colors to wear when dealing with sick people. She cleared the judgmental thoughts from her head as she led her to the sunroom. "Let's have a seat in here this time. It's a more comfortable place to visit."

Madeline smiled courteously as they took a seat on the couch and piled her briefcase and purse at her feet. "It's a heck of a winter out there. I wasn't sure I'd be able to make it with all the snow we've been getting."

Carol groaned in agreement. "It's been a doozy so far. I think I've paid the snow removal company more this year than I did for the whole season last year, and we're not even done yet."

"It's crazy. My poor husband is so sick of it. Thankfully, it's him who has to shovel and not me." Madeline chuckled. "There are somethings I am glad to leave to him. I'll cook as many dinners and wash as many dishes as need be as long as I don't have to shovel the darn laneway."

Carol chuckled. "I don't know which is worse."

Madeline's laugh had an alarming touch of anxiety to it.

"Are you okay?"

Madeline straightened in her seat and took a deep breath. "I'm good. I wanted to come by to check on Theo, and to see how he's doing. I know you've been faxing the results from his checkups over to the office, so that's not what I'm here for."

Carol nodded and pursed her lips, preparing for what she now feared would be bad news. "Of course not. Marco has them all in the library right now. They have their history lessons today. I think they're starting into the Aboriginal history. They should be out for lunch any minute really."

"I should get this out before they come in then." Madeline looked even more nervous now.

"Okay, get on with it," Carol urged her. "Is his mother asking for him back?" She couldn't help but to voice the fears that were creeping up inside her.

Madeline shook her head somberly. "No, no. She's not."

Carol breathed a sigh of relief. "Oh, good. I'm so glad." She rested her hand on her chest and leaned back into the couch.

"Carol," Madeline started, "Theo's mom is dying."

Carol sat up straight again, her relief quickly returned to worry. Her eyes shone with tears, primed and ready.

Madeline cleared her throat. "The doctors said they don't expect her to last a full week. The reason she asked CAS to take him was because she had gotten so much worse. As you know, she was using a lot of drugs and was struggling through her advancement to AIDS for a while."

Carol sat perfectly still, realizing that she was going to have to find a way to make Theo understand without pushing him back into silence.

"She loves Theo very much." Madeline shifted in her seat and reached down to her purse. "She asked me to bring this to him." She pulled out a smaller, purpler version of Clifford the Bear and held it up for Carol to see.

A silver chain was strung around the bear's neck with an oval locket on the end. Carol reached her hand out and touched it delicately. "This?" She looked to Madeline for the answer and let go of the locket.

Madeline had tears in her eyes now too. "She put her picture in one side and a picture of her holding him as a baby in the other." She clicked the locket open.

Carol exhaled slowly and wiped at the tears that had escaped her eyes before leaning forward and cupping the locket in her hands. She stared at the images. The photo of Theo and his mother was a close-up shot of them. His mother had her nose pressed against his, and they were smiling with their mouths open. The photo of his mother alone must have been taken before she was sick and using drugs again because she looked full of life with no pock marks on her face and a wide, toothy smile. Carol swallowed hard. "It's beautiful."

"She wanted him to have something to remember her by. She figured that Clifford could have a little girlfriend bear or a little sister bear that carried the token of their time together." Madeline took a deep breath and exhaled loudly. "She doesn't want him to go to the funeral. She asked that specifically."

Carol nodded. "I'm glad actually. I don't think he could handle it. We only just got him talking to everyone recently. Until now, he's been so selective about who he feels safe with."

Madeline cleared her throat and sat up straight. "I'm glad he's coming through that phase. I really want him to be happy."

"Us too. It's tough when they are so broken that they can't talk. Marco and I were worried for a little while that there might be some larger issues that we would have to deal with. I just don't know how I'm going to tell him."

Madeline stiffened in her seat as she heard the kids chattering in the foyer and coming closer. She quickly said, "I think you should wait. There's no harm in waiting until he's a little older."

Tyler and Maggie walked by the sunroom holding hands. Curtis and Bradley weren't far behind them, each of them commenting on how hungry they were.

Marco came up behind them with Theo walking just in front of him. "Hurry up, buddy. They're going to take all the food!" He reached down and playfully tickled Theo who squealed and giggled. Marco stopped when he noticed Madeline. "Oh, hey. How are you?" He rested his hand on Theo's shoulder to get him to turn into the sunroom.

"I'm good, thank you." Madeline stood up and turned her attention to Theo and crouched down with her hands on her knees. "Hi, Theo. Oh my gosh, you've gotten SO BIG!" She spoke in a silly, tiny voice and emphasized her words.

Theo's face lit up when he saw her. He squealed and ran to her, wrapped his arms around her neck and hugged tightly. "I miss you, Maddy."

"You were listening all that time after all." She turned her eyes to Carol and then Marco. "I asked him to call me Maddy when we first met. Spent a few days trying to get you to say it, didn't I?" She tickled his stomach and laughed along with him.

Marco tousled Theo's hair. "Oh, he's a talker now. That's for sure. Aren't you, little buddy?"

Madeline let him go and stood to grab the stuffed bear from the couch. "Your mommy sent me with a gift for you." She turned back to Theo and held out the bear.

Theo's eyes lit up and filled with tears simultaneously. "Is she here?"

Madeline shook her head. "No, sweetie. She couldn't come today. But she wanted me to bring you this little bear. She says that Clifford will love having a little friend." Madeline crouched down and offered the bear to Theo.

He took the bear slowly. His chin was quivering as he tried not to cry. He hugged the bear and petted its head.

"Your mommy thought that Lizzy would be a good name."

Theo smiled. "Clifford and Lizzy." He giggled.

Madeline opened the locket for him. He stared at the pictures happily.

"Do you know who that is?" Madeline pointed to the baby.

Theo shook his head.

"That's you."

He looked at her in disbelief. "No."

Madeline chuckled. "Yes. It's you. And that's your mommy. She wanted you to have this special locket too. She says that Lizzy will take great care of it, so you have to be careful with it. Okay?"

Theo touched the photo gently before closing the locket. He closed his hand around it very carefully. "I will."

"Go on and show Tyler. I bet he is going to love it." Carol motioned with her head for Theo to go to the dining room with the other kids.

"Yeah," he said excitedly as he turned and bolted from the room.

Marco waited for Theo to be gone from earshot before asking, "Are you okay? Is everything okay?"

"Everything here is certainly fine. You two have done such a great job with him. He's so vibrant compared to how he was when I dropped him off in the fall." Madeline nodded her approval. "I'm very happy to see it."

Carol stood. "Thank you for saying so. We think he's improved quite a bit as well."

"Is Lizzy his mother's name?" Marco asked. "I'm still trying to sort out the bear and the meaning behind what just happened. Is everything okay?"

Carol shrugged. "Just another day, really. We have some bad news to prepare Theo for in the coming months."

Marco seemed to understand as his expression grew solemn.

"I should get going," Madeline said. "They're calling for freezing rain again tonight. I want to get home before it starts."

"Of course," Marco said, stepping aside. "Drive safely. And thank you for coming by."

Carol followed Madeline out to the foyer to send her off. "Just when I thought things were getting to a smooth flow. Nothing is ever easy around here."

Madeline looked at her curiously. "I meant what I said. There's no reason to tell him right away. I think you can let him know when he's older."

"Yes, but how is it fair for me to decide that for him?"

Madeline made a *tsk-tsk* sound. "It wasn't you who decided. It was his mother. She doesn't want him to go through the pain right now. Just consider it a gift to a dying woman. Maybe this is a way for her to keep living a little longer, if not in life then in his dreams of being reunited with her."

Chapter Thirty-Six

CAROL & MARCO

Ten and a Half Years Ago
October 1987

The autumn air was unusually warm as Carol made her way to the picnic tables in the back grounds of Dalhousie University. The unusual temperature was making her hair even bigger than it was after she'd fluffed, primped, and sprayed it before leaving the house. The leaves had changed their color but still hadn't fallen, creating an otherworldly atmosphere for her as she glanced around for Marco. She was supposed to be meeting him to plot their midterm project. They had been dating for a few months now, but she still felt like a childish sixteen-year-old girl with a crush on the high school football star when she was around him. In actual fact, it was worse when she wasn't with him. It seemed that all she did these days was daydream about what it would be like in the future together. She would spend countless hours imagining the children they would have—she wanted at least four—and the dinners and parties they would have at their home, her family's estate.

They first crossed paths in their History of Medicine class. She felt like a giddy teenager when she saw him, tall, macho, and Italian. Built like a football player, he seemed to have an endless supply of intoxicating colognes and charm. She hoped he didn't take her for some desperate old cougar. He was considerably younger than her, she thirty-six to his twenty-eight. She wished that wouldn't matter, but it kept her from asking him out for the first two years of their university degree program. They were studying to become registered nurses. She already had several degrees, and had finished her PhD in psychology shortly before they met. Marco was planning to get a Master of Social Work and had joked about getting a degree in psychology just so he could understand Carol's complexities better. She never knew if this was a compliment or if she should smack him, but he was so darn cute that she couldn't help but giggle when he said it.

By some stroke of luck, earlier in the semester, they were paired together to write a paper on the HIV and AIDS crisis with an aim on how to address the epidemic. It was this project that was bringing them together this early October day.

"So what do you think about examining it from the sociological standpoint? I mean, don't you think it would be interesting to delve into the question of *why* so many people are ignoring it and refusing to acknowledge it as a crisis? I want to understand why there is such a reluctance to fund research for medications. Personally, I don't understand it." Marco squinted as he spoke, shielding his eyes from the rays of sunlight that were creeping between the colorful branches of maple trees next to the picnic table they'd chosen to sit at. "Why is everyone so afraid of it and how can we, as human beings, not do everything possible to find a way to help the people who have HIV or AIDS?"

Carol contemplated his angle. "I think that could work. I think we should learn about this ACT UP group that started down in New York in the spring. They're in the news, and they're advocating for a national policy and for access to experimental drugs. I think we can learn a lot from them."

Marco continued excitedly, "And we can link the social issues and misconceptions to the science and try to debunk them."

"Like?" Carol was jotting messily on her yellow notepad.

Marco, without missing a beat, sat up on the top of the picnic table with his feet planted firmly on the bench. "Like the fear issue. People still don't know how they can get it. So many people still think it's a gay disease. There's so much hatred toward people who have HIV. It's alarming. I'd like to explore why, and to prove that there is no reason to fear people who have it. And I'd like to explore options to bring it back to love. You know?"

Carol smiled at him. It was in moments like these that she was relieved of her feelings of insecurity around him, these moments when he dove into an idea and chattered about it excitedly, almost anxiously. Her eyes stung and her chest filled with heat as she listened to him dream up a house where people who were shunned by their loved ones could come to find a new life. As the fantasy grew larger, so did his stature. He sat up taller and taller, explaining to her how they could theorize about a place where people who had lost their families because of the hatred and bigotry could come to find shelter and support.

"People must feel like they've lost when they get diagnosed. I think it would be an innovative approach to offer a home where people could find themselves again. A place where there is living proof that there *is* life after diagnosis. Because there *will be* life after diagnosis." Marco stopped and looked at Carol who was welling up with tears. "Are you okay?"

She swallowed. "I love that you want to save the world. What a dream to have."

Buoyed by the compliment, Marco puffed his chest out. The corner of his mouth pulled slowly into a smile. "I think we can design our project as a sort of proposal to a funding body. You know? Pitch to the professor the idea to have a house like that. We would need to do the historical, sociological, and medical sections of the paper, which is what he wants. But we could make it a creative paper that we put together as a sort of business proposal. Maybe someone could then use it someday to actually impact change."

Carol leaned in and kissed him. "It's going to be the best project he's ever seen."

Chapter Thirty-Seven

CAROL, MARCO, & MAGGIE

Eight Years Ago
May 1990

"I'm sorry," Maggie whimpered in her tiny voice. She wouldn't look up from the doll clutched in her hands. Her cheeks were stained with dried tears.

Carol sat down on the floor, cross-legged, and pulled Maggie into her lap. "Sorry for what, sweetie?" She ran her hand along the bandage on the doll's left arm.

"Isabella was sick. I was just trying to help." Her voice wavered as she tried to be strong.

"That's very kind of you to have helped her when she needed it," Carol said.

Maggie stifled a sob and pressed on the doll's bandage. "My mommy said to stop crying. She said it makes everything harder. I thought that if I stopped, she wouldn't make me go away."

"Crying is good for you. It's a healing power that we all have deep inside us. It's like our own magic power. When we cry, we heal. Did you know that?"

"No."

Carol kissed the side of her head lovingly and hugged her tight, fighting back tears of her own. "Oh, Maggie. You are so brave. Did you know *that*?"

Maggie shook her head to say, "No." She kept fidgeting with Isabella.

Carol pointed at the doll. "You are so brave because you tried to take care of your friend. There's nothing wrong with that. You're a good girl."

"No," Maggie argued. "Mommy and Daddy said I'm a bad girl for playing with dirty things and for ruining everything. They *said*."

"You didn't ruin anything, sweet girl. Believe me when I say that. You are perfect. Never feel bad for helping someone in need. The best kinds of people are the ones who would risk everything to make someone else feel better. You're one of those people."

Maggie stopped crying and wiped her cheeks.

Carol hugged Maggie tight. She felt the seed of hatred growing in her stomach as she held this beautiful six-year-old girl, crying in her arms. She wanted to drive all the way to Toronto to slap Maggie's parents, but she knew she never would. In a twisted way, she felt she owed them for giving her her first child. "We're going to be the best of friends, you and me." She stood Maggie on her feet so she could look her in the eyes. "I mean that. You're my number one lady and always will be."

Maggie blushed and hugged Isabella to her chest, rocking from side to side. "And Isabella."

Carol laughed. "She's my number two lady." She patted the doll on the head. "She'll never be before you."

For dinner, Marco made them his famous pasta and meatballs. At least, that's what he called it. They each had a big bowl in front of them, and sat cross-legged on the floor to watch cartoons while eating. Carol had gone to the store earlier in the week to buy nearly every children's movie ever made, hoping that at least one of them would make Maggie happy. She was glad to see that the entire collection was a hit.

As the chosen movie, *An American Tail*, came to an end, Maggie turned to Carol and Marco and asked, "Do you think I'll ever find my family again?"

Carol choked on her wine. She wished she'd pre-watched the movies. She hadn't planned on any of them being about a young mouse being lost at sea and then setting off on an emotional journey to find his lost family.

Marco smiled warmly and rested his hand on Carol's knee so as to say that she could relax while he answered the question for her. "You will. It may not be the family you at first expect or want, but I believe that you will find family again. And I believe that you will be loved. Always."

Chapter Thirty-Eight

IT WAS SATURDAY, March 12, a week before Marco and Carol's anniversary. When Carol went up to the sitting room after breakfast, she found a slim-fitting, long black dress; an elegant black clutch with sparkly, silver chains for straps; and a black crystal brooch lined with diamonds placed neatly on the couch, positioned as though a woman were laying sexily on the sofa, waiting. With the dress was a note that read: *Dinner at Fernando's at 6:30. Let me spoil you.* Fernando's was the local Italian restaurant—Marco's favorite—and the fanciest place in town.

Carol got Maggie to help style her makeup and hair. She hadn't been this excited about an evening out in a long time.

"You're stunning," Marco said breathlessly as she came down the stairs to meet him in the foyer.

She blushed. "Thank you." She took his arm as he outstretched it for her. "Sir," she said, smiling and nodding as she stepped from the last stair. "You look very handsome." She reached her hand out delicately and ran her fingers down the seam of his blazer. He was wearing the same black tuxedo he'd worn on the night of his graduation from university only seven short years before. They had made some wonderful memories in that tux. She cleared her throat softly and smoothed out the flap she had ruffled. "Very handsome," she repeated.

Marco grinned and kissed her cheek. "Shall we go and frolic with the Italians?" He grinned and used his best British accent as he always did when he was trying to sound fancy.

Using the same accent, she said, "Enchanted. That sounds lovely." She took his hand and curtsied as he led her proudly from the foyer. As they exited the front door, Carol called back to Maggie and the boys, "Don't wait up!"

MARCO BEAMED AS he escorted Carol to their reserved table at the center of the window section of the restaurant, sliding her chair under her as she sat.

"Why, thank you." Carol gave an impressed look as she set her clutch beside her plate and waited for him to sit across from her.

"Only the best for tonight. It's not every day that we get to celebrate us and all that we share. I look forward to this night every year." He picked up the wine menu and read the names, specifically seeking the Chianti section. When the server came to the table, he selected a Ruffino.

Carol leaned forward and ran her fingers along the back of Marco's hand. "You spoil me so well."

They spent the evening sitting across from one another, giggling and talking about the kids, the past, and the future while gazing lovingly into one another's eyes.

As they finished the dessert course, she started telling him about when Bradley came out to see her after they got back from the police station. He seemed irritated as she told the story, so she considered stopping, but shrugged it off and assumed he was just tired. This was the first time in ages that she felt like she could let loose, and she wanted to embrace it.

Marco smiled and chuckled minimally throughout the story. She was somewhat disappointed that he wasn't as amused by her telling of how panicked she was and how she tried to hide the joint from Bradley.

"And then I threw…" She waved her arm to demonstrate how she threw the joint over the veranda.

"Carol, watch—" He was cut off by the clatter and commotion of her wineglass falling as she swiped it over during her animated storytelling. The table shook as she bumped it while trying to rescue her glass. Red wine splashed across their plates and onto the white linen.

"Shit," she said. She grabbed her glass up as quickly as she could, barely saving any of the wine from spilling.

"Come on, let's get going," Marco said, taking his napkin from his lap and tossing it onto his plate.

She slurred her words as she spoke, taking time to get each syllable right. "I think I'd like another glass before we go." She raised her hand to motion the waiter over to the table. She looked at Marco brazenly and tried to blink flirtatiously, but appeared more like she was struggling to keep her eyes open.

"No. I think you've had enough. You're already drunk. Stop before you embarrass yourself any further," he said angrily, grumbling under his breath.

"Excuse me, but I'll decide when I've had enough," Carol said. She picked up the empty bottle of Chianti she had been drinking and closed one eye as she tried to see if there was anything left in it. She set the bottle down with a hollow thud and struggled to say, "You're lucky this is empty. I would have poured myself another." She narrowed her eyes at him, waiting for him to come back with another retort. He just sat staring blankly at her. Finally, she added, "It's good for the circulation."

"Yeah, one to two *glasses*, not *bottles*!" Marco said, slapping the table.

"Do not threaten me," Carol warned, slapping the table in return and pointing her finger in his face.

Marco sat back, startled, embarrassed that he had lost control of his temper and of the scene they were making, looking over his shoulder to see who had noticed. Carol mistook this withdrawal to be a win for her side of the argument and smiled smugly as she drank the last of her wine.

"I'll go get the car." Marco stood up abruptly and accidentally bumped the table with his lap, causing the bottle of wine to wobble and the glasses and silverware to rattle.

"Jeez," Carol said, reaching to steady her glass and the bottle. "Calm down."

Marco stopped beside her and leaned down so she could hear him clearly without having to raise his voice. The firm and emotionally void way he spoke sent a chill down her spine. "Do not patronize me, Carol. I am not one of these kids who thinks that you can do no wrong. I *know* you. I am telling you as someone who loves you that I think you're making a huge mistake. It's time to clean yourself up." He turned his gaze to meet hers and glared at her, silently challenging her to disagree.

She stared back defiantly and unsuccessfully tried to hide her flinch at his words. She cleared her throat and smoothed out the skirt of her dress, breaking eye contact to do so. "Okay, I'm ready to go now." She bit the inside of her bottom lip to keep from crying. She was not going to let Marco win. He stepped back to let her stand. She shakily picked her purse from the table and coiled its silver chain in her hand, clutching the purse tightly to her chest in a dainty fashion. "Excuse me," she said as she struggled to keep her balance while walking to the door.

When they got to the car, Carol refused to make eye contact. She didn't want him to see that he'd gotten under her skin. She slammed her door as she got into the passenger seat and shot a hateful look at him. "Thanks for a lovely dinner, dear," she said sarcastically. She hated herself as she said it, but she turned her eyes forward to dismiss him.

Marco grunted in frustration as he slammed the car into reverse and pulled back, squealing the tires. He slammed on the brakes, jolting them both in their seats before speeding out of the parking lot and onto the road. "It's like you're incapable of participating in life without it. You're a psychologist for Christ's sake. You should know the signs. How do you not see it?"

She closed her eyes. It helped her ignore him. She couldn't stand to listen to, what she considered to be, his ridiculous claims. He was so off base that she wanted to slap him.

MARCO TOOK A deep breath as he sped the car out of town. Marco didn't like that he'd upset her, but he was pleased to see that she'd lost the arrogant expression she'd worn during their argument. Usually, when her expression went from fiercely angry to sorrowful and sad it meant that she felt guilty.

Marco grumbled under his breath for the rest of the drive home, glancing over at her every now and then to see if she was listening. As he drove, he considered that perhaps a fight was what they needed. Perhaps this would help her evaluate how she'd learned to cope and she would get better now. She needed help, and he knew that he couldn't force her. All he could do was push and hope for the best. And then he had a fleeting thought. *Maybe I shouldn't have said anything until she was sober.* He wondered if she would ever change. For years, he had been trying to hint that she shouldn't smoke like a teenager anymore. And he never liked drunks. His father was a drunk. What if she didn't love him enough to quit? Did he need to leave to get her to hit bottom? Would that even make a difference? And what then would happen to the kids? He couldn't leave. What had to happen to get through to her, to shake her?

Chapter Thirty-Nine

TYLER WAS OUT for a midmorning walk to clear his thoughts, a routine he had gotten into when the group therapy sessions became more invasive. He found that wandering the property and watching nature would clear his mind and help him process the emotions that were stirred up in him or in the other kids at the house. He had developed a habit of internalizing other people's struggles and feeling their emotions, unsure of which parts he owned and which he did not. These morning walks helped him put all the pieces together. Since the snow wasn't fully melted yet, he usually walked up the driveway to the road and then back. Today, he stopped near the line of maple trees.

It was a cold day near the end of March, and the sun was shining bright but doing nothing to warm him. He was wearing his faded blue jeans with flannel built into them and his black, heavy, gray-wool-lined sweatshirt with a plaid hood over top of a long-sleeved cotton shirt, but he could still feel the chill. The air, despite being cold, was refreshing, and with each breath he exhaled in a slow-moving cloud, he felt more alive and more connected to the world. Satisfied with the clarity and peace of this moment, he took a deep breath and let it out heavily.

"Tough group the other day, eh?" Marco asked. The soft gravel and sand quietly crunched beneath his shoes as he walked toward him. His breath hid his face as he exhaled.

"It wasn't too bad actually. A lot to process, but not too bad overall," Tyler said, taking another deep breath and turning to face the trees again.

Marco stopped beside him and turned his gaze in the same direction. "What are we looking for?"

"Nothing. Just enjoying the smells and general shape of the branches. I love the way they look as they're spidering across the sky like they're reaching for something."

Marco turned his attention toward the branches. "It is a beautiful sight. A reason to be grateful for winter, I guess." He smiled. "Are you sure nothing else is up? Maggie had some pretty emotional things to say. I'd guess some of that is percolating in there," Marco said as he lightly tapped the side of Tyler's forehead and nudged him with his elbow. "I'd guess it even more because you and Maggie have barely spoken for a week now."

"Yeah, I guess," Tyler said, nudging back. "I don't know what to do about any of that. She wants me to be this television version of a boyfriend, and I don't know how to be that."

"Yeah, women and girls, believe me, they're crazy. That's part of what makes us love them, though," Marco said, wrapping his arm around Tyler in a jovial gesture. "Totally crazy."

Tyler laughed uneasily. "I'm not always sure I love them, though. That's part of what confuses me. Right now, I think I want to be gay. But I don't want to say anything to Maggie because I don't know. I just don't know." As he made this admission, he felt himself instinctually shrinking away from Marco. He wasn't used to talking openly about his sexuality with the people at the house, and he held on to a deeply rooted fear of rejection.

Marco kept his arm around Tyler, smiling down at him and gently squeezing until he looked him in the eyes. "You're double out of luck then. Guys are nuts, too, so I guess it just shows that love is the crazy thing, but we can't live without it. It's fundamental to life."

Tyler felt his anxiety leaving his body, and he stopped pulling away from the embrace. "I've been having lots of dreams."

Marco gave Tyler an intrigued look. "Dreams? Dreams about...?"

Tyler shrugged. "About the past. About important people from the past."

"Your parents?"

Tyler scoffed. "No, definitely not them. About someone I loved. The more I dream about him, the less I think I'm bi and the more I think I'm gay."

"Ahh... Hence the confusion." Marco paused to think for a moment. "I'm not sure what I can say that will help you make that decision. That's something you're going to have to figure out for yourself. But what I can say about guys is that we're complicated and don't open up about what's really going on enough, and girls...girls are crazy. They open up about so much, but they expect us to guess the things they don't share. It's intense. And if you try to offer solutions to their emotional woes, heaven help you."

"Yeah, I think that's pretty accurate. Is Carol like that?"

Marco choked and inhaled, mimicking a wince as he said, "Oh, boy. Answering that could get me killed."

"I won't say anything to her. Help me out. I like Maggie, but she's driving me crazy. I've never been anything but moody, so I don't get why she thinks that I would change all of a sudden."

Marco sighed. "I know, buddy. Girls are crazy like that. I feel like a broken record, but it's true. Just the other day, I tried to give Carol a little bit of advice on how to handle her emotions in a healthier manner, and I'm lucky she didn't bury me in the backyard."

Tyler pushed Marco away. "You're hilarious. She would never do that. You guys are like a rock."

"It's true that we're pretty solid, but we're human, so we still have our differences and I'm a man—hence, I make sense and am pretty rational—and she's a woman, so...what is she?" Marco said in jest.

Tyler laughed and rolled his eyes, repeating his lesson of the day: "She's crazy." They walked quietly with their hands in their pockets. "You know this advice was really terrible, right?" Tyler chuckled.

"Hey, I don't have to hit the nail on the head every time." Marco winked and nudged him. "I think we're all crazy, but that's what makes the journey so worth it...to be able to learn about all the crazy we don't yet know."

Tyler took a deep breath and let it out in a fluster as he tried to find the right words. The perplexed expression on Marco's face didn't help. It just made him feel more anxious. Self-consciously, Tyler looked up at the sky.

"Spit—it—out." Marco spoke with deliberate pauses for effect.

"I've been having stomachaches a lot." Tyler felt his breathing get a little easier.

"Stomachaches are natural. I don't think there's—"

"It's not just a stomachache. It's a *stomach*ache." He hoped Marco would pick up on the subtly. He didn't want to spell it out for him. He was embarrassed to be talking about it in the first place. Marco still looked confused, so he went on. "Everything that goes in comes out liquid." He cringed as he said it. He couldn't bring himself to call it what it was. Something about the word "diarrhea" always felt so disgusting to him.

Marco's face lit up as though a lightbulb had gone off. Tyler was relieved that he wouldn't have to say it.

"How long have you been having stomachaches?"

Tyler smiled when Marco played along. "It's been a week now. I was hoping it would stop. Maybe it will."

"Let's keep an eye on your weight and let me know if the stomachaches continue. There are medications that can help control the diarrhea."

"Yuck, you said it." Tyler scrunched his face up.

"Big-boy words for big boy problems," Marco said. "If it lasts for a month or if you lose ten percent of your body weight, it becomes a serious issue. It's called wasting syndrome. There are medications to stimulate your appetite and control the...stomachaches."

Tyler frowned and said, sarcastically, "The fun never ends, does it?"

Marco draped his arm over Tyler's shoulders. "You never know. With a little bit of medication to get your tummy under control, the fun could be dried up in no time."

"That's nasty." Tyler playfully shoved Marco away. "Seriously nasty."

Marco winked. "Nasty but true. Don't be worried about wasting. It's not guaranteed you're dealing with that. For all we know, the food's been too rich for you lately and your tummy is reacting. It's perfectly normal to have some crappy days."

"Ew!"

"I couldn't resist. I don't get near enough chances to use crappy puns on people."

"Stop!" Tyler pretended to stomp ahead of Marco.

"Sure, I'm sorry. That was really crappy of me." Marco winked and raised his hands up in mock self-defense.

"What if it is wasting and you're making all these jokes about it?"

"Then I'll feel crappy." Marco roared with laughter. "The only thing you can really do is laugh. Sometimes that's the best solution. Laugh and keep putting one foot in front of the other, and try not to crap your pants."

Chapter Forty

GIRLS' NIGHTS: CAROL used to host them at least once a month back when Janie was alive. They would get together in the sitting room outside Carol and Marco's room to talk about the boys, their hopes and dreams, celebrities, new inventions that caught their interest, things they'd read, and often, much to Carol's disdain, sex. When Janie died, Carol got so caught up in the whirlwind of the funeral, mourning, supporting the kids, and then getting Tyler and Theo oriented into the house that she had lost touch with the bonds she had before. Somehow, she'd allowed herself to become more of a neglectful parent than a loving and trusted confidante. And as much as it pained her to admit it, she had essentially forced everyone to stop saying Janie's name rather than encouraging them to hold on to her memory all because she couldn't shake the last memory she had of her.

The girls' nights were multipurposed. She was able to feel like she had a connection to Maggie and Janie that went beyond teaching, counseling, and caretaking, and she was able to sneak little secrets out of them that let her know what was really going on between the kids. The girls had never caught on because she never betrayed what she heard. She just made note of what types of things she and Marco should start looking out for or if there was anything they needed to act on.

This night was multipurposed as well. She needed to repair the damage she'd done to her relationship with Maggie and to try to bring happier memories of Janie back into the fold. She also wanted to know how serious Maggie and Tyler were getting. When she asked Tyler, he sloughed it off as though it wasn't anything too serious, but she knew Maggie would be several steps ahead of him. Really, this night was a sort of damage control. She needed to know if she could form these genuine bonds without using drugs like she had with Tyler. She needed to prove Marco wrong. She needed to prove to him that she was capable of engaging with the people around her on a personal level while sober. Ultimately, girls' nights were being reborn out of her own desire to prove to Marco that there was no reason for her to quit smoking weed or drinking wine.

The sitting room was decked out with pillows and blankets. Piles of snacks covered the coffee table and littered the floor around it. Carol and Maggie had raided the cupboards downstairs for all of the popcorn, potato chips, licorice, and pop they could find. They'd even snuck up to the "man cave" to raid their secret stash of mini chocolate bars, laughing and squealing as they ran through the halls with bars spilling out of their hands.

For Christmas, Santa had brought Maggie a flannel onesie, and had opted for a very light and airy cotton pajama pants with a button-up shirt and a drawstring for Carol that would allow for venting when her rare, but nevertheless uncomfortable, hot flashes came to bathe her. "Maggie, I'm sorry you've felt trapped with your feelings about Janie. I should have tried harder to work through my own demons there, and I should have welcomed and encouraged memories about her. I just don't know how to get that image out of my mind." She closed her eyes and saw Janie's lifeless, tortured face as clear as if she were staring straight at it again. She cleared her throat as memories of her own panic and screaming filled her. She had been distraught as she pulled Janie down from the rafters in the basement, scraping her hands against the unfinished edges of the shelving unit Janie had stood on before hanging herself.

Maggie could see how Carol was struggling, so she reached out and took her hand in hers.

"I want you to be able to celebrate her. I do. Maybe when it's with me, let's start small. Let's get together once a week to share some laughs about her for half an hour."

Maggie brightened. "Maybe that will help you replace the bad images with fun ones."

"I think it might." Carol smiled. "Let's start."

Maggie went first. She laughed as she told Carol about the time she and Janie had replaced the shampoo in Bradley's bottle with mayonnaise. They had giggled hysterically and waited for hours for him to come out screaming about it, but he never even noticed. They'd found it even funnier when they realized he'd had several showers with it before they had to confess in order to get the angry reaction out of him. "Janie laughed so hard, she peed herself."

Carol took a deep breath as she wracked her brain for a happy memory about Janie. She closed her eyes tight and took several deep breaths in an attempt to squeeze the familiar image of death from her mind. She stammered a few attempts at starting into a memory, but couldn't come up with anything concrete. She opened her eyes. They were wet. She looked to the floor in shame and took Maggie by the hand. "I'm sorry, honey. I can't..." She sighed.

"Don't be sorry. I know it's tough. For now, let's just embrace when I share memories about her. Maybe that will help you find yours again. In time." Maggie patted Carol's hand gently. "Like you always say, 'We don't have to fix it all in one day. Let's take it in strides.' Sound good?"

"Sounds good."

Maggie sat up straight and shared a few more memories that she had of Janie. She and Janie had been boy-crazy since they first become friends. Well, actually, Janie had introduced that to Maggie. Janie was always talking about being sexually frustrated, especially when she would watch Bradley working out or coming in from a jog.

When Maggie broke up with Bradley, Janie nearly slapped her for giving up her chance to snuggle up to him.

"And those abs! How are you giving up those abs!? Are you nuts?" Janie had shouted.

She used to tell Maggie all about her dreams for the future, always saying that there would be a cure coming out any day now. Janie was sure she would have a family of her own someday, no matter what. She wanted a family more than anything else in the world.

Somehow the conversation had found its way to parenting and pregnancy. Carol wished she'd been paying more attention when it started, so she could have tried to steer it somewhere else.

"Didn't you ever want kids?" Maggie asked.

"Oh, honey, that ship has sailed. I'm a little too old for any of that now," Carol said, biting her lip to keep it from quivering. She wished she could steady herself to these questions without feeling so caught off guard.

"You're only fifty—"

Carol raised her eyebrows. "Careful. If you ever want to have privileges again, you'll cushion your guess."

Maggie laughed. "Oh, I meant thirty-five."

"Ha, smart girl."

"Whew, dodged a bullet there," Maggie said, pretending to wipe her brow.

Carol forced a smile and watched, only half listening, as Maggie suggested names for children and possibilities for a future. The world felt foggy around her and everything muffled. "Do not cry," she told herself in a whisper.

"...don't you think?" Maggie asked.

Carol panicked for a moment, realizing she had been daydreaming through most of the conversation. "Think what?"

Maggie gave her a curious look. "Weren't you listening?"

"I'm sorry, honey. I dazed off I guess. Consider it an old-age moment. What were you asking me?"

"I wanted to know if you believed it would be okay for me to have kids someday. I've been reading that there are special types of treatments that make it possible." Maggie smiled. "I think I'd qualify to do that. And I think Tyler and I will make such great parents. You've got the calm one and the—" She paused to find the right word. "—the less calm one."

"Ever the diplomat," Carol said. She could think of a few better adjectives to use for Tyler, but she kept them to herself and stuffed some popcorn in her mouth as extra assurance that she wouldn't blurt one out.

"Do you think the treatments are good?"

Carol nodded emphatically. "I think there are risks." She tried to sound enthusiastic. "Of course, I think science is coming out with new possibilities all the time, but it's important to know that the use of zidovudine only reduces the risk of mother-to-child transmission. There are a lot of factors to take into account. It's not a sure thing yet, but it will be by the time you're ready to have kids." Carol hesitated to continue, reminding herself that this was a night about silly dreams and hopes. She didn't need to cast doubt over Maggie's. Her lungs tightened as she fought the urge to protect Maggie from setting herself up for heartache. She took a deep breath and exhaled slowly. "I think you'll be a wonderful mom someday, Maggie. I do. I think we need to be careful about what we expect from the future." She cursed herself as she said it, and her heart sank when she saw the brightness fade from Maggie's eyes.

"I just want to believe that it *could* happen."

"I know, sweetie. I don't want to squash the dream. It is possible. One day, you will be able to have a family of your own."

Maggie looked up, glaring into Carol's eyes defiantly. "But not with Tyler."

The anger in her voice startled Carol, stripping her of her defenses. "Maggie, I didn't—"

"But you did. You're so convinced that he's going to die. How can you call yourself a doctor when you don't believe that science could actually save him?"

Carol reached for Maggie's hand, trying to stop her from standing up. "Don't go, Maggie. I didn't say it wouldn't be with Tyler. You're projecting that on me."

"You didn't say it, but you meant it. Aren't you supposed to be encouraging us to believe in the future? Aren't you supposed to keep us from giving up when it gets tough?"

"I am and I do," Carol said. Her tone was sharper than she wanted it to be. Now was not the time to become defensive. She softened her voice. "I am sorry, Maggie."

"What if Tyler hears you talk like that? He's actually starting to believe that he'll live long enough for a new drug to come out to get his viral load in check and reverse his status. Negative thoughts and stress will just make things worse."

As Maggie stormed from the room, Carol couldn't help but to resent her. She couldn't fix this. It was clear that Maggie had been bottling this up for some time now, and of all nights for her to unload, she'd chosen girls' night. "Selfish. Epic failure," Carol muttered. The thought of Tyler dying made her stomach turn. She didn't want Maggie to expect him to live, but she didn't want to think about him dying either. She took a handful of ketchup chips and stuffed them ungracefully into her mouth, crumbs cracking and falling down the front of her shirt. She stayed on the floor, leaning against the couch with her legs outstretched. The chips echoed irritatingly in her head as she munched them, worrying that Marco was right and wishing that she was stoned.

Chapter Forty-One

THE DAY WAS perfect. The sun was shining brightly, and the temperature was warm enough that she and Tyler could be comfortable without any clothes. That was Maggie's plan. She'd been planning it for weeks now. The day she would ask Tyler to take her virginity had finally come. It was just like all the movies she loved. She even wore the dress she'd picked up with Carol back at the mall, the one that made her boobs perk up and sat high above the knee, hoping it would be a good incentive. A warm, beautiful day where they could lay a red-and-white checkered blanket in the tall grass, enjoy a picnic, and make love for the first time. She ate her egg salad sandwich so fast that she nearly choked. For a brief moment, she was irritated with how much food she packed for them. It took so long to finish it and even longer for the moment to come. She'd been worried at first that Tyler didn't like what she'd made because he kept complaining about a stomachache, and it was possibly the slowest she'd ever seen him eat.

She brushed her hair back slowly and tucked it behind her ear using only her middle finger, smiling and biting her bottom lip as she met his gaze. "I never thought I'd fall in love here," she said. She wanted him to make the first move, and surely she had made it clear enough that she wanted him. Every moment between her offering herself to him and his taking the cue and leaning in for a kiss made her chest ache. At last, he leaned forward, and they kissed and rolled back onto the blanket.

"I want you to," Maggie said, taking Tyler's hand and sliding it up the front of her dress. "I'm ready."

He kissed her, pushing his tongue into her mouth passionately, their breathing and her gentle moans drowning out the rational side of his brain. She moved her hands to his pants and began to pull at his belt.

"No," he said, "I can't. This isn't smart."

"Oh," Maggie said, surprised. "I'm sorry."

"Don't be sorry. I really want to. Believe me, I do. It's not smart, though. I'm just scared because of my hep C and your viral load is really low, and we have no condoms. What about superinfection or reinfection or whatever? I won't risk you."

"Okay," Maggie said. She felt both embarrassed and loved at the same time. She knew that what he was saying was the right thing to do, yet she couldn't help but feel rejected.

"Let's just keep it PG for now," Tyler said, refastening his belt and gently sliding her dress back down and smoothing it out. "I don't want us to change. I love what we have. Let's keep this, and if we decide to go further, let's do it when we've had time to make the choice and make sure you're safe by using condoms."

"I have it too," Maggie said. She immediately regretted it. "I know it's different, but I meant... Ugh," she said, giving up and standing to repack the picnic basket.

Tyler took a deep breath and smiled away the brief scowl that took over his face. "I know what you mean. We are in the same situation, but it will mean more to both of us if we wait."

"I just thought this is what you wanted," she said, her voice trailing off.

The look of complete shock on his face took her by surprise. "Me? How could... Why did you think that?"

"Because you're a guy, and that's apparently what you think of every ten seconds or something like that." She smirked as she said it, realizing how ridiculous she sounded. "Oh, my gosh. This is so embarrassing."

"I was a prostitute. You do remember that, right?"

She nodded.

"Sex doesn't mean anything to me. It's just sex. And I kinda hated it the whole time I was having it before. You know? I always felt ashamed after it was done." He hugged her. "I don't want to be ashamed with you."

She hugged him back tightly. "That makes sense. It really does." They stayed in their embrace until the sun started to set. She wished they could stay and watch it dip behind the horizon, but she knew that Carol would be worried. "We should go back soon."

He kissed her forehead. "Shhh," he said, nodding toward the sun that was now half-hidden by the forest. "Just a little while longer. I wanna remember this."

Chapter Forty-Two

THE SMELL OF Marco's famous pasta sauce wafted from the kitchen and into the hall, slipping delicately into the TV room where Carol and the kids had gathered to watch reruns of *Friends* while waiting for dinner. Carol's stomach rumbled as she caught a whiff of his garlic- and thyme-infused sauce. "Mmm," she said, "I'm starving." She rubbed her stomach and leaned back in her spot on the couch. "I hope it's ready soon."

"Seriously." Bradley grabbed his stomach with both hands and leaned back as well. "As soon as Marco said he was making his pasta, I decided not to have any snacks this afternoon. I'm dying. It's like torture."

"Theo and I snacked anyway," Tyler said, smiling deviously at them from where they sat lounged on the floor, leaning on pillows. "If there is food, I will eat."

"You haven't had enough of Marco's pasta yet then," Bradley said. "It's honestly the best thing I've ever eaten. I don't even care how many calories it has when I eat it. I save myself for it so I can get more in."

"I didn't snack either," Maggie said, blushing. "I snacked last time and was sad when I got full because I wanted to keep eating."

"Guess who just got their Fanshawe acceptance letters!?" Curtis said, announcing himself proudly as he stepped into the room.

"Oh, shit," Bradley groaned. "Are you sure they're not rejection letters?" He sat up straight as Curtis handed him his letter. "I don't want to open this." He fidgeted with the envelope, twirling it about to see it from all angles. "It feels like a rejection."

"How can you tell that?" Maggie walked over and snatched the letter from his hands. She examined the envelope similarly to how he had, smirking as she brought it close to her ear and pretended to listen to it. She shook her head. "I'm sorry, Bradley. I think you're wrong. It sounds like an acceptance letter to me."

"Hearing problems so young?" Bradley said as he stood and took the letter back.

"Well, hell," Curtis said. "I have been waiting too long for this." He eagerly ripped his envelope open and pulled the letter out, bending and nearly ripping it as he did. "Congratulations Mr. Richards," he read, "You've been accepted to Fanshawe. We're excited to help you begin to *Unlock Your Potential*. We look forward to welcoming you to the Adventure Expeditions and Interpretive Leadership program in the fall." As he finished, he leapt in the air and cheered, "Yahoo!"

"You're such a goof. That's wonderful news, Curtis," Carol said, standing to give him a hug. "Congratulations!"

"Thank you. Now all I need to know is if Bradley got in."

"No pressure," Bradley said sarcastically. He slowly opened the envelope, peeling the flap back delicately and milking the tension in the room.

Curtis was still dancing excitedly on the spot from his news and the anticipation of Bradley's. "Seriously, open the damn thing already." Het let out an exasperated sigh as he waited. "You're killing me." He grabbed at the letter so he could open it himself.

"Okay, okay," Bradley said, shaking Curtis off and turning away with the letter. "Let me see it first." He paused to read it to himself first, leaving the room in suspense. Maggie, Curtis, and Carol were moving in to read over his shoulder. He shifted away again, hiding the letter from sight. "Congratulations, Mr. Holmes, you've been accepted to Fanshawe. We're excited to help you begin to *Unlock Your Potential*. We look forward to welcoming you to the Broadcast Journalism-Television News program in the fall. We also," he continued with a smirk on his face, "would like to commend you on your stellar application that far outshone that of Curtis Richards—"

"Ha-ha, very funny," Curtis said, slapping Bradley on the chest and taking the letter from him. "Let me see that thing."

"I guess my hearing's not too bad after all. Congratulations," Maggie said, hugging Bradley tight. "And to you," she said to Curtis as she turned and hugged him too. "It's going to be sad without you guys here all the time."

"We're the first to graduate high school and go off to college from here," Curtis said proudly. "It's going to be really exciting. I bet Carol will let you guys come visit us in our apartment, right? Like a normal family."

Carol smiled. "Absolutely. I don't see any reason why not. It's going to be a really fun learning curve for all of us. And you two will be coming back to visit us often and for all the holidays." She hugged them both one at a time. "Just because you're becoming college men doesn't mean you get to avoid your family."

"Dinner—is—ready," Marco announced from the doorway.

"Did you know that you're catering to the first two graduates of the New Life house? And, conversely, the first two to get into college." Carol pointed at Curtis and Bradley. She beamed as she said it. *Graduates*. Their success cemented the positives of what she and Marco had been trying to do in stone. They were doing a good thing. Her eyes glistened with tears of joy as she presented the boys to Marco in a show of pride.

"Congratulations, guys! That's fantastic. Quite the honor," Marco said, grabbing them both in a joint hug. "Three cheers to you both. Let's go eat. I'm starved."

"You're starved?" Bradley said. "I think my stomach ate half of itself having to smell it all afternoon."

"Try being the one in the kitchen with it. It's ten times worse, I swear. Pretty exciting that it turns out to be a celebratory dinner."

"I'll be in in a few minutes. I just have to run to the washroom first." Tyler was hugging his stomach with both hands.

"Are you okay?" Marco asked. "Is the medication not working?"

"I'm good. I just need a few minutes." Tyler quickly excused himself and darted down the hall toward the washroom.

The rest of the kids cleared out and filed into the dining room, leaving Carol and Marco in the hall. "You hid their letters this morning, didn't you?" she said, leaning into him and kissing his cheek.

He smiled. "Me? Not me. I would never."

"How did you know it would be good news?"

"I just knew. They're great kids. Who wouldn't want them?" he said, smiling and kissing her. "I just took a chance really. If anything, tonight could have been a consolation dinner, but I'm glad it can be a celebration instead."

"To brighter futures."

"To brighter futures indeed," Marco said. He kissed the top of her head and slapped her butt, sending her skipping forward and giggling. "Now get in there and eat!"

Chapter Forty-Three

"YOU KNOW, I'VE been thinking more about what I want to do," Tyler said, leaning back in the swing and giving it a gentle push. "A lot about it."

Carol matched his lean, eager to hear more. "How so? What great things do you want to do?"

Tyler slowed the rocking of the swing and turned to look her in the eyes. He was smiling genuinely, and his eyes had wetted enough to host a twinkle as he spoke. "I think I want to write. My sister used to tell me that I had so much to offer in ways of wisdom. And since then, I have a lot of life experience to share too."

"Okay," Carol said, intrigued.

He sat up, excited by the idea as it became clearer to him. "Yeah. I've been writing a bunch of stuff down in the journal you got me for Christmas."

Carol winked. "That Santa got you."

He waved her hand off as she tried to pass the joint to him. "I want to get this out before I get too stoned. I've lost way too many trains of thought out here."

She gave him a look of amused surprise and continued smoking it to herself.

"Okay, the one that *Santa* gave me," he said, emphasizing "Santa" to placate her. "What if I don't die right away? What *if* I have more time left than I've been planning for?" He squirmed a little in his seat as he said it out loud. He took a deep, relaxed breath and sat taller in his seat.

Carol's smile was smug yet playful. "Well, I'll be," she said. "I never thought I'd see the day." When Tyler rolled his eyes, she patted his arm gently. "I'm kidding, sweetie. I'm really pleased to hear this. What will you write about?"

"I think I'll write about this," he said, pointing at the house and all around him in a fluid motion. "I won't include our evenings here of course, but I'll write about my life at home and then on the streets and how I came here and the way this place works. I think people need to know about places like this."

"So you think a nonfiction? Like a memoir?"

"Yeah," he said. "I think I've stayed on track long enough." He took the joint now. "I thought that writing fiction would be fun at first, but I think that writing my life story would be better. Fact is that I *am* going to die young."

"And? What does that have to do with writing fiction versus nonfiction?"

"I may never have a chance to tell my story. I won't get to have kids, so my legacy ends with me. But if I write my memoir, then I have a chance to be remembered."

"Hm," Carol said, breaking eye contact. "I love that you've found something to be passionate about. It's refreshing that you're finally thinking about the future and not zeroing in on your death all the time."

Tyler laughed. "Yeah, I can be pretty dark, eh?"

"Yeah, you sure can," she said. "You sure can."

They sat in silence, both considering the future as they shared the remainder of the joint. As Carol butted it out and put it into her tin, Tyler jolted and cried out enthusiastically, "Oh! I almost forgot."

The sudden volume and fervor with which he spoke made Carol scream and drop the tin to the ground. "Jesus Christ," she said, cursing and looking at Tyler with wide-eyed terror. "What the fuck did you do that for?" She sat clutching the swing to keep her balance. Irritated by his grin and laughter, she continued, "What the fuck is wrong with you? I could have had fuckin' heart attack." He laughed harder, so she leaned forward and slapped him on the arm.

"Language," he said, wagging his finger back and forth in the air and mocking Marco. "I don't think you should be so giving with your eff-bombs."

"Well what the hell'd you do that for?" She started to laugh now, realizing the ridiculousness of her reaction. "I'm stoned. You can't do that shit to me. I think I might fall over if I try to pick up that damn tin now," she said, motioning to where it lay between their feet.

He bent down to pick it up for her, and she slapped him on the back of the head. "Hey," he said, sitting up and handing her the tin, pretending to hold his head in pain. "You could have given me a head-attack."

"You're an ass," she said, tucking the tin into the front pocket of her hoodie. "Now tell me what that was."

"What 'what' was?" He looked at her with genuine confusion.

"What do you mean what 'what' was?" she said. "*That.*" She pointed at him and rolled her hand in the air to remind him of the whole ordeal.

He thought for a moment. "Hm," he said. A smile slowly crept across his face.

"You don't even remember, jerk," she said. "I almost died so your brain could fart. Great." They slipped back into a giggle fit. "Stop," Carol said. "I can't breathe." She started to make croaking sounds in the back of her throat as she laughed. "Oh, shit," she said finally as the laughter subsided.

"Oh!" Tyler said again, slapping her arm gently. "I remember."

"Say it, don't slap it," she said, looking down at his hand, which was still slapping her in tiny repetitive movements.

He stopped. "I thought of something else that I might be good at someday." He paused. "Someday... I like the sound of that."

"Do tell," Carol said, getting comfortable on the swing again to listen. "I love hearing you talk about the future." She watched him bubble with excitement over his newfound belief in life. A confusing rush of sadness and pride crept through her in the form of a body buzz, tingling its way through her arms, back, and chest. She brought the blanket up above her head and subtly wiped the tears from her cheek as she lowered it back down to tuck it by her chin and then faced him again, blinking away any remaining emotion.

"I think I'd be good at working with kids. So maybe something like that. Like what you do here," he said with sincerity. "I think I'd be good at it."

"I think you would too," she said. "Just don't go taking any lessons from me, or you'll find yourself staying up late to get high with them."

"Hey, this is great. Why wouldn't I want this?"

"Because if it were any other kid, someone would probably find out, and I'd be losing my license, this house, and go to jail." She reflected on the statement for a moment, contemplating the reality of it. "I really could lose everything for this."

Tyler's smile faded. "I will never do anything to jeopardize you or this place."

"I know," she said, patting his knee. "I just get startled by the thought sometimes is all. I'm just saying it out loud to make myself feel better. Sometimes I just need to say it to feel that reassurance. Besides, you're too much like me to say anything."

His smile perked back up as he blushed. "You know that you're more of a mom to me than mine ever was, right?"

"Don't say that," she said, feigning support for his mother and looking away again so he couldn't see the effect his words had on her.

"It's true," he said. "If a mother is supposed to make you feel safe, like you belong in the world, like you're loved, like you have a purpose...like you matter. You are that to me. You gave me the journal that gave me hope for a future. Even if I don't live, my story will."

She exhaled slowly and deliberately, fighting off the wave of sobs she could feel vibrating in her chest. "Jesus, scare me half to death and then try to get me crying. You're batting a thousand tonight." She patted his knee without looking at him.

He took her hand and gently squeezed it. "I mean it. Thanks for believing in me." He stood up with his blanket, poised to leave. "I'm going to get to bed. See you in the morning."

"You're welcome. You're a good kid," she said. Her voice squeaked and wavered as she said it. She took a deep breath and held it, her body trembling as she fought back the tears, until he was in the house. At the sound of the slamming screen door, she buried her face in the blanket and cried. When she finally regained control of herself, she lit another joint and reflected on Tyler's plans for the future. She smiled as she replayed his excitement in her mind. *Finally*, she thought, *he found his purpose.*

Chapter Forty-Four

MARCO SMILED AS Carol pulled out the joint, and for the first time in a long while, he was conflicted about whether he truly wanted her to give it all up. They had always had so much fun when they'd smoked up together. He could remember when they were in university, and they would get stoned before philosophy class or times like right now when they would smoke up behind the dumpsters at the mall, waiting for the theater to let them in. The innocence and the giggles that came with the experience were moments he never wanted to lose, and in this moment, he found himself wondering if they could find those same joys without it. Had they ever laughed and gone into giggle fits without being high?

"What's the matter?" Carol asked, tapping his shoulder and waving the now-lit joint in front of his eyes. A light rain had come through while they were eating dinner, and now the air was humid and pressed against them like a comforting hug. "You're not mad, are you?"

He shook his head as he came back to reality. "What do you mean?"

"You disappeared there," she said, still holding the joint out for him to grab. "You looked like you were troubled. I'll toss this if it's going to affect our do-over. I can't call a mulligan on a mulligan, can I?"

He shook his head again. "Nah. I just dazed off, I guess. Don't throw that thing out. You crazy?" As he took the joint from her, he shielded it as if he were protecting it.

She chuckled. "Imagine how dazed you'll be once you've had half of it." She nodded at the joint.

"Jesus, I know. I feel like a teenager again. Hiding out behind the theater to get stoned," he said, laughing as he coughed and passed it back to her.

"Me too. I like the naughtiness of it. We're so good naturally that it feels right to be bad." She winked and pushed on his chest. She slid her hand down to his waist and held on to his belt, teasing him as she suggestively tugged on it.

He knew she had no intention of opening it right there, but the simple suggestion aroused him regardless. "You are a brat," he said slowly, leaning in and kissing her cheek. "A complete and total brat." He leaned against her as he took the joint into his hand and tried lifting her dress.

She giggled and pushed him away. "I don't know what you're talking about."

HE HELD THE erection for the entire movie. Carol helped by grazing it with her fingers every so often, teasing him of what was to come. He hadn't felt this way since they'd first started dating. He couldn't remember the last time he'd had an erection that lasted longer than thirty minutes let alone an entire movie. On the drive home, he pulled the car down a dead-end road where they could have sex in the back seat like they had done when they were young. It was a lot more complicated than he'd remembered, but he was glad they put the effort in, and he was pretty sure she was too.

Chapter Forty-Five

"OKAY," BRADLEY SAID. He was standing beside Tyler, holding his hands outstretched in front of them both, creating a frame. Tyler cocked his head a little to the right as he joined Bradley in peering through his hands to the soccer ball that sat ten feet in front of them in the grass. It was the last game of the day, and Tyler was up for a potentially game-winning penalty kick.

Tyler put his hands out in a similar fashion to Bradley and said, in a mocking tone, "You are the ball. I am the ball. The ball and we are one."

Bradley rolled his eyes. "Be whatever you want to be as long as you listen to what I'm saying."

Tyler laughed and put his hands back down.

Bradley bumped him playfully. "So...you are the ball," he said in jest. "Seriously, though. When you're running to it, make sure you land so your left foot hits the ground after you've wound your right foot back and as it's coming back toward the ball."

Tyler nodded and kept nodding for the entirety of Bradley's speech. He had been placed on Bradley and Carol's team for the day of sports. This was the last game they were playing. They had already played softball, capture the flag, and ultimate Frisbee. Bradley had surprised Tyler with how supportive he was on a sports team. He didn't get frustrated if they fumbled or if any kind of mistake happened. He simply gave a pep talk, a high five, and an atta-boy. Tyler even found himself attracted to Bradley in this element. It was like all of the things that made him a jerk faded away, and he turned into this nice guy. Needless to say, this was not his first pep talk of the day and Bradley was as friendly and jovial as he had been for all the others. Tyler was pretty sure it wouldn't even matter if they lost.

"Did you get that?" Bradley asked.

Tyler looked to the ball. He hadn't been listening. "Hm," he said. He nodded and patted Bradley on the shoulder. "So I just—" He lunged forward. "—kick the ball?" he said, grunting as he sent it hurtling toward the net.

Bradley laughed and threw his hands in the air before clutching the side of his head as he watched in awe.

Marco jumped to block it, but it blew by him and into the net.

Tyler turned around smugly, smiling and playfully swiping imaginary dust off his shoulder. "No sweat, Cap."

"I knew you could do it," Bradley said, reaching up and clapping his hand to Tyler's. "That was sweet."

Tyler chuckled. "First time a jock actually gave me props in a sport."

"Jocks aren't all bad, you know. It's about the team, the sport, the fun. If you're on a team, you're treated pretty well," Bradley said. "Teammates are some of the best bonds you'll ever have." He frowned briefly as he said it. Tyler knew it was because he hadn't heard from any of his teammates since the whole ordeal with their coach. It was as though he'd been completely forgotten.

Bradley quickly replaced the frown with a smile. "Let's celebrate! To your first Sports Day at New Life and to your first game-winning penalty kick." Bradley shook him gently, cheering as Carol came running over squealing and waving her arms in grand-standing fashion.

"It's true," Tyler said, nodding and making playful smug faces. "I'm pretty awesome."

"Tyler, you lead us out in the cheer," Bradley said once they were huddled together.

"Nah, that's the coach's job." Tyler nodded at Bradley. "That's all you."

"Not when you win the game for the team. This is all *you*."

Tyler blushed. "On three, let's do it all together."

Carol and Bradley nodded in agreement. They placed their hands in the center of the huddle, interlocking with one another.

Tyler started, "One, two, three..." They rocked their hands up and down excitedly as he counted.

"GO JAYS!" They tossed their hands in the air and broke away from the huddle in a boisterous show of team spirit.

"Congrats, guys," Marco said, walking up to them with Curtis and Maggie. "We Eagles are gonna let you bask in the glow of your triumph for now. We'll be demanding some kind of a rematch later this summer. No one told us you had a ringer on your team." Marco grabbed Tyler by the shoulders from behind and gave him a gentle shake. "Great kick, Tyler."

"Thanks," Tyler said, awkwardly patting Marco's arm as it stretched across his chest to wrap him in a hug.

Marco pulled away from him, but kept his hand on his shoulder. "Let's all go get cleaned up. The losing team—Maggie, Curtis, and I—will make dinner."

Carol snickered. "You mean call for pizza."

Marco shot her a playful look. "Dinner is dinner." He kissed her on her sweaty cheek.

"Extra meat and cheese, please," Tyler said as they moved toward the house.

THE KIDS JOINED Tyler in the sunroom to watch him reenact his penalty kick, over and over.

"And then, I just ran and..." Tyler smiled and paused for effect and to get Theo to laugh. He winked and pretended to kick the soccer ball, raising his arms in a victory chant. "Yeaaahhh, he scoooooorrrrres."

"What is that?" Maggie asked, pointing at his waist.

He glared at her and moved away. "Nothing."

"But I saw a dark mark there." She pointed at his side and reached her hand out toward him to lift his shirt, but he slapped it away.

He looked down at her angrily and stepped away. "It's a bruise. Haven't you ever seen one before?" He looked nervously at Bradley and Curtis who were now watching them. He was angry with her for drawing attention to him. He had a flash of his younger years, when he would have to hide and pull away from his teachers and friends and deny the bruises his father had put on him, and filled with shame, which quickly turned to rage.

Maggie recoiled from the hate in his eyes. "You don't have to be so mean about it," she whispered. She looked to the ground, embarrassed that she had reached out.

"Bradley, let's go get some plates set. The pizza guy is coming up the drive," Curtis said, keeping his eyes on Tyler and Maggie as he tapped Bradley on the knee to get him to follow.

"I'm sorry," Tyler said. "I banged my side on the elliptical as I got off the other day. It's just a bruise. I'm sensitive when it comes to defending them."

"Okay," Maggie said, continuing to sulk.

He sat down beside her on the bench and wrapped his arm around her, pulling her in close. "I'm sorry, Maggie. I don't mean to be a jerk," he said. He kissed her forehead. "I guess the apple doesn't always fall too far from the tree."

"Don't say that. You're not like him. I refuse to draw a line between you and your father." After a moment, she added, "You're awfully defensive about a simple bruise." She kept her eyes on him, waiting for him to tell her more.

"Forget it. I think you triggered some memories or something. It's fine. I'm fine," he said. He felt guilty for lying, but it was better than the embarrassment he would feel for telling the truth, so he made peace with the lie and kissed her to change the topic.

"Pizza's here!" Marco announced as he emerged from the foyer carrying a stack of aromatic boxes.

"Yay," Tyler said, jumping up to help him. "I'm starving."

"You should have extra," Marco said, eyeing him. "You're lookin' skinny."

Tyler blushed. "Yeah, I've been working out a lot. Gotta keep fit for the lady." He winked at Maggie playfully and she blushed.

Marco eyed him suspiciously, doubting his reason.

AFTER THE PIZZA had been devoured and the kids were cleaning up, Marco pulled Tyler aside to ask about his weight. He had watched with keen interest as Tyler struggled to eat his meal. When Tyler had first arrived, he would have eaten six or seven slices, but today, he barely ate two. They stepped into the sunroom to talk. "How's your weight? Have you been keeping tabs on it?"

Tyler shrugged. "It's low."

"How low?" Marco was not going to let him shrug this off. "Carol weighed you when we first spoke about your stomachaches. We can weigh you again, but I'd like for you to let me know. Have you been watching?"

"Yes. It's low. I've lost something like twenty pounds."

Marco's eyes widened. He'd hoped to keep his reaction subtle, but had failed. "That's concerning, Tyler. We really need to get you in to see Dr. Benson. Are you still having diarrhea?"

Tyler squirmed and made a face.

"Come on. It's time to put on your big-boy pants. This is serious stuff."

Tyler wouldn't look Marco in the eyes, but he nodded.

"We'll get you in to see the doctor in the morning. In the meantime, please try to keep eating even if you don't feel hungry. Carol's going to get you upstairs on the scale, so we have an accurate account of how much weight you've lost."

"Okay." Tyler backed away from Marco. "Can I go?"

Marco sighed and let Tyler excuse himself to the kitchen to help clean up. He closed his eyes and rubbed his forehead, taking a seat on the couch to stare out the window. The lights were off. The faint glow from the dining room kept him grounded. He watched his own reflection as he tried to stymie the worries that were mounting deep within him. He wasn't ready to lose another one. He closed his eyes when he noticed tears in the eyes of his reflection, and pretended they weren't there.

Chapter Forty-Six

TYLER—ALONG WITH all of the kids—was struggling to finish his final school project before the big camping trip Curtis had planned. A prerequisite for the trip was that their end-of-year projects be handed in before leaving.

Maggie had taken on a literature review and analysis of William Golding's novel *Lord of the Flies*. Curtis had prepared a history paper on the Norse people who had inhabited L'Anse aux Meadows in Newfoundland. Bradley had written a paper on the history of sports medicine. And Tyler, Tyler had decided to write his memoir. He was cursing himself for it now. It had proven to be a much larger endeavor than he thought it would be.

"You look lost," Curtis said, sitting down across from him at the dining room table. Tyler was using the laptop and was surrounded by a stack of printed pages and a mess of pens. He looked like he was writing a dissertation. Curtis eyed him up and down. He hadn't showered; his hair was a mess and unwashed; he had a dirty plate and a half-empty mug next to the emptied coffee carafe. "You're like one of those drunken playwrights from back in the day." He fanned the stack of pages with his thumb, grimacing at the amount of work it indicated.

"Thanks, asshole," Tyler said, laughing. "It's stressful trying to finish this."

"Your memoir?"

"Yeah."

"That's a big project," Curtis said, grabbing the stack of papers and, this time, scanning through them. "I better be in here." He winked.

"You might be. I'm stuck on how to end it." Tyler took a deep breath. "It's frustrating. How do you end your own memoir when you're still alive?"

"I guess by saying that life goes on. Or something like that. I'm not much of a writer."

"But does it?"

Curtis's smile faded. "Don't start with that again. Of course it does."

Tyler sighed.

"Speaking of all that... What did the doctor say?"

Tyler knew Curtis hated asking. He also knew that Curtis had been worried about whether Tyler would be healthy enough to go on the camping trip.

"Just that I need to keep eating, take these medications for wasting, and try to remain positive." Tyler looked away to keep from making full eye contact. He didn't want to tell the whole story. Truthfully, he was still trying to process it.

Dr. Benson told him that he was worried about how fast he was wasting. He had turned to Carol and Marco then to say, "This is usually an indicator of the late stages of the disease. I'm sorry I don't have better news for you."

He also pointed out Kaposi sarcoma lesions on Tyler's chest and waistline, forcing him to come clean about the few weeks he'd known about them and the time when Maggie had tried to point one out. He didn't like talking about them. They made him feel dirty. Apparently, the good news was that his blood work was okay, and that he was in the clear to start chemotherapy after the camping trip.

After Tyler went out to the waiting room, Carol and Marco stayed with the doctor to talk further. A few times, he thought he could hear arguing, but the voices were muffled. Neither Carol nor Marco told him what they had stayed back to talk to the doctor about, and he pretended not to care. He replayed the words "late stages of the disease" in his head over and over on the drive home, and somehow managed to keep from crying until he was alone in his room.

"I guess this isn't the time to get all sentimental with it. I think I've done a good job about telling my life story. I never should have decided to write it in such a short time," Tyler said, changing the subject back to his memoir and hoping that Curtis would forget about the doctor.

"Just because you're handing it in now doesn't mean you can't go back and fix it up later," Curtis said.

"You're right," Tyler said, nodding and feeling content. "Sometimes I forget that this is a school. You know? It's a school, it's a hospital, it's a therapist's couch, it's...it's...it's a family." Tyler felt uncomfortable finishing the sentence. It did feel like a family, but he felt corny saying it nonetheless.

"It's totally all of those things," Curtis said, smiling brightly. "It's nice to see you waking up to that."

Tyler smiled. "I think I know how to end it."

Chapter Forty-Seven

CURTIS

Four Years Ago
June 1994

"But how? But...but how did you?" Curtis's father, Ryan, stuttered as he tried to find the right way to ask all the questions he had. He was still reeling from the news Curtis had just shared. They were supposed to be going camping in a few hours, and somehow the worst news he could imagine was sprung on him. Now they sat on the couch with their bags packed and piled on the floor in front of them, seemingly stuck and going nowhere.

Curtis aggressively rubbed his forehead with the tips of his fingers. Tears dropped straight from his eyes down to his knees, skipping his cheeks altogether. "I don't know." His voice wavered as he tried to think of what could have happened.

"Was it drugs?"

"I don't know." Curtis's tone was more impatient now as he grew tired of the questioning.

"Sex? Have you been having sex?" Ryan put his hand on Curtis's shoulder to encourage him to look up. He didn't know why, but he felt like he needed to know how it happened. He hated the thought of his young son having sex, but he wouldn't be surprised by anything Curtis did anymore.

Curtis pushed his hand away. "Don't. Just don't." He stared angrily into Ryan's face, challenging him to try again. They were at a standoff. One of the many they'd been having over the last year since Curtis started hanging out with an older, wilder crowd.

"I'm trying to understand, Curtis. That's all. I need to understand."

"What about what I need?" Curtis yelled. His voice cracked. "Does that matter?"

Ryan took a deep breath to keep from reacting. "Curtis, what you need is all I've ever cared about. Let's just take a minute here. I want to help." He'd had to walk on eggshells for most of the last year whenever it came to questioning Curtis, so he was getting better at diffusing the confrontations before they escalated too far. It wasn't the first time he had to take the passive role, and he was sure it wouldn't be the last.

"I don't know how I got it. It might have been from sharing a needle at a party. It might have been from sex. *I don't know.*" Curtis teared up again. "What the fuck am I gonna do?"

Ryan cleared his throat, another technique he'd learned to employ to keep from saying something contentious. He hated swearing, and before Curtis started hanging out with these druggy friends of his, he hadn't liked it either. It was another subtle reminder of just how much of his son he'd lost. "Was it with a boy or a girl?" He hated asking. He never wanted to be the parent who asked his kid what their sexual preference was because he didn't want to be the parent who cared, but he knew what communities HIV was more prevalent in.

Curtis shrank away. "I don't want to talk about this. Can we just talk about something different, please? *Please.*"

Ryan wrapped Curtis in a hug, squeezing tighter as Curtis tried to pull away. "Curtis, it's going to be okay. We're going to get through this." He blinked feverishly to stifle the tears but was unsuccessful. He exhaled slowly and kissed the top of Curtis's head and repeated, "It's going to be okay."

Curtis tried again to pull away, but Ryan, who was of a similar slender build but with more muscle, pulled him back again. Curtis tried to speak, but a bubble of spit burst in his throat as he began to cry, causing him to choke briefly and swallow. He allowed himself to collapse into Ryan's hug, pulling his knees up to his chest and sobbing in the fetal position.

When Curtis's tears quieted, Ryan encouraged him to sit up to look him in the eyes. "I'm not going anywhere, Curtis."

Curtis sniffled and wiped snot from under his nose. "What am I gonna do?"

Ryan thought for a moment and then said, "What are *we* going to do. *We're* going to pack these bags in the truck and get to our camping trip. I think a weekend of nature will help us find those answers." He slapped Curtis lovingly on the knee and stood up.

"But I'm sick... I can't."

Ryan looked at him in the familiar, loving way that he always did when Curtis said he couldn't do something. "And that's supposed to stop you from living?" He blinked to keep the wetness in his eyes from becoming tears and then smiled and clapped his hands together. "Get your pack. The world is waiting."

Chapter Forty-Eight

CURTIS

Four Years Ago
July 1994

Ryan came hurriedly into the kitchen, covered in grease and stinking of motor oil and holding a light-blue pamphlet in his hand like a trophy. "You'll never guess what I found today, buddy. It looks perfect."

Curtis was digging in the fridge for the milk jug; he looked over his shoulder at his dad and nodded toward the table where two plates sat on placemats with large, clear drinking glasses. A pot of macaroni and cheese was bubbling on the stove beside a frying pan, sizzling with sliced hot dogs. He had made dinner and set the table, hoping that pretending life was normal would make it real.

Ryan had been working late nearly every day since Curtis told him he had tested positive for HIV. He had been trying to make enough money to take them both on a two-week camping trip in August for Curtis's birthday. The plan was to make life continue as normal and to make sure Curtis didn't return to the friends he had been hanging out with, the friends that Ryan kept blaming for Curtis's misfortune.

"It wasn't a new shower, was it?" Curtis chuckled at his own joke and plugged his nose, pretending that Ryan was stinking up the room.

"Ha! Funny. That's what work smells like. You'll see. One day." He held the pamphlet up for Curtis to see. "It's a place for positive kids. Kids like you."

Curtis scowled and recoiled. "You want to get rid of me? Things were just getting better."

"Don't say that. I don't want to get rid of you. We talked about finding some kind of a camp or a group you could go to, to relate to other people going through this..." Ryan didn't know how to finish, so he waved his hand instead. "You know."

Curtis scraped the hot dogs into the pot of macaroni and stirred choppily, trying to hide his frustration. "I thought we decided I would stay here. That I'd do treatments and we'd camp and sort it out ourselves." He didn't like the whiny sound in his voice, but he didn't try to change it. "I don't want to leave."

Ryan took his seat at the table as Curtis slopped several big scoops of macaroni onto his plate. "Curtis, I know you want to stay here. But I can't take care of you the way you need."

"Health care is free. What's so hard? It's not like you have to do anything."

"Sit down, Curtis. There's a lot to be said for going through a hardship with likeminded people who are going through the same thing. I think you'll grow into such a strong man if you go to this place. My gut says it's the right place for you." He slid the pamphlet on the table to rest beside Curtis's plate.

Curtis slid it back, refusing to give in. He didn't want to go anywhere. His friends were here. His dad was here. His whole life was here. "You can't make me go."

"Actually, Curtis, I can. I am your father. You are fourteen years old, and I can sign you into this house if I want to." Ryan was stern.

Curtis hated Ryan's therapist—whom he'd been seeing since soon after Curtis had announced that he was HIV positive—for suggesting that he take a more active role in parenting. All it meant was more rules.

"Legally, it's my decision. But you and I don't work like that." Ryan softened his tone. "I don't want to be the type of parent who makes decisions for you. I want you and me to talk about it like men, and to consider it like men. I want us to make the decision together. Whatever the decision is."

"Fine. I'll think about it. How long would I be gone?"

"You'd finish your schooling there. Once you graduate from high school, you could come back here. But I think you'll have bigger dreams by then."

"That's a long time." Curtis put his fork down and leaned away from the table. "I'm not hungry anymore."

"Oh, Curtis. Don't be like that. I'm trying here. I'm trying to help us navigate through this." Ryan stuffed his mouth with a forkful of macaroni; cheese dribbled down his chin, and he wiped at it with a napkin. "Just think about it, okay? How many people your age are you going to meet who are going through the same thing? This is a one-of-a-kind place that can offer you so much more than I can. I'm just a mechanic who likes to camp. I don't know about this disease or how to incorporate it into your life. I want to know. I want to. I think we could both learn so much from them. I want you to have the best life you can have. And I think this New Life House is the place where you can get it." He paused and squeezed Curtis's hand, seeming to think this would make him more willing to consider it. "Think of all the camping we could do in the summers out along the coast. I could save up my vacation time and come out there, and we could discover all kinds of new places."

Curtis frowned but took the pamphlet. His dad wasn't usually so adamant about things, so his curiosity was piqued, and the thought of leaving and reinventing himself was at least a little appealing. "Thanks." The front of the pamphlet had a picture of an old-looking mansion that seemed to be in the country. He flipped it open, hoping to get an idea of whether it was in a city or not. The majority of the information talked about HIV- and AIDS-related facts, the homeschooling curriculum, and the promise of life after diagnosis. He paused on this phrase that appeared in large font, made to look like handwriting, set apart from the rest of the words. *There is life after diagnosis.*

"What is it?" Ryan leaned over and tried to see what Curtis had fixated on.

"I'll go. I'll try it." He liked the sound of it: *life after diagnosis.* It wasn't the end of the world, and it was the first time he actually believed that it might be true.

Chapter Forty-Nine

CURTIS

Four Years Ago
November 1994

"I hate this place. I don't even know why I agreed to come here. I miss my friends. My *real* friends." Curtis groaned and crossed his arms across his chest. He wore the same familiar scowl he'd had glued to his face since he arrived at the beginning of September. This was not what his dad had promised it would be like. There was no mention of therapy or being forced to talk about his feelings in front of these other kids. He had just started feeling comfortable opening up, and now this new kid was here. He shot Bradley, who quietly scoffed and rolled his eyes in an air of machismo indifference, an irritated glare.

JANIE ROLLED HER eyes and glanced at Maggie who was staring shyly, but not discreetly, at the newest arrival, Bradley. He was sitting beside Curtis, unamused by his outburst. It was his first week at the house, so he wasn't being forced into sharing yet.

Janie wondered what tales Bradley would have to tell, imagining that some steamy encounter with a high-end prostitute landed him here. She loved to daydream and to make up fantasy-based stories for everyone. Back when she lived in Edmonton, she would spend hours at the mall watching people walk by so she could make up stories about where she imagined they'd come from and the lives they'd lived. It was always more fun than the truth. She much preferred making stories up, and usually Maggie did too. But today, she couldn't seem to get her friend to play along. She coughed to get Maggie's attention.

Maggie looked at her and blushed, offering a smirk as a defense. During therapy, they would never dare share even a whisper, only looks and eye rolls. The real dishing came afterward. They would steal away to a quiet corner of the house to gossip about their theories behind Curtis's back. He was the only other kid who'd joined since they'd been there, and he was always so secretive that they had come to really enjoy writing his story for him.

"I hope he doesn't turn out to be some bore," Janie had said one afternoon. "Like, I hope he got it from a blood transfusion gone awry caused by a rock-climbing accident up in the Yukon."

"Oh, that sounds so exciting. I think that's the best scenario. Very plausible too." Maggie giggled and leaned into her friend. "Or if he was all cut up from a fall and had to save the life of his climbing partner, who was positive, and the blood seeped into his hands as he saved him."

Janie nodded emphatically. "Oh yeah, and that act of heroism was his ultimate undoing. Yes. I like it. Perfect."

They had been sorely disappointed when Curtis had explained how he had contracted HIV. He had shrugged it off, saying that he had loved to party and made a few stupid choices. He hadn't even been able to pinpoint how he'd gotten infected. The girls decided that the mystery surrounding his actual method of infection was license enough to continue speculating. It kept him interesting.

CURTIS STOMPED HIS foot again. "I feel like he just lied to get me here. Like he just pretended that this was the best thing for me when it was really the best thing for him."

Carol smiled sympathetically. "Curtis, your father calls you every day still. I think if you were to examine the evidence objectively, you would see that he still wants you in his life."

"Then why did he convince me to come here? I'm never going to be able to do any of the things I dreamt about doing." He fought back tears. He hadn't wanted to leave his life behind.

"Things like what?" Marco asked. "What kinds of things do you want to do that you can't do here?" He leaned back in his chair and crossed his legs. "I would like to think that we would try to make those things possible. All you have to do is voice it."

Curtis sighed. "It doesn't matter. I probably can't do it anyways."

Bradley had finally had enough. "Okay, man. Just give it up. Try working your whole life to be an athlete and having that snatched away.

You can go sling burgers and live in hippy camps all you want. I'll never get to be on a sports team again."

"Who told you that?" Carol asked.

Bradley shrugged and refused to answer.

Carol made a note on her pad of paper, reminding herself to talk to Bradley about this misinformation about his future in a one-on-one session.

Marco asked again. "What is it that you want to do?"

"We can't camp here. We can't hike. There's nothing. It's a house in a field in the middle of nowhere, and my dad knew that. I couldn't be any further away from where I want to be."

Marco smiled and exchanged looks with Carol. "You never know. Anything is possible. There's always tomorrow, kids."

"I guess we're done?" Janie asked, motioning to stand up.

Marco chuckled. "What makes you think that?" He, too, stood to leave.

"The *Full House* moment usually comes at the end." Janie giggled and linked arms with Maggie as they strode out of the library.

As Curtis got up to leave, Marco half jogged across the circle to get a moment alone with him. "Curtis, I'm sorry about what you're feeling. I know it must be hard to adjust to this."

Curtis tried to hide that he was annoyed by Marco. He didn't want to get into trouble, and he didn't want to have to justify what he felt. He pursed his lips and stared blankly at Marco, waiting for the cliché pep talk.

"Come on a walk with me."

"What," Curtis said indignantly, "to the row of maples midway down the driveway? No thanks. You're joking if you think I'll agree to camp there."

Marco laughed. "Such a cynic you are. Go get your coat." He laughed again as Curtis sulked off to the foyer to get his coat and shoes. "I'll meet you out on the back veranda through the kitchen."

WHEN CURTIS GOT to the veranda, he found Marco standing in the grass beyond it, staring at the field. He rolled his eyes and stomped down the steps, annoyed that Marco would think he would be excited by a virtually treeless field.

"Great. Let's go." Marco gently slapped Curtis on the back and started to walk away from the house.

Curtis followed reluctantly, staying a few feet behind.

After about five minutes, Marco glanced over his shoulder at Curtis who was still sulking, much like he did every day. He slowed his pace to match Curtis's. "You know, if you look up when you walk, you can see more. You can get a better idea of where you're going." He nudged Curtis.

Curtis took a deep breath and exhaled loudly and raised his head. They had just come over a small hill in the field. He could make out a forest in the distance. His heart skipped a beat as he started to understand where they were heading. "Are you...?"

Marco followed Curtis's awe-struck gaze to the forest. "Yeah, Curtis. I am. I'm taking you to our forest."

"Our?" Curtis was speechless. He had barely looked out the window since he'd arrived with his dad. When they had driven up the laneway, he had glanced behind the house and had seen nothing but a huge field filled with tall, unkempt grass that resembled hay.

"It takes about twenty minutes to walk to the edge. In the winter, it takes about double that because the snow gets tough, but it's still worth it then. There's about two hundred acres of woods back here. All of it perfect for camping."

Curtis's face lit up as he listened to Marco. He stared at the forest with a sense of longing he hadn't felt in a long time. He imagined himself sleeping in the middle of the trees with a small campfire burning beside him. He didn't want Marco to think he would give in so easily, but he couldn't stop the smile from spreading across his lips.

"You're in for a treat." Marco clapped his hands together and quickened the pace, knowing now that Curtis would stop dragging his feet.

They made it to the forest in good time with little chatter between them. Curtis reached his hand out to touch the bark of a tall, white birch as they left the field and stepped into the trees as though he needed to feel it in order to believe it was real. He stopped beside the tree, still fingering the bark, and looked at Marco who had not stopped to wait for him.

"Come on, that's not what I wanted to show you." Marco waved for him to follow.

Curtis continued deeper into the woods with Marco. He looked around in wonder, loving the sights and the smells. The soft, sweet scent of dead leaves rose from the earth as they crunched beneath his feet. He took a deep breath through his nose to savor their pleasant, musty aroma that reminded him of home, still smiling. He found Marco standing before a large maple tree, several feet in diameter. It dwarfed all of the trees near it, making them seem almost insignificant. It stretched up high, poking out above the forest ceiling. A few leaves clung to the branches up above. "Wow," he said, stopping beside Marco.

"It's great, isn't it? Something majestic about it." Marco watched Curtis, who was staring up at the tree wide-eyed, and then wrapped his arm around him. "Life isn't always what we want, but we can make good things come out of what we have. We may not be able to offer you any mountains to climb, but we have this: a place where you can come to find solace and feel connected to your dreams and your dad whenever you want."

"Really?"

"Well, as long as you tell us that you've come out. We do want to know where you are. And you can't skip classes, but yeah. You can come out here. Let this be your place, your temple if that's what you need it to be."

"Thank you." Curtis couldn't think of anything more profound to say, so he repeated himself. "Thank you."

"And how about you give some thought to leading camping exercises out here."

"Are you serious?" Curtis couldn't hide his excitement now.

"Yeah. Why not? Teach us all a thing or two about surviving in the wild. Bring us into your world. Let us know you."

Curtis immediately started thinking of things to do on a camping trip as a group. He looked back up at the tree, still intrigued by it. He leaned forward and held his hand against its trunk. He closed his eyes and smiled. "I'm gonna love this place."

Chapter Fifty

"YOU ALMOST READY, slowpoke?" Curtis called from the doorway of Tyler and Theo's room, where Tyler was frantically stuffing whatever clothing he could find into his duffel bag.

"Yeah, yeah." Tyler didn't look up. He just kept grabbing clothing, balling it up, and stuffing it in. "I know, I know," he said. "I should have packed yesterday. I *know*."

Curtis laughed. "Yeah, but let's not live in 'shoulds.' Make sure to pack some warm stuff, sweaters and pants. It'll get cold at night."

Tyler rolled his eyes. "Are you serious? It's like thirty degrees out there."

"Yep, sure am," Curtis said, slapping his hand on the doorframe.

Tyler startled at the sudden slap. "Yep, sure am." He mocked Curtis under his breath, grumbling and pulling some T-shirts from the bag to make room for a hoodie. "I'm Curtis, and I'm the peppiest morning person ever born."

Unbothered by Tyler's pouting, Curtis chuckled and skipped off down the hall to pester the others. He called back over his shoulder, "Make sure you can fit that on your rucksack. They get real heavy real fast.

"Maggie, tell me you're ready," Curtis said, stopping to lean against the doorframe to her bedroom.

"Of course," Maggie said, zipping her duffel bag closed.

"Awesome. Tyler is pretty much the only person not ready then." He grinned proudly. It was always the camping newbies who floundered, and it was his job to break them in.

Maggie giggled. "I bet he's the first one to crack this year."

"I don't know. He's been homeless, so I think camping is going to be a piece of cake for him," Curtis said. "My money's on Bradley again this year."

The kids had been doing these camping trips into the woods at the back of the property ever since Curtis's first summer there. It had become a part of their annual routine. The third weekend of June every year, they would traipse off into the wilderness so Curtis could lead them on some kind of exercise to connect with nature. Every year, it kept his dream alive.

Curtis loved that Maggie had always enjoyed the trips. The first year, Janie had a full-scale emotional breakdown in the middle of the weekend. Having grown up around shopping malls, makeup, and all things pretty, camping was a bit of a culture shock for her. When she got tree sap and pine needles stuck in her hair, it was all over. Last year, Bradley had thrown a rather memorable temper tantrum, which ended in him flipping the food-prep table over. It wasn't even his first year. He had been stubbing his toes on tree roots, dealing with dirty clothes and bugs in his tent. It took a tiny little "suicide bug," as the kids called it, flying into the corner of his eye to set him off. He screamed obscenities about how ridiculous the whole weekend had been, stomped around in circles, slammed his fists, and eventually flipped the food-prep table into the dirt. It was the most severe reaction of any of the kids. Even Janie had done a better job of keeping her composure. She mostly just screamed when wildlife got near her and cried when her fingernails and hair got dirty on the first day, knowing that she wouldn't be able to shower for two more.

"I'll catch up with you later," Curtis said, slapping the door lightly and again skipping off down the hall to check his room for anything he might have missed on his first two checks.

He glanced around the room. His bed was made, and the covers had been pulled tight to avoid any creases or wrinkles. He had a stack of three novels on his nightstand: *The Call of the Wild, Into the Wild* and his newest addition, *A Walk in the Woods*. They all fit a theme: Curtis's theme, outdoor adventures. The blinds had been pulled open, letting the morning sun wrap the room in its joyful hug. His eyes moved across to Bradley's side of the room where the blinds were still pulled closed, his blankets had been crudely tossed overtop his bed simply to give the illusion of having been made, and an open can of stale pop sat on his nightstand with a *Sports Illustrated* magazine. The stark differences between them never failed to amuse Curtis.

Heading back into the hallway, Curtis called out a warning for the remaining stragglers to finish packing and get downstairs for breakfast. "Fifteen minutes!"

"Thanks for the warning, buddy," Marco said, walking quickly down the hall with his and Carol's bags in his arms, stopping briefly to put Curtis in a playful headlock. "You be easy on us this year. Let's not walk forty miles before we find a place to sleep, please?"

Curtis smiled devilishly and followed Marco downstairs. "It has to be a different spot each year so we chart new territory. That's half the fun in adventure camping."

In the dining room, Bradley sat huddled over a bowl of cereal. His gray Blue Jays T-shirt stretched tight across his shoulders, creating a ripple through the big, blue 15 and slightly obscuring the last name of Shawn Green, his favorite right fielder.

"Come on, Bradley! Look alive!" Curtis said. He clapped his hands excitedly as he bounced through the dining room and into the kitchen, bringing with him a burst of energy and noise. The door swooshed back and forth obnoxiously after him.

Bradley, half-awake, looked up from his bowl with a spoonful of Cheerios inches from his mouth and scowled. "Seriously, I am the only one actually eating breakfast already. *Buddy!*" he shouted so Curtis could hear him from the kitchen.

"WHAT'S THAT, BIG guy?" Tyler said, coming into the dining room from the kitchen with a plate of english muffins covered in a thick layer of Cheez Whiz.

"I'm eating. How much more alive does he want me to be?"

"Yeah, he's a little extreme this morning," Tyler said, sitting down across from Bradley.

"A little? You crazy?" Bradley said. Both boys laughed.

"Everyone hurry up and eat, so we can get this show on the road." Curtis pushed his way through the swinging door with a bowl of cereal and a piece of toast. He was wearing a half-untucked, brown-and-black plaid flannel shirt, with the sleeves rolled up to his elbows, overtop of a white T-shirt and faded blue jeans.

Tyler found himself staring at him, enjoying how much he resembled Chad. "Hey, Curtis, are there any hollowed-out trees in the forest?"

Curtis looked at him curiously. "Yeah, I guess so. Oddly, I'm not actually sure. Why?"

Tyler's cheeks flushed red. "Oh, just wondering." He laughed at the inside joke that only he understood.

IT TOOK A while, but Curtis eventually got everyone to finish eating and out the door. They had a long walk to the spot he'd picked out. He had spent many days walking into the forest to find the Knowing Tree and to ponder the best spot to set up camp. Carol had denied his request to force everyone to make their own shelters using trees and branches. He tried for weeks to convince her, but she wouldn't budge. She kept citing the risks involved and that they were supposed to avoid activities where they could get seriously cut and bleed while on Combivir. He needed to come up with a backup plan that would make up for having to sleep in tents, and there was only one spot where he could fully clear his head of all the clutter. That's where the Knowing Tree came in handy.

They walked for a little over an hour into the woods, past the Knowing Tree and past the small creek a little beyond it, before they came to a clearing that was lined with voluptuous pine trees of various ages. He had fallen in love with this space when he found it. The clearing was shaped like a crude circle and offered plenty of room for everyone to set their tents up around the center, where he imagined a large bonfire.

"Okay. First things first," Curtis said, stopping in the center of the circle and setting his rucksack down. Pointing to the middle of the clearing, he announced, "This is where the fire pit is going to be. We'll need people to head out and get some firewood and some to go off and grab rocks to circle the pit. Who wants to do what?"

Maggie raised her hand. "I'll take Theo to get firewood." She quickly took Theo by the hand and led him off into the woods before anyone could object. "I'm sure I saw a spot back a ways."

Curtis chuckled, knowing full well she was going to find a spot to pick up sticks that was far enough away that she would miss out on lugging any heavy rocks.

"I'm just gonna sit down for a few minutes, okay?" Tyler said, dropping down onto his rucksack.

Curtis frowned and took a deep breath. "You gotta give the experience a chance. Hunting and gathering is half of the experience of being in the wild," he said excitedly. He knew he was basically talking to a wall when it came to convincing Tyler to do something he didn't want to, but he had been taught to keep trying. This was his chance to show off his leadership skills.

Tyler sighed. "I will. I swear, Curtis, I want to have the whole experience. Save something for me to do. I just need to take a break. I'm beat. Let me dig the hole or something."

Curtis nodded. "Okay." He could hear a hint of urgency in Tyler's request, making his exhaustion seem genuine.

"YOU OKAY?" CAROL asked, stopping beside Tyler.

He wiped at the sweat dripping from his forehead. "Yeah, I'm just wiped. Not used to such crazy hikes." In truth, he was nauseous and felt like he was going to faint, and all the talking was making it worse.

She looked him over, trying to assess his level of fatigue. "Okay, just take it easy then," she said. She patted his shoulder and tossed her rucksack down beside him. "I'm an old lady, so I'll rest too." She plopped herself down. "I can micromanage from here just fine."

Marco laughed.

Carol's head snapped around to catch him. "What's funny over there, huh?"

"Oh, what? Me? I'm just—" Marco said, pointing at himself and spinning around to look for someone else to blame. "—going to go find some rocks for the fire pit." He chuckled as he dropped his rucksack and quickly scurried off into the woods. "Come and help me carry the heavy ones," he said, waving for Curtis and Bradley to follow.

Carol turned back to face Tyler, who was still dripping with sweat. "Are you sure you're okay? You're a mess."

"Ha, thanks. I try," he joked. "I'm fine. I'm just really hot. I'll be fine."

Carol continued to look him over nervously.

"I'll be fine. Just let it go," he said. He was irritated by her attentiveness. He liked that she cared, but he wished she wouldn't smother him with it. And with the heat, he was chafing and sweating and coming closer and closer to a temper tantrum every minute. "I just need time to relax and shake it off...in silence. Please."

Carol nodded and zipped her lips with her hand. They both leaned back and looked up.

Tyler watched the clouds slide across the sky, morphing into new shapes as they reached the edge of the trees that guarded them. He closed his eyes for a few moments, enjoying the burning feeling as they were wetted by his lids. When he woke, he first noticed that the sun had nearly set. Camp had been set up, the hole for the fire pit had been dug and a small fire was crackling in it. It took him a few seconds to realize where he was when he sat and saw the small tent city that circled him. He was lying in front of his own tent, which had been set up.

"Hey, you're awake," Curtis said, walking over and handing him a cup of coffee. "Here."

Tyler took the coffee and asked Curtis groggily, "Was I asleep all day?"

Curtis laughed. "Yeah, man. I've never seen someone sleep for an entire day just to get out of setting up their tent." He winked and nudged Tyler with his foot to let him know he was kidding. "Seriously, though. How are you? You looked rough before. Still do."

Tyler scoffed. "Thanks, jerk. I don't know what happened. I just felt awful. Just hearing people talk was making me feel like I was gonna ralph. The only thing that made it all go away was to close my eyes." He took a big gulp of coffee. "And thanks, I'm okay. I'm sorry I didn't dig the hole." He pointed at the fire.

"Oh, God. Forget about it. Take it easy. It's just a camping trip," Curtis said. "I make a big deal of it, but tell us if something's wrong."

"Sounds good. How about I fill the hole at the end of the weekend?"

"Works for me," Curtis said. "I'm gonna go get dinner started. I'll meet you over by the fire."

"Sure," Tyler said, groaning as he stood up. He picked his rucksack up and tossed it into his tent before heading over to sit by the fire.

Curtis was standing at the foldup table slicing potatoes, adding onions and garlic, and wrapping them individually in tinfoil. He called these his "rustic fire potatoes." Maggie was sitting near the fire, staring at the flames intently with an almost hypnotized glow in her eyes. Theo was with Carol, wrapped up in a blanket. Marco and Bradley were over by Bradley's tent talking. Tyler figured they were talking about college again. It seemed to be the only thing Bradley talked about anymore. It was like all of a sudden he had fallen in love with the idea of moving off and joining the world. Like he had decided there was a future after all.

"Hey," Tyler said, sitting down beside Maggie.

"Hey, sleepy." She smiled. "How was your nap?"

"It was lovely. It could have been longer, but I thought I'd grace you all with my presence for at least a few minutes this trip." He winked and nudged her leg playfully with his.

Maggie laughed. "Are you feeling okay? I've never seen anyone do that before."

"What? Sleep?"

"No," she said. "You know what I mean." When he didn't answer, she added, "You slept all day on the ground. It was almost scary how deeply asleep you were."

"I used to sleep on the ground all the time," Tyler said. "It must have been a comfortable reminder of where I come from."

Maggie pursed her lips and didn't respond.

"Are you okay?" he asked.

"It's nothing. I was just worried. I don't know how to explain it."

Tyler frowned. "I was just tired. I've never been that tired before."

Maggie returned her gaze to the flames. "I love watching them dance. It's soothing in a way."

Tyler agreed and leaned back into his chair, wrapping his arm around her and pulling her close. "I'm not going anywhere," he whispered.

She smiled.

Bradley and Marco joined the circle just as Curtis started putting the potatoes on the fire. The sun had nearly vanished by now, and with it, its warmth. Carol bundled Theo in a hoodie and sweatpants and wrapped him in a blanket. The temperature seemed to drop instantly as the sun disappeared.

"I'm freezing," Maggie said, hugging herself and rubbing her arms. "I think I need to put some pants on."

Curtis stood up to address the group, using his best authoritative tone. "Everyone best bundle up. Try not to get a chill."

"I'm fine," Tyler said, pulling the zipper on his sweater up. "These are my bundles."

"You seriously didn't bring anything warmer than that?" Curtis asked, frowning at Tyler who wore a pair of baggy shorts, a T-shirt, and a lightweight zippered hoodie.

"Well, how was I supposed to know that winter would come back in June?"

"This is Canada. What did you expect?" Bradley said from behind Tyler, laughing and squeezing his shoulders before stepping away from the group.

"God, Tyler. How reckless can you be? You could get sick," Curtis said.

"Ha! That's funny," Tyler said sarcastically. "I think that ship has sailed, dude." He laughed again.

"Don't worry, bud. We'll take care of ya," Bradley said, arriving back to the circle with a pair of track pants and a hoodie. "Wear these. I have a bunch of stuff with me, so it's cool."

"Thanks, man," Tyler said as he stood and took the clothes.

"No worries. Curtis forgets that not everybody is as organized as he is." Bradley gave Curtis a friendly wink. "Ain't that right?"

"We have to be smart about our health. It's important. More so for us than for some regular person going camping. You can't screw around with this," Curtis said.

"I know, Curtis. I know. Relax. I'll get changed." Tyler backed away, mocking a fearful submission.

Curtis stoked the fire. "Good."

CAROL CAME OVER, sensing an argument. "What's the problem?" She stopped Tyler from walking away and looked to Curtis for the honest answer.

Curtis fumbled with his words. "It's fine. Bradley gave him something to wear."

Carol turned her gaze to Tyler. Her eyes were fierce, and her mouth was curled into a tiny *O* as she inhaled and tried to keep her cool. "You didn't bring anything warm to wear? Tyler!? Where's your head?" Her voice was harsh. Her hands trembled by her side. She cleared her throat and closed her eyes to keep from shouting.

"It's okay, Carol," Bradley offered. "I gave him in a pair of sweats that I brought and a sweatshirt that will fit under his hoodie. He'll be fine."

She knew he was trying to help, but she couldn't let this go. Not after what the doctor had told them barely a week before. She only agreed to allow Tyler to come on the camping trip because Marco and Dr. Benson had convinced her that Tyler's condition was getting worse, and that it might be the last chance for him to get out and have some fun with the other kids.

"What's the point anyway?" Tyler said angrily. "Does it even matter if I do everything right? I'm still *sick*. And now I'm *dying*." He stomped his foot as he shouted.

"Don't say that. Do you really want to speed this up? Are you trying to get worse?" Carol wanted to walk away from the argument, but now that she'd started, she didn't know how to stop. She was infuriated with him.

"Carol—" Bradley tried to calm them down, but she waved him off.

"It's like you're just giving up." Her voice cracked as she fought off the urge to cry.

Tyler flinched and brought his hand up to rub his chest, right where she knew his lesions were. "No, I'm not. Can I just go get changed please?" Tyler's eyes were moist now and glistened in the campfire light.

"Fine." Carol waved her hand dismissively. "Go."

After Tyler stomped off to his tent, Maggie finally spoke. "Is it true? Is he dying?" She had tears streaming down her cheeks but was managing to keep her voice steady. She wiped aggressively at her cheeks. "Tyler told me that it was nothing serious, and that it would clear up with medicine."

Carol turned to Maggie, realizing what she'd done. She hadn't meant for everyone to find out like this. She frowned. "I'm sorry. Let's all forget about this for right now. He's not doing well, but there's always hope. We just have to keep him positive and mindful of his health. It's just one of the sucky realities of this disease." She excused herself to her tent before any further questions could be asked, and so she could cry in private.

THE NEXT DAY, Curtis led the group in survival activities. He had gotten Carol to agree to let them build a shelter using the items they could find in the forest. She had been reluctant to allow them to sleep in them, but she did see the benefit in having everyone partake in building one as a group. Curtis prefaced the activity by telling them all that this will save their lives should they ever find themselves lost in the woods.

"I'm pretty sure Curtis is the only one here who will ever end up in a situation like that," Tyler said, leaning into Maggie. The temperature hadn't fully rebounded, so he still wore Bradley's sweatpants and hoodie.

The group was kept busy for the entire day with building the shelter. For Tyler's part, he did not take any breaks. He made sure he was actively participating from start to finish. Curtis was impressed with Tyler. He knew Tyler didn't want to miss out again and have it look like he was purposely wimping out on the camping weekend. He also knew that Tyler wanted to care about the trip just because it was important to him.

Following the shelter being built, Curtis announced that they would be playing a game of hide-and-seek. Curtis gave Theo a wink during this speech, knowing that the person who would get the most out of the game was him. They played right up until it was time to get ready for dinner. Marco and Curtis prepared the meal while everyone else took time to either journal or quietly reflect on the day. This was something Carol had mandated for everyone. She told them that she wanted each of them to try to find something out about themselves that they didn't already know. She even included Curtis's Knowing Tree into the exercise, telling them all to go and find it at some point and let it guide them, which totally thrilled Curtis. They spent the rest of the evening gathered around the campfire, telling stories and singing songs. Curtis strummed on his guitar, and Marco used branches as drum sticks.

As the sun set, a damp chill washed its way through camp. Tyler still wore Bradley's outfit and now wrapped himself in a blanket. Despite the roaring fire, he couldn't keep from shivering.

Tyler was the first to go to bed. Carol forced him to go to his tent so she could wrap him in an extra blanket. His teeth chattered uncontrollably as she tucked the blanket around him.

"He's shivering more than I'm comfortable with," she whispered to Marco when she came out of the tent. "I think we should consider taking him back to the house. It's too dangerous." She found herself wishing they'd never brought him camping in the first place.

"We'll keep an eye on him, but I think you're right. You should talk to Curtis. Get him on board, so he doesn't feel like we're hijacking his last camping weekend," Marco said as he rubbed her back. She leaned into him and took a deep breath, enjoying the peppery scent of his skin.

Carol thought about the promise she'd made to Tyler, that he would love camping. She didn't want to steal this from him. "Let's just wait for now and see how he does tomorrow." She and Marco returned to the fire to sit with the other kids, though she kept her eyes fixed on Tyler's tent as though she were expecting some kind of crisis to unfold.

"CAROL, ARE YOU okay?" Maggie asked, taking note of her distance. She followed Carol's gaze to Tyler's tent. "Is he okay?"

Carol shook her head. "He's fine, dear. I'm just lost in my thoughts."

Maggie watched Carol intently to judge whether she was being honest or not. She determined that she was lying. Carol never made eye contact when she was lying, and she wouldn't make it now. "It's dangerous for him to be out here, isn't it?" She could feel her chest tightening as she grew anxious.

Carol shook her head again. "Not always." She looked her in the eyes this time, making Maggie feel relieved for a moment before she looked away again and said, "I'm sure he's fine."

Maggie sat worrying about Tyler and planning out the argument she wanted to have with him for being so careless as to refuse to bring anything warm to wear. She was already irritated that Bradley was the one, of all people, to give him clothes to wear. She hated seeing him in Bradley's sweatpants and sweater. She wondered if Tyler liked wearing them, but shook the thought from her head almost as quickly as she'd let it enter. *He hates Bradley,* she reminded herself. She didn't even know how to begin planning the argument about him lying to her about what the doctor had said. Why had he hidden it from her? It seemed so unfair.

THE NEXT DAY it started to rain. They set up a tarp so they could have somewhere dry to sit other than their tents. They made a few treks into the woods to play hide-and-seek as the angry-looking clouds offered a plethora of shadows and dark corners to hide in.

Tyler spent most of the day sleeping and woke only to eat dinner, which he did groggily and with minimal enthusiasm. When Curtis tried to get him to stay up after lunch, he explained that, to him, the air seemed to be filled with a haze that not only affected his vision but his hearing. "It's like everything you're saying is muffled, like you're talking into the wind. It's exhausting having to ask everyone to repeat themselves. I just need to lie down."

Curtis nodded and forced a smile, wishing that things were different.

"I feel like this is the worst camping trip we've gone on," Curtis said, sitting beside Bradley on the log he was using as a bench. He was frowning and had lost the upbeat spunk that had been driving Bradley insane for the last three months. He stared across the campfire to see Carol leading Tyler to his tent to encourage him to lie down again. From this angle, Tyler appeared to be fifty years his senior with the way he shuffled along with his hunched over and feeble movements.

Bradley gently slapped his friend on the shoulder. "It's okay. Just take a step back and appreciate it for what it is."

Curtis leaned away and stared at him in surprise. "Are you friggin' kidding me?!" he said, laughing. "Where the hell did you learn that crap?"

"Oh, some old guy said it to me when I was freaking out once," Bradley said, nudging him with his elbow.

Curtis sighed. "We're the same age."

"Actually, you're a month older than me. Face it. You're an old guy." He pushed Curtis's shoulder. "The trip is still a lot of fun. Tyler's not feeling well, the weather sucks, but no one has freaked out and the bugs aren't making anyone cry. You should count your blessing in a way."

Curtis rolled his eyes. "Yes, I should definitely count my blessings that the most butch guy here isn't running around squealing that bugs are touching him." He nudged Bradley back playfully. Both boys laughed for a moment before their attention drifted back to Tyler and Carol. She was checking his temperature with her hand, and he was trying to swat it away. Marco was nearby, holding an extra blanket that they could only assume was going to be wrapped around Tyler once they finally forced him to bed. An unsettling thought came to Curtis then. *I wonder if they're only staying out here because of me.*

"He looks really sick," Bradley said, interrupting Curtis's thoughts before he could delve too deeply into them.

"Yeah." Curtis looked down. He fidgeted with his hands and kicked at the dirt.

"What's up?" Bradley tapped his foot against Curtis's to get his attention.

"I just don't know if I should cancel this whole thing."

Bradley shook his head. "No."

"Tyler's sick. If I'd known, I never would have brought everyone out here. You know?"

"Yeah, but you can't cancel it. You've been planning this all year."

"I have. But I won't be able to live with myself if Tyler gets worse...or..."

Bradley scoffed. "Seriously? Don't go there. Just because he's sick doesn't mean he's going to die." He knew he'd said it too loud when Curtis shrunk in his seat as though to avoid being seen by the others. As a gut reaction, Bradley shrunk as well. "Sorry," he said quickly.

"He's sicker than you and me. His immune system is way more challenged, so we have to be aware that it really *could* mean death for him if he were to get too sick," Curtis whispered. "It makes me sick to think of it."

"You're the man. I'll support whatever you decide," Bradley said. He paused for a moment before adding, "Just don't whine to me all year that you didn't like your last big camping trip at the house when we get back and find out that he was just being a pussy."

When Carol stepped back out of Tyler's tent, Curtis was waiting for her. "I think we should head back first thing tomorrow," he said before turning and walking away, not waiting for a response. His decision had been made. Leaders have to make sacrifices for the greater good of the group.

Chapter Fifty-One

"HOW ARE YOU feeling?" Carol asked, motioning for Tyler to take a seat on the examination table. She ordered him to come up for a physical as soon as they got back from camping, but he went for a nap instead and slept from the time they got back until after dinnertime. She finally went and forced him to get up and follow her to the exam room. If she wasn't so concerned, she would have lectured him for it.

"I'm all right," Tyler said. "Just tired...and freezing. And that annoying cough is back." He shivered and rubbed his hands on his arms to warm himself up. He was wearing a zip-up hoodie and heavy sweatpants. "Are you cold?"

Carol scoffed. "I have hot flashes every other hour. I think I've forgotten what it means to be cold." She pulled out her stethoscope and put the tips in her ears. "Take off your shirt, please."

Tyler unzipped the sweater to reveal his chest for her to place the cold chest piece on. "I wore this sweater so I wouldn't have to freeze." He smiled as she listened.

Carol tried her best not to look at the lesions that he was trying to hide with the hoodie. "Take a deep breath and exhale slowly." She slid her arm around him to place the piece on his back without making him take his shirt off. "Again." She listened intently, keeping her expression blank as she did. She picked up her notepad and jotted down some shorthand that he couldn't make out. "I'm going to call Dr. Benson. I think he needs to come in and check you out. Your lungs sound like they're holding fluid again. And you look like hell." She frowned as his shoulders sank. He seemed to have aged many years over the course of the camping trip.

"Okay," Tyler said. "Is it bad?" He zipped up his sweater and shivered again. His eyes had dark circles forming around them despite the sleep he had gotten.

Carol shook her head. "I don't know, Tyler. With everything Dr. Benson said the other day, I just don't know. We have to remain positive, though."

Tyler laughed. "That won't be hard."

Carol glared at him. "You know what I mean."

"Jeez, take a joke."

"I'm sorry. I'm having a hard time finding the fun in any of this right now. I'm genuinely worried." She placed her hand on his shoulder. He felt very thin despite his sweater.

"Marco, Bradley, and Curtis left this morning for London. They'll be back Monday night. They're off to find an apartment."

"Yeah, I remember them talking about how early they had to wake up to catch their flight."

Carol smiled. "Yes. They had a lot of complaining to do this morning when I drove them to the airport. It was comical because I also had to wake up but for no benefit."

"Peace and quiet for a weekend. That sounds like a pretty great benefit."

"You're right. There's an upside to that for sure. Speaking of peace and quiet...I want you to take it easy. Take lots of calories. You're too thin."

"Ouch," Tyler said jokingly. "I worked hard for this physique."

"Go binge watch some *Party of Five* or something," Carol said, waving him off.

He blushed. "That one time I watched it...jeez." He laughed and then quietly said, "I might."

"I want you to rest," she said sternly. "I'm not kidding about that."

"I might work some more on my memoir." He stood and followed her toward the door.

She looked at him suspiciously. "I thought you handed that in already? You were supposed to before the trip."

"I did," he said. "I think I can expand on parts. I've decided it's a living document." He coughed weakly and then let out a deep, chest-rattling cough. He covered his mouth with his hand and felt the warm spray of phlegm wet his skin.

Carol frowned. "Go to bed first. I'll call Dr. Benson and see if he can come in soon."

"And I'll write up a storm."

She smiled as she pulled the exam room door closed behind them. "You're going to make a mighty fine writer one day."

He stood a little taller. "Thanks. I think I just have the one book in me, though, like this is the book I'm meant to write."

"I look forward to reading it. Maybe that's what I'll do while Marco is away." She led him to the stairs and down to his room, tucked him into bed, and drew the curtains closed. He succumbed weakly and closed his eyes before she could insist again that he should sleep. She stood watching him for a long time after he fell asleep. His breathing was labored. He looked so peaceful yet sad. She sighed and switched off the light to leave him undisturbed.

Chapter Fifty-Two

"WHAT A DAY," Carol said as she, Marco, Bradley, and Curtis walked into the front foyer. She tossed her car keys in the glass bowl that sat on the stand near the door. She had waited for their flight to get in for more than an hour longer than expected.

"The delays were crazy. I can't imagine waiting for that long with nothing to do," Bradley said, sighing as he tossed his bag down on the floor.

Carol pointed at it. "Bring that upstairs. I don't want to find it down here when I head up to bed later."

"But it's so much closer to the laundry room here."

"Whining will get you nowhere." She pointed at the bag again. "Upstairs with it."

"Fine." Bradley sighed, picked up the bag, and slowly made his way upstairs.

"I can't wait to sleep," Curtis said, grabbing his bag and heading toward the stairs. "Thanks for picking us up, Carol. Good night." He waved as he started up the stairs.

She smiled and waved back. "My pleasure. Good night."

"Why can't they all be polite like that?" Marco said quietly, smiling as he did.

Carol laughed. "Seriously."

He tossed his bag down on the floor where Bradley had initially placed his. "I'll bring it up when we go," he said defensively before she could say anything.

She walked toward the fancy living room. "So how'd it go?"

"It went really well. I'm surprised how easily they came to agree on a place."

"Those two get along so well, it scares me sometimes," she said. "Curtis has a way with Bradley that I don't think anyone ever has."

Marco nodded. "They seem to really respect each other. It's great to see. It's sad that they'll be so far away."

"They better be coming home for holidays. They don't just give up their family because they're college boys." She waved her finger in the air like a school teacher. "I won't have that."

They took a seat on the couch in the fancy living room. The coffee table was covered in papers. Sitting prominently in the middle of the papers was an unopened bottle of red wine. "Would you like a glass?" Marco said, pointing at it.

Carol waved dismissively. "I don't think I'll have any. I just had it out in case I felt in the mood when we got back from the drive. I think it will put me right to sleep."

Marco stopped in his tracks, staring at her. "Carol Taylor turning down wine. Well, I never..."

"Oh, hush." She laughed. "I'm reading Tyler's memoir. It doesn't feel right to drink while I read it."

Marco nodded and picked a stack of pages up and read a few sentences. "Seems like deep stuff."

"Yeah. It's pretty heavy, but it's good." She leaned back into the couch. "Tell me more about the trip, the apartment, the school."

"They're going to get into so much trouble," he said excitedly.

She frowned.

"Good trouble, but trouble. It's going to be so refreshing for them to experience the world again out from under the stigma of their disease. They don't have to wear it like a badge there because they'll be anonymous. I almost envy them the opportunity to start anew, but I wouldn't give up what we have here for anything in the world." He reached out and held her hands. "This is where I want to be, but I can definitely see the allure of a big city."

"That will be really great for them. I'm sure it will provide new challenges in learning how and when to share their status with people. But I think they'll do just fine."

Marco smiled. "A chance to be normal."

"And how will the apartment details work?"

"We are signed on as the guarantors. We have to send a copy of the lease to the agency we're getting the funding grant through to make sure there are no hiccups. I think it's going to be a great thing."

Carol breathed nervously. She didn't want to imagine any of the kids leaving the house. "They're our first kids to move off to college. It's kind of scary. I'm excited for them but terrified."

Marco leaned forward and kissed her forehead. "It's a big moment for all of us." He pulled away and smiled at her and said, "The evolution of our family."

She smiled back. "I called Dr. Benson. He's been swamped with other patients. Says he'll be in tomorrow. He couldn't get away from his other patients before then."

"How's Tyler doing? I was pretty worried while we were away."

"His lungs don't sound good. He's been sleeping mostly since you left."

"Wow," Marco said, "That's a lot of sleeping."

She nodded. "I'm worried."

No sooner had she said she was worried did Bradley appear in the living room, his face as pale as snow.

"Bradley, what is it?" she asked, standing up quickly.

"I was going back to my room after brushing my teeth, and I can hear Tyler coughing really bad. I went in and got Theo out and put him in our room with Curtis." He paused to catch his breath. "It sounds really bad. Like I think you need to come check him."

"We're coming," Carol said. She rushed quickly past him.

He stepped aside to let her by easily. "I tried talking to him, but he couldn't even answer me. He just kept coughing."

"Thanks, Bradley," Marco said, patting him on the shoulder. "We'll take care of him." He rushed after Carol to Tyler's room.

BRADLEY FOLLOWED CLOSE behind and stood in the doorway to watch. Tyler's coughs sounded wet and full, and each one made Bradley flinch.

"I need my stethoscope. Bradley, can you run and grab it please? And a thermometer. And an icepack," Carol said, turning to face him. Her voice was loud and urgent.

"Yeah, of course. I'll be right back." He turned and ran up to the third floor and dug through the examination room in a hurried frenzy. On the way back downstairs, he skipped every other step to get there faster. Marco met him at the door. "Here it is," he said as he handed over an armful of supplies.

Tyler was moaning in discomfort now and twisting around in the bed. The sight of him terrified Bradley, but he couldn't do anything but stand and stare.

Carol attempted to listen to his lungs while Marco took his temperature. She rubbed her hand on his forehead, wiping the sweat away and smoothing his hair down while cooing to him. "Shhh, shhh. It's okay, sweetie. You're going to be okay."

"We need to move him into the quarantine room," Marco said as he pulled the thermometer from Tyler's mouth.

"What is it?" Carol asked, looking up briefly while continuing to rub Tyler's forehead.

Tyler moaned again and coughed. Phlegm sprayed from his uncovered mouth and stuck to his lip.

Carol wiped it away.

"We need to get him cooled down. Fast. It's at one-o-three." Marco frowned and looked over at Bradley. "Go on to bed, please. Thank you for all your help. We're going to get Tyler into the quarantine room down the hall. You don't have anything to worry about. We just need to get him to a sterilized environment."

Bradley nodded. He still didn't know what to say. He backed away slowly, still staring at Tyler. He could only wonder in horror, *Is that what it's going to be like for all of us?*

Chapter Fifty-Three

THE QUARANTINE ROOM—Tyler's new room—was next to Carol and Marco's. It was easily self-contained. The decorations were plain. The bed had buttons to raise the head or foot. They had acquired a mobile bed table from the hospital when they first put the room in the house. It sat pushed to the side, awaiting his lunch, which Carol had asked Marco to prepare when the doctor was gone.

The only way in or out of the quarantine room was through a six-foot-long by four-foot-wide glass box that went from floor to ceiling, just inside the door of the room, that they called the sanitization chamber. Marco used to complain that they had gone overboard with it, but Carol remained adamant that they needed a quarantine room just like it if not better. The sanitization chamber was there so that anyone entering the room could disinfect their hands and put on protective gear before going any further if they were sick. They'd put it in as a sort of panic room in case one of the kids fell ill and needed extra protection for their weakened immune system like Tyler now did. They never considered what would happen if two kids got sick at the same time and hoped they'd never have to. This was the first time they ever had to use it. And perhaps the more somber reason for adding the room was to be able to qualify as a hospice. They didn't want any of the kids to have to die in a hospital, away from everyone they knew. The quarantine room allowed them the dark fortune of dying at home.

DR. BENSON ENTERED the room from the sanitization chamber. He moved to Tyler's bedside and checked his pulse. "Pulse seems normal. That's good." He shuffled Carol out of the way so he could check his vitals. He was hooked up to the heart monitor, and a breathing tube was strung under his nose.

"It took us nearly an hour to get his temperature down last night. The fever was very high. He gave us quite a scare."

"Hi, doc," Tyler said weakly. He opened his eyes to see the familiar face. He looked fatter than he did the last time he had seen him.

"You've gotten skinny," Dr. Benson said, gently squeezing his wrist. "All skin and bones."

Tyler allowed himself a fleeting moment of hope that this was all simply due to extreme weight loss.

Dr. Benson removed his stethoscope from his bag and listened to Tyler's lungs with a morose expression glued to his face. "Hm," he said. "Hm."

Tyler closed his eyes. They burned when he shut them, but it felt worse to have them open.

"Just rest. I'll do my tests. You don't need to talk," Dr. Benson said as he lifted Tyler's gown to check his torso and the lesions, to see if they had spread since the last visit. He kept his expression flat to keep from exposing his feelings. "Have you noticed shortness of breath throughout the month before you got sick?"

Tyler thought about it for a moment and then nodded. "A little."

Dr. Benson frowned. "Okay, big guy. Thank you. I'm going to go outside and talk to Carol and Marco, but first I'm going to get Carol to draw some blood. We need to determine if your counts and white blood cells are high enough to allow for chemotherapy, okay?"

Tyler nodded again and swallowed.

Dr. Benson moved out of Carol's way as she moved in to take the samples. "It's going to be a little prick."

"Well then I'm not interested," Tyler said, laughing weakly. He winced and coughed. "Oh, don't make me laugh."

"That was all you, you dirty bird. Keep your mind out of the gutter, and maybe you won't hurt yourself." She slid the needle into his vein and collected the samples, five vials. When she was done, she taped his arm with a cotton ball and pressed her hand over the wound firmly. "We'll be back soon." She followed Marco and Dr. Benson into the sanitization chamber.

"I'M VERY CONCERNED," Dr. Benson said as soon as the door clicked shut. "I'm going to get these samples to the lab right away. I'll swing by on my way back to town." He took the Ziploc baggie that Carol had placed the vials in. "I can't know by looking at him, but my guess is that chemo won't be an option right now. We'll see what the lab says."

"Is there something you'd like us to give him for the fever?" Marco asked, reaching his hand out and squeezing Carol's shoulder. "Last night was tough. He was very uncomfortable and moaning in pain. If it happens again…"

Dr. Benson reached into his bag. "I suggest we administer trimethoprim and sulfamethoxazole. I think Bactrim will be the best option here. I will send over a prescription. I brought some tablets here with me on the off chance. I'm sorry that we have to use them. I fear that he has Pneumocystis pneumonia. To make a formal diagnosis, I'd have to order a chest X-ray, but I'm not sure I want to take him out of here and to the hospital in his current condition. He's exhibiting all of the symptoms, so I'm going to go out on a limb here and say that PCP is what we're dealing with."

Carol closed her eyes to keep from crying and took a deep breath. Marco squeezed her shoulder a little tighter.

"I think we should get an intravenous drip hooked up to keep him hydrated. Perhaps, you can get that set up today. Do you have the drip bags?"

Marco nodded. "Yes, we do. We have a full stock of everything. Perhaps you could request the hospital send some more over in a week?"

"Sure. I can do that. I'll let you get back in there with him. I'll call you when I know more."

"I'll show you out," Marco said, opening the door for him.

"Thank you." He turned to Carol. "I wish this were under more pleasant circumstances. Take care."

"Thank you, doctor," Carol said, waving and pushing the door closed behind them. She turned to the sink and scrubbed down before reentering Tyler's room. She sat on the edge of his bed and took his hand in hers. "Sweetie, are you awake?"

He blinked his eyes open. "Yeah. I am."

"I'm sorry you invested so much to have me here only for me to screw it all up," Tyler said. He took a deep breath, trying to stop his tears. "It's all my fault."

"Having you here is the best investment we ever made," Carol said with conviction. "Don't ever doubt that." She grabbed his hands and squeezed tight, staring intensely into his eyes. "And none of this is your fault. Life happens, and we have no control over that. The only thing we have control of is how we deal with it, and you brought yourself here, so I'd say you're dealing with it pretty well."

Tyler's bottom lip began to quiver violently as he fought back tears. "I'm scared."

She held her breath.

"I don't want to die," he said. He began to sob uncontrollably. "I don't even know what I believe. I need more time. Please don't let me die. *Please.*"

Carol struggled to control her breathing. Tears filled her eyes. "Tyler...I..."

"*Please*," he begged. Tears stained his cheeks. He squeezed her hands tightly. "What's going to happen to me? Where'm I gonna go?" His voice was shrill and desperate.

Carol gasped for a breath and held her hand over her mouth as she tried to keep herself together. "Tyler, sweetie. I don't know. I don't know. We're going to do everything we can. I promise. I promise you." She took a deep breath and held it again and willed her tears to stop. She couldn't think of anything else to say.

He wrapped his arms around her tightly, hugging her and burying his face in her shirt. His fingers pinched the skin on her back as he clung to her.

She welcomed the pain as it distracted her from crying.

"I'm not ready," he said, sobbing. "I'm not ready."

Chapter Fifty-Four

THE HOUSE HAD quieted significantly since Tyler had fallen ill. Curtis and Bradley had all but forgotten that they were moving at the end of the summer. They spent most of their time outside in the back fields tossing the football around or watching the world beyond the row of maples speed by as if nothing else mattered. Maggie spent most days teaching Theo to read or watching *Rugrats* on constant repeat. Marco would move between kids, talking to them and trying to keep on top of how they were feeling while keeping the house running, preparing meals and ensuring that everyone went to bed on time. The constant bickering and laughter was absent from the house, and for the first time, Marco found himself understanding its nickname: *the Death House*. It never seemed more relevant than in these quiet moments when he stood in the empty living room. The lights in all of the common areas were off and had been for most of the month. Nobody wanted to accept reality, so everybody either hid in their rooms or outside until it was time to eat and then they disappeared again.

Carol practically never left Tyler's side. Most nights, she would sleep in the chair beside his bed. From time to time, Marco was able to convince her to join the house for dinner or to come to bed with him. He even purchased a baby monitor that they left in Tyler's room to persuade her that she could leave him long enough to sleep and spend time with the others, but she was never really present unless she was with him.

IT WAS JULY 23, and summer was nearly half-done. The kids hadn't been able to see or talk to Tyler since he was put into quarantine on June 28.

"Tyler, I'm going to raise your head up a bit," Carol said, reaching her hand to the button on the side of the bedframe. "It might be nice to sit up for part of the day today?"

Tyler opened his eyes slowly, squinting. "Maybe just a little bit, okay?" he said weakly. "I don't feel too good." He shifted to balance himself on his elbows while she raised the head of the bed about eight inches. "That's good," he said, letting himself fall back against the pillow. He was drained of energy from having held himself up for those thirty seconds that it took for Carol to raise the bed.

Carol slid her hand from the button, moving it up to rest it on his forearm. "Would you like some ice? How's your mouth?"

"Yes, please."

Carol reached down to the mini fridge beside the bed and retrieved a small metal container of ice cubes from the freezer compartment. She had taken to giving him crushed ice a week earlier when the thrush had gotten worse. He kept complaining about a constant burning sensation in his mouth and throat. The ice seemed to work to soothe the pain.

"Thank you," he said, opening his mouth as she spooned some of the ice in. Her hands smelled like marijuana. He smiled. "You toked early today."

She let out a short laugh, pulling her hand away and placing the spoon and ice bucket onto the bedside table. It clanged and rattled as she set it harder than she intended. "A girl's gotta cope."

Tyler's bronchial tubes rattled as he laughed, and so he coughed. He covered his mouth with his hand. When he pulled his hand away from his mouth, she noticed a small spatter of blood. Her heartbeat quickened as she snatched up a few tissues to wipe his hand. Seeing him deteriorate before her eyes was more difficult than she had imagined it would be.

"I'm sorry," he said. Embarrassed, he looked away and toward the window on the other side of the room.

"Don't be silly. There's nothing to be sorry about," Carol said as she finished wiping his hand and tossed the tissues into the garbage. She was glad for this moment to catch her breath. Without him looking at her, she could take her deep breaths to regain composure unnoticed. She could see that the Kaposi's sarcoma lesions had spread. He had one on his hairline near his right ear, she could see two on his neck and one on his throat near his collarbone, and several now dotted his arms.

He turned to face her again. "Thank you for being here."

"Of course, sweetheart. I wouldn't be anywhere else." She squeezed his arm gently. She wanted to turn away so he couldn't see her cry, but she kept his gaze.

"Don't do that," Tyler said, pleading with a faint chuckle. He placed his left hand over Carol's.

She laughed and wiped the tears. "I can't help it sometimes. You've become a great friend, and I hate seeing you like this."

Tyler forced a shaky smile. "You know. You're the mom I always wanted. I never got the chance to have a mom who taught me anything."

"Oh, seriously. Don't do *that*," Carol said, rolling her eyes.

"It's true. My mom hid behind her bible and allowed my dad to torture me with it. She never stood up and told me what was right or that she loved me or that she wanted me to be happy. Nothing. I never had that until I came here... Until I met you."

Carol squeezed his arm again, this time with both hands. "You're a jerk. You know that?" she said, tears now dripping from her cheeks onto the metal hand rail on the side of the bed. She leaned back in her chair, wiping her eyes with both hands. "How can you tell me not to cry and then say stuff like that?"

"Why hasn't anyone else come in to see me?" Tyler asked after a few moments of silence.

"They want to. We don't have the masks and coverings yet. Marco is working on getting them from the hospital."

"Why can you come in then? That doesn't make a lot of sense. Is it that they don't want to?"

"They want to. Believe that. I think they're driving Marco nuts with how much they ask. He's doing everything he can. The first couple of weeks, you were really sick, so we couldn't risk it at all."

"I'm still really sick."

"That's true, but you're conscious for more of the day now. You were sleeping most of the time the first couple weeks in here." She felt like she was making excuses.

"I guess that all luck runs out eventually. Good, bad, it doesn't matter," Tyler said. He blinked, fatigue setting in. "I think I'll take a nap if it's okay."

"Sure it is. I'll be here. I've been reading a new book," Carol said, tapping the cover of *Fried Green Tomatoes at the Whistle Stop Café* by Fannie Flagg. She knew she'd read a little bit but mostly she would watch Tyler as he slept. It's how she put herself to sleep most days now. She would watch his chest rise and fall with each breath. Sometimes, he would take a small breath and, before exhaling, he would follow it up with an exaggerated, deep breath. She found the rhythm soothing. He looked so peaceful when he was asleep and so pained when he was awake.

"Can I have a little bit more ice to fall asleep with?"

"Definitely." She spooned some more ice into his mouth.

"Thank you." He closed his eyes and sucked on the ice.

She stood and kissed him on the forehead, surprising even herself. She wasn't the type to be this nurturing. "Sleep well, little angel," she whispered.

Chapter Fifty-Five

THE RADIO WAS on quietly in the corner to break the deafening silence that had been following Marco around all summer. He was sitting at the desk in the office reading through a thick file of papers, wearing his thick, rectangular framed reading glasses and with a highlighter in his hand and the lid in his mouth. He was researching medications and possible treatments to ask Dr. Benson about.

"Wow, you really did good work on this place," Bradley said from the doorway.

Marco perked up, glad that someone was finally present. "It's been an uneventful month. I've had a bit of time to obsessively clean."

"Yeah, I remember when we couldn't see the walls or desk because of all the papers and boxes. Seriously, the place looks great." Bradley looked around the unrecognizable office. The boxes with old files and papers had been moved up to the attic for storage. The round meeting table was now in the far corner. A couple of armchairs and a small coffee table sat on a round throw rug in the center of the room. Everything was dusted, swept, mopped, and decluttered.

Bradley sat in one of the chairs. "I wanted to talk to you about Tyler."

"Okay, sure," Marco said, getting up from the desk and moving to sit next to him. "What's on your mind?"

"I think you and I should drive to the hospital to pick up the gowns and other attire they seem to be incapable of sending over."

"I think we need to let the hospital take care of its process. We can't interfere with them. They'll get the stuff to us."

Bradley, frustrated, raised his voice as he spoke. "You don't get it, though. We need to go in there. Curtis is beating himself up every day because he thinks it's all his fault, and nothing any of us says is gonna change that. And Maggie barely talks to anyone but Theo; she's shut right down. And I think that if anyone is gonna get Tyler to snap out of it, it's me. I just have to challenge his ego a couple times, and he'll jump out of that stupid bed." His eyes were red and wet. "We need to go in there. And if we can just drive to the hospital to get the stuff, they won't be able to say no. *Please.* Let us in to see him."

In this moment, Marco was impressed by Bradley. "The hospital hasn't said no. They're understocked. I'll talk to Dr. Benson today. Maybe he'll have some extras. He's coming in to see Tyler later, so let me see if he thinks Tyler's immune system is doing better and then we can maybe even skip the masks and hospital garb."

Bradley's eyes lit up. "Really? You think we could?"

"Let me talk to Carol and Dr. Benson first. Don't go telling anyone yet because it might be that you and I have to make a trip to the hospital. Let's just wait and see."

"Deal. I'll keep it under wraps if you promise to get us in there soon. It's torture to know he's behind that door but we can't go in."

"I know it is. He's lonely. He's been asking about you guys, so he'll be happy to have the company. We just don't want to compromise his immune system any further than it already is."

"Thanks, Marco. You'd be doing us a solid by letting us deal with it. You know? We're all just bottled up with stuff. So thanks." He stood and walked to the door. Before exiting, he turned to Marco and said, "I've never wanted someone to be happy more than I want it for Curtis. He's my best friend, my brother. I don't want him to live with regret about this. He thinks Tyler blames him."

Marco nodded, signaling that he understood. After Bradley left, Marco leaned back in the chair and stared at the desk across the room with the open file next to his coffee mug. "Damn it," he said, tossing the highlighter to the desk. It clacked off the top and onto the floor. "Great. Of course," he said, defeated. "Gimme a break... something... *come on.*" Feeling as though the walls were caving in around him, he threw his hands up to cover his face and screamed.

Chapter Fifty-Six

"KNOCK, KNOCK." DR. Benson announced himself as he poked his head through the sterilization chamber door into Tyler's room.

"Hi, come on in." Carol sat up in her chair and set her novel down.

He stepped inside and closed the door behind him, leaving Marco in the sterilization chamber washing his hands and arms. Dr. Benson wore a mask, covering his signature graying mustache, and a pair of blue rubber gloves. "Thank you, Carol. I'll just do a few checks on Tyler's vitals, and then we can all have a chat." He moved over to the bed and placed his medical bag between Tyler's knees. "Hi there, kiddo."

"Hey," Tyler said. His voice was raspy from his dry mouth and throat. He grimaced, his discomfort obvious.

"Let's get you some ice," Dr. Benson said, reaching down to the fridge and pulling the bucket of ice from the freezer. He took a scoop and placed it inside Tyler's reddened mouth and upon his lumpy tongue. "Your mouth and throat are looking a little rough. Perhaps we can get a moderate painkiller prescribed to help with any discomfort you're feeling. We'll take good care of you." His eyes were pulled into a squint as he smiled warmly beneath the mask.

"Thanks," Tyler said, nodding. He looked wearily at the doctor's mask and gloves.

Dr. Benson held his hands up as if to show off the attire. "Oh yes, excuse me please. I have a bit of a cold right now, so even though I've sterilized, I feel it is prudent that I add the extra protection for you." He unzipped his medical bag and removed a stethoscope and manual-inflation blood pressure monitor and then set them on the bed next to Tyler's legs. He performed his checks of Tyler's vitals methodically, checking the heart monitor and intravenous drip before packing his items back into his bag. He took a seat in the chair Carol had been claiming since Tyler had fallen ill.

Carol and Marco moved to the other side of the bed. She stood by the head of the bed, holding Tyler's wrist with one hand and rubbing the top of his head with the other. Marco stood beside her, gripping the brace bar tightly.

"You're making me nervous," Marco said, loosening his grip on the bar.

Dr. Benson folded his hands in his lap before beginning. "I got the results of Tyler's blood work yesterday. And given the severity of the thrush and lesions he has, it is not looking good. I'm very sorry."

Tyler closed his eyes, knocking tears free and sending them slowly down his cheeks. His chin wrinkled and trembled as he fought back a sob. He exhaled long and shakily.

Marco took Tyler's hand and squeezed it tightly. "Is there anything we can do? I've been reading about different trial drugs that aren't legalized yet. Can we talk about getting on those trials?"

"I'm afraid that trials are not always successful. If you could send me the information about them, I can check into them and see if Tyler would be a good candidate, but I don't want to hang our hats on that," Dr. Benson said, glancing over at Tyler.

Carol kept her hands on Tyler, trying to soothe him.

"This is the worst part of my job. I'm truly very sorry. Let's not give up. Marco has found some possible trials. Let's wait and see if those are viable and keep a little faith."

Carol, struggling to think of something to say, leaned in and kissed Tyler on the side of his forehead. "It's okay to cry," was all she could come up with. He let out a soft sob, wrapping his arms around her arm as she hugged him, burying his face in her shoulder.

"I'm sorry, Tyler," Dr. Benson repeated, standing up and gently squeezing his arm. He moved toward the sterilization chamber to exit. Marco followed.

ONCE OUTSIDE THE room and into the hallway, Marco addressed Bradley's concerns. "He hasn't been able to see the other kids in a month." Marco's voice cracked. "How are we going to explain this to them?"

"Why hasn't he? You have a sterilization room."

Marco frowned and lowered his head, ashamed. "We thought it would be best to wait until he was feeling better so they didn't have to see how bad it had gotten. We didn't want them to get scared."

"I'd suggest letting Tyler and the kids visit, one-on-one. It's a tough time, but I think the risk of anyone making him worse is not as significant now. I think it's important for you and Carol, and Tyler and the kids, to prepare for saying goodbye. I don't think he has much time left," Dr. Benson said, frowning. "I want to believe that the trials you've researched will prove useful, but Tyler's condition has worsened so fast that I fear there won't be enough time to administer them to any effect."

Marco stared blankly past the doctor as he processed what this meant. As he came to understand that Tyler was going to die and that they had sheltered the kids from it for so long that all they had left to do was say goodbye. He felt a knot of nausea growing in his stomach. They weren't protecting them at all. "We failed them," he whispered, still not looking at the doctor.

"What do you mean? You two do such great things here."

"We thought we were protecting them all by keeping them apart. We failed them. This is going to hurt them more than seeing him throughout the month would have."

"You did what you thought was right. True, you needed to keep him shielded from any potential health risks, but you wanted to keep them from seeing the horrors of what could happen to them one day. It's a tough choice, but I think you made the right one."

"Now, I have to go and tell those kids that their friend, their brother is going to die. They're never going to forgive me," Marco said, turning to hide his face as he began to cry.

"They will, and you will, find a way through. That's the thing about these things. Families come together and find compassion for one another," Dr. Benson said. He moved toward the stairs. "I should get going. You're going to have your hands full for a while."

"Sure, okay, let me show you out," Marco said, stepping toward the stairs to follow.

"No, no, Marco. It's okay. I know the way. You have other things to worry about."

Marco nodded, and Dr. Benson disappeared around the corner and down the stairs. The hall was empty again. Marco could hear the soft and muffled beep of the heart monitor attached to Tyler. "God, I'm such an asshole," he muttered, wiping tears from his eyes angrily. *I'm supposed to protect these kids. They trust me for that, and I failed them. I fucking failed them.*

WHEN NEITHER MARCO nor Carol showed up to make dinner, Bradley took on the role of caretaker and recruited Maggie to help him make dinner for everyone. Maggie welcomed the distraction from her worrying. She desperately needed something that would help her hide from the fact that she was losing Tyler. They fed all of the kids in the dining room and prepared dinner trays for Marco, Carol, and Tyler, leaving a covered dinner tray outside their bedroom doors.

Bradley left a small handwritten note for both Carol and Marco on their trays.

Everything's going to be okay. There's always tomorrow.

Chapter Fifty-Seven

AT DINNER, MARCO and Carol told the kids that there was little chance for Tyler to make it through and that they would all be able to go in and spend some time with him. The reactions they got were mixed. There were a lot of tears and some confusion as to why they could sanitize and go in now but not before.

"The risk was too high," Marco explained. "We were trying to limit any possible afflictions to his immune system, but now that the doctor has informed us that his body is shutting down regardless, we feel it's imperative that each of you spend some time with him. He misses you."

"Why didn't the treatments work for him?" Curtis asked. His voice was shaky. He didn't look up from his plate when he asked.

Carol cleared her throat, but Marco answered for her. "I think we just caught it too late. His lifestyle before coming here was one where he continually compromised his health, lack of nutrition, and no treatments. I think it was just a perfect storm of events with terrible results."

Carol nodded at Marco, thanking him for stepping in.

Maggie couldn't take listening to it anymore. She scoffed and referred to their request as a "ludicrous goodbye ritual" before storming up to her room.

Bradley followed, barging in and trying to convince her to change her mind, hoping to talk some sense into her. "You can't miss this opportunity to say goodbye. It's so rare to have, and you can't."

Maggie only stood firmer in her position. "I will not give him permission to die. If we all say goodbye, he'll give up. Right now, he needs to fight."

"You can't be that naïve," Bradley said sharply. "I refuse to believe that you're so lovesick that you're going to ignore reality. You're not that girl."

Maggie visibly flinched. "I just can't go in there and see him like that. Does that make me a coward? That I can't bear to see what it looks like when the guy I love is dying. I don't wanna know that's like. Ever." She sobbed, covering her face with her hands.

"Maggie, do you really want to have this regret?" Bradley asked.

"I get so much strength from the way I remember Janie. When she was so full of life. Carol can barely hear Janie's name without falling apart because she saw her at the end. I don't want that to happen for me with Tyler."

"That was different. It was suicide. There's no comparison." Bradley was impatient. "I'm not going to beg you. This is ridiculous."

"I just can't see him like this... I just can't." She wiped her face and looked out the window. Staring out at the line of maples that Tyler had so often been fixated on, she found herself understanding their appeal.

Bradley tossed his hands in the air, frustrated. "You're taking this from him, too, you know."

She ignored him and kept her eyes locked on the trees.

"I hope you change your mind."

"I won't."

"You sound just like him. So impossible."

Maggie smiled then and turned to look Bradley in the eyes. "Good. He's giving me strength already. It's working."

Bradley frowned as he prepared to leave. "I just want you to know that we'll all be here for you when you realize how dumb you're being. I'll try to let Tyler down gently."

She flinched again. She wasn't used to Bradley being so curt with her, but she was not going to give in. Deep down, she hoped that her choice to stay away would encourage Tyler to get better.

Chapter Fifty-Eight

CAROL COULD HEAR the sound of the toilet flushing behind the bathroom door just before Marco emerged with a forced, half-hearted smile.

"Hey," he said softly as he walked toward the bed. "Whatchu thinking about?"

"Oh, I don't know." She was sitting in bed, looking at the open pages to the same novel she'd been staring at all summer. Her breasts were barely covered by the dark-blue sheets.

"Come on. Let's talk." He stripped his clothes off, dropping them in a heap beside the bed, and climbed in beside her. He pulled the chain to the lamp on his side of the bed, brightening where he sat as well and bringing his loving face into full view. He kissed her shoulder and moved in to hold her, not caring whether the sheets covered him or not.

"I can't stop thinking about Maggie," Carol said, closing her book. "That poor girl has suffered so much. I just don't know how I'm going to get through to her this time."

"*We*. We will get through to her, Carol," Marco said. "This is an awful time for all of us, and we will get through it as a family." Marco understood the relationship that Carol and Maggie shared very well. He had always admired their bond.

"I expect that her natural inclination is going to be to hide away."

"Then we need to keep her engaged," Marco said, hugging her tighter. "It's going to be a team effort, but we can do it. Maggie will be okay. We will be okay."

"I wish she wouldn't be so pigheaded about saying goodbye," Carol said. Her chin trembled, and tiny little dimples exploded across it as she rambled on. "I can't understand how one girl can lose her health, her family, her friends, and then come here and lose the two people who showed her how to be herself and still be okay," Carol said, her voice cracking and the words beginning to get lost in the sobs.

"Shhh. It's okay, babe. We all miss Janie, and we'll all miss Tyler. We'll get through this. Together," Marco said, soothing her, rubbing her back and kissing the top of her head. "We'll get through this, and Maggie will get through this. We have to respect her decision no matter how tough."

"But she's making such a stupid mistake."

"And that's life. We need to let her live it. Isn't that the point of all this?"

Chapter Fifty-Nine

THE DAY'S WEATHER was gray and gloomy, raining off and on from the time the sun rose. It seemed as though the dampness had seeped into the house and everyone in it. Bradley took a deep breath before turning the knob on the door to Tyler's room, exhaling loudly. The force of his exhalation sent a wave of calm through his body. "Hi—" He stopped short of the rest of his sentence when he came nearly face-to-face with Carol, who was sitting on a plastic chair in the corner of the sanitization chamber. She smiled warmly and stood to greet him.

Bradley glanced around the room and noticed Tyler in his bed through the glass wall. "What is this? I didn't realize there was a separate room before *the room.*"

"It's a sanitization room. It's where you'll have to wash up really well, and if you feel like you've had a cold at all, please wear gloves and a mask as well; otherwise, just wash up and get in there," Carol said, pointing to all of the items he would need.

"I haven't been sick," he said. He took his ring and watch off and left them in a dish beside the sink, offering his rationale, "I don't think I could have gotten all the germs off these." He scrubbed his hands and arms thoroughly, the way he had been taught by Carol when Tyler first got sick. This was how he washed before preparing the meals over the last weeks.

"I'm going to be in here. It's also pretty well soundproof, so I won't be able to hear you when you're speaking to him. If you want, though, I can come in to support you while you're in there."

"No, it's okay. Thank you." Bradley dried his hands off quickly and moved toward the door.

As he entered Tyler's room, his breathing seized as the beeping of the heart monitor and the swishing of the oxygen pump surrounded him at their full volume.

"Hey," Tyler said, smiling and waving him closer.

Bradley hadn't realized that he'd stopped a few feet from the end of the bed. The raspy sound in Tyler's voice caught him off guard.

"Hey," he said, stepping forward to stand beside him. He stared at the dark lesions on Tyler's neck and face. He wasn't expecting him to look any different than he had in June. He stifled tears as his eyes moved from the lesions to his gaunt face and the sunken in appearance of his eyes. His once slim and borderline-athletic frame now appeared frail and sickly. Bradley couldn't fight the urge to stare.

Tyler patted the bed so he would sit beside him. Seeming to notice Bradley's hesitation, he said, "Relax. I won't break. Sit."

"Does it hurt?" Bradley asked, lowering himself slowly onto the edge of the bed. He cringed as his weight caused the mattress to raise Tyler up.

"No," Tyler lied. He then offered some truth. "It just makes me tired."

"Liar," Bradley said, lightly slapping him in jest.

"It's not really. Just the thrush. That's what hurts," Tyler said. "My muscles too. They're achy. Nothing too major."

"Maggie's not coming," Bradley said abruptly, looking away from his face as he did. He didn't want to see his reaction; it would be too painful.

"Is she mad at me?"

When he looked back to Tyler's eyes, his own filled with tears. "She's not mad at you. She's just refusing to accept..." His shoulders sank as he understood that this friend, who he was sitting with, *was* going to die.

"That I'm dying," Tyler said, finishing for him. "It's okay. You can say it."

"I'm sorry, Tyler. I tried to convince her to come, but she's afraid to see you like this. She wants you to get better, but she also doesn't want this to be her last memory of you."

Silence. The sad songs of birds feeling trapped by the rain came into the room, muffled by the closed window.

"Are you angry with her?"

"I'm frustrated. Hurt, I guess... No, tell her that I'm not angry. I don't want her to have any regrets. Tell her I understand. Perhaps more than she knows."

"Really? You do?"

"Yeah. It's a horrible memory to hold on to. I'd rather she remember that one time I was nice." Tyler winked to get Bradley to laugh.

Not missing a beat, Bradley slapped the bed and said, "That one time was a good day." His tone became solemn again. "I'll tell her."

"I don't want to let Maggie hijack our visit." Tyler forced a smile and changed the subject. "When I met you, I was like 'he's gorgeous, holy shit,' but then you turned out to be straight, and I kinda tucked my gayness aside for Maggie. But if you'd even hinted, I would have been all for it." He laughed.

"Wow," Bradley said, blushing. "I don't—"

"I know you don't, jerk. I'm dying, so I don't care if you know I think you're hot. Just accept the compliment."

Bradley blushed again. "I do accept it. I have no problem with it. I don't know why I felt like telling you I don't swing that way."

"Don't worry about it. I'm pretty tough to offend. Unless you call me a fag. That shit makes me nuts," Tyler said, winking and nudging him.

"Oh, God," Bradley said, rolling his eyes. "How ridiculous, eh?"

"It kinda sucked when you turned out to be like the kids who picked on me in school, though."

Bradley frowned. "I'm sorry I was such a jerk."

"Don't worry about that either. I think it actually helped us, you know? I think that us having a friendship now feels more rewarding than if we'd been friends from the get-go," Tyler said.

"Yeah, I think so too. I'm gonna hold on to the memory of those kids in the mall and how you freaked them out for forever. That was awesome. Pretty sure that's when I started respecting you."

"Totally. And seriously, back to the 'you're hot' thing," Tyler said.

Bradley laughed. "Come on, man."

"You're gonna find a hot chick. There are so many girls—and guys— who would chomp at the bit for a chance with you, so don't give up on that."

"Thanks, Tyler," Bradley said, offering his hand out to shake. "Nah, I'm just kidding." He dove in for a hug. "Take it easy, and keep fighting. I hope you get better, so I can tease you about being attracted to me for the next thirty years once you're not facing death and get all shy again."

Tyler hugged him back, breathing in gently to get a whiff of Bradley's cologne.

"There's a big lineup, so I'll let the others come in. Everyone is eager to see you."

"Except Maggie," Tyler said, frowning.

WHEN CURTIS ENTERED Tyler's room, he had to stifle his panic. He didn't know how to talk to someone who was dying.

"Hey, Mister College," Tyler said, calling to him. "How's the weather?"

"It's good."

"Good enough for camping?"

Curtis froze when he heard the question, mortified at the thought. "I...I...guess so..." He slowly made his way to stand beside Tyler.

"You haven't gone for any more trips? Seems like a waste of the summer to me," Tyler said, looking toward the window. The curtains were open a crack, revealing the gray and damp world outside. "I guess today wouldn't be such a fun day for it, though."

"Okay, Tyler. I need you to get better," Curtis said. He rubbed his forehead to comfort himself.

Tyler turned to look at him. "I don't know if I can."

"You need to," Curtis urged, "I know it's selfish, but I just can't deal with this." He ran his fingers into his hair and pulled on a handful, his substitute for a stress ball.

"This isn't your fault," Tyler said, reaching out and nudging Curtis. "You can't control this any more than Dr. Benson or me or Carol. It's just fuckin' shitty luck."

Curtis wasn't satisfied with this. "You wouldn't be sick if you hadn't come on the camping trip. You would have been fine if it wasn't for that damp, awful weekend."

"*That* was an awesome weekend. And I was sick long before it."

Curtis glared at him, infuriated. "How could you say that after what's happened?"

"Just like I did," Tyler said. "I had never gone camping before. You all thought I would relate it to being homeless, but camping was way more fun. I never had s'mores before or slept in a tent or any of that. If I hadn't gone, I might be dying without knowing what any of that's like."

Curtis was silent. He didn't know how to refute Tyler's perspective. It was, after all, Tyler's take on the experience.

"I don't blame you. I think that everything happens for a reason. Not because of some God or anything but because the universe has a set plan. I got sick because my health was fading. It was bound to happen. The doctor told us that I was getting worse, that there wasn't much time left."

"Carol and Marco knew? Why didn't they tell us?"

"I asked them not to. I didn't want everyone walking around pitying me. I wanted to feel normal still." Tyler laughed cynically.

Curtis was silent as he tried to understand why they went camping given Tyler's condition.

"So you see, it was never your fault," Tyler said. "You did me a favor by giving me an experience I would never have had otherwise. You helped me live. Thank you for that."

Curtis exhaled. "Don't thank me. I don't wanna be bawling when I walk outta here past Carol."

Tyler smirked. "Suck it up, princess."

Both boys laughed. "Give me a hug, asshole," Curtis said, slapping Tyler gently on the chest. "I'm gonna miss you." They embraced in a tight, comforting hug.

"You're a great friend, Curtis. Keep being you."

When they separated, Curtis's eyes were red and wet. "Damn you. Now, I'm crying."

"Did I ever tell you that you remind me of the guy who gave it to me?"

Curtis recoiled. "What? Don't say that. I don't want to remind you of someone horrible like that. How could you say that?" He wiped messily at his cheeks.

Tyler raised his hand to get him to quiet down. "Relax, Curtis. It's a good thing. *A really good thing.*"

"How can it be? I remind you of some guy you prostituted for who gave you this fucking thing that's killing you. You're *dying*, and *I* remind you of the guy who did it. Like what the fuck?"

"I wasn't prostituting when I got it."

"What?" Curtis was surprised by this. He hadn't understood the situation that led to Tyler contracting HIV as well as he'd thought. "Didn't you say...?"

"I don't like opening up all the time," Tyler said. "I fell in love with a guy that my sister and I knew. His name was Chad. He was outdoorsy, laidback, charismatic, and always made me feel like I mattered."

Curtis could hardly keep up with his tears and now his nose started to run. "I didn't realize."

Tyler smiled. "He was a really amazing guy. He didn't know he had it. We lived on the streets together before he OD'd. That's when I turned into a big mess out there. I never met anyone like him again until I met you, so I mean it as a compliment. You're really great, and I think you'll make the world a better place for anyone you meet just like he did. So don't worry about me. You already did that for me. Now you can do it for someone else."

"Jesus, Tyler." Curtis's throat made a croaking sound as a burst of tears broke through his defenses. "I'm a mess now. That's the best thing anyone's ever said to me."

"I've thought it for a long time. I just felt weird saying it. I guess knowing that I'm dying makes it easier to say. And I guess that's why I was never able to fully fall for Maggie. She's nothing like him."

Curtis hugged Tyler again and then stood to leave. "I know you don't believe anymore, but maybe you'll get to see Chad when you go."

"Maybe." Tyler touched the tattoo on his neck, turning his head so Curtis could see it. "I got this the day of his funeral. Maybe that means something."

"What does it say?"

Tyler's lips trembled. His eyes shimmered. "Forever in love." He pressed his hand firmly against his neck. "It's the most truthful thing I know."

"I'd like to think it means that he'll meet you there. Wherever there is. You know? That he's been waiting for your happy ending."

Tyler smiled again and swallowed hard. A single tear slid down his cheek. "That's a nice thought."

"I wish things were different. So different," Curtis said.

"Go live your life. You have so much to do." He waved as Curtis stepped back into the sanitization chamber.

WHEN CURTIS WAS back in with Carol, she asked, "Are you okay?"

With a blank expression on his face and an emotionless tone, he replied, "I don't know."

Carol watched him, unsure of what to say. She wanted to reach out and hug him but stuttered in motion and stopped herself. He nodded awkwardly at her and left, closing the door behind him and leaving her alone in the glass encasement.

Thinking that Tyler must be feeling drained, Carol stepped in to ask him if he'd like to have a sleep before continuing, but he refused. "I'm okay. I've waited long enough."

"Are you sure?"

He nodded. "I'm tired, but I don't wanna miss anyone."

Carol was unsettled by the way he said it as though he knew something she didn't, as though he may be running out of time.

MARCO WENT IN with Theo. "I figure Theo and I can visit with you together. The trio back together again," Marco said, smiling and bouncing Theo gently up and down on the bed.

"Totally," Tyler said, reaching out and giving Theo a high five.

"Ty, Ty. I miss you," Theo said, holding on to Tyler's hand. "Where you been?"

Tears danced in the corners of Tyler's eyes. "Right here, Theo. I've been right here."

"Why?"

Tyler looked past Theo to Marco, confused and silently begging to know why Theo didn't know.

Marco panicked, desperate not to have the conversation now. "We don't know how to tell him. We figure it will be easier to tell him if you actually do..."

Tyler nodded. "Okay." He turned his attention back to Theo. "I want to thank you, little guy."

"Why?"

"That's your word of the week, I bet."

Theo looked up over his head, nearly tipping backward, to see Marco as he, too, laughed.

"Thanks for reminding me how to be a big brother, and for reminding me that I want to be part of a family," Tyler said.

Theo looked confused. Marco took a deep breath and exhaled slowly to stop himself from crying.

"Fist bump, li'l dude," Tyler said, slowly raising his hand. It trembled, but he kept it up to get an excited fist bump from Theo before setting it back by his side. He smiled, tears now falling from his cheeks to the pillow.

"Don't cry," Theo said, leaping forward and laying on Tyler's torso, wrapping him in a big hug. "Don't worry, be happy," he said, imitating the toy fish plaque that Curtis had in his room.

Tyler tried holding his breath, but couldn't stop the tears from coming. He began to weep, wrapping his arms around Theo. "It's okay to cry sometimes," he said between sobs. He looked to Marco to rescue him, pleading with an expression of exhaustion for Marco to take Theo out.

Picking up on the cue, Marco stepped forward and lifted Theo up. "Come on. Let's get you out of here."

"Thank you," Tyler said, waving to Theo as Marco took him to the sanitization chamber and passed him off to Carol before returning.

"That was tough," Marco said, offering a smile and a light tap on Tyler's leg as he sat down on the bed.

"Yeah…it was," Tyler said. "I never knew how tiring this would be."

"Do you want me to come back later?" Marco asked, motioning to stand up.

"No, no. Please. Stay," Tyler said, reaching his hand out to indicate for Marco to sit. "Don't go."

"Okay. I'm not going to be much easier to listen to."

"That's okay. I want to hear what you have to say. I always do."

"You know, I've never met anyone who's had as much of an impact on this house as you," Marco said, looking into Tyler's eyes. "I seriously never have."

Tyler exhaled slowly, still trying to keep himself together. "Gosh."

"Yeah, gosh," Marco said, laughing. "I think you coming here has been the best thing that's ever happened to any of us. Carol is opening up more, and Bradley and Maggie and Curtis and me. And all of us. You're too important to this place, and to us, to die. I'm having a hard time accepting any of this. I can't believe that God would put you here to make such a difference and then take you away before all the possibilities have been realized." Marco paused for a moment to collect his thoughts as he found himself rambling. "Wow, that was a mouthful."

Tyler laughed.

"I've been searching for possible treatments, and if you just hold on a while, they can run some tests and find one that might be compatible. I just need you to hold on for a little bit."

Tyler's eyelids were puffy and heavy. "I'll try. I'm exhausted right now, though." He blinked slowly. Fatigue was setting in, and he was embracing it.

"I'll let you get some sleep. We can talk about possible treatment options later," Marco said, rubbing Tyler's thigh as he stood to leave.

"Don't let me sleep. Tell Carol to come in," Tyler said anxiously. He opened his eyes again to wave as Marco stepped into the sanitization chamber.

CAROL ENTERED THE room slowly, wringing her hands together in a fierce and deliberate manner. She noticed that he had grown much thinner; she could see the point of his shoulder bones through his medical gown.

Being able to see his elbow bones so clearly, she would have thought they were swollen if she didn't know how much weight he had lost and that his arms had simply grown slimmer than the width of his elbows. She wondered why she was only noticing these changes now. Was she truly this blind?

Tyler opened his eyes, sensing that Carol had entered the room. "Hey," he said weakly, trying to sit himself up.

"Let me help," she said, wrapping her arms around his torso and helping to shift him farther up so he could rest against the raised head of the bed in a sitting position. She sat on the edge, beside him, and took his hand in hers. She was exhausted from trying to keep herself together for the other kids as they visited.

He squeezed her hand. A single tear slid from the corner of his eye. "I don't think I'm scared anymore." His eyes were full with tears that seemed to jump as he spoke.

"How can you not be afraid?"

"I just... This is what I came here for." He squeezed her hand again. "Thank you for letting me have a family, for letting me have a home for this. I was so scared to die like Chad did. I didn't want to die like that. Alone. Out there."

She frowned and let her own tears flow freely. "I wish you'd come here for something else." She swallowed a ball of mucus in her throat noisily.

Tyler squeezed her hand until she looked him in the eyes. "Thank you for letting me live."

Carol brought her hand up to cover her face as she cried. She wished she could be stronger for him. She cleared her throat and pushed the tears away and looked him in the eyes again. "If I'd had a son, I would have wanted him to be just like you." She wiped at her eyes again.

Tyler let go of her hand to cover his mouth as he coughed. He closed his eyes. His voice was strained as he said, "Thank you. I wish my mother had thought the same."

"She will have that regret her whole life. I know she will."

"I guess we all have those in the end." Tyler opened his eyes. "If you get to talk to my sister, can you tell her that I'm sorry? I want her to know that I wish I'd been there for her. I wish I'd gone to see her after I was kicked out. If I'd just stayed away from all the drugs, I could have been a brother to her still. I'm just so sorry." His breathing sounded alarmingly heavy and rushed.

Carol nodded. She didn't know if she could speak without bawling. She was holding his hand in both of hers and petting it methodically, almost frenetically. She felt guilty listening to his regrets while wishing that she could light up a joint. Her chest felt so tight. She needed to relax so she could breathe again.

Tyler cleared his throat and winced in pain as the thrush burned. He squirmed to get comfortable without success. His muscles ached and throbbed.

"Tyler..." She felt her heartbeat quicken as she noticed the sense of urgency in his eyes. It was as though he knew he was leaving. "There's so much I want to say to you," she said, trying to keep her words clear through her anxious stutter.

Tyler forced a soft smile and squeezed her hand. "Shhh," he whispered as he closed his eyes. With a few short breaths, his chest stopped rising, and he was gone. It seemed too easy, too perfect. Her stomach tightened and turned as the reality gripped her. She breathed in after what felt like minutes of breathlessness, and choked on a lump of spit in her throat.

"Goodbye, sweet boy," she whispered, leaning forward and gently kissing his forehead. She began to sob with her lips still pressed against his face. The sounds that escaped from her seemed foreign. "Ffff, oh, wow," she said, standing up and wiping the tears and snot from her face with both hands. "Oh, fuck." She gasped for steady breath as she wept, exhaling shakily. "Hnnn...Fuck..." She pushed the chair away from the side of his bed and tucked herself on the floor beside the bar fridge, and leaned against the wall. As she sat there on the floor for what felt like hours, the tock of the grandfather clock down the hall seemed to echo around her. She started to feel that her heartbeat had found a rhythm with it. Outside the room, the hall was empty. The sky was still gray, and the air was heavy. She was alone.

Chapter Sixty

MUCH TO MARCO and Carol's surprise, they were able to reach Tyler's mother and sister to tell them about his death and planned funeral. Telling them was harder than Marco had expected it would be, but not as hard as it was when they showed up for the funeral and asked to meet the other kids to learn about how his life was before he died. Carol offered to put them up in a room in the house, but Mrs. Nickels quickly rejected, insisting on staying in the hotel in town to be able to see a little bit of the town he'd lived in. They knew it had less to do with that than it did with her fear of the kids. The funeral service was small. The only attendees were those who lived at the New Life House, the priest, Dr. Benson, Nurse "CC" Conrad, Rachel, and Mrs. Nickels. Most of them had an opportunity to stand and read or speak about Tyler. Rachel had written a heartfelt goodbye to him that she was barely able to read without sobbing. Mrs. Nickels cried only a few times. She sat rigid with an air of stoicism while she learned about who her son had grown up to be.

When the service was over, Mrs. Nickels moved to stand next to Carol and Maggie who were standing beside the large photograph of Tyler at the front of the church. "I think that Ty's dad will come around. He will regret this choice," Mrs. Nickels said. "I know he is a firm man in his beliefs, but I truly believe that he will regret this."

"I don't understand how you could love someone who threw your son out of your life," Maggie said.

In any other situation, Carol would have tried to scold Maggie for being so rude but not today. She was glad that someone was doing it. It made it less likely that she would make some kind of foolish emotional display in front of everyone herself.

"I know it's difficult to understand sometimes," Mrs. Nickels said, stopping to face Maggie. "I love them both so much. It hurts my heart how different they are. I wish that Bruce had learned to love Tyler. I really do."

"Tyler was the best thing that ever happened to me," Maggie said, wringing a handkerchief with so much intensity that the palms of her hands were red and sore.

"I'm sorry that you are going through this," Mrs. Nickels said, frowning.

"Why didn't your husband come?" Carol asked, deciding that Maggie wasn't digging hard enough.

"He's still angry." She looked down from the confrontation. "I am embarrassed to say that he still denounces Tyler as his son."

"That brings real anger to my heart," Carol said. "I have been raising that boy for almost a year now, and I have never been so proud of anyone in my entire life." Her voice cracked; her chin trembled. She imagined her life without Tyler, and her heart sank. "I don't think I've ever truly known heartbreak until the day he said goodbye."

"That goes for me too," Nancy said. "I think back to when Tyler was thrown from my home every day. That was the last time I saw him…" Her voice broke and she dabbed a tissue into the corner of her eye. "I've lain awake so many nights, worrying that he was all alone and wishing that I could have done something to change what happened. I would see Bruce sleeping so peacefully and want to scream at him. I will never understand how he could be so hateful toward his own son."

"Are you still with your husband?"

"Yes."

"How?" Carol asked, forgetting her manners and her professionalism, letting her emotions get the better of her. "How can you love a man who separated you from your son?"

"I ask myself that question all the time," Mrs. Nickels said. Her voice was heavy; she sounded defeated. "I try not to judge him. I know God will take his actions into consideration when he reaches the gates of Heaven."

For a moment, Carol wondered if Mrs. Nickels was also referring to Tyler. She noticed that she began to stand taller as she stood in her convictions. It was as though her faith gave her the strength to shake the struggle. Carol had always been somewhat awestruck by people who could so blindly follow a religion based on a book that had, since its inception, been so easily changed on the whim of powerful men. In this moment, she was impressed by the strength that Mrs. Nickels seemed to get just from talking about it.

"I love my son, and I love my husband. I just wish they'd loved each other. We all would have been so free."

"I DON'T KNOW why he never came to see me," Rachel said, frowning. She was sitting with Curtis in the fancy living room. Her mother had tried to get her to come back to the hotel with her, but she insisted on going back to the house for the reception to learn about Tyler's life before he died. "We were like best friends. I hoped every day that he'd come and see me. Maybe wait for our parents to be gone and come over. But he never came. And I started to think that maybe he hated me because they kept me and threw him away." She ignored the tears that stained her cheeks and made her mascara run, looked to the ceiling and took a deep breath. "I loved him so much."

"He didn't hate you," Curtis said, hesitating as he reached out to pat her shoulder.

She noticed his hesitation and shook her head. "I'm not like my parents. I'm not afraid of you." She nodded toward his hand, which remained suspended in midair.

He smiled. "Oh." He put his hand back down without making contact with her. "I just wanted to reassure you that your brother missed you. He and I used to talk a lot, and he spoke really highly of you. And of Chad..." He hoped he wasn't crossing a line with her.

She teared up again. "I haven't seen him in so long. I'm so angry with him. He ruined my brother and then just disappeared."

"What do you mean disappeared?"

Her expression was puzzled. "Well...Ty ended up here. And where's Chad? He's not here, so he has to have left. My brother loved him. He never would have ended things."

Curtis frowned. "You don't know?" He took a deep, exasperated breath. "Tyler loves him still."

"What? How could he?"

"Tyler told me about him before he died." He choked up as he said it. *Died*. "Chad died of a drug overdose sometime when they were living on the streets. It really messed Tyler up, and he loved him right up until the moment he left." He couldn't say it again. *Left* was better.

She started to cry again, covering her mouth with a shaky hand.

Curtis put his hand comfortingly on her shoulder and squeezed gently. "Would you like the Whistler T-shirt that he wore all the time? I think it was Chad's. Maybe a good memory of both of them for you?"

She looked up. Her cheeks were splotchy and her eyes red. She didn't nod or speak, but Curtis knew she wanted it. He excused himself briefly and returned with the neatly folded, dark-green T-shirt with navy-blue letters outlined in white.

"The ends of the sleeves and waist are all tattered, but you can tell it was well loved." He handed the shirt to her. On top of it, he included a printout of Tyler's memoir and a photograph that he'd found on his bedside table. The corners of the photo were softened and creased, small water dots had discolored some of the scenery, but Tyler, Rachel, and Chad were clearly visible. They were standing inside a hollowed-out tree in a forest.

She picked up the photograph. "Oh, wow. I remember this." She cleared her throat, preparing to tell the story. "This was taken in Stanley Park. We used to sneak out and get high with our friends. We'd play hide-and-seek sometimes. Because—"

"Because who doesn't want to get stoned and play hide-and-seek in the forest?" Curtis said, smiling. "I would have loved that. I never knew Tyler liked the woods and the outdoors."

Rachel nodded emphatically. "Totally. We used to go there all the time. I kept looking for him there after he was kicked out, but he never came." She paused and then got back on track with her story. "He and Chad first kissed in that tree during a game of hide-and-seek, and I found them. So that's where the three of us really got to know each other because I finally got to know for sure that Tyler was gay."

"I thought he was bi..."

She rolled her eyes. "Oh, please. Don't tell me you bought that whole bisexual thing. He tried to say that so my parents would accept him better, but I never saw him truly appreciate a girl. It's just what he says so he'll fit in better. He likes guys." She frowned. "Liked." She wiped at a tear. "Anyways, we went to the tree to get a picture of all of us one time because we thought it was a really cool way to commemorate that moment. I can't believe he still has it."

"I think he'd love you to have it." Curtis smiled.

"Thank you," she said as she wrapped her arms tightly around him.

"Oh, and...uh... Try not to say that you don't think he was bi near Maggie."

"Who?" She pulled away from the hug so she could see his face.

"The redhead. She fell in love with him, and they dated. Apparently, they even came close to having sex."

Rachel shook her head. "I won't say anything. I promise. But wow. I can't believe he almost made it with a girl. The old Tyler—the Tyler that I knew—would have gagged at the thought." They laughed together.

"I just can't imagine him with a girl. I thought maybe you and him but not a girl."

"Ha, we're not exactly each other's type," Curtis said.

"He might not have been yours, but you're definitely his. Look at Chad in this picture. You kinda look alike."

"Wow, you're right. We do. I never really saw it before."

"I almost thought you were him at first. I was a little sad when you weren't. Not because you're you but because I was hoping they were together until the end..." She closed her eyes.

"I think you should read this too." He tapped his finger on the printed pages.

She opened her eyes to look down at the typed document in her lap. "What is it?"

Curtis flipped a few pages. "It's his memoir. He wrote it for you." He pointed at the dedication.

For my kid sister, Rachel.
Thank you for being you.
Hopefully, we can meet again someday in the trees.

Her hands shook as she ran her fingers delicately over the inscription. When she finally made a sound, it was a deep sob that started in her stomach and broke in her throat. She covered her mouth and nose as she cried, rocking back and forth in an instinctual attempt to soothe herself.

"I'm sorry," Curtis said, again afraid to reach out and comfort her. She kept sobbing and rocking, so he hesitantly rested his hand on her shoulder. "I'm sorry," he said again.

"CAROL," RACHEL SAID, stepping into the living room after knocking lightly on the door. "Can I talk to you?"

Carol sat up in her seat, straightened her face, and cleared her throat. "Hi, dear. Yes. Of course you can."

Rachel smiled warmly and moved into the room to take a seat beside her. She placed the T-shirt, memoir, and photo in a pile on the coffee table as she sat.

Carol sat uncomfortably, waiting for Rachel to speak, unsure of what to expect.

"This might sound weird, but I want to say thank you."

Carol breathed in and held it, blinking to keep from crying.

"I mean. Really. Thank you. I'm so happy my brother found this place. And that you were here to take care of him. Nobody wanted to do that back home." She frowned and focused on her hands, which were folded neatly in her lap. "I think it's great that he had a place to call home and people to call family before he…"

Carol took Rachel's hands in hers and patted them gently. "It's okay, dear. Thank you. That means a lot. He was really special. We were happy to have him here."

"I know you paid for him because my parents wouldn't." She said this in the same manner that Tyler would have, as a direct and rational fact.

"Rachel—"

"I just want to say thank you. You didn't have to do that, but you did it for him. I'll never forget that."

"—I'll never forget *him*," Carol said, forcing a smile.

Rachel hugged her, whispering in her ear as she did. "Please keep doing this. You saved him."

Carol pulled away to look her in the face. "Where did you—"

"I overheard you saying that you weren't sure if you were doing any good with this. That maybe this whole thing was better on paper than in real life."

Carol let her smile fade. She didn't know what to say.

"You gave us the chance to say goodbye. Without this place, we never would have known what happened to him. And he would have spent the last year of his life living on the streets. That's reality." Rachel squeezed Carol's and then stood with her belongings and moved toward the door.

"You remind me of him. So wise beyond your years," Carol said.

Rachel turned around, with tears in her eyes, and said, "Thank you. That makes me proud."

"I WOULDN'T SAY goodbye," Maggie said, her hands shaking as she wiped at her tears with a tissue. "I feel like I robbed us both. What kind of person does that?" She hated herself for being so cowardly. All he wanted to do was say goodbye, and she refused him. She hid in her room and pretended it wasn't happening in a selfish attempt to avoid the sorrow of his death, but now she was here mourning him anyway. "I will regret that decision for the rest of my life."

"Maggie, I've never really been happy that you fell in love with him, but I get it. He was an amazing guy, and if there's one thing I've learned about him it's that he wasn't angry. He cared about you a lot, and I can't see him being angry that you were afraid. Or that you wanted to remember him in better times." Bradley handed her a tissue.

"Thank you," she said, blowing her nose into the tissue gracelessly.

"It's like a freakin' sob fest here." He stood up and paced in front of the couch.

Maggie cleared her throat. "He loved this room. He used to say that it was like being in church but without all the judgment and hatred." She smiled as she thought of him teaching Theo about the church for the good people.

"Well then, when you're in his church, you should stop judging yourself so critically. Nothing could be more blasphemous." Bradley forced a soft smile to show that he was trying to be supportive.

"You're right." She straightened in her seat. "And, besides, his sister is here. She must be feeling worse. I should try to be respectful of how she's feeling."

Bradley shook his head. "Oh, forget about that. Grieve the way you need to, but don't hate on yourself. Tyler loved you. Focus on that."

She stood to give him a hug. "Thank you, Bradley. You're a good friend. Truly."

He hugged back, closing his eyes and enjoying the moment for what it was.

CAROL HAD ESCAPED the house to sit on the back veranda. She couldn't take anymore crying or emotional outbursts. Her heart was aching so badly that she, at one point, feared she may literally be having a heart attack. She wished it were nighttime already so she could smoke a joint. The funeral had nearly destroyed her, and the reception at the house had been draining her energy ever since. Talking to Nancy had fired her up with anger, but talking to Rachel had been the drop in her already full bucket that had threatened to unravel her. She was sitting here now, hoping against all hope that she could hold it together a little longer.

Bradley stepped out onto the veranda to join her. "Hey, Carol."

She glanced over at him. She couldn't hide her irritation that he had found her. She felt it on her face but didn't have the energy to hide it.

"I'm not here to cry," he said, sensing her hesitation for him to join her.

"I'm sorry, Bradley. I didn't mean to look at you like that."

"It's okay. It's been a hard day." He stepped toward the swing. "You know how Tyler used to say that he thought this was the Death House *and* the New Life House?"

She took a deep breath and thought, *Not this. Not now*, but said, "Yes."

"Well, I've been thinking about it, and it *is* like the Death House here."

She sighed and rolled her eyes, preparing to tell him to stop talking like that, but he jumped in before should could speak.

"But not for the reasons the townies say. It's because that's what we learn about. We learn how to go gracefully. You can't have life without death, and here, we learn how to live and that death is, truly, inevitable. We don't have the curse of feeling immortal like everybody else."

Carol held her breath as he spoke, in awe of the maturity and reason he was employing.

He sat beside her on the rickety, old porch swing, seeming strangely calm. "We can either mope around in fear and grief, or we can try to be like Tyler and *live...*"

Chapter Sixty-One

CURTIS COULDN'T QUITE grasp the fact that his friend was gone. He had been struggling to cry, to show even the slightest emotion. Guilt hung over him as he tried to figure out why he wasn't crying. He knew he felt sad, and he knew that he cared for Tyler. He found himself continually staring at photos of him to try to encourage the tears. It was as though he was numb or stuck, and it made him feel like he was suffocating. He wanted nothing more than to break down and cry just like everyone else was. Now, he stood at the Halifax Airport with Marco. Bradley and Carol had wandered off to find the washroom. The day had finally arrived for Curtis and Bradley to move to London, Ontario, to start college.

"What's the matter, Curtis? You're about to board a flight to your dream. Perk up a bit." Marco squeezed Curtis's shoulder.

Curtis looked up at him without responding. He felt his eyes getting hot and wet, and instantly began fighting the very release he'd been willing. He exhaled deeply and shifted his position, so he could turn away. "I just miss him."

Marco wrapped his arm around Curtis and squeezed him again. "It's okay to cry, Curtis."

"I just wish he was still here."

"I know," Marco said. "You know he'll always be with you, right?"

Curtis rolled his eyes. He didn't like the hokey direction Marco was taking this.

"I mean it, Curtis. You can't tell me that you don't view the world a little differently since knowing him. It's the things that he taught us and the ways that he changed us that will keep him in our hearts, and with us."

"Thanks, Marco." Curtis put his arm around him and returned the caring squeeze. "I wish I could cry. It would feel so good to just let go."

Marco laughed and stood so he could look Curtis directly in the eyes. "There's a time to cry, and there's a time to move on. It just means that you're at the moving on part."

Curtis thought it over. "Hm."

"Didn't he give you a task?"

Curtis took a deep breath and exhaled slowly. "Yeah, he did. He asked me to make a difference for kids like us. The way I did for him."

"Then I think you've got your marching orders." Marco gently pinched Curtis's chin. "You are a great guy, Curtis. And Tyler saw that. He doesn't care that you're not crying. He's probably glad for it."

"He did hate when there was too much sappiness," Curtis said, pushing a smile onto his face and clenching his teeth to keep it from slipping.

"That's the spirit."

"What's the spirit?" Bradley asked, slapping them both on the back as he arrived. "I kept it on my hands just for you."

"Awe, you're disgusting," Curtis said, pulling away.

Bradley shrugged. "I thought it was rather generous of me."

"You're going to be such trouble out there, aren't you?" Marco said, hugging Bradley.

"Nah, not me." Bradley feigned innocence.

"I'm gonna miss you, bud."

"We'll be back at the holidays. That's not too far away," Bradley said. He pulled away from the hug. "Where's Carol?" He scanned the crowd for her face.

Marco looked around as well. "Wasn't she with you?"

"For like two seconds. She got distracted by something and went off to it and said she'd meet me back here."

Marco shrugged. "Who knows? She could be anywhere."

Carol leaned her head between them, startling them as she said, "Who are we looking for?"

Marco nudged her playfully. "Some ol' lady."

"Oh, schnap!" Bradley said, clapping his hands together.

Carol scowled at Marco. "You watch it there, bucko. I can still whoop ya."

Marco laughed, mimicking fear.

"We gotta go through security. The line is getting long over there," Curtis said, pointing.

Carol pulled him into a tight hug. "You take care of yourself and Bradley. You know he's going to need some of your guidance to keep out of trouble." She pulled back and brushed his hair from his forehead.

"I will."

She turned to Bradley. "And you make sure this guy lets loose and has some fun every now and then. Don't let him turn fifty before his time."

Bradley hugged her tight. "I will."

"Now, go on. Give us a call when you land and get to the apartment," Marco said, sending them off to the security line.

"Bye!" both boys said in unison, waving as they picked up their carry-on luggage and moved into the line.

CAROL AND MARCO stood at the edge of security, smiling and waving until they disappeared from view. Once the boys were gone, they let the smiles fade and be replaced with worry. Had they done everything they could to get them ready? Were they going to understand the importance of saving money to buy food and to pay bills? Were they really ready to face the world?

As though they were reading each other's minds, they blindly reached for one another's hands to offer comfort.

Carol leaned her head against Marco's shoulder, still staring intently at the place where their first two graduates had stood moments before. "I'm going to miss them so much. The house is going to be so empty."

Marco pulled her into him with one arm. He kissed the top of her head and closed his eyes to embrace the moment. He appreciated the bittersweet feeling that it brought for him, a mixture of excitement, worry, and sadness. Most of all, he was proud. They'd dreamed about the day they could send their first two kids back into the real world to begin their new life. He hadn't known what to expect, but he liked it. It felt complete.

"Do you think they'll be okay?"

He smiled. "I think they'll be happy. And I think they'll be great."

They stood for another few minutes, staring at the doors to the security line, and then made their way toward the exit. "Where'd you disappear to earlier? We were starting to think you'd gotten lost or something."

Carol shook her head. "I just thought I saw something interesting on the bulletin board."

"And?" Marco asked.

"And what?"

"Was it interesting?"

"Oh, no. It was nothing. Let's go home."

Marco eyed her suspiciously. "Hm," he said. He tried to guess if she seemed high, wondering if she'd snuck out to smoke a joint before sending them off.

"Hm, what?" she said defensively.

"Just seems like you're hiding something."

"It's nothing, Marco. Honestly. Just trust me. Please."

Marco shook his head. "It doesn't sound like nothing. I don't understand why you can't tell me what you saw. It doesn't sound like something I would like."

"Can we just let it go?" she said, letting go of his hand as they exited airport and entered the parking garage. She sounded more exhausted than she did frustrated.

Marco slowed down so she could walk ahead of him and frowned. "Sure." Had she really lost the ability to face everything? He didn't want to keep fighting about this. He wasn't sure he could stay if she kept using drugs, but he didn't know how to leave. He slowed down further to watch her as she walked, holding back tears as he feared that they were ending.

Chapter Sixty-Two

CAROL SIGHED AS she took another toke from the joint in her hand. As she sucked on it, the red embers pierced her eyes against the night sky. She was on her third joint of the night. She choked on the smoke; tears dribbled from the corner of her eyes. "Shit doesn't work anymore," she muttered, shifting her position on the swing, the hinges squeaking as she did. She stared out into the darkness and wiped at her face as she tortured herself down memory lane.

Twenty-Five Years Ago
June 1973

"Oh, dear, please. It would be so lovely to spend the evening together. I know I'm not quite as exciting as your friends in town, but it would just be so nice to spend some time with you," Carol's mother, Veronica, said. Her hair was thinner now, so she wore a scarf to cover the balding spots caused by the chemotherapy.

"Thanks, Mom, but I have to get to town. The girls are waiting down at the Lasso for me. I don't get home often enough, so they miss me. Thought I'd go out with them." Carol blushed as she told the lie. She had a boy waiting for her at the Lasso, and he was promising to bring an ounce of weed with him. All she had to do was finish supper with her parents and get to town. She had tried to leave right after dinner, but her mother had insisted she stay for tea and dessert, and now they found themselves on the front porch, having the same old talk.

"We miss you, too, you know. Do we have to say it to get you to stay with us?" Veronica spoke in a soft, almost weak, voice.

"I'm sorry. Maybe we can next week. Would that be okay? I'll come back up from Halifax a day early so I can sleep over too." She barely noticed the sad, dejected look in her mother's eyes as she skipped off the porch and toward her car.

"Love you, Caroline," her mother called after her, waving. She stood weakly to watch as her daughter got into her car and sped off down the driveway.

"SHE DIED OF a broken heart." Carol's father's voice was filled with contempt. He glared at her through his squinted gray eyes. They were in the kitchen the day of the funeral. The reception had ended, and everyone had gone home. "You, you were too good to stay home for one night, to spend just one night with your mother. She was sick for Christ's sake." He slammed his hand on the table.

Carol jolted at the sound it made. She had never witnessed him so angry before. She exhaled slowly as the tears began to fall. She wouldn't look him in the face. She felt guilty for refusing her mother that night on the porch. If only she could have that moment back. "I'm sorry, Daddy. I'm sorry."

Her father scowled and shook his head. Tears glinted in his eyes. This was a first too. "You disappoint me, Caroline. Your mother always had such hope for you, but I knew better. I knew what you were." He looked past her now as though she no longer mattered. "You and your girlfriends and boyfriends down at the bars in town. People talk, you know. You're one of those damned modern-day hippies. Doin' all those drugs and boozin'. Cool kid, huh? Good for you. Pray that you never have any children to disgrace you on your deathbed. Your poor mother. How she wept for you. How she prayed for you. An embarrassment. You're lucky you're my only child, or I'd be leaving you nothing. As it stands, I'm not sure what you'll do with all that you get. What will you become, I wonder? What will you do to our name? Nothing I bet. I bet you do nothing and become no one. All you do is take and destroy." He got up from the table. "You can show yourself out," he said over his shoulder as he left her standing in the kitchen alone. He died less than a year later. They had never truly patched their relationship, and she'd been trying to prove him wrong ever since.

CAROL CRINGED NOW the same way she had when she had been speaking to her father that long-ago night. She wished she'd known it would be her mother's last night. How she would have done things differently if she had. She only half listened to the things her mother had said during that last dinner, forcing smiles at the appropriate times. In truth, she didn't care about her mother then. She felt like she was a burden, like she was impeding her from living life. "Ha," she said aloud, nearly startling herself at the sudden volume. How ridiculous she felt now, knowing that the boy she had rushed to meet had only been in her life for a week, long enough for her to smoke all his weed and then dispose of him.

The light in the kitchen flicked off, leaving her in further darkness. Marco must have come downstairs to make sure the front door was locked up and the lights turned off. He didn't trust her to do anything anymore. It seemed like he had all but left her with the way he treated her now, with such disregard.

"I'm sorry, Mommy," Carol said, whining to herself and to the empty veranda. She thought of Tyler and wished he was there. She wished he would tell her to smarten up. Strangely, she thought she might actually listen to him if he did. "I wish we could have that evening now." She butted the joint out, crying as she did. *If I could just do it all again, I would have stayed. I swear it. I would have stayed.*

Chapter Sixty-Three

IT HAD ONLY been a rushed nine months that they'd known him, but it felt like Tyler had been in their family for years. The hole he was leaving in the house was glaring, and everyone sensed it. The rooms felt dimmer, the halls seemed to echo, yet everything seemed quieter. Carol was convinced that she'd witnessed the spark in each of the kids disappear. It was as though no one wanted to look anyone in the eyes anymore for fear of getting too close. For the fear of losing each other was greater than the joy of having one another.

Bradley and Curtis had been in college for two weeks. Maggie had fallen back into herself and hardly talked to anyone except for Theo. The house felt emptier than ever.

Carol hated how she could feel Marco's eyes on her every time she went downstairs to the veranda at night. He would look at her with such contempt when she would come back stoned. He'd barely touched her since they'd left the airport. Every time he looked at her with such disgust and contempt, she felt the urge to take as many drugs and drink as much alcohol as would be needed to become invisible, to join Tyler and Janie. She finally understood how Janie came to make the decision she did. She wiped at a nervous tear threatening to slide from her eye.

Lately, she had been plagued with doubt over her decision to smoke joints with Tyler. *What if I made it worse? What if that somehow made him go faster? What if it is all my fault?* she wondered. *And what if we hadn't stayed on that camping trip? Maybe he wouldn't have gotten so sick.*

Here she was, lying in bed next to her partner in life and in love, and she could barely feel him. She knew she was shutting down and pushing him away, but she didn't know how to stop. She could feel everything slipping away from her. The scariest thing for her was that she wasn't sure she cared anymore. The heavier life got, the more she wished it would all fall away. It was the exact feeling she'd had when she saw the bulletin board at the airport.

"Hm." She sat up straight, having a sudden moment of clarity. She flicked her lamp on, trying not to wake Marco as she moved. She carefully rummaged through the papers in the drawer of her bedside table until she found the pamphlet.

"Here you are," she said in a whisper. She looked over at Marco to make sure he was still sleeping. Once she was sure he was still asleep, she pulled her glasses from their case and a black pen from the drawer. She took a deep breath and unfolded the pamphlet, taking care to read every word and making sure that she understood the legend and its associated codes: S = speaker, D = discussion, O = open to the public, C = closed (for members only), T = topic, GL = gay and lesbian, and CL = candlelight. She took a deep breath and started circling viable options. When she was done, she set the pamphlet on her bedside table and finally managed to fall asleep.

"SO THAT'S THE thing you saw that was interesting?" Marco said, pointing past her. He was sitting up and smiling with tears in his eyes.

Carol blinked to adjust to the sunlight that now filled their bedroom. He had opened the blinds. The smell of fresh coffee made her nose twitch. She sat up and moved her eyes to where he was pointing. There, on her bedside table, sat a fresh cup of coffee beside the pamphlet. She pressed her lips together. She still didn't understand why she took it or what had prompted her to notice it from across the room in a crowded airport. The pamphlet was a beigey color with a truly plain design on it. The biggest thing on it was the "NA" on the front. She picked it up and fondled it for a moment and then handed it over to him. "Yes, that was it. I just wasn't ready to talk about it. I wasn't even ready to think about it." She shrugged and folded her hands in front of her, digging at her cuticles with her thumbnail.

Marco took a shaky breath as he ran his fingers over the front of the pamphlet. His hands were trembling, causing the paper to vibrate. He took a deep breath and exhaled slowly as he unfolded it to see a list of Narcotics Anonymous meetings with locations, times, and various codes. "I'm really proud of you," he said as he saw the circles Carol had drawn around three of the meetings.

She forced a smile. "I don't even understand it yet."

"That's okay," he said. "That's totally okay." He wrapped his arms around her and pulled her in tight. "I love you, Carol." He kissed the top of her head.

"Ditto," she said, hugging his arm and closing her eyes as she leaned into his chest. She wanted to stay like that forever. "They're all in Halifax. It would mean almost an hour of driving each way. I don't know if that's okay."

"Nothing's ever been more okay."

She smiled and said, in a whisper, "Okay... Okay."

Chapter Sixty-Four

One Year Later
September 12, 1999

A lot happened in the year that followed Tyler's death. They had welcomed a new young girl into the house, Emma, who turned ten years old a few months before moving in. Being so close in age to Theo, she really helped pull him out of his shell. Maggie had just recently moved to Halifax to attend Dalhousie University. It was as though they had a fresh, clean slate to start over with.

Carol stuck to her guns about attending Narcotics Anonymous meetings in Halifax and managed to stay clean. She and Marco threw out all paraphernalia to do with marijuana and everything related to alcohol or wine. She'd accepted the decision to give up weed, but wine was harder. She held on to one bottle until she was about six months clean before becoming willing to get rid of it. She had a good cry the day she and Marco uncorked it and poured it out in the forest at the base of the Knowing Tree. And from that point on, she knew she would never drink again.

Her home group—main NA meeting—was having a celebration for her this night to celebrate her first year of continuous clean time. Marco had flown Curtis and Bradley back for the weekend, and Maggie had driven up from Halifax. Carol wasn't sure she wanted all the attention, but it was really nice to pretend like everything was back to normal for a few days.

"There you are," Curtis said, stepping out onto the back veranda to join Carol on the porch swing. "I've been looking for you everywhere."

She smiled up at him and took a sip of her tea. "Have a seat with me," she said, patting the seat beside her.

"Gladly," he said, plopping himself down. The metal springs squeaked, and the swing bounced them about messily. "Oh, jeez." He put his arms out to balance himself.

Carol braced her tea, trying not to spill it from the vibrations. "You sit like you've been standing for years."

They watched Theo and Emma as they played with another boy, about the same age, on the new slide and jungle gym Marco had put up a couple hundred feet from the veranda in the back field.

"Theo looks so grown-up."

"Just turned six," Carol said proudly. "He speaks so clearly now and is turning out to be quite funny. He's trying out a bunch of different types of humor. Some gross and some genuinely funny, some disturbing too." She cringed as she recalled his filling the toilet bowl with earwigs earlier in the summer. She'd nearly had a stroke when she went to pee.

"And who's that other little boy? You guys didn't mention anyone new."

"Believe it or not, but that's Wade, a boy from town. We held a workshop a few months ago, and his mother really took interest in bridging the gap between the kids and the locals. He's here on a play date. His mom picks him up in about an hour." Carol checked her watch, squinting in the bright afternoon light to see it.

Curtis's eyes grew wide and his mouth slacked open. This was not the same Carol. "You mean...?"

Carol gave him a playful "hush up" look, rolling her eyes. "Yes, I know. We actually went outside the bubble to interact with the townies. The response was mixed. There are still a lot of prejudices, but it's so wonderful that Wade's mother has taken to bringing him here to play with Theo and Emma. It almost feels normal around here."

Curtis sat back in the swing. He needed to take a minute to absorb what he'd heard. He watched as Wade chased Theo and Emma in a game of tag like he had nothing to fear. His eyes filled with tears. He cleared his throat and blinked them away. "How is Maggie doing?" He looked to where she sat, near the jungle gym on a swing set next to a wood-framed sand box.

Carol's eyes flicked to Maggie and she took a deep breath. "She's okay. It's amazing how much can change in a year. Theo is so different and Maggie and all of us really." She stopped to reflect on this. "I wonder how much Tyler has to do with all of the changes."

Curtis chuckled quietly. "He has everything to do with it. I feel like a better and stronger man for having known him. Even Bradley does. Despite their fighting and bickering, I think Bradley really grew from it."

Carol leaned into Curtis and gently tapped his shoulder with her head. "I think Maggie will find strength while she's in university. She's already loving it at Dalhousie. It's nice that she's not too far. She wants to teach elementary kids. I think she'll be good at that."

"Me too. I think that's what she was always meant for." He paused to enjoy the sentimental moment with Carol. "Do you think she's forgiven herself yet? I hate to think that she carries guilt around for having refused to see him still."

"I think she will eventually. Someday, she may even let herself fall in love again. But she's got her whole life ahead of her with no rush." She smiled as she said it, knowing that Maggie had such a long way to go and all the time in the world. "She has a lot of growing up to do before she'll truly find herself."

Curtis looked at Maggie contentedly. "I think Tyler might have taught her about resilience and stubbornness. She'll be fine. I'm sure of it."

"I'm not religious, but sometimes I feel like Tyler was an angel, like he was put at the New Life House to teach me—and all of us—something about something. Something about life. I think everything happens for a reason. And that Tyler came to the house to find out what it was to have a family while showing each of us something about the same. I feel like I lost a son, a best friend, a mentor, and a truly loveable individual," Carol said, sitting up straight as she finished. They sat in each other's company for another few moments before Carol got up. "I have to go panic about what I'm going to say tonight."

Curtis laughed. "You'll be great. Don't worry."

"Thanks," she said, waving before disappearing into the house, passing by Marco—who was on his way out to the veranda—as she entered.

"SO HOW ARE you holding up out there?" Marco asked, taking a seat beside Curtis. He had a sparkle in his eyes that Curtis hadn't seen before.

Curtis made room for him. "I'm doing really good. I think I figured out what I want to do."

"That's great. What are you thinking about?"

Curtis hadn't told anyone but Bradley about the idea yet. He had been so excited to tell Marco and Carol, but he wanted to make sure the idea was reasonable first. He'd spent the last three months researching its viability.

"Well, don't keep me waiting. Patience is not a virtue I have a lot of." Marco slapped Curtis gently on the leg.

"Well, it would mean I go for a business degree once I'm done my Outdoor Adventure diploma." He paused to watch Marco's face, checking to see if he would balk at the idea of spending more money. Deep down, he knew he wouldn't.

Marco just sat bright-eyed and smiling, waiting for the rest of the plan.

"Once I have that, I would start an Outdoor Adventure or Wilderness Tours program that would only offer tours and services for positive people."

Marco's eyes grew wider as did his smile.

Feeling like he needed to justify it still, Curtis spoke quicker. "I would have to check into having a staff who would travel with the group. Like a nurse and some other people to make sure no one would get sick." He flinched as he said it.

"Wow, that's great, Curtis. I'm really proud of you." Marco stared at him in amazement. "Seriously."

Curtis smiled, showing all of his teeth. "I want to run it with the spin that it is a positive experience for positive people. I think that's what Tyler was getting at. He wanted me to know that it was an experience that not all positive people get to participate in because of the higher health risks and general misinformation, but if I design an outdoor adventure company that caters to positive people and promises a positive experience, I think it will help people as well as make a lot of money. This is something that would be so great for people, especially kids. I can see it being strengthening for people," Curtis said with such enthusiasm that he barely breathed until he finished and had to take a deep, exasperated breath.

"You realize this will out you to the world. It won't be your choice who knows anymore," Marco said, leaning back in the porch swing beside Curtis.

"I'm not ashamed anymore. I am who I am, and I would rather proudly make a difference than hide in the shadows fearing rejection."

"That's a great sentiment. I'm really happy for you, Curtis. Truly." They made eye contact and shared an impromptu moment of silence.

"And at least I won't have to go through the awkward 'coming out' stage when I'm dating someone. I think that by me running the business, it will explain itself. No fuss, no muss."

"Oh yeah?" Marco asked.

"Yeah."

"And what's Bradley think about your plan? With you two living together, I could see him feeling some extra pressure or fearing being outed."

Curtis paused before answering. "It's still a bit of a touchy subject to be honest. We have talked about it a lot, and he's not sure what he feels about it yet. He's been dating a few girls but is afraid to get intimate with any of them and is equally afraid to open up to them to allow them any insight on why he's afraid."

"And does he see the benefit in not having to tell them if the company was to make it known for him?"

"See, I don't see how it would do that to him. He doesn't have to admit that he has it just because I do," Curtis said. "Bradley and I had this argument earlier in the year. It was pretty messy. We weren't sure that we'd keep living together. Lately, though, he's been coming around. He even told me that he might want to run a sports program through the company so other kids who have HIV won't have to miss out on team sports like he had to."

"Wow, that's great progress."

"He's not such a boy anymore as he is a man," Curtis said.

"There's a lot to be proud of in him...and you."

"Thanks. I still think we wouldn't be as far along as we are if it hadn't been for Tyler. It's his presence that spurred all of this." Curtis fanned his arm out to point toward the house to imply that Carol's getting clean and his and Bradley's maturity was a direct reflection on Tyler.

"I think you're right. He had a lot to do with it, and now it's all about what *we* do with it."

CAROL STOOD BESIDE her sponsor at the front of the room, looking out at the crowded room in the church basement in downtown Halifax. There were close to sixty people in attendance. Marco and the kids were in the front row, smiling up at her proudly.

Her sponsor was a short woman with long white hair and who dressed like a hippy in a leather vest, flower-patterned blouse, and faded bell-bottom jeans. She was holding Carol's one-year medallion, fidgeting with it and running her fingers along the number 1, which was embossed on the front. She looked out at the crowd and said, "My name's Sheila, and I'm a grateful, recovering addict."

"Hi, Sheila," the room responded in unison.

She looked up at Carol and smiled with tears in her eyes. "Carol. I'm so proud of you."

"Thank you."

Sheila chuckled and said, "No, no. Shhh." She flapped her hand in the air to get Carol to stop. She gently squeezed her arm. "You get to say thank you *after* I make you listen to some nice things about you."

Carol took a deep breath and prepared herself for it. "Oh, dear." She laughed nervously.

"You'll be fine. Suck it up." The room filled with warm laughter. Sheila waited for it to subside before continuing. "Carol, you've been through a lot in your life and in this year. You've taken on a really important, but not always easy, role in your life." She motioned to the front row. "I think it makes you stronger, and I think that now that you're working on your recovery, you will be able to be that much better at it. And I know that's important to you."

Carol nodded.

"I think the reason you're still here is because you come to meetings, you do service, you reach out to people, and you work your steps. It's a simple program, and you're doing it. You're doing it one day at a time." Sheila paused. "You know, I was outlining the one on the front of the medallion with my finger. This is an important year, a huge stepping stone. It's where the rest of your life begins."

"I've had a lot support from the people here," Carol said, interrupting.

"And with some inspiration from friends who have passed." Sheila smiled softly at the insinuation.

Carol exhaled slowly, trying not to cry.

"Now, for your next year, I wish for you to learn to forgive yourself. And maybe even love yourself. That's my wish for you."

Carol wiped at a runaway tear.

"You've made it this far. Now, it's time to keep going. I love you, and I'm so honored you asked me to work through your recovery and your steps with you. I am in awe daily. Just remember to take it one day at a time. Give me a hug." Sheila reached her arms out excitedly and squeezed Carol tightly before handing her the medallion and taking a seat.

The room erupted with cheers, whistles, and applause. Carol stood clutching the medallion to soak the moment in and to think of what to say. The room quieted. She looked at Marco, who sat beaming with pride and joy next to Curtis, and found the courage she needed. "Hi, my name is Carol and I'm an addict."

"Hi, Carol," the room said, again in unison.

"I want to thank the members of this group for helping me believe in a new way to live. And for helping me find it. And none of this would be possible...me celebrating a year clean...if it hadn't been for my beautiful partner, Marco, and our family." Carol nodded toward the kids and Marco who sat in the front row. "My recovery was made possible by those of you here and those who we've lost. I'm so grateful."

The room erupted with applause and cheers again as the members of her home group and her family celebrated her achievement.

"Way to go, Carol!" Bradley shouted over the voices.

The clapping quieted so she could continue.

"I haven't come to believe or 'found God' yet," she said, making air quotes with her hands. She paused for a moment to reflect upon her first year of recovery, glancing around at the faces from the New Life House until, finally, her gaze met with Bradley's, and she smiled. "But I'm a work in progress. You know, I just keep telling myself that everything's going to be okay and that there's always tomorrow."

Acknowledgements

There are so many people I owe huge thanks to, including all of my friends and family who have listened to me go on and on about this book and journey for the last few years. You have all shown me such love and encouragement throughout this process. Thank you. Truly, deeply, thank you.

Thank you to Raevyn and Jason and everyone at NineStar Press who took a chance on me and this book, this dream. I am so grateful for all of the effort you've put into making this book become what it is. And I will be forever touched by the kindness with which you met all of my green questions as we embarked on this journey. A huge thank you to Natasha Snow for the amazing cover art that encapsulates the very essence of the story so beautifully.

I am so grateful to my amazing team of beta readers – Glen Hartle, Ginny Kerr, Sabine Modder, Kayla Lavoie, Gilles Benoit, Carole Cantin and Noreen Fagan – who selflessly and passionately jumped on board to read the second and fourth drafts of this novel. Your insight, feedback and energy for this project buoyed my soul. You are a group of heroes to me.

I'd also like to thank Nadine McInnis whose work I greatly admire and who graciously agreed to be a mentor to me for this novel. Your guidance, comments and willingness to be a part of this journey was and remains inspiring and incredible.

As hinted at in the dedication, my biggest thank you goes to my husband, Glen, who made this dream possible. Without your support, dedication and pure awesomeness, I don't know that this book would be happening right now. Thank you for always supporting me and for believing in me even when I felt like I was a disaster.

And for the fantastically awesome group of people (forty-seven of you, I believe the count was) who volunteered to read and critique my first chapter amidst the querying stages of this book: thank you. You helped make the hook that much better. You all rock.

I dreamed this book up when I was eighteen years old. At the time, the SARS epidemic was in full swing, and I was in the middle of my chemotherapy treatments. I caught a fever and found myself quarantined in a hospital room for a week with limited visitors. That experience bore the genesis of this story. While the story has changed since then, I am thrilled to have had the chance to bring to life for others to read these characters that have lived with me for years.

About the Author

Sean holds a diploma in Professional Writing from Algonquin College (Ottawa, 2009). He found his love of writing at the age of ten when he released his first miniseries via Duo-Tang folder to his family and friends. Further to *Life at the Death House*, he has another four novels outlined and is working on draft one of a fifth. He specifically enjoys writing stories that deal with how people react to hardships, exploring how they come through it for better or for worse. Common themes include addiction, mental health, sexuality, grief and hope.

In December 2016, he launched the Pontiac & Ottawa Valley Writers' Circle (POVWC) under the umbrella of the Pontiac Artists Association. He continues to coordinate the efforts of the POVWC and is enjoying the blossoming of a strong creative writing community.

Sean lives on a farm in Bristol, Quebec, with his husband, Glen; their dogs, Suzie, Maxwell and Walker; their goats, Tyrion and Arya; and their llamas, Shadow and Angie.

Email: seankerr84@gmail.com

Twitter: @SeanEDKerr84

Website: www.seankerr.ca

Also Available from NineStar Press

Connect with NineStar Press

Website: NineStarPress.com

Facebook: NineStarPress

Facebook Reader Group: NineStarNiche

Twitter: @ninestarpress

Tumblr: NineStarPress